OUT FOR BLOOD

Mal's beast lifted its head at the familiar scent. *Blood.* The crowd erupted in a wave of deafening sound.

Mal leaped, kicking time back to its normal speed. Chrysabelle's heartbeat pounded in his ears as her breaths grew shallow and her blood scent overwhelmed his control.

A woman screamed, 'Brutus, behind you!'

But Brutus turned too late. Mal landed on top of the varcolai, crumpling him to the ground. He drove his fist into the shifter's face, breaking his nose. Beside them, Chrysabelle clutched at her throat, her mouth open as she gasped. Blood bubbled up from the slices across her neck. 'Mal,' she whispered. Her eyes rolled back, the whites showing between her barely open lids.

'Hang on,' he whispered back, struggling to keep the beast controlled. So much blood.

Brutus shifted to his half-form and snarled, showing off prehistoric fangs. He swiped a hand at Mal.

Ducking the claws, Mal blocked the hand with his forearm, then jammed his elbow into Brutus's stomach.

The shifter exhaled a *whoof* of air at the same time Chrysabelle's pulse went silent. Mal froze. He flicked his gaze toward her, afraid of what he'd see. What he already knew.

Blood trickled from the corner of her mouth. She stared unblinking. Her brilliant comarré glow was gone.

KRISTEN PAINTER

House of Comarré
Blood Rights
Flesh and Blood
Bad Blood
Out for Blood

OUT FOR BLOOD

House of Comarré: Book 4

KRISTEN PAINTER

orbit

www.orbitbooks.net

ORBIT

First published in Great Britain in 2012 by Orbit

A CIP catalogue record for this book
is available from the British Library.

ISBN 978-0-356-50210-6

Typeset in Times by M Rules
Printed and bound by CPI Group (UK) Ltd, Croydon, CR0 4YY

Papers used by Orbit are from well-managed forests
and other responsible sources.

 MIX
Paper from
responsible sources
FSC
www.fsc.org
FSC® C104740

Orbit
An imprint of
Little, Brown Book Group
100 Victoria Embankment
London EC4Y 0DY

An Hachette UK Company
www.hachette.co.uk

www.orbitbooks.net

For Judi McCoy:
A wonderful friend, a great mentor,
and a fabulous writer.

You left us too soon.

Even in darkness, blood shines in a way that cannot be ignored. It always rises. It always fights. It always conquers.

— ACACIUS, GREEK SCHOLAR

Chapter One

Deep in sleep, Chrysabelle curled against a cold, steely form that paralleled her own. The oddness of that burrowed through her consciousness and tugged her toward the surface. She reached behind her. Her fingertips collided with a hard midsection.

A body. In her bed.

Years of comarré training kicked in. Coming awake, she twisted and looked directly into dark, familiar eyes. She stared, a thousand responses firing across her synapses, the foremost being relief. She blinked twice and shed the remnants of sleep enough to find words. 'You're in my bed.'

Mal nodded, irises sparking silver. 'I do have to sleep occasionally, you know.' A lilting smile curved his mouth. 'I'm glad you finally woke. How are you feeling?'

She ignored the question, not sure enough of an answer to give him one, and pushed to a sitting position, gathering the coverlet around her. In doing so, she exposed him. He wore only pajama bottoms she didn't recognize. The names scrawled over his skin glared back from his chest and arms. Somehow she managed to look away, scooting to the edge of the bed until her toes touched plush ivory carpeting. 'How long have I been out?'

'Not long. About a day and a half.'

She rubbed her forehead, then pushed the hair out of her eyes. 'That's long enough. What happened? I don't remember much beyond going to see Atticus, then ... ' She squinted, trying to think. She'd gone to Dominic's signumist to replace the signum Rennata had stripped off her back. Before that, they'd been in New Orleans, retrieving the ring of sorrows. She'd needed the ring's sacred gold for her new signum. But her memory faded not long after she'd lain down on Atticus's table. After the first puncture of his needle. She shook her head. 'There's nothing after that.'

'Nothing?' The bed moved as he shifted. 'You're sure?'

'Positive.' She kicked her foot out, rubbing her toe through the carpet fibers. The signum arching over her foot glinted back. 'Everything fades to black after Atticus started stitching the signum into me.' She rolled her shoulders, examining the way her body felt. There was an eerie lack of pain. She turned to look at him. 'I take it you brought me back here when he was done?'

Mal nodded. 'After Atticus said it was okay to move you. Velimai helped me get you settled.'

'Did anything else happen? I should be in pain.' A lot of it. 'It takes longer than a day and a half to recover from new signum.'

'Yes, something else happened.' Mal growled his displeasure. 'Not long after we got you into bed, you decided you were well enough to visit the Aurelian. I only found out because I smelled blood. Velimai and I had to break the door down. That's when we discovered you'd opened the portal on the bathroom floor.' He shook his head, eyes flaring silver. 'Of all the foolish things. You should thank that wysper. She made me go after you—'

'What?' Chrysabelle cringed. Why didn't she remember any of this? 'You went through the portal again? You know what happened the last time—'

'Chrysabelle, the Aurelian *killed* you. I found her cleaning blood off her sword and you on the floor, bleeding from a gut wound. No pulse. No breath. You were *dead*.' He peered at her more intently. 'Or at least I thought you were.'

'Obviously, I wasn't.' Or was she? That might explain why she couldn't remember anything. But how was she alive now? 'Besides, you knew I was going to go see her to find out as much about my brother as I could. That was the whole point of getting the signum.' But how had she found the strength for a trip to the Aurelian so soon after getting them? There was no way she would have been healed enough for that. She hugged the coverlet a little tighter and turned to see him better. 'Do you know if she told me anything?'

He looked down at the bed for a second, then shook his head slowly. 'You told me she knew your brother's name but wouldn't say it so you could hear it, or something like that. I wish things had gone differently for you. I really do.' A black determination shone in his gaze. 'If I ever see the Aurelian again, I will kill her for what she did to you.'

Fortunately, Mal would never get that chance, so his threat didn't worry her. 'Not telling me my brother's name isn't really a crime punishable by death.'

'She *killed* you. How is that not upsetting to you?'

Chrysabelle spread one arm out wide. 'Do I look dead? You must have misunderstood what happened.'

Tension tightened his jaw. 'I misunderstood nothing. I carried your lifeless body back here.'

'Maybe I just passed out.'

'And had no heartbeat and no breath?' He rolled his eyes. 'Is cheating death a comarré power you never told me about?'

'No, of course not.' She pulled her arm against her side and hunched her back, her skin suddenly too tight. The need to stretch was overwhelming. 'There has to be an explanation for what happened.'

'There is. You were dead.' With a shake of his head, he lay down again and stared at the ceiling. 'Stop ignoring what happened.'

But she wasn't ready for that truth. It implied things had gone wrong with the gold. That melting the ring of sorrows hadn't removed its power like it should have. If she didn't concede something to Mal, he'd never let this conversation end. 'I'll admit everything's not a hundred percent right.'

'When is it ever?' He shoved off the bed and padded across the room to stand by the French doors going out to the balcony. He pushed the curtains aside. The sun had just set, leaving the world awash in purple shadows. He peered out, then let the curtains drop and turned back to her, crossing his arms over his bare chest as he leaned against the doors.

She tossed the coverlet aside, wrapped the sheet around her like a strapless dress, and walked to him. 'Let's not go looking for trouble. I survived a killing blow. That's something to be thankful for.'

'I agree, but' – he shook his head – 'you don't seem like yourself.'

Her brow furrowed. 'In what way?'

'The way you . . .' He shrugged. 'It's nothing, I guess. Just the leftover stress of it all. Never mind. I'm sure you're *fine*.'

She ignored his sarcasm. 'Absolutely.' But she wasn't and she knew it. He was giving her an out, but he didn't believe his words any more than she did, and that knowledge hung in the air between them. A shard of thought pierced her mind, but it was a shadowy, hollow awareness she wasn't ready to acknowledge. And telling Mal her suspicions would only mean he'd rant and rave. That would solve nothing. What was she going to do? Have the signum removed from her skin because of a hunch? Having them torn out once was enough.

'You're still a bad liar.'

She tried to smile. 'See? Nothing's changed.' She rubbed her eyes and yawned. 'I'm starving.'

His eyes went completely silver. He turned toward the balcony as his face shifted into the hard, angled mask of a noble vampire.

She lifted her chin. 'So are you. I felt how cold you were when you were beside me.'

He kept his eyes focused on the horizon. 'I'm fine.'

'Now who's the liar?' The urge to touch him, to soothe him, surged through her. Instead, she walked back to the bed and occupied herself with straightening the coverlet. 'Let me get a shower, then I'll get you some blood. Will you ask Velimai to make me something to eat?'

His face human again, he nodded and looked toward her. 'Of course. I guess you'll want to see Damian after you eat. He's at the freighter, guarding another—'

'Tatiana's comar is at your freighter?'

'Yes. I know you don't remember, but you said his name

before you passed out. You must want to talk to him about something.'

She sank down on the bed and tried again to recall what the Aurelian had told her, but nothing came. 'I must have thought he could help me find my brother.' She shook her head. 'I'm not up to seeing anyone yet. Maybe in a day or two. Right now, I just want to shower, eat, and feed you. Then I need to do some thinking.'

He tipped his head to one side as if suppressing the urge to say something. 'Your call, but don't you think it's possible the Aurelian told you something Damian might be able to help you with? Maybe he knew your brother?'

She shrugged his words away. 'Without knowing more than the singular fact that I have a brother, how can he help me? I have no name to give him. No idea who my brother's patron might have been. Nothing.' She sighed. 'It's so frustrating.'

'What if Damian *is* your brother?'

She glared at him. 'He's not. Don't you think I'd know if he was?'

'No, I don't. You didn't even meet him when he was here. How could you know?'

'Stop pushing. I'll talk to him, I will. Just not yet.' She rolled her shoulders again, trying to alleviate the uneasiness coursing through her. Mal's insistence wasn't helping her mood.

'Are you sure you're okay?' He studied her as if she might suddenly grow a third eye.

'I'm well enough, considering,' she lied, nerves fraying slightly. 'Please, just leave me alone to shower, okay? I'll feel better after I eat.'

He held his hands up and headed for the door, grabbing a T-shirt off the end of the bed as he went.

She sighed. She'd apologize for snapping when she went downstairs, but he must understand she wasn't quite herself at the moment. Why did he have to push so hard?

When the door closed, she walked to the bathroom, dropped her robe, and stared at the signum Atticus had replaced. Nothing about them looked any different than her other marks, and yet she knew that the gold had changed her. For better or worse remained to be seen.

Chrysabelle wasn't fine – that much Mal knew. Her glow was different. Darker. He also knew that what she didn't want to talk about – the power from the ring of sorrows being somehow responsible for her surviving the Aurelian's sword – wasn't just going to magically wear off. He never should have put his blood into her, never should have let her get the signum replaced, never should have let her go to the Aurelian alone. *Never never never. Weakling.*

He snorted in anger as he plodded down the steps from her suite, half agreeing with the voices. As if he had any control over any of those things. He'd no more let her die than she'd let him stop her from doing what she wanted. And now there was a price to pay.

How high a price? Who knew. But having the ring's power coursing through her had to mean more than just keeping her alive when her life was threatened. That was too simple. He ducked into the hurricane shelter room that had served as his sunproof sanctuary and changed into his T-shirt, jeans, and boots. Power had a way of exacting a price for its use. Tatiana was proof of that. *So are you.*

He shut the door behind him and headed down the hall and into the kitchen. Velimai, the wysper fae who'd been

Chrysabelle's mother's assistant, sat at the table with a cup of tea, scanning her e-reader. It was good she'd stayed on after Maris's death. He didn't like Chrysabelle being alone in this huge house, and with Velimai's vampire-killing voice, the fae offered good protection should Tatiana come calling.

Velimai looked up when he came in. She signed something he didn't understand, then pointed toward the upstairs.

'Yes,' he answered, guessing at what she'd asked. 'She's awake. And hungry. And a little cranky.' *Who wouldn't be around you?*

The wysper offered him a wry smile, set her reader down, and headed for the refrigerator. She pulled out a few things, then gave him a questioning look and a nod toward Chrysabelle's rooms as she went to the counter.

He pulled out a chair and sat, his back to the wall. 'She's in the shower. Should be down shortly.'

Velimai stopped seasoning a steak to give him a good, long look. She slowly mouthed, *'You look tired.'*

'I am.' Tired of always being at odds with Chrysabelle's stubbornness. 'And frustrated. She doesn't want to talk about what happened.' He tilted his head back until it touched the wall, then closed his eyes. 'Or what's still happening. Or going to happen, depending on how you look at it.'

Two soft clinks on the tabletop brought his head back down and opened his eyes. Velimai tapped the top of the whiskey bottle she'd put there with a squat glass, then glided back to the range where the grill was heating.

'Thanks.' What he really needed was blood, but that could wait. *No, now.* He'd had enough practice in delaying his own gratification. Another hour or so meant nothing. He poured a couple centimeters of whiskey into the tumbler and tossed them back. The burn felt good. Substantial. Something he could quantify. Unlike Chrysabelle, who continued to bewilder him. 'We'll have to discuss it sooner or later.'

Velimai nodded. The steak sizzled as she laid it over the grill, the scents of searing, bloody flesh reminding Mal of his human days. A muted whir filled the room as the vent kicked on to suck up the smoke. She put down the tongs she'd been using, came back to the table, scrawled something on an e-tablet, then held it out to him.

She'll talk when she's ready. You & I know it's the ring in her system. Maybe your blood too. But what can you do until she's ready? Fight with her? No use.

Mal set the e-tablet down and leaned back. 'No use is right. I just can't help but wonder what the final cost of all this is going to be.'

Velimai sighed and went back to the steak.

'The final cost of what is going to be?' Chrysabelle cinched her robe a little tighter as she entered. Her hair was dry. Maybe she'd changed her mind about showering. The look in her eyes said she understood perfectly well what they were talking about.

He didn't want to fight with her. *Do it.* But neither did he want to ignore something so critical. Velimai glanced at him, her expression plainly asking him to drop it. But he couldn't. This was too important. This was Chrysabelle's life. Her future. 'The final cost of what's going on with you. With the ring's power in your system.'

'The ring's power was destroyed when Atticus melted it down. I told you I'm fine. If you can't accept that, maybe you should go.'

He canted his head to one side, trying to quell his building frustration. 'Chrysabelle, don't be—'

'It's my house,' she said quietly. 'I'll be whatever I want to be, understood?'

He rose, thankful there was no sun in the sky to keep him captive here. 'Let me know when you're ready to be someone who wants to face reality, because if you think the ring's power and my blood in your system aren't somehow responsible for you still being alive, you're wrong. And we need to figure out what else it means before something new happens. Tatiana's still out there. The first sign of weakness in you and she'll exploit it. You think she won't?'

Her face went slightly ashen. 'You don't want me to have a moment's peace, do you?'

'Of course I do.' He tried not to growl in frustration but failed. 'I just want to figure this out. To help you.' *Help yourself. Bite her. Drain her.*

She crossed her arms like a shield against him. 'Yes, I know how you help. Like the time you followed me to the Aurelian. And the time you put your blood into me to save my life. Your help is never really that helpful, is it?'

He came closer, staring down at her maddening glow. 'You're still breathing, aren't you?'

'Yes. And I'm tired of the air smelling like vampire.' She turned away. 'Go home, Mal. When I'm ready, I'll come find you.'

Every cell in his body ached to fire back, but he stayed silent despite the voices trying to pry his jaws open. He stalked out of the house and slammed the door behind him. The voices raged like drunken carnival revelers.

Maybe the voices were right. Maybe it was time to let Chrysabelle go. Let her deal with her life on her own.

If only he could get his heart to agree.

Chapter Two

Corvinestri, Romania, 2067

'She is the most remarkable child, isn't she?' Tatiana gazed into the perfect face of her daughter, Lilith.

The kine doctor swallowed and glanced at Octavian, who sat in one of the nursery's rocking chairs. 'Yes, she is ... exceptional. If you wish, I could test a sample of her blood, make sure she carries no human defects.'

'Defects?' Tatiana scowled. 'What is that supposed to mean? The only spot on her is the birthmark on her hip.' She pulled down Lilith's pantaloons enough to show off the perfect crescent moon shape.

The doctor inhaled and took a step back. 'Nothing untoward, I promise you. It's just that human children are immunized against human diseases. We have no way of knowing if Lilith needs these things or not.' He smoothed the pockets of his white coat. 'I meant no disrespect of any kind. Clearly she is a ... superior being.'

Tatiana kept her gaze on him, narrowing her eyes slightly and saying nothing until he squirmed a little more. Kine were so easy to control. 'No blood tests.'

'My love,' Octavian said. 'The tests might not be such a bad idea. We want the best for her. That includes the best care. You don't know what she might have picked up from her mother.'

Tatiana turned toward the vampire who'd become inseparable from her since his recent turning. She'd come to rely on him far more than she'd ever relied on anyone else. It unnerved her, but she chose not to dwell on it. 'You think she could be in danger from a human illness?'

He shrugged and pushed out of the rocker to stand beside her. He stroked his finger down Lilith's pink cheek, his eyes sparking silver. 'We don't want to take any chances with our precious girl, do we?'

If only Tatiana's own father had cared so much about his daughter. Lilith wasn't even Octavian's blood. 'No,' she said softly, drinking in the fatherly affection he displayed toward her adopted child. 'Only the best for her.'

Octavian smiled and gave her a wink. 'Only the best for *both* of you.'

The doctor visibly relaxed. 'So you would like to proceed with the tests?'

Octavian nodded, his face suddenly stern. 'Harm this child in any way and I'll kill you myself.'

'Yes, my lord.' The doctor paled. 'I'll just get my bag.' He shuffled away to rummage through his things.

Octavian guided Tatiana toward the divan. 'Sit. You'll both be more comfortable.' She did and he sat beside her. 'Any word from Lord Edwin on this ball the House of Bathory is giving in your honor?'

She shook her head, unable to keep a slight smile off her lips. 'You're trying to distract me.'

He leaned back and crossed his legs. 'Is it working?'

'Maybe.' She shifted Lilith from her arms to her lap. 'He sent word earlier. I meant to tell you. The ball is a week from today. At Lord Syler's mansion in Čachtice.'

Octavian wrinkled his nose. 'Slovakia? Can't say as I find that appealing.'

She laughed. 'You're such a snob. It's lovely, I assure you. And in hosting this ball, Syler confirms his alliance with the House of Tepes.'

'Yes, but it means we have to travel.' His gaze lit upon Lilith. 'We must be heavily guarded. Every precaution taken.'

A subtle throat clearing interrupted their conversation. The doctor stood before them, syringe in hand. 'I'm ready whenever you are.'

Tatiana took a voluntary breath. 'I want to know everything you're going to do before you do it.'

'Of course, my lady. I'm simply going to do a heel stick and extract the blood from there. I doubt the child will like it, but in one so young, it's the best way.'

'Very well.' She moved the blanket swaddling Lilith so that her little feet were exposed.

The doctor pulled a nearby chair closer and sat, then swabbed Lilith's heel with antiseptic. 'Keep her still as best you can.' He held her foot in his fingers and slid the needle in.

Lilith's eyes flew open and a piercing wail erupted from her throat. The doctor winced. Tatiana raised her hand to shove him off her child, but Octavian caught her wrist before she could strike.

'What are you—'

'This must be done.' He shook his head, eyes bracketed with concern. 'It hurts me to hear her cry, too, but it's for the best.'

'For the best,' the doctor reiterated. 'Almost done. There now.' He slid the needle out and twisted a cap over it to seal the vial. 'There, there.' He patted Lilith's stomach.

She caught his finger in her tiny, flailing fist and latched on. The doctor smiled. She brought his finger to her mouth and began to suck on it.

'She's just hungry,' he said. 'That's all – What the ... ' He tried to yank his hand away, but Lilith held fast. He cursed. 'She's bitten me. The little beast has her teeth in me!'

Octavian leaped up. 'How dare you!'

'Beast?' Tatiana snarled as her face shifted and her fangs descended. She clamped her hand over the doctor's arm, holding him in place. 'You took her blood. Now she'll take some of yours.' She pulled him closer so she could aim her silver gaze into his mud-brown kine eyes. 'Apologize for calling her such a horrible name or you'll pay with more than blood.'

The doctor trembled, his eyes flicking from Tatiana to Lilith to Octavian. 'I ... I apologize for my disrespectful comment. It will not happen again.'

Tatiana tightened her grip, causing the doctor to whimper as his bones ground together. 'You're lucky to still be alive, kine.'

Octavian snorted in agreement.

'Yes, my lady.' The doctor nodded, doing his best to get as far away as he could while in her grasp.

A popping sound announced the release of his finger from Lilith's mouth. Blood trickled from two red pinpoints on the pad of his index finger.

Tatiana released him as well. 'Go now while you still can. I want those results immediately.'

The doctor gathered his things with great haste, depositing the vial of blood into his waistcoat pocket. 'Of course, my lady.'

Octavian kissed her cheek. 'To make sure that's all he does with her blood, I'll accompany him back to the lab and stay until the tests are completed.'

She nodded. 'A wise decision.'

He took the doctor by the elbow and began to escort him out. 'And don't think I won't kill you if you make one false move.'

Tatiana curled Lilith into her arms and rested farther back into the divan's depths, comforted by the knowledge that she was no longer the only one with her child's best interests at heart.

Everglades, New Florida

Creek notched the kickstand down on his V-Rod and hopped off his bike. The last time he'd been out to his grandmother's had been in a last-ditch effort to keep Chrysabelle from bleeding out after having her signum stripped off her back. As a tribe healer, his grandmother had known what to do, but Mal hadn't liked it. Neither had Chrysabelle.

This time, Creek was the one who needed help.

He climbed the steps of the small, wood-paneled house to knock on her door. Not that there was a need to announce himself with Pip around. His grandmother's fifty-pound mutt barked like the house was on fire anytime a person, vehicle, or gator got within a few yards of the place. 'Pip, settle down. Mawmaw, it's me, Tommy.'

One last bark and the door opened. 'Shush, Pip, you'll wake the dead.' Rosa Mae Jumper peered up at Creek through the thick lenses of her glasses. 'I know who it is.' She smiled and held her arms out to him. 'Come here, child.'

He gave Pip a quick head rub, then bent to embrace her, inhaling the soft violet scent of the homemade sweet acacia perfume she wore. 'How are you, Mawmaw?'

'Just fine.' She let him go only to take his hand and lead him into the kitchen. The aroma of browned meat greeted him, making his stomach grumble. 'I've got a venison roast in the oven. Sit down and you can eat supper with me.'

'A whole roast? I thought Mom was still on night shift.' The table was set for two. 'You and Pip eating formal tonight?'

Without looking at him, she tsked. 'Foolish boy, that setting's for you. I knew you were coming. Don't I always?'

Yes, she did. He smiled and took a seat at the kitchen table while she went to the oven. Mawmaw knew all kinds of things that most people never had a clue about. He hadn't planned on eating here, but she'd be more amenable if he did. Plus, eating her cooking was no hardship after his years of prison food. Damn, he was glad the KM had gotten him out of there, even if they did hold it over his head like a thousand-pound weight.

While they ate, he got her to tell stories from his childhood and managed to keep the conversation to lighter topics, but the way she looked at him said she wasn't that easily fooled. At last she cleared the plates, set a pan of scraps down for Pip, and motioned for Creek to join her on the back porch. He took the rocker next to her, the paint worn off the seat and arms from use. She lit a cigarette and offered him one.

He shook his head. 'Those'll kill you, you know.'

She inhaled long and slow before letting out three perfect smoke rings. 'So will those damned blood eaters you chase after.'

He laughed softly. No hiding anything from her. 'I don't know what you're talking about.'

'I'm sure you don't. Just like I don't feel the air of power coming off you.' She took another puff. 'Nice of you to visit.'

In other words, get on with it. 'I need your help, Mawmaw.'

'You tired of working for those people?'

He shifted. The way his grandmother sensed things ... 'Those people got me out of jail. Paid Una's tuition.' Kept his sister, Mawmaw, and his mother safe, too.

'You didn't answer the question.'

He sighed and watched a red hawk float on a thermal. 'Sometimes, yes, I am bone-tired of working for them, but a deal's a deal.'

'Uh-huh.'

Time to change the subject. 'I need a charm made.'

Pip came out licking his chops and flopped at Mawmaw's feet with a contented sigh. She stared out at the swamp that made up her backyard. 'What kind of charm?'

He dug into his shirt pocket, extracted the three black feathers he'd been given, and held them out to her. 'This kind.'

Pip lifted his head and gave a short, growling bark.

Rosa stopped rocking. The ash on her cigarette grew a little longer while she studied his offering. At last, she tapped the ash off and set the cigarette into a coffee cup filled with a little sand. 'I don't know what you're involved with these days, Thomas, but that's nothing for you to play with.'

'I'm not playing. I need the protection.'

'You need to leave that woman alone.'

'It's too late for that now.'

She turned enough to see his eyes. 'It's never too late.'

He stared at the words HOLD FAST tattooed across his

knuckles. 'It is. I saved her life. She's sworn to protect me now.'

His grandmother dropped her head as if praying, her eyes squeezed tightly closed for a moment, and she sighed hard. When she raised her head, Creek swore there were tears in her eyes. She held out her hand. 'These are from her?'

He gave her the feathers. 'Yes.'

She turned them over in her fingers. 'This is dark magic, child. And dark magic can't be trusted. It's fickle. Like a woman.'

'I know. That's why I'm here. She told me to come to you.'

All expression vanished from her face as she looked up at him. 'Did she call me by name?'

'No,' he reassured her. 'She didn't say your name.'

Relief lit her eyes. 'Maybe she truly doesn't mean any harm, then.' She turned the feathers over again, looking for what he didn't know. 'They feel . . . false.'

'They're real. I saw her pull them from her hair.'

'Not what I meant.' She frowned. 'I'll make the charm. You're going to need it if what you've told me is true.'

'It is. I wouldn't lie to you.'

She gave him a sideways look. 'But you'd step over the truth if you had to.'

'There are some things you shouldn't know.' Like the full details about his work as a Kubai Mata, defender of mankind, killer of othernaturals, and enslaver of desperate mortal men.

She got out of her chair. Pip was on his feet a second later. 'Yes, I know, it's for my own protection.' She motioned with a tip of her head back toward the house. 'Come inside. Let's get this charm made.'

An hour later and missing a little blood, Creek rode away

from his grandmother's, the charm dangling from a leather cord around his neck. He'd promised to visit more often but knew that promise was emptier than he meant it to be. His life was unsettled, his time not his own, and judging by the flock of ravens overhead, none of that was about to change any time soon.

Chapter Three

Paradise City, New Florida

'Madam Mayor?'

'Yes?' Lola Diaz-White looked at Valerie, her administrative assistant, and away from her inbox, currently overflowing with e-mails from citizens expressing their fear or in some cases harassment from their human neighbors or their disapproval of how she was handling the othernatural situation from both sides, or reminding her elections were less than a year away. It was enough to make her wonder if re-election was worth it.

'Alden Willamette is here to see you, and the police chief is still waiting.'

Willamette was a city councilman. No doubt he'd been getting the same kind of e-mails she had. He was a good man, honest, and one of her most stalwart supporters. She pinched the bridge of her nose, trying to stave off the headache building behind her eyes. 'Send Alden in first.'

The man came in a few moments later, shutting the door behind him. 'Lola.'

'Alden. Please, have a seat.'

He stayed standing. 'I'm fine. This won't take long. I'm sorry about this, I really am, but' – he reached into his suit jacket, pulled out an envelope, and laid it on her desk – 'effective immediately, I'm resigning.'

Her jaw slacked. 'You can't just resign. It's not like you can be replaced that easily.'

'I'm sorry. I am. I didn't mean to do it this way. Things just came to a head these last few days. As of today, though, I've tied up all my loose ends.' With a labored sigh, he finally sat. A thousand emotions rolled through his eyes. 'Lucinda's fae. Three-quarters.'

Again, Lola's jaw went south. She sat back slowly. His wife had always been unnaturally beautiful. His daughters, too. And there had always been ... something curious about them. His revelation explained so much. 'I understand you have a lot to deal with, but why does this mean you have to resign?'

He looked up, the only emotions left on his face anger and pain. 'We've been married twenty-one years and she never bothered to tell me until the night of Halloween when she couldn't keep it a secret any longer. Now she's taking the girls and moving to New Orleans. Says it's a haven city and the only safe place for them.' He ran a hand across his face. 'Do you know there are three fringe vampires in our neighborhood? Three. They look at my girls like they're sizing up their next kill. And Kaleigh – you know teenagers – she's ready to fight every time she thinks her little sister is being threatened.' He stood and walked to the windows. 'Lucinda's right about moving them. She and I have a lot to work through, but my kids are the innocents here.'

'I understand that more than you know.' She joined him at the windows. Being mayor meant she had power, but Lola had never felt so helpless in her life. Despite her connections and her pull in this city, she was no closer to holding her grandchild in her arms. Her half-vampire grandchild.

He glanced at her, but she didn't elaborate. Her grandchild was her business. 'I'm sorry to see you go.'

'Thanks.' He frowned. 'I'll be here another day or two if you need me.'

'Don't worry about it. Just take care of your family.'

He was quiet as he turned toward the door. Then he stopped. 'You know, if I could become one of them, I would. It would make everything so much easier.'

The words startled her, because she'd begun to wonder the same thing. 'You would?'

'Absolutely. They're faster than us, stronger than us, they out-live us. Why would anyone not?'

'A varcolai killed my daughter.'

'Because your daughter was human. If she'd been other-natural, she'd have at least had a fighting chance.' He shook his head. 'Face it. They're superior. I'd rather join them than become a slave to them.' He held his hands up. 'Mark my words. The tide will turn. Humans will become vampires as much as they can because that's the only choice. Fae and var-colai will side against them. War will come if peace isn't found first. Being in a haven city seems more and more like the only way a mortal like me will survive.'

She said nothing, just stayed at the windows after he shut the door behind him. His words slowly soaked into her. She turned and stared into her city. The fall of twilight meant the city looked almost normal, but during daylight it was impossible not to notice the damage left behind by Samhain night. The broken buildings and scorched streets were being repaired, but life would never be the same for any of them after that night. Would people desert her city if she couldn't protect them?

She leaned her head against the glass. How could she protect her citizens when she was as vulnerable and human as they were?

Maybe Alden was on to something about humans becoming vampires. It was like he'd somehow sensed the small thoughts creeping into her mind. Her excursion this evening might help her make sense of it all. Maybe show her the right decision. Or present her with an opportunity. She already knew what her *abuela* would say.

'Mayor?'

At Police Chief Vernadetto's voice, she turned. 'What can I do for you?'

He gestured toward her desk with the hand that held his hat. 'Did you read my report?'

'No, not yet. I've spent the day wading through e-mails and taking phone calls from concerned citizens. My apologies. Can you sum it up?' She went back to her desk, sat and began to dig out the paperwork.

He nodded. 'Long story short, several of my night patrol teams have been repeatedly harassed – hunted, you might say – in the bayside area. To the point that they've all requested reassignment unless they're allowed to use deadly force. Problem is, I can't get any human officers to go down there.'

'And the teams that are being hunted? What are they? Varcolai?'

'Varcolai are the ones doing the harassing. My teams are all fringe.'

'Vampires? Being harassed?'

'Most nights the odds are twenty to two. Not even a vampire can deal with that many shifters.'

She shook her head. Her city was in deep. 'What's your solution?'

'Deadly force. Make an example.'

'And cause a riot.' She tapped her fingers on the desktop. 'Pull whatever varcolai patrolmen you have and put them down there. Let them deal with their own kind.'

He nodded. 'Will do.'

She was about to ask why he hadn't done that already when Valerie buzzed the intercom. 'John and Luke Havoc are here, ma'am.'

'Send them in.' She stood. 'Chief, if you'll excuse me, I have another matter to attend to.'

He nodded and left as John and Luke entered.

John dipped his head in greeting. 'You sure you want to do this?'

'Positive.' A frisson of emotion zipped up Lola's spine. 'This child is my flesh and blood, my *familia*. There is no question about what I'm willing to do to get her back. None. And I owe it to Julia.'

'I get that. Family is important to us, too,' John answered. 'You ready, then?'

'Yes. Let's go.' She would have gone on her own if she didn't recognize the foolishness in that.

'Wait,' Luke said. 'I know I'm new to your employ, but I still have to tell you this is one of the dumbest things you could do.' John started to say something, but Luke held his hand out to silence him. 'But if it were my kin, I'd do the exact same thing. I just don't want you getting hurt. You have a city to run, after all.'

'A city in which both human and othernatural citizens are looking to me for guidance. If I show fear in this situation, what will they think? How will they take it if their mayor is too cowardly to face a vampire even if it means rescuing her grandchild? I must do this.'

Luke nodded. 'I understand.'

She straightened a little, buoyed by his words. 'He has no reason to hurt me. We are joined by blood now. We share a common interest.'

'He may see you as a threat,' John said. 'And not to belabor the point, but he's a vampire unlike any other. He can daywalk. He lives in a freaking abandoned church, a place no other vampire can comfortably set foot. He's not predictable in any way.'

'Then we are alike in that manner, because I doubt he expects me to come to his door.'

'No one expects that,' Luke muttered.

'That's the point,' she responded. 'Now take me to Preacher's.'

'Welcome, sir.' The butler bowed and moved to the side to let Doc enter his new home. Leaving the freighter behind wasn't something Doc was completely ready to do, but since he'd killed Sinjin and become the Paradise City pride leader by default, moving into Sinjin's old crib was kind of a requirement.

'Lose the *sir*,' Doc said, his gaze roaming the penthouse, trying to take in every bit of the lux joint at once.

'Yes, sir. Er, my apologies, si—' The butler stiffened, his face reddening.

'No worries.' Big worries, actually, but Doc wasn't going to give the man grief for doing his job. Figured Sinjin had a butler. Man always did have a big feeling about himself.

The penthouse spelled that out pretty well, too. Made perfect sense this was where Sinjin had lived. Leopards liked height. Doc was no exception to that. What he didn't like was everything else that came with this joint. Like the butler. Like being leader of the Paradise City feline varcolai pride. And being husband to Sinjin's old lady. That last bit was not sitting well with Fi, not that anyone could expect it to. Doc had spent the last two days trying to calm her down, when he should have been here, figuring a way out of this mess.

Wasn't like he'd planned on taking Sinjin out. Doc shook his head, no longer seeing the fully loaded pad around him but instead replaying the fight between him and Sinjin, the moves slowed down in his head, each punch, kick, roll, and grab like part of a choreographed dance that had gone horribly wrong when he'd suddenly gone up in flames and turned Sinjin into barbeque. The memory of that night brought a rush of heat to Doc's skin. He popped another ketamine just to be safe.

Why the hell had Sinjin thought that framing the vampires for fake comarré deaths was a good idea? The beef between Sinjin and Dominic wasn't a secret, but killing off Dominic's counterfeit comarré was no way to go about settling things. Doc had no love for the vampire either, but those girls didn't deserve to die for it. No one did. Except maybe Dominic.

Now the mayor had even more ammo against othernaturals, especially since the first fake comarré killed had been her daughter. Dammit. This was such a mess. Doc didn't know where to start fixing things. When he hadn't been calming Fi down, he'd been searching for a loophole that would free him from being pride leader, but he'd found nothing. If the pride leader challenged you and you took him on in a fight and killed him, you were the new pride leader. Plain and simple. Black and white. Done deal.

'Sir? I mean . . . ' The butler cleared his throat. 'How would you care to be addressed?'

'Doc is fine.' How much did a place like this cost anyway? Did the pride really have that kind of cash?

'I wouldn't feel comfortable with that.'

Doc turned to the butler. 'Look, I don't feel comfortable having a butler, so we both need to compromise, you dig?'

The butler nodded.

'You have a name?'

'Isaiah.'

'Good name.' Doc nodded. 'My grandmother would have approved.'

Isaiah smiled. 'Thank you. May I call you Mr. Mays, perhaps?'

With a deep inhale, Doc shook his head. 'You call me Mr. Mays and I'll be looking for my father. How about you call me by my full name, Maddoc.'

'Such a civilized name for an alley cat,' a voice purred. Another feline presence filled the space, and Doc turned, his gaze landing on the person who'd caused the heartache in his relationship with Fi these past few days.

Isaiah gave her a little head bow, then held his hand out toward her as he addressed Doc. 'Maddoc, this is Heaven Silva. Your wife.'

Chapter Four

Velimai's mood hadn't improved since Chrysabelle had thrown Mal out, so Chrysabelle walked outside to meet Creek after the guard at the front gate had called with his arrival. She perched on the fountain's edge in the center of the circular drive, trailing her fingers through the water and listening for the sound of his motorcycle over the fountain's gurgling.

The bike's rumble preceded him and a few seconds later, he drove through the estate's open gates and parked a few feet away. He climbed off the bike, set his helmet on the seat, and smiled. 'It's good to see you. You look healthy.'

'Good to see you, too. And I am healthy. I guess. What brings you by?' She had nothing against small talk, but her mind was elsewhere.

'Straight to it, then.' He sat beside her on the fountain's wide ledge. 'Look, this is hard for me to tell you, but try to remember at this point, I'm just the messenger. I want you to understand that.'

'Okay.' Had to be Kubai Mata business. Creek always seemed so apologetic about it. 'What's going on?'

'Samhain evening, my sector chief informed me that the Castus have the vampire child.'

She nodded. 'We already know that.' She'd kicked Mal out and yet she'd just said *we*. Like the two of them were a unit.

He nodded. 'I figured you did.' He worried a small hole near the knee of his jeans. 'The KM want you to get the baby back.'

'Why me? Why don't they send their own warriors in?'

'We're too obvious. Too detectable. Nobles would scent us out immediately – if we even got past the city wards.' He jerked a thumb over his shoulder. 'Those sacred brands? They make our blood smell sour. Ask Mal, he'll tell you.'

She shook her head. 'The KM has resources. They could figure something out.'

He sighed. 'They have figured something out. That they want you to get the baby back. I'm sorry, Chrysabelle. I know you probably have no desire to go back there.'

She studied him. The bend of his mouth and the way he sat a little hunched over told her he wasn't enjoying this. 'And if I refuse?'

He dragged a hand over his Mohawk. 'They'll start by eliminating Mal.'

She laughed sharply. 'If the nobility can't kill him, I'd like to see the KM try.'

His gaze shifted and his voice lowered. 'Then they'll come after you. I'm powerless to stop them.'

Anger ripped through her. 'I've done nothing to them. They have no reason to involve me in this.'

He sat back. 'That's not totally true. You haven't returned the ring of sorrows to them.'

'Why should I even care about returning a ring to an organization I know so little about? If I even still had the ring.'

He stood and paced a few steps away. 'I don't know much about them either, and half of what I do know, I question.' He raised his hand as if to stop himself from talking.

'Then why keep working for them?'

He looked sideways, like someone might be watching. 'I owe them, Chrysabelle. Big time. For my freedom. For things they've done for my family.' He shook his head. 'They own me. At least for a little while longer.'

'No one should be indebted like that.' Her anger with him defused. She understood exactly the position he was in. 'You have to find a way out.'

He exhaled, his words quiet. 'I can't. Not yet.'

'Do they know what I've done with the ring?'

'No.'

She stood, ready to go back inside. 'Then tell them.'

Something close to fear shadowed his eyes. 'That's calling down trouble.'

'I can handle it. And I want them to know they don't control me. So tell them exactly what I did with their precious ring and that there's nothing you can do about it. Then maybe they'll leave you alone.'

'Nothing will make them leave me alone.' He spoke the words quietly, his tone resigned.

Her anger on his behalf grew. 'In fact, tell them I want nothing to do with them and will consider them enemies if they contact me again.' She turned and headed back to the house.

'Chrysabelle—'

She spun back around. 'I don't mean you, Creek. You can contact me, but not on their behalf. I like you. You've been a good friend to me.' More than that. He'd saved her life more than once. Fought at her side. Kissed her. She tempered her anger for the sake of their friendship. 'If the Kubai Mata want that child, they'll need a new plan. I'm done being a pawn for the greater good.' She paused. 'So should you.'

By the time she reached the front door, the sound of Creek's motorcycle had already begun to fade. She slammed the door behind her and stormed into the kitchen. Her anger wasn't completely at the KM for wanting her to do their bidding. No, much of it was at herself for pushing Mal away. Velimai glanced up from where she was setting plates of dinner on the table.

'That was Creek,' Chrysabelle said. Like Velimai hadn't heard when the guard had called. She threw herself into one of the kitchen chairs, her temper darkening with each passing minute. Why was she so afraid of facing things? Why did Mal raise such emotion in her? Answering those questions meant coming to terms with what she was feeling. Something she was so not ready to do.

She wished Velimai would just sign something. Anything to break the stoniness that had settled over the house since she'd thrown Mal out. Velimai sat, intent on her dinner. Chrysabelle cut a bite of steak and stuffed it into her mouth, but all she tasted was anger. Enough. She swallowed and set her fork down. 'I didn't mean for things to go that way with Mal. He just has a way of . . . pushing my buttons.'

Velimai looked up from her meal, putting her silverware aside to free her hands. *How did you mean for things to go?*

'I don't know.' She slid her plate away. 'Why do I do that? Why does everything with him have to be a battle? Why does he always find a way to do exactly what I don't want him to do?' She lifted her gaze toward the ceiling for a second. 'Why do I even care?'

You two are very much alike. You need each other. Both seeking something that can't be found alone.

Chrysabelle pursed her mouth. 'Riddles don't help.'

Velimai shrugged and went back to eating.

Chrysabelle's appetite was gone, Velimai's words ringing soundlessly in her head. 'I should get Jerem to take me out to the freighter and apologize. Plus I owe Mal blood.' And she could fill him in on what the KM was up to. She stood, dropping her napkin onto her plate. 'Will you tell Jerem I need the car? I'm going to shower first, but then I want to go out to Mal's.'

Velimai nodded.

Chrysabelle turned away and almost ran across the living room and up the stairs. What did Velimai think she and Mal were seeking? Freedom? That was true. But did they really need each other? The thought of being without him upset her. Did that mean she cared for him? If she did, why did she fight with him this way? Why did he always set her off so easily? She would not travel the same path as her mother. Falling in love with a vampire had gotten her mother nothing but years of misery. And ultimately, death. Not that Dominic was so awful, but something had gone wrong between them. Enough that Maris had ultimately chosen to live alone rather than with him.

Chrysabelle pushed through the doors to her suite and didn't stop until she was naked under the pulsing jets of her shower. She would visit Mal, apologize, and give him blood. Then she might as well talk to Damian and see what she could find out. Mal had said the comar was at the freighter. Why, she couldn't imagine, but if Mal had done it to keep the comar out of her hair while she recovered, then she owed him one. The floral scent of her shampoo did nothing to soothe her. If Damian was with Mal, where was Saraphina, the comarré who had run away with him?

She rinsed the soap from her hair and skin. Maybe Mal had her, too. If so, Chrysabelle might be off the hook for giving him blood. In fact, if Saraphina stayed with him, Mal wouldn't need Chrysabelle's blood at all.

The bittersweetness of that thought brought an unexpected ache to her soul. She leaned her head against the slick marble wall, closed her eyes, and let the water beat down onto her.

Holy mother. Maybe Velimai was right. Maybe she did need him. She shook herself and shoved those thoughts away. There was too much to deal with right now to worry about something as insignificant as feelings. Like finding her brother.

Nothing pressed on her so much as finding him and fulfilling her mother's wish. After everything Maris had done for her, getting her brother home was the least Chrysabelle could do. To know that she had family, *real* family – not just the preordained brothers, sisters, aunts, and uncles of the comarré life – made her long to know him with a yearning that sprang from her soul. She *would* find him. No matter what it took.

An hour later, she walked up the gangway to Mal's abandoned freighter, wearing both sacres, a pair of wrist blades, and a new attitude. She would not let Mal upset her. If he wanted to talk about what had happened at Atticus's, she would politely steer the conversation in a new direction until such time as she felt comfortable dealing with whatever Mal thought was going on.

The ship, as always, was dark and deserted, lit only by the weak solars that dotted the never-ending labyrinth of passageways. 'Mal? It's Chrysabelle.' As if he wouldn't know.

She had a general idea of which way to go. Her heightened sense of smell helped a bit, too. Mal's dark spice pervaded the ship's space, but it was stronger in some directions than others. She followed the path she remembered in her head, taking a flight of stairs that seemed familiar and taking a turn that looked right, passing corridors and doors that, one after another, seemed to blend together.

Frustration building, she called for him again. 'Mal! Hello? Anyone?'

A shimmering image burst through the wall ahead of her and turned into Fi. 'Hey. What are you doing here?'

'Fi, I'm so glad someone's here. I'm trying to find Mal. I think I got a little turned around.'

The ghost girl frowned. 'Last I saw him, he was at your house. Did he leave without telling you?'

Chrysabelle sighed. 'I may have thrown him out.'

Fi's face was blank for a moment, then she laughed. The laughter faded fast. 'Men suck.'

Chrysabelle's brows lifted. 'Something going on with you and Doc?'

'I take it Mal hasn't filled you in on what's been going on?'

'No.' Not that she'd given him a chance.

'Walk with me to the galley.' Fi's feet hit the floor a second after she became corporeal. She turned down the closest corridor. 'Long story, but the short version is he's the new Paradise City pride leader, and that job comes with a wife.'

Chrysabelle easily matched the shorter girl's stride. 'And you don't want to fill the position?' She'd thought the varcolai and Fi were crazy about each other, but maybe she'd been wrong.

Fi shook her head. 'The position's already been filled by the previous leader's wife. When Doc killed Sinjin – who was the one killing off Dominic's comarrés, in case you hadn't heard . . .'

'I hadn't. Go on.'

'Anyway, when Doc killed him, he inherited everything that had been Sinjin's. Including the guy's wife.'

'What?' Chrysabelle stared in disbelief. 'That's rather archaic.'

'That's pride law. The same set of rules that kicked Doc out of the pride have now put him in charge of it.'

'Wow.' Chrysabelle took a moment to process. What else had happened in the last few days that she didn't know about?

'Wow is right. Freaking sucks is more like it.' Emotion thickened Fi's voice. 'Where does that leave me?'

'Well, you still love him, right?'

'Yes.'

'And he still loves you, right?'

'I suppose.'

'Fi, come on.'

She blew out a long, hard breath. 'Yes, he still loves me.'

'So why can't you and Doc just explain things to this woman? I'm sure she'll understand. She probably doesn't want to be married to Doc any more than you want her to be.'

'Hmph. I wouldn't count on that. Pride marriages among the ruling class are pretty old school from what Doc's explained to me. Sinjin didn't marry for love. He married for alliance. This woman's father is the leader of one of the biggest prides in existence. Riling her up would be a very bad thing.'

Chrysabelle looped her arm around Fi's shoulders. 'There has to be a way to work this out.'

Fi shrugged, conveying about as much positive energy as a burned out match. 'Whatever.' She glanced up at Chrysabelle.

'So what's going on with you? Doc and I came by to see you, but you were out cold and Mal didn't want to hear about anything. All he could do was focus on you. He's into you pretty hard. Like you don't know that.' Suddenly her face brightened. 'Did he tell you how he feels? Is that why you kicked him out?'

'No, that's not why. I kicked him out because he wanted to talk about something I didn't. But now I know he was probably right, even if his timing sucked.'

Fi nodded as she stopped and opened a door. 'You want a cup of tea?' She stepped over the threshold and flipped on the solars, illuminating the galley.

'Sure. Might as well hang out and wait for Mal.' The last time she'd been in this kitchen, she hadn't even really known who Mal was. That felt like years ago.

'You can always go relieve Damian for a bit if you want. I'm sure he'd appreciate the break.'

'Mal told me he was here. Relieve him from what?'

Fi filled the teakettle. 'He's guarding that vampiress who defected from Tatiana. Darciana or Dulciana or something.'

A chill settled in Chrysabelle's gut as she took a seat. 'Daciana?'

'Yeah, I think that's her name. We've got her locked up in one of the storage containers in the far hold.' Fi lit a Sterno pot and set the kettle over it. 'You know her?'

'Yes, but her husband is the one you have to watch out for. He's very ambitious. Like a male version of Tatiana.'

Fi leaned against the counter. 'According to Daciana, Tatiana killed her husband. That's one of the reasons she wants asylum.'

Chrysabelle narrowed her eyes. 'I don't buy it.'

'Me neither.' The ghost girl smiled. 'You want to go talk to her?'

'I don't think—'

'You know, she showed up on your doorstep.' Fi waggled her brows. 'Wanted us to let her into your *house*.'

Chrysabelle's fingers stroked the leather crisscross of her sacre straps. 'Did she now?' Annoyance pushed her to her feet. 'Couldn't hurt to ask a few questions, could it?'

'That's what I'm saying.' Fi capped the Sterno. 'What if she refuses to answer you straight up?'

Chrysabelle flicked one wrist blade out. 'I can be pretty persuasive when I want to be.'

Chapter Five

The rabble split with appropriate respect as Mal shoved his way through the crowd outside Seven. *Fools*. Wearing his noble face no doubt helped, but the crowd's respect meant nothing. He was on a mission. Finding a new blood source was the first step in distancing himself from Chrysabelle. *Blood blood blood*. Loosening her hold on his hunger would make it easier to need her less. Might even help him forget what being next to her in bed had felt like. He hoped.

The fringe working the velvet ropes outside the door held a hand up. 'Cover's a buck fifty.'

'A hundred and fifty dollars? Dominic's lost his mind.'

The fringe shrugged. 'It's Friday, my brother. All the freaks wanna play, and for that, you gotta pay.'

'I am not your brother.' One of the two hulking varcolai bouncers behind the fringe snickered. Mal glanced up, wishing for the old days when Seven's entrance was a dimly lit doorway with easy-to-glamour guards. Easy for him anyway. No other Tepes vampire he knew could use their persuasion power on varcolai or fae.

'Not technically, but we *are* both vampires—'

'Whatever.' Mal pushed past. 'Dominic owes me. You want my cover charge, get it from him.' Dominic *did* owe him, although Dominic might not see it that way. Mal's blood had taken the place of Dominic's with the witches. That had to be worth something. *Or nothing. Just like you.*

Wisely, the varcolai bouncers let him pass. Maybe they knew who he was or maybe they knew Mal's relationship to Doc. Either way, he entered without further obstruction. Once inside, he quickly found Katsumi. He would have rather found Mortalis, but the shadeux fae didn't seem to be around.

She arched a brow at him. 'Please tell me you've come to take on a few new opponents in the Pits.'

'Like hell. Where's Dominic? I need to talk to him.'

'In his office.' She sidled closer, her jasmine scent creeping over him. 'But maybe I can help you.' One black polished fingernail glided down his arm. 'What do you need?'

Blood. 'For you to back off.' He walked away, shaking his head. Maybe the side effects of navitas had begun to set in. Being resired was known to cause insanity. Tatiana was proof of that. Katsumi seemed to be sliding in that direction.

Someone grabbed his sleeve. He spun, instantly defensive. 'I told you—'

A petite blonde, one of Dominic's comarré, dropped her hand from his arm and bent her head. 'I'm sorry to upset you, master. I saw you talking with Ms. Tanaka. I thought you wanted company.'

'Don't call me master,' he snapped.

The girl cringed and backed away. Her signum, such as they were, gleamed dully in the club's low lights. 'My apologies for—'

'Stop.' Mal sighed. Bloody hell, he was a monster. *Yes, you are.* 'I didn't mean to ... When you first grabbed my arm, I thought you were Katsumi.'

The girl lifted her head. She wasn't unattractive, but she was no Chrysabelle. 'You're a friend of Ms. Tanaka's? I see that you're noble like her.'

He exhaled derisively. 'I was noble before her grandparents were born.'

'Of course, sir.' She nodded, her long blonde curls swaying. 'Are you in need of blood?'

Yessss ... drink drink drink. 'Yes, but I need to speak to Dominic first.'

Her eyes widened slightly. They weren't as blue as Chrysabelle's. 'I can take you to Mr. Scarnato, if you'd like.'

'I can find my own way there.'

Her head dropped again. 'As you wish. Have a pleasant evening.' She curtseyed and began to leave.

The voices whined at the loss of the blood, cursing him in every language they spoke. 'What's your name?'

She looked up, hope brightening her face. 'Alice.'

He bent slightly, peered into her eyes, and added a touch of persuasion to his voice. 'Go home, Alice. Forget this place exists. Go back to school and do something meaningful with your life.'

Her pretty face contorted with insolence. 'Don't use your powers on me, vampire. We're warded against that. You think Dominic's stupid?' With a snort, she twisted on her heel and stormed off, her previous coyness gone.

Well. That was interesting. Made sense Dominic would protect his comarré from vampire influence. Wouldn't want any of them being persuaded to become someone's pet for free.

But fringe didn't have the same powers nobles did, so who was he protecting them against? Tatiana's return? Or the newly resired Katsumi? Either way, Dominic was smart. Shady. But smart.

Mal made his way to Dominic's office. He sensed Dominic was alone. Good. He didn't want an audience for the conversation he was about to have. He knocked and a few seconds later, Dominic bid him enter. Mal did and saw that he'd been wrong about Dominic being alone. Seated in front of Dominic's desk was a leanly muscled, dark-haired vampire Mal didn't recognize.

'Am I interrupting something?' He glanced at the other vampire. Definitely noble, not quite Dominic's age but not a vampling either. How had Mal not sensed him?

'No, no,' Dominic assured him. 'This is Luciano, my nephew. He's come to help me run things here. Every night, Seven gets busier. It's good to have family you can trust.'

'Luciano.' Mal nodded at the other vampire. 'Are you St. Germain like your uncle?'

'No.' Luciano grinned. 'I am House of Paole.'

That explained not being able to sense him. Paole vampires were undetectable to other vampires. Sneaky bastards.

Dominic leaned back in his desk chair. 'Luciano is a *caedo*.'

A chill skittered down Mal's spine at the word. He tensed, instantly on guard. He'd been hunted by *caedo* many years ago. Unsuccessfully, but hunted nonetheless.

Luciano threw his hands up. '*Zio, per favore.* Why would you tell him that?'

Dominic waved Luciano's concerns away. 'Malkolm is anathema. Like us. You worry for nothing.' He stood and walked out from behind his desk and laid his hand on Mal's. 'This man sacrificed his blood for mine. That is a debt I have not yet repaid. He will say nothing, will you, Malkolm?'

'No.' He kept his eyes on Luciano, who didn't look quite convinced yet. 'So long as you're not here for me.'

Luciano frowned. 'Why would I be here for you? I'm here because my uncle needs me. And because I grew tired of life as the nobility's errand boy.'

Errand boy? How about killer? *Like you.* The *caedo* were an elite force of vampire assassins. They did the dirty work other nobles didn't want to soil their hands with but were willing to empty their accounts to pay for. 'Dominic said you were anathema like us. What did you do?'

Luciano's eyes sparked silver. 'I quit.'

No one quit the *caedo*. Except by death. That explained Luciano's reluctance to have his profession revealed.

Dominic gestured toward a chair. 'Sit, my friend. Let us share some wine to celebrate Luciano's arrival.'

'Wine isn't what I need.' Nor did he need to carry the weight of any more of Dominic's family secrets.

'Ah, I see. There is something else I can help you with?'

'I need blood. From one of your comarrés.' Damnation, it pained him to say those words.

Dominic went back behind his desk and sat. 'I would be happy to do this for you, except ... ' He stared at Mal expectantly, and when Mal didn't say anything, he finished, 'What about Chrysabelle?'

And there it was. The question he'd known would be asked. Mal sat, buying a little time to form an answer. 'She's still recovering. I don't want to bother her.'

Dominic lifted his brows. 'That hasn't stopped you – or her – from the exchange in the past.' He shrugged and lifted his hands. 'I don't want to do something that might upset her. You know she's like family to me.' He leaned toward Luciano. 'She's Maris's daughter, the comarré I spoke of earlier.'

'Marissa? *Sì.*' Luciano nodded.

What Mal knew was that Dominic wasn't going to let it drop until he got a better answer. 'I need to put some distance between us. Her wishes.'

'Ah.' Dominic absently tapped his fingers on the desk. 'She is just like her mother, that one.' His hand went still. 'Any time you need blood, you have only to come to me. As I'm sure you would extend yourself to me, should I need anything.'

So a favor for a favor. Fine. He should have known Dominic wouldn't give without getting something in exchange. Mal had no desire to return to pig's blood. 'Haven't I proven that in the past?'

'You have.' Dominic pressed the intercom on his desk. 'Send one of the best comarré up.'

'Yes, sir,' a female voice answered.

Mal shifted. He hadn't wanted to do this with an audience, but neither did he want to be alone with a human with an open vein. Chrysabelle could fight him off. One of Dominic's comarrés could not.

'Do you wish privacy?' Dominic asked.

'No.' He forced himself to relax.

'Please.' Dominic held his hand toward a secluded corner of his office that held a chair, low table, and love seat. 'I don't care to be watched while I dine either.'

Without further argument, Mal got up and went to the seating area. A few minutes later, someone knocked.

'Come,' Dominic called.

The door opened. 'You sent for me, master?'

Son of a priest. Of all the comarré Dominic had, Alice was the one who got sent up?

'Yes,' Dominic answered. He pulled a knife from a desk drawer and held it out to her. 'Take this, get a glass from the bar, then fill it for my guest there.' He gestured toward Mal. She didn't look, but Luciano watched with interest.

With a hesitant movement, she accepted the dagger. 'May I ask why, master?'

Bloody hell. Mal growled softly, causing her to turn. 'Because I can't drink from the vein.'

'You,' she whispered. A flash of anger passed over her face, quickly disappearing into a mask of obedience. 'As you wish.'

'Do you know each other?' Dominic asked.

'No,' Alice said.

'Yes.' Mal crossed his ankle over the opposite knee and leaned back. 'I tried to use my powers of persuasion on her in the club. She didn't care for it.'

Dominic laughed. 'I'm sure she explained that my comarré are warded against that. Trying to get a replacement for Chrysabelle?'

'Something like that.' Mal held eye contact with Alice, challenging her to say otherwise. Tired of the games, he pointed to the chair next to him. 'Sit.'

She did as he asked, setting the glass on the low table. 'Now what?'

'Nick your vein and hold it over the glass.' How simple was she?

'Why not just bite me? It's so much simpler.'

'I told you I can't drink from the vein.' *Can and should.*

Indignation rolled off her in waves. 'Do you think I'm not worthy?'

Every muscle in his body tensed. He reminded himself he'd thought this a good idea. 'I do *not* drink from the vein.'

'Alice,' Dominic barked. 'Do as he asks without question. Do not make me speak to Katsumi about your training.'

'Yes, master.' Disgust in her eyes, she held out her arm and pricked her wrist with the dagger. She yelped, biting her lip. Red beaded up, perfuming the office with the coppery scent of faded roses. Human blood. She turned her wrist over and the glass began to fill.

Mal waited until the blood was an inch from the top. No point in not getting as much as he could if he had to endure this torture to get it. 'Enough.'

'Like I could give you any more,' she whispered, pressing her fingers to her wrist and lifting her chin as if she'd just provided him with the finest vintage wine France had to offer.

He took the glass and chugged it without ceremony. The blood held none of Chrysabelle's sweetness or power. There was no sharp burst of pleasurable pain as his body came to life, no beating heart, no need to draw breath. Just the sensation of being full and the numbing of the voices, something human blood had always done. He set the glass down and stood. Time to go home. Check on the comar and see about the vampiress being held captive in the freighter's hold. 'Dominic, my thanks.' He tipped his head at Luciano.

'Whenever you need it,' he reminded Mal. Luciano lifted his hand in farewell.

Alice stared up at him intently, obviously waiting for him to thank her as well. 'Feel better?'

'Not much.' He hadn't stopped thinking about Chrysabelle once. 'I've had real comarré blood. This isn't it.'

Chapter Six

'Prick me again and I'll have your fingers cut off,' Tatiana snarled.

The modiste jerked the pin away from the gown's bodice. 'I'm so sorry, my lady. I will be more careful.'

'Yes, you will be.' Nothing irritated Tatiana more than inactivity. Standing on this platform before these mirrors, being fitted for a gown to wear to the Dominus ball, was not the best use of her time. Not when she could be in New Florida hunting down that comarré whore and finally taking possession of the ring of sorrows. With that power, Tatiana would be utterly unstoppable, and protecting Lilith would be as easy as breathing. If Tatiana still breathed.

Octavian strolled in. His eyes silvered as he took her in. 'You look glorious.' He stopped by Lilith's crib, leaning down to coo soft words and tickle her belly. Pride swelled in Tatiana at how good he was with her. She'd been so right to turn him from the kine head of her household staff to her vampire paramour. 'Sweet child,' he whispered. He kissed her tiny fist, then came to Tatiana's side and kissed her cheek. 'Hello, my love.'

'Octavian, don't keep me waiting. How did her blood tests come out?'

'Everything's fine. With the strains of vampirism in her system, the doctor doesn't think any of the usual immunizations will be necessary.'

'Excellent.' Relieved, she glanced at Lilith's crib. 'I'd hate to subject her to that kine again.'

'He's not such a bad fellow. But enough about him.' He took her hand and held her arm out. 'I know nothing about women's fashion, but you do wonders for this dress.' He winked at her as he released her hand.

She smiled and smoothed the skirt. 'I do, don't I?' She studied the gown. Deep purple silk corseted her torso with a heavy crusting of diamond embellishment purposefully designed to conceal two slender blades that could be whipped out at a moment's notice. From her waist, the gown flared so that it flowed around her like water when she walked. Let Svetla's pale blondness try to compete.

'You look like the queen you are.'

'I'm having a tiara made to match. Diamonds and amethyst.'

'As you should.' He glanced at Lilith. 'And for our little one?'

'Lavender silk and a headband stitched with diamonds and amethyst as well.'

He nodded. 'Like mother, like daughter.'

She glanced at the seamstress and her helpers, reluctant to talk about private matters in front of them but eager to find out if Octavian had news from Daciana. 'Any word from our associate?'

'Unfortunately, no.' He grasped his hands behind his back

and walked forward a few steps. He released his hands, clenching them into fists. 'I have no clear way of making contact, despite our new advances.'

Since declaring computers and communication devices no longer off-limits in the House of Tepes, Tatiana had been frustrated by how few members seemed interested in using them. She was slowly learning to use them herself and understood these things took time, but how could anyone not want to take advantage of the technology? 'That's very disappointing. Do you think . . . all is still well? It's been nearly five days.' And no word from Daciana. Anything could have happened to her. Tatiana swallowed down the building emotions. This was what came of allowing herself to care about others. She reached for the locket around her neck, comforted by its weight in her hand.

Octavian shook his head as if to dispel her thoughts. 'I'm sure everything is fine. You know I'm willing to take care of this in person, if you wish. I can leave immediately. Just say the word.'

'I can't spare you. With the ball approaching, I need you here with me. Especially when . . . ' She studied the kine around her, looking for listening ears. 'All of you, outside until I've called you back.'

'Yes, my lady.' The modiste motioned for her helpers to leave.

As soon as the doors closed, Tatiana stepped off the platform to face Octavian. 'I'd love to have you check on Daciana, but I suspect the council has eyes on me.' She threw her hands up. 'I hate that those pompous fools can affect me this way. After all I've been through with them, the way they fought me becoming Elder, the way they made me wait after Ivan's death, the way they doubt me and question me at every turn—'

Octavian took her hands in his. 'You're Dominus now. One

of the council yourself!' He held her gaze. 'There's *nothing* they can do against you.'

'Not openly, no. Just because they must accept me publicly doesn't mean they won't still try to tear me down in private. With the ancient ones so firmly on my side, I have no doubt jealousy will drive at least one of them to oppose me. More than one, I'm sure.'

'My darling.' He shook his head. 'Let them try. What can they do? You think the Castus will not punish any who dare come against you? You watch. The rest of the families will be your dutiful servants at the ball.'

She pursed her lips. 'For show, yes. But what they plan behind closed doors—'

'Again, I say let them. Let one attempt something. I'm sure the Castus will make an example of them the rest will not soon forget.'

An idea flared in her mind. She smiled, her fears ebbing as the new thought formed. 'Or we could make our own example.'

His face lit up, his whiskey eyes going silver with joy. 'You are the most brilliant woman I've ever known. I'll work on that immediately. Do you have a preference?'

'Oh, yes.' She laughed, giddy with purpose. 'Svetla.'

After he'd parked his bike inside the machine shop, Creek pulled the rolling door closed and locked it. The shop that he'd turned into his headquarters looked about as rough as any other building in downtown Paradise City, but that was the idea. No one would ever guess the place was so secure. Being back in his childhood neighborhood was no joy, but it afforded him great access to the othernatural lowlifes from whom he was duty-bound to protect humanity. Walking past the shop's open area, he hung his leather jacket on a hook on one of the sleeping loft's support columns.

He leaned against the big steelwork sink in his makeshift kitchen and stared at the glass block window above it, letting Chrysabelle's words sink in. As much as he agreed with her, there was nothing he could do. The KM owned him for now. Sure, he'd rather live out in the Glades near his mother and grandmother. Someday, he would. Someday when his debt to the Kubai Mata was paid. At least, that's what he liked to tell himself.

He grabbed a beer from the fridge and loped up the stairs to his bedroom. From there, he climbed through the one unboarded window to sit out on the fire escape. He wished Chrysabelle had been more receptive to his message from the KM, but he understood. Completely. She'd been through a lot. He hadn't expected her to want to go after a vampire child when it meant putting herself in Tatiana's path again. Chrysabelle deserved to be able to do what she wanted to do. Even if that included Mal. At least she hadn't shut Creek out entirely, although he'd given up on his feelings for her. There was a bond between her and Mal he couldn't penetrate.

He should probably stop thinking about her. Not that she was the only woman on his mind lately. He settled onto the grated steps of the fire escape, twisted the beer cap off, took a pull, then set the bottle beside him. From inside his shirt, he tugged loose the charm his grandmother had made. It was warm from being against his skin. His grandmother had wrapped the three black feathers in leather and silver, sealed the knots with blood, said words over it Creek didn't understand, then passed the whole thing through the smoke from an assortment of dried herbs and other things Creek didn't remember.

He lifted it to his nose and inhaled. A faint hint of the soulless woman's briny, ocean-air scent remained. He turned the charm over in his fingers. 'Yahla,' he whispered. If not for the proof in his hand, he'd think she'd been a dream.

'You called?'

He started, nearly sending the beer clattering to the asphalt below as he twisted to look toward the voice.

She perched on the stairs above, her head cocked to one side, eyes bright and blinking, body hugged in bits of black leather and low-slung jeans. 'I am here.'

He stood and moved against the rail to put a little distance between them. 'I see that.' For a deadly aberration, she was unquestionably hot.

'You have no need to fear me now.' She bobbed her head toward the charm. 'Your grandmother is a wise woman.'

He tucked the charm back inside his shirt. 'Yes, she is.' And he was a fool for not telling this one to leave him alone.

She rose and walked slowly down the steps. 'You have thought of me.'

It wasn't a question, but he answered anyway, unable to keep the word from leaving his mouth. 'Yes.'

Almost toe-to-toe with him, she stopped, an odd smile curving her lips. The long feathers of her hair shifted like silk in the breeze. 'Do you find me beautiful?'

'Yes.' Again the word was spoken before he could think otherwise. It was like she pulled the truth from him.

Her hand lifted, her fingers coming to light upon his chest. They were warm through his thin T-shirt. 'I can make you forget her,' she whispered.

He didn't doubt that. He also didn't doubt she could do a whole hell of a lot of other bad things to him. 'I don't know who you're talking about.' Could she read his mind?

'The gold one. She is not for you. Her blood is not your blood as mine is. We are of the same people, you and I. We are kin.'

'She's just a friend.' He drew away to the side of the fire escape and found his voice as soon as her touch left him. 'And you're a myth. A story my people tell.'

Her eyes darkened until not even the light from inside his bedroom reflected in them. 'You're Kubai Mata. How many people believe in you?'

She had a point, but it wasn't one that made him like her any better. Irritation popped his jaw. 'You should go.'

Her head tipped to the side and she blinked a few times. 'You are angry with me, but I am not the one who bound you to the Kubai Mata's promise. You did that to yourself.'

'I did it for my family.' Was every woman in his life going to come down on him for that?

She came a little closer but didn't touch him again. 'Your reasons are enough. But I am sad that you deny yourself for them.' Her lip curled in disgust. 'The Kubai Mata.'

'I don't deny myself anything.'

'They rule you. They are your master.'

'They got me out of *prison*.'

At the word, her mouth softened again. 'You did not deserve that place for what you did.'

'I agree, but the jury thought otherwise.'

She spat. 'And none of them tribe. None of them your people.'

'No.' She had a point, but all that was in the past now.

Her hand reached out and her fingers bunched in the fabric of his T-shirt. The space between them disappeared. She pressed against his chest and her pulse vibrated through his body, so fast it was like a shudder. Tendrils of heat curled around his muscles, brushing against his nerve endings with soft insistence. 'I am your people.'

'Yes.' She was. He was half Seminole. She was born of Seminole myth.

Her lids fluttered as her hands slipped higher up his chest. 'And I can set you free of the Kubai Mata.'

He shook his head, her mouth dangerously close to his, her eyes impossible to look away from. He wanted her. Right down to the soles of his feet. 'I ... I can't be free of them until my family is safe.'

She threw her head back and laughed, the sound a soft *caw-caw-caw*. 'I have promised to protect you.'

'It's not me I'm worried about. My sister, my mother, my grandmother. They're my concern.'

Her hand flattened down hard on his chest. 'You think I would hurt them?'

He looked into her eyes, searching for a reason to answer otherwise, but he seemed destined to always speak the truth around her. 'Yes.'

She pushed away, but he grabbed her hand, unwilling to let her go. Unwilling to dismiss the possibility that she could do what she said. 'Give me your word. Your promise. Tell me you'll protect them, too. Otherwise, I want nothing to do with you anymore.'

Her eyes were wild, her mouth slightly open as her chest rose and fell. 'What do you give me in return?'

Reluctantly, he released her. 'What do you want?'

Instead of answering, she stepped back and dragged her hands through her hair, then held them out, her palms full of feathers. 'Take these to your grandmother. Have her make charms for each of them.'

He took the feathers and tucked them into the pocket of his jeans. What had he just agreed to? And why didn't he care more what the answer was?

'You are a good man, Thomas Creek.' She flattened herself against him, her breasts soft through the leather top she wore. Her hands came up to stroke the column of his neck, the shaved sides of his head, each caress dragging him toward the line between control and abandon. She leaned up and touched her mouth to his, just enough contact to pull a groan from his throat.

Instantly, his emotions returned to the day he'd stepped free of the prison grounds. Every want and desire he'd ever had while trapped inside that steel and concrete hellhole now burned in him again. Nothing mattered but possessing Yahla. His hands tightened on the bare skin above the waist of her jeans. 'I'm not as good as you think I am.'

She laughed, the same birdlike sound as before, then pulled his head down to hers and kissed him with a fire that ignited every wicked thought coursing through his brain. When she released him, he was panting. She smiled and took his hand to lead him back through the window and into the bedroom.

'You saved me. And now I am going to save you.'

Chapter Seven

The lights of Umberto's restaurant lit up the night like a burning ember in an ashtray. The last time Lola had come to Little Havana, she'd been here to identify her daughter's body. Pain pierced her heart as the car drove on. She hadn't planned on coming back so soon. If ever. It wasn't that she'd abandoned the neighborhood of her people; she'd just . . . risen above it. Her *abuela* had pushed her to get out. To better herself. To join the ranks of the successful. *If you can't beat them, join them*, her *abuela* had always said. And join them Lola had, despite the cost to her personal life.

Little Havana was one of the least desirable places to live in Paradise City. For her, it represented everything she'd clawed her way out of.

And yet, this was where she was from. Where her daughter had lived. Where the father of her grandchild made his home. What kind of man was this vampire named Preacher?

John Havoc, the captain of her security team who was currently seated beside her, had told her everything he'd known about the man. Which wasn't much, but it certainly painted a picture. Preacher was the only vampire anyone knew of who could daywalk or tolerate religious symbols. John said the man had been a marine and a medic, that he'd inadvertently turned himself through an infusion of blood during the Great War.

'It's just up ahead.' Luke Havoc pointed from the front seat. 'Around this corner.'

Her heart rate sped up. John turned his head toward her. 'Don't be nervous. Luke and I are here to protect you.'

She'd forgotten about the varcolai's heightened senses. 'I suppose he'll be able to hear my pulse, too?'

John nodded. 'Yes. But that's okay. You're coming in peace. Not to harm him.'

'I suppose.' The car rolled to a stop and parked. Her driver would stay here to guard the vehicle. In this part of town, there might not be a vehicle to come back to if he didn't.

Luke got out and waited for them on the sidewalk. John held the door, then closed it behind her. They flanked her as they approached the abandoned Catholic church where Preacher made his home. She crossed herself as Luke knocked on the church's arched double doors. The stucco was cracked in numerous places, the painted trim had faded in the sun, and what little remained of the once-beautiful stained glass windows told her the building's glory days were long past. 'I went to Mass here as a child,' she told no one in particular. 'With my *abuela*.' Who would die all over again if she knew there was a demon living in the sanctuary now.

Luke knocked a second time, but there was still no answer. He walked to where she and John stood. 'It's possible he's out feeding.'

Lola shuddered. 'This was a bad idea.'

One of the front doors shot open, its rusted hinges protesting.

A man wearing fatigues and sporting a shaved head stood inside, a gleaming blade in one hand. He bared a set of fangs smaller than John's and Luke's, but no less frightening. 'What do you want?'

She cleared her throat and stepped forward. John put his hand on her arm, but she hadn't planned on going any farther. 'My name is Delores Diaz-White. I believe you knew my daughter, Julia White.'

The vampire froze, becoming so still he seemed almost inanimate. Then the hand holding the knife lowered to his side. 'Yes, I knew her.' His voice was quieter. Almost sad. The emotion surprised her.

'I also understand you and she had a child.'

His brows lifted slightly, only to collapse back down as he narrowed his eyes at her. 'What do you want?'

'Just to talk. May I come in?'

His gaze went to John and Luke. 'I don't like shifters.'

'They'll stay out here.'

'Madam Mayor—' John started.

She held up her hand to silence him, then addressed the vampire. 'They'll stay out here so long as I'm in no danger.'

Preacher nodded. 'My word.'

She studied him for a moment. 'You'd better mean that. Harm me and I'll have this building burned to the ground with you in it. Understood?'

He grunted what she assumed was a yes and moved a few steps back into the church.

With a last look at John, she entered the sanctuary. The white plaster walls and Stations of the Cross seemed in good repair, although the handsome wood floor was in desperate need of polishing. Dust draped most of the pews and much of the ornate interior, but a bank of vigil candles flickered at one side of the altar. The area there looked well used. The floor even had a little shine to it.

The door shut behind her.

She turned at the sound, very aware at being closed in with a creature who might actually kill her. Her heart began racing anew. She exhaled, the breath much less steady than she'd wished for. 'I suppose you know I'm nervous, being able to hear my heartbeat as you can.'

He kept a little distance between them, watching her like she was the dangerous one. 'I can.' A few steps closer and he stopped. 'So you're the mayor.'

'Yes.' Did that help or hurt? His face revealed nothing.

'Julia told me that.' He studied her hard.

What else had Julia told him?

'I suppose you think you're brave to come here. *Stupid* might be a better word. How do you know I won't hurt you?'

She wanted to retreat but forced herself to stand firm. 'You gave your word.'

The distant candle flames reflected in his eyes like tiny stars. 'And you believe the word of a vampire?'

A bead of sweat trickled down her rib cage. 'You're the father of my grandchild. That makes us blood.' *Ay Dios mios*, why had she used that word?

He snorted. It sounded almost like a laugh. 'You might be as crazy as I am, lady.'

'Lola, please.'

'Lola.' He slipped the knife back into its sheath on his belt. 'They call me Preacher.'

'So I've heard. Is that what you prefer?'

'It suits.' He walked past her, up the main aisle and toward the altar. She followed. At the first pew, he genuflected, then sat. He tipped his head toward the open space beside him.

She bent and crossed herself as well, then took a seat on the same pew with a little distance between them.

'You're a religious woman?' he asked.

'I don't get to Mass as often as I used to, but yes.'

He nodded slowly. Approvingly.

Desperate to fill the silence, she blurted out, 'You live here.'

'You know that already or you wouldn't have come looking for me here.'

'Yes,' she answered. He slung his arm over the back of the pew. If he stretched out his fingers, he probably could have touched her shoulder. She forced herself not to slide away. 'Did you love my Julia?'

'Yes. I married her.'

Lola's mouth opened. 'You did?'

'Right here in this church.' He lifted his head toward the altar. 'Mariela was born here, too.'

'Mar-Mariela?' Lola stuttered around a knot in her throat. 'That was my mother's name. So Julia had a little girl?' Tears burned her eyes. She looked upward and blinked, letting out a long breath and, with it, a silent prayer that her grandchild was safe, wherever she was.

'Beautiful baby.' Preacher's voice cracked.

She glanced at him, caught him wiping his eyes. 'I'm so sorry for what we've both been through. I'm sorry Julia didn't feel like she could come to me when she found out she was pregnant. I tried to be a good mother, I did, but—'

'She wanted to. I stopped her.' He leaned forward and rested his elbows on his knees. 'I couldn't picture a scenario where it ended well.'

Lola folded her hands in her lap and studied the gold and onyx ring on her pinky.

He straightened. 'I effed up. I'm sorry.'

She shook her head, barely believing she was having this conversation and who she was having it with. 'Actually, you didn't. I can't picture a scenario that would have ended well either. Not then. Now, with what I know, maybe.' She shrugged. 'The past is passed. I want to focus on the future.'

'Is that why you came?'

'Yes. I know the child, Mariela, was taken from you. I know that the beings who now possess her are far more powerful than any human.'

Anger flared in his eyes. 'You know who has her? Tell me and I'll hunt them down.'

'I don't think it's that simple. I'm told the ancient ones have her. The creators of your race.'

The anger spread from his eyes to settle onto his face. 'Don't ever lump me in with any of them, understand? I'm not like them. Vampires disgust me. They're parasites in need of the kind of cleansing only a stake through the heart can bring.'

Confusion swept her. 'But you are one.'

He snarled. 'I never meant to be. If I'd known what I was doing, I would have gladly died instead.' He stood and paced toward the altar. 'Now I live with this curse every day, trying to do God's will by cleansing those who kill humans. The only good being a vampire has brought me is the power to protect my mortal brothers.'

It felt like a sign. With renewed courage, she spoke. 'Then you'll understand why I'm here. As a human, I'm vulnerable. Weak. Outmatched by those I must go up against.' With Willamette's and her *abuela*'s words chiming in her head, Lola rose and said another silent prayer, this time that John's and Luke's hearing didn't extend into the sanctuary. 'I want you to help me get Mariela back.'

He nodded. 'Just tell me what you want me to do.'

She took a breath. 'Turn me into a vampire.'

'So you are the man who killed my husband?' Heaven stood atop the step that led into the sunken living room, dressed in a one-shoulder python-print minidress that revealed more of the grieving widow than it covered. The last time Doc had seen a woman who looked like her, he'd been flipping through one of Fi's fashion magazines. Lean, dark, dangerous, and beautiful. High maintenance. Totally Sinjin's type.

'Yeah.' He inhaled, the exotic scent of jaguar filling his nose along with the flowery fragrance of some perfume. Or hair products. Or skin lotion. Hard to tell with a woman like that.

Her eyes flickered from tawny brown to green-gold, showing off her varcolai side. His answer angered her. Her spike heels clicked down the steps until they were on the same level. 'Is that all you have to say for yourself? *Yeah*?' She mimicked his American accent with obvious disdain before shifting back to her Brazilian lilt. 'You killed my husband and you cannot even apologize? Or perhaps you are not sorry?'

'I *am* sorry. I didn't mean to kill Sinjin. He attacked me and—'

'He challenged you and you accepted. You knew what was at stake.'

'*He* came at *me*.'

'They say you went up in flames. Burned him to death.' She eyed him warily as if looking for fire to burst off his skin. 'Varcolai can't do that.'

'And neither can I,' he lied. Since he'd started popping ket-amine, the emotions that caused the flames had been so mellowed out that even at his most angry, nothing happened. 'It was just a weird power brought on by Samhain.'

She crossed and uncrossed her arms, obviously unsettled. 'You could have let him go. Let the police deal with him. At least if he were still alive . . . ' She ground her teeth in anger and turned away.

'If he was still alive but in police custody, you'd be pride leader by default.' He plopped down on the couch – his couch now – and kicked his feet up onto the glass coffee table. 'I get it. You're bunched up because you're not the boss. You should have spilled your plans to Sinjin before he decided to up and kill some innocent women. Or maybe you knew what he was doing.'

She spun back around, gold bangles jangling on her wrist as she lifted her hands in expression. 'I had no idea.'

'You had *no idea* what your husband was up to.' He raised a brow, then snorted softly. 'I take it this was a political marriage only, then.'

She lifted her head slightly. 'I cared for Sinjin, but you know how it is with pride leaders. Marriage is for making alliances.' She sat at the far end of the big sectional, crossing her feet at the ankles and tucking them to the side. 'I knew he was intent on stirring up the city against the vampires.' The way she pro-nounced *vampires* gave it an extra syllable. *Vam-pi-years.*

'Would you have stopped him if you'd known how?'

She nodded, eyes downcast. 'I would have tried. Sinjin was not . . . an easy man to have his mind changed.'

Doc snorted again. 'You don't have to tell me.'

She looked up. 'He kicked you out, yes?'

'Yes.'

'And now you are pride leader.' Her fingers twisted the rock that was her engagement ring. 'And my husband.'

He shifted forward. This was just the opening he needed. 'Look, I know you didn't sign on for this – and I'm sure you never agreed to get hitched thinking you'd have a stranger for a husband a few months after you said *I do*. I'm cool to have the whole thing annulled or whatever needs to take place to make the marriage go away.'

Her fingers stopped fussing with the ring and her head jerked up, her spine straightening like a rod had been shoved through it. 'You think I am so easy to get rid of? Do you know who my father is? Rodrigo Silva. The São Paulo pride leader. He commands more than ten thousand varcolai. Do you wish to anger him? Because I'm sure he would love to hear how you so casually desire to toss me aside.'

Dammit. 'That's not what I meant. I was trying to do you a favor.'

'A favor. Pah.' She spat air at him, flicking her fingers. 'We are married. You must accept that.' She crossed her arms and stared away from him, muttering in Portuguese.

'Look, you don't understand. I have—'

Her head whipped around. 'What is the matter with me? Do you not find me attractive?'

'Of course you're attractive. You're beautiful.' Some of the anger left Heaven's face. Thank Bast Fi wasn't here. 'But it doesn't matter what you look like, because—'

'Ah, I see now.' She raked her gaze down his body, head waggling back and forth. 'You do not like the girls, eh? You prefer men – is that it?'

'No! Hell no.' He growled softly. This was so not going how

he'd pictured it. 'Listen to me. What I'm trying to tell you is I'm already in love with another woman.'

'Love.' She waved her hand at him. 'An emotion that comes and goes.'

'Heaven, she's my fiancée. I plan to marry her.'

He waited, watching the words sink in. Her expression went blank; then her eyes took on the greenish gold of her true nature.

'So the rumors about the ghost girl are true?' Her mouth twitched into a grimace.

'Yes.'

She shook her head. 'You will not marry her. Because if you do, I will kill her.'

Chapter Eight

Chrysabelle followed Fi down into the freighter's hold, each of them carrying a rechargeable flashlight taken from the galley. The solars were still lit but growing weaker as the night wore on. The last thing either of them wanted was to have the light fail while they were confronting an aged, noble vampire. Fi could turn ghost and escape, but Chrysabelle and Damian, no matter what their training, were still human.

Chrysabelle squinted, testing her night vision. It was decent but starting to fail. She couldn't speak for Damian, but he'd been without a patron for long enough now that her guess was they were both suffering from a lack of bite. Their heightened comarré senses were diminishing with each passing day.

Damian. Why had she said his name during her recovery? What had the Aurelian told her that made her unconscious mind focus on him? Could he really be her brother? She'd not seen him during the time he'd been quartered at her home. Did he remember her? Hopefully he'd know something that would help her solve this mystery.

Fi made circles with her flashlight beam. 'You'll have to

throw your weight against the door. Hinges are for crap. I just ghost through unless I'm bringing him food.'

'You've been taking care of Damian?' She wasn't sure why that surprised her. Fi was young and sometimes did things that showed her age, but that didn't mean she wasn't without feeling. 'What's he like?'

'He's nice. Angry. Like you were when you first got here.'

'I wasn't angry.'

Fi laughed. 'And honey badgers are cuddly.' She smiled at Chrysabelle. 'It's okay, I get it. Change sucks. Who doesn't know that better than me? He's not so much angry at the world as he is angry that Saraphina betrayed him. I think he may have been a little sweet on her.'

'Betrayed him how?'

'Apparently running was his idea. He called her a lifer. Said she hadn't wanted to leave, but he thought once she saw what life could be like, she'd be okay. She wasn't. When Daciana and her husband came to the house, Saraphina helped them subdue Damian.'

Chrysabelle shook her head. 'I know – knew – a lot of comarré like that. They can't see past the life they're living to the life they could have.' Her head whirled with thoughts. Where would she be now if she hadn't run after Algernon's murder? Pawned off to another patron? Sent back to the Primoris Domus for the breeding program?

'You still with me?'

She nodded. 'Just thinking. Does Damian . . . look like me?'

'Sure, I guess, if you mean in a blond hair, blue eyes, gold tattoos kind of way. Otherwise' – Fi pursed her lips – 'it's hard to say. Damian's tall and handsome and has nice—' Fi blushed and shrugged. 'All you upscale comarrés look the same to me.'

'Technically, I'm only a comarré in looks now since my last trip to the Aurelian.'

Fi glanced at Chrysabelle's clothes. 'And your looks haven't changed. You still wear your hair in that braid, still wear white all the time. There are other colors, you know.'

'I know.' She sighed. 'What is it you said? Change sucks.' And as much as she was ready for it, she didn't know where to begin. 'Maybe I should cut my hair. Try to wear color. I wouldn't know where to start.'

Fi slowed and pointed with her flashlight beam. 'We're here.' She stopped and turned to Chrysabelle. 'You want some ideas on changing? I'd be happy to help. You know I love clothes and you have the kind of money that makes shopping an orgasmic experience.' She grinned like she was already emptying Chrysabelle's accounts. 'Let's run this Daciana down, see what she knows, then we'll map out a plan to revitalize Paradise City's retail economy.' Her eyes rounded with happiness. 'Hey, maybe Damian will let me make him over, too! It would be fun to put him in some leather pants and—'

Chrysabelle laughed. 'How about I get to talk to him first?'

'Got it.' Fi jerked her thumb at the door. 'You want to shove that thing open? I'll hold your flashlight.'

'Sure.' She handed the torch over, then planted her feet and popped her shoulder into the door. It flew open easily. The space beyond was pitch-black. 'You left him without lights?'

'No way.' Fi stepped over the threshold and flipped both flashlight beams into the darkness. In front of them sat a big metal storage container, its doors blackened and twisted loose from their hinges. A lamp lay on its side near a cooler.

There was no vampire. And no comar.

'Holy mother, they're gone.' A cold hand squeezed her heart.

Why hadn't she listened to Mal and come to talk to Damian when he'd suggested it?

Fi danced the lights through the space. 'How the hell did she get out of there?'

'Did you search her before you locked her up?'

'I didn't but I think . . . ' Fi shook her head dejectedly. 'No. None of us did. We were too much in a hurry to find Creek. If she's done anything to Damian—'

Chrysabelle grabbed her flashlight back and helped Fi search the space. 'If she's done anything to him, we'll kill her together. He might be my only chance to find my brother.'

'I don't see a body. She must have taken him.'

'She'd be smart to keep him alive.' Chrysabelle turned back to Fi. 'Where would she go? She's got to have a place to hole up before dawn.'

Fi scratched her head. 'She might not care about that yet. She might want revenge for being locked up.' She bit her bottom lip. 'She could have heard Doc and me talking about going to the pride headquarters. Do you think she'd go after him there?'

'If she's crazy enough to work for Tatiana, she's crazy enough to do anything. Let's go. My car and driver are outside.'

'Awesome. We should leave a note for Mal, let him know.'

'Good idea.' One apology was enough to owe him.

They hustled back to the galley where Fi dug up a pen and a scrap of paper.

'Here,' Chrysabelle said. 'Let me.'

Came to apologize. Found Damian and vampire gone. Think she's headed to pride HQ, as are Fi and I. – C

With Fi on her heels, she ran down to Mal's room and stuck the note between the door and the jamb. 'All right, let's head over there and warn Doc.'

Fi's directions and Jerem's enthusiastic driving got them there in less than twenty minutes. Not a sign of Daciana or Damian along the way. Not that she'd expected to see them on the sidewalk.

'Here.' Fi leaned through the car's partition to point to a building at the end of the block.

'This is pride headquarters? Looks like a nightclub.' The sign above the door said BAR NINE.

Fi sat back. 'It's both.'

Jerem parked the car, his eyes on Chrysabelle in the rearview mirror. 'After Sinjin lost Seven to Dominic in a poker game, he opened this place. The nine is either supposed to be for a cat's nine lives or the fact that Sinjin wanted to be two notches above Dominic. Take your pick.'

Fi put her face against the window to look at the top of the building. 'Pride leader gets the penthouse.'

'Doc up there?' Chrysabelle asked.

She shrugged and slipped farther into her seat. 'Lights are on.'

Jerem unlocked the doors. 'You're sure you want to do this?'

'We have to,' Chrysabelle answered.

'You want me to go with you? I'm not feline, but I *am* var-colai.'

'I thought so,' Fi said. 'What kind?'

'Ursine.'

'You're a pig-shifter?'

He growled softly. 'Ursine means bear.' His gaze went back to Chrysabelle, waiting for her answer.

'The pride has no problem with me. We'll be perfectly safe.'

His gaze flickered over Fi. 'There might be an issue if Doc's new wife is there. Maybe Fi should stay with me.'

Fi grunted. 'I kinda hate that that might be a good idea.'

'You might also want to leave your weapons behind. At least the visible ones.'

'No.' Chrysabelle hooked her hand through the strap of one sacre. 'I'm not willing to acquiesce that much.' She put her other hand on the door handle. 'I'll only be gone long enough to make Doc aware of this new situation.'

She got out. The soft, muted sounds of music emanated from the club and a small crowd milled around the entrance, but it was nothing like Seven's madness. She took a breath to steel herself. Get in, see Doc, get out. That's all she had to do.

With a purposeful stride, she made her way to the velvet ropes and the pair of bouncers guarding the front.

The smaller of the two stepped into her path, blocking her from going beyond the ropes. 'No mortals.' His gaze went briefly to the handles of the twin sacres pecking over her shoulders. 'And certainly not mortals packing steel. Sorry, sweetheart.'

She wished she had Mal's powers of persuasion. As it was, her comarré charm wasn't going to be enough. A good lie and a little bravado might be, though. 'Mortal? Do I look like a mortal to you? Check your night vision.'

'So you're comarré, so what. We don't need your kind here.'

'Oh no? Tell that to your new pride leader, then. Maddoc's hired me as personal security.'

'That right?'

She leaned down, putting them eye to eye. 'Turn me away. See how long your job lasts after I explain to Doc how helpful you've been.' She held his gaze without blinking. 'He's looking to clear some deadwood anyway.'

A muscle in his jaw spasmed. 'Yeah, fine, whatever.' He unsnapped the rope and held it open.

She slipped through. She hadn't expected that to work, but with Doc being new on the job, maybe they didn't know him well enough to know what he would and wouldn't actually do.

Samba music pulsed through her as she made her way inside. Large plush seating areas and potted palms dominated the perimeter, but the two-story dance floor in the center held a riotous crowd moving in a way that only creatures with superior flexibility and extra vertebrae could. From the second-story wraparound balcony, more patrons watched, drank, and conversed. Maybe Doc was up there, keeping an eye on things.

She looked for a way up and found an elevator. Unfortunately, it also had a bouncer. The upstairs must be a VIP area. Definitely where Doc would be. Maybe the same approach would work with him. She pushed through the crowd, accidentally bumping someone.

A glass smashed to the floor.

She turned to apologize. 'Sorry, I—'

An enormous shifter stood behind her. Sandy blond hair brushed his wide shoulders. 'Who let the vampire's toy in here?'

She pulled up to her full height, but she still didn't reach his chest. 'I'm no one's toy.'

'Did your master send you or did you come seeking revenge on your own?'

'What? No. The only thing I'm seeking is Doc.'

Two massive, clawed hands grabbed her by the straps of her sacres and lifted her into the air. Gold eyes stared back at her, the pupils reflecting green. He tipped his shaggy head back and roared. Pain erupted in her ears.

She fought her instinct to stick one of her wrist blades into him and shut him up. Instead she put her foot against his thigh and pushed. He didn't budge. There had to be a way to resolve this without creating an incident. 'Please, put me down. I don't want to hurt you.'

He shook her, rattling her brain. '*You* don't want to hurt *me*?' His short burst of laughter faded into something much more menacing. He pulled her closer, his hot breath wafting over her. 'Your kind got our pride leader killed, vampire whore. Now you come here, to the heart of us, bearing weapons? Taunting us?'

A crowd circled around them. Heads nodded at his words. 'Make her pay, Brutus,' someone shouted.

Brutus untangled his right hand from her sacre straps and clamped it around her throat.

Being choked had a way of making a person no longer care about creating an incident.

She reached for a blade.

Chapter Nine

Chrysabelle's scent draped the freighter's corridors like holiday bunting, causing the voices to whine. Mal called her name, expecting to run into her at any moment. 'Chrysabelle? You here?' But he couldn't sense her, and her lack of answer confirmed she wasn't on the ship. She had been here recently, though. There was no other way her perfume would be so strong.

'Fi, come out here.' Maybe she knew. He called a second time but still no answer or appearance. Where were they? He walked the corridors, listening, but the ship was a tomb. He couldn't even pick up the comar's heartbeat down in the hold. An eerie sense of something gone wrong gnawed his bones. *You should know.*

Following the traces of Chrysabelle's scent to where it was the strongest brought him to his quarters. Jammed into the door frame, a piece of paper shone dully in the fading solars. He pulled it free and read the note, the words filling him with dread.

Pride headquarters was not a good place for Chrysabelle. Mal doubted that Sinjin had been alone in his plan to kill comarré and place the blame on the vampire population. There had to have been other pride members who'd thought it was a good idea. Maybe even helped Sinjin plan the attacks.

For her to go strolling in there, even if it was to warn Doc ... What if Doc wasn't there? What if she ran into someone Sinjin had been in collusion with?

Son of a priest.

He dropped the paper and took off running. Pride headquarters wasn't that far away. With fresh human blood in his system, he could get there faster on foot than by car. The abandoned port disappeared behind him and the miles sped by. Under the cover of night, the few pedestrians he passed barely noticed him as anything more than a sudden breeze.

He slowed a block away from Bar Nine, recognizing Chrysabelle's car. He tapped the window.

Jerem powered it down and tipped his head in greeting. 'Malkolm.'

Fi leaned through the partition from the backseat. 'Hey, Mal. I guess you got Chrysabelle's note.'

'She inside?'

Fi nodded. 'About a minute ago. You just missed her.'

He looked at Jerem. 'Why didn't you go in with her?'

Lips pressed firmly together, he frowned. 'She wouldn't let me.'

'Typical,' Mal muttered. 'I better check on her.'

'You want me to come?' Jerem asked. 'You might have a better shot of getting in if I'm along.'

'No, I can manage.' His powers of persuasion would open the doors. 'I know one of the guys who works the front.' *Liar liar liar.* 'Stay here and protect Fi.'

'I don't need protecting,' she called out, but he was already moving away from the car.

The bouncers walked toward him as he approached but stayed inside the velvet ropes. He held his hands up as a show of peace. 'Not looking for trouble, just a friend.'

The short one snorted. 'No friends here, vampire. Turn around and go back the way you came. This is varcolai territory.'

Now close enough to make good eye contact, Mal let power come into his voice, doing his best to direct it toward both shifters. The blood in his system helped. 'I'm a feline varcolai, just like you.'

'No, you're ... ' The bouncers stared, round-eyed and wavering.

He pushed harder, causing a small ripple of dizziness in the back of his brain. 'I smell like earth and musk, the scents of a shifter. My eyes reflect the same gold that yours do. Welcome me to the club, then forget me.' *We wish we could.*

Fogged with persuasion, the pair nodded slowly. The big one unhooked the rope from the stanchion and moved aside. 'Welcome,' he mumbled.

'Welcome,' the shorter one added.

Mal darted inside, hoping the persuasion held. He paused to lean against a wall in a small alcove until the residual vertigo passed. Chrysabelle's blood would have prevented him from taking such a hit from so small a power drain. Human blood just didn't pack the same punch as what flowed through her veins. He inhaled. She was definitely here. A few seconds later, loud voices emanated from the club's interior. Someone was unhappy. He straightened and listened closer.

And heard Chrysabelle's voice. Damn it.

He spun out of the alcove and charged through the crowd. Finding her wasn't difficult. An enormous varcolai held her aloft by her throat and the crisscrossed straps of her sacres. The next few moments seemed trapped in time like insects in amber.

The varcolai roared in fury, the crowd around him calling out encouragements. Chrysabelle snapped a blade from her wrist sheath. He yanked back the hand from her throat, letting her dangle by her straps. Claws sprang out from his fingertips.

Her arm shot forward, her blade burrowing between his ribs. His clawed hand flew toward her, slicing across her throat. He dropped her and reached for the blade in his side. Blood spewed everywhere as she fell. Mal's beast lifted its head at the familiar scent. *Blood*. The crowd erupted in a wave of deafening sound.

Mal leaped, kicking time back to its normal speed. Her heartbeat pounded in his ears as her breaths grew shallow and her blood scent overwhelmed his control.

A woman screamed, 'Brutus, behind you!'

But Brutus turned too late. Mal landed on top of the varcolai, crumpling him to the ground. He drove his fist into the shifter's face, breaking his nose. Beside them, Chrysabelle clutched at her throat, her mouth open and gasping. Blood bubbled up from the slices across her neck. 'Mal,' she whispered. Her eyes rolled back, the whites showing between her barely open lids.

'Hang on,' he whispered back, struggling to keep the beast controlled. So much blood.

Brutus shifted to his half-form and snarled, showing off prehistoric fangs. He swiped a hand at Mal.

Ducking the claws, Mal blocked the hand with his forearm, then jammed his elbow into Brutus's stomach.

The shifter exhaled a *whoof* of air at the same time

Chrysabelle's pulse went silent. Mal froze. He flicked his gaze toward her, afraid of what he'd see. What he already knew.

Blood trickled from the corner of her mouth. She stared unblinking. Her brilliant comarré glow was gone.

With a roar that shattered glass, Mal set his inner beast free. The inked names spread over him like a rush of water, drowning his humanity until he clung to the last shred with his fingertips. Through his red-tinged vision, he watched fear fill Brutus's eyes, watched as the beast subdued the varcolai with a fist to the temple, then punched a hole in the shifter's chest and ripped out his heart. The varcolai reverted to his lion form as he died.

'What the hell is going on here? Mal?'

At the familiar voice, Mal forced the beast back into its chains and found a modicum of control while doing his best to ignore the suffocating pressure of Chrysabelle's death. He turned to see Doc standing behind him, his face a mask of horrified disbelief. Mal got to his feet as the beast retreated further. He unclenched his hand to point at the dead lion, dropping the heart. It landed with a wet thunk at his feet. Varcolai blood dripped from his fingers. 'He *killed* Chrysabelle.'

Doc's eyes flickered gold. 'Pick her up and bring her to my office *now*.' Then he gave a few instructions to a man in a shirt marked SECURITY. 'Close down this side of the club and get this taken care of.' Finally, he addressed the crowd. 'Get the hell over to the other side of the club or go home, but you can't stay here.'

Reluctantly, the crowd began to move. Mal scooped Chrysabelle's body into his arms. *Dead dead dead.* She was warm and redolent with the honey-sweet perfume of blood. He wanted to hold her against him, kiss her forehead and wait for her to return to him, but instead he followed Doc to a nearby elevator. Once the doors closed, Doc spoke.

'Dammit, Mal, I did not need this. Not with everything else going on.' He looked at Chrysabelle and cursed softly. 'I can't believe she's dead.'

'She's not dead.' Warm blood seeped from her throat through the fabric of his sleeve.

'Bro, she's dead. Look at her. Listen to her, for Bast's sake. She's got no pulse.'

'She's not *permanently* dead.' *Too bad too bad too bad.*

Doc shook his head as if Mal were crazy. 'What the hell made you two think coming here was a good idea?'

'Chrysabelle came to warn you that the vamp in the hold escaped. She thought the vampiress might come after you in retaliation. I came after Chrysabelle as soon as I found out. I never would have let her come alone. You think I'm stupid?'

Doc kept shaking his head. 'I don't know what I think anymore.' He glanced down at Chrysabelle and swore again. 'For real, man, I don't hear any breathing.'

'Because there isn't any. She's dead.'

Doc lifted an eyebrow. 'You just said she wasn't.'

'I said I didn't think it was permanent.'

'Maybe you are stupid.'

'Look, the Aurelian killed her and—'

The elevator doors opened into a wide vestibule. Two men guarded a set of double doors.

'Get that office open,' Doc commanded.

The man on the right sprang into action, pulling the door wide. 'Should I get Barasa?'

'Don't get anyone,' Mal answered. 'She's fine.' *Finally dead.*

The men were varcolai; they could sense the lack of life in her as well as he could. He hustled past them into the office.

Doc paused before entering. 'We're not to be bothered.'

'Yes, sir.'

Doc locked the door behind him. 'Put her on the couch, then tell me again how her being dead is okay with you?'

'It has to do with the gold from the ring of sorrows.' Mal eased her onto the black leather sofa, then kneeled beside her. Where his right sleeve hadn't been torn by his transformation into the beast, his skin was soaked with her blood, causing the names there to writhe. 'When the signumist melted it down, she thought that would erase the ring's power. It didn't. Instead the power transferred to her.'

'What kind of power?' Doc stared down at her.

'She didn't know, but whatever it is, it brought her back to life after the Aurelian ran a sword through her.'

'I hate to tell you this, but I don't think it's working.'

'It will.' It had to. Mal brushed hair off her forehead. Her signum sparkled in the overhead lights. 'Give it time.'

'Sun's gonna be up soon. Just how much time are you talking exactly—'

Chrysabelle gasped, her body bowing off the couch as though yanked upward on a thread. She collapsed back down, breathing hard. Her eyes opened, and after a few seconds, she pushed herself up. 'What happened?'

Mal sank back onto his heels in relief, but the emotion passed quickly. No way was she getting out of talking about what had happened this time. As sternly as he could manage through the joy of her returning to him, he answered, 'You died. Again.'

Chapter Ten

'Grigor will come with her.' Tatiana studied the invitation under the desk lamp's glow. Octavian's penmanship was beautiful. Too bad it had been wasted on Svetla's name.

Seated beside her at his desk, Octavian finished the last invitation with a flourish, then looked up. 'Let him. He *is* invited.'

She sighed. 'I hate that he is.'

'It would seem odd to invite the Elders without their Dominus as well, don't you think? And if he comes, we'll find a way to distract him. Besides, the idea is that we're bringing the Dominus here for the courtesy of meeting Lilith before the ball. The Elders are just a bonus.'

Tatiana tucked the invite into its envelope and laid it on the desk beside the others. 'A brilliant bonus. If this plan works—'

'It will.' He smiled. 'I thought of it.'

She swatted him. 'Don't be cocky, my pet. If this works, the rest of the plan must still be perfectly aligned.'

He tugged her onto his lap. 'Everything will go off beautifully – you'll see. Once we have Svetla here, you'll use your powers of persuasion to plant the seed of kidnapping Lilith in her head. The moment she acts on it, you'll alert Sam—'

She pressed a finger to his lips. 'Don't speak his name. We mustn't call him before we need him.'

He nodded, pressing a kiss to her finger before she removed it. 'Forgive me. My excitement got the best of me. You'll alert *him*, who will catch Svetla in the act and strike her dead.' He nipped Tatiana's neck, his pleasure at thinking up such a cunning plan obvious. 'There's no vampire alive who would come against you after hearing about that.'

She rolled the hem of her blouse between her fingers. 'I agree, but fitting the pieces of this puzzle together is going to be difficult.'

'You worry too much.' He frowned. 'Or are you still concerned about Daciana?'

Unsettled by the reminder, she rested her head against his. 'I will be until I hear from her.'

'It's good that you have this new project to distract you, then.' He held out the four envelopes, each addressed to the other noble houses. 'You have messengers waiting?'

'Yes. The House of Rasputin's will go out today, the others tomorrow. I just hope Svetla's as eager to see Lilith as I think she'll be. I'd much rather accomplish this before the others arrive.'

He shifted beneath her, moving so that they faced each other more. 'But if the other Dominus and Elders are here to witness the ancient one's actions, it can only benefit you.'

'True.' She stroked his cheek. 'Protecting you from Grigor's and Svetla's mind reading isn't going to be easy. They get one jot of a thought about what's going on and they'll kill you without hesitation.'

He patted the breast pocket of his jacket. 'I have the potion from Kosmina. She assures me it's what the kine in St. Petersburg use to keep their masters from knowing their thoughts.'

Tatiana clucked her tongue. 'I can't believe you're willing to trust your life to a kine.'

'My darling,' he cooed. 'If something happened to me because the potion didn't work, whose wrath would Kosmina face?'

She smiled. 'Mine.'

Through the opening of her blouse, he traced the curve of her breast with his finger. 'Knowing that, do you think she'd give me something that might fail?'

'No.' When he put it that way, it did seem rather convincing. 'How is it you always know what to say to me?'

'Because,' he said, drawing her closer and nuzzling his mouth against her collarbone, 'I only want your happiness.'

She unbuttoned her blouse, inviting him in. 'You are my happiness. You and Lilith. I cannot imagine my life without either one of you. The words sound odd even to my own ears, but having a child again has changed me. I want you both around me always.'

He pulled back, an unexpected look in his eyes. 'Are you implying . . . No, never mind.' He laughed like he'd made a mistake. 'My emotions make me foolish.'

She cupped his face in her hands, keeping his gaze on her. 'Am I what? Say it.'

He tried to turn away.

'Say it,' she commanded again.

'Do you . . . love me?'

She held his gaze for a long moment. She cared for him deeply, but love? She loved Lilith. Did she also love Octavian?

Yes, she did. He was her lover, but also her child, sired by her own hand. How could she not love him? 'I do.'

He went utterly, completely still.

For a moment, she faltered. Had she misread his affections? Maybe he didn't feel the same way she did after all. She took her hands from his face and pulled back, instantly assessing how she might retreat with her dignity intact. The first spiny tendrils of anger sprang to life in her belly. 'I—'

'I am honored. And unworthy,' he breathed. He laughed, a great boisterous sound of joy. He hugged her tightly, picking her up and twirling her around the room.

'Put me down this instant!' But relief swept through her. She had not made a foolish decision after all.

At their noise, Lilith began to cry from her crib.

Tatiana slapped his chest. 'Now look what you've done.'

Octavian kissed her firmly, then let her go. 'She's only crying because it took you so long to answer me.' He went to Lilith's crib and cradled her in his arms before returning to Tatiana. 'We make a handsome family, don't you think?'

'I do.' Tatiana nodded. 'Handsome and powerful.' Recognizing him as her consort would give Octavian the most protection she could offer. If anyone harmed him, she'd be able to come after them with no questions asked.

Let the Dominus and their Elders come. She was ready.

Yahla sprawled across Creek's chest, her rhythmic breathing warming his skin. His right arm curved around her body, his hand splayed on the small of her back, the feathers of her hair soft on his shoulder. His other hand held the charm his grandmother had made. Without it, he'd be dead by now.

He touched the charm to his lips, kissing it and saying a silent thank-you to Mawmaw. Was it wrong to thank your grand-mother for making the best sex of your life possible? He stifled a laugh so as not to wake Yahla.

She inhaled a sleepy breath and stretched, stiffening for a moment against him, then melting back down until their curves rejoined. 'You are awake?'

'Yes. I slept a little.'

'Did you dream?'

He nodded. 'Of you.'

She lifted her head and smiled. 'Did you do to me in your dreams what you did to me in your bed?'

'You're a wicked woman, you know that?'

She turned onto her back so that her head rested on his shoulder. 'I am whatever you need me to be, Thomas.' Her fingers drew small circles on his thigh. 'Wicked. Willing. Wanton.'

'Yeah, well, maybe I did.' It had been a long damn time since he'd had a night like last night. One that had left him limp and drained of every ounce of built-up need. The only need he had now was Yahla. He wanted her beside him all the time.

'What else do you desire?'

'A simple, peaceful life.' It was true. He'd had enough trouble these last years to never want another problem again. But that wasn't going to be the way of it as a Kubai Mata.

'You're thinking of them, aren't you?'

'Them?' He knew who she meant, just didn't want to talk about it.

'Don't pretend with me. The Kubai Mata. Your masters.'

'Don't call them that.'

She shifted to look at him. The wildness had returned to her eyes. 'Why, when that is what they are?'

He pushed up to his elbows. 'I'm done discussing this. You know I can't do anything about it.'

Her smile returned, this time bent and odd. 'But I can. And I will.'

He shook his head. 'Enough. There's nothing to discuss.'

The scrape of the metal door being rolled back sounded from downstairs. Creek leaped from the bed and put a finger to his lips for Yahla to keep quiet. He'd locked the door. How had someone picked it without him hearing? He tugged on his jeans and grabbed his crossbow.

No footsteps. Whoever was downstairs was either really quiet or hadn't come inside. He notched a bolt into the bow and went to the edge of the loft. 'Don't move or you're dead.'

Argent's green eyes stared back at him. 'I doubt that very much.'

Creek dropped the bow. 'Sector Chief. I didn't realize it was you.'

'Obviously.' The dragon-shifter turned his attention to Creek's V-Rod, running his fingertips over the gas tank before glancing up again. 'If you're waiting for me to come up there, you'll be waiting a long time.'

'Yes, sir. Be right down.' He dropped the crossbow onto the bed so he could yank on a T-shirt. Yahla looked less than pleased to be left alone. He held up a finger to say he'd just be a minute. Argent probably just wanted an update. Which wouldn't take long since there was nothing to tell. Shirt on, he bent, planted a kiss on her calf, and jogged down the steps. 'So, what brings you by?' Unexpectedly. His favorite way to be visited.

'Have you spoken to the comarré about recovering the child yet?'

'Yes. She's not exactly interested in taking that job.'

Argent didn't seem fazed by the news. Instead, he crouched to examine the bike more closely. 'Speak to her again. If she still refuses, kill the anathema. That will persuade her.'

Creek ran a hand over his Mohawk. 'I don't think killing him will have the effect you think it will. Might be better if you gave me more info about the baby. Something to help convince her the child is worth saving.'

Argent blinked the inner eyelids of his half-form. 'Need I remind you the comarré still owes us the ring of sorrows? I will not bargain with her. She will do as the KM commands.'

'About that.' Creek planted his hands on the counter behind him and prepared for the worst. 'She wants you to know she melted the ring down and used the gold to replace some lost signum. As in she had the gold stitched into her skin.'

Argent jerked like he'd been struck by lightning. Creek had never seen him react that way before. Then the dragon-shifter shot to his feet. 'That stupid woman. The KM cannot allow one person to have that much power. Such a deliberate act can only be construed as aggressive and must be—'

'She only did it because she needed the signum replaced. She's not trying to take over the world, so just relax.'

Quicker than Creek could track, Argent backhanded him, cracking his jaw and snapping his head back. 'Know your place, tribe.'

A second later, Yahla dropped down from the loft, landing right behind Argent. Stark naked. Her eyes were the same non-reflective black they'd been earlier. Creek forgot the pain in his face. Call it a hunch, but his gut said things were headed south. She tipped her head at Argent, studying him like a bug on a leaf. 'You will not touch him again. Nor will you tell him what to do anymore.'

Argent bristled, but after a quick glance, he ignored her. 'Who is this? A whore? If you have needs, fine, but see to them outside your home.'

Hatred twisted Yahla's face. She opened her mouth much wider than should have been possible and screeched her displeasure. Raven-shaped shadows danced around her. 'He is not yours to control any longer.'

Turning, Argent shifted to his half-form, causing bone-spiked wingtips to burst from his shoulders and talons to erupt from his fingers. Creek moved slowly, positioning himself so that he could keep eyes on both of them. Splotches of scales covered Argent's visible skin, and his slit pupils took on a predatory gleam as bright as Yahla's were dull. 'You're not human.'

'You do not scare me.' Her head moved in short, jerky increments. 'Nothing scares me.'

'No?' Argent inhaled as he curved his body upward, then thrust back, expelling a stream of fire.

'No!' Creek yelled, but he was too late.

The fire engulfed Yahla, and she disappeared in a hiss of flame, leaving a pile of charred feathers behind. Creek stared, unable to take in what had just happened.

Argent regained his human form, smoothing his suit jacket like nothing unusual had just happened. He put his back to her remains. 'You have wretched taste in women. There will be no more of that, understood? Now clean that up and get back to work. I want the comarré on a plane to Corvinestri tonight.'

'How can you just kill a woman like that?'

Argent gave him a strange look. 'She wasn't human.'

'And that's an excuse?'

His brows furrowed. 'This conversation is over.'

Catching a small movement, Creek stayed put, his hip anchored to the countertop. He pointed behind Argent. 'You might want to turn around.'

The burned feathers lifted into a small tornado, exploding into a swirling, cawing mass of ravens. A few seconds later, Yahla walked out of the midst of them, a few feathers drifting to the floor. Her eyes were dull, black pits. No white. No reflection. Just bottomless holes. She walked toward Argent, spreading her arms like she might take flight. Then she opened her mouth in the same unnaturally wide way she had before.

This time, she inhaled.

A strange shimmery substance floated off Argent and disappeared down her gullet. He seemed frozen as the color left his scales, his hair, his eyes, until he was as washed out as an old photo left in the sun. Yahla closed her mouth and swallowed.

Argent collapsed to the floor.

She stepped over him on her way to Creek. 'Now you are free of him.'

Creek pushed away from the counter to crouch beside the sector chief's lifeless form. He felt the man's neck. No pulse. 'You killed him.'

'I took his soul. He no longer deserved it.'

'Undo it.' Cold panic gnawed at Creek's belly. The same feeling he'd had when his sentence had been read. 'Now.'

'I cannot. Nor would I.'

Sweat stuck Creek's shirt to his back. 'Holy hell. You can't just kill people. Especially not a Kubai Mata sector chief.'

She stood very close, forcing him to look at her. 'You are afraid I have done something bad.'

'You *have* done something bad. Something that's going to make you an enemy of the KM. Something that could send me back to prison.' His gut rolled over at the thought of being charged with another murder. He would *not* go back to prison. 'How do you think I'm going to explain this? You think the KM isn't going to check up on him when he doesn't report back?'

She leaned over and cupped his face in her hands. The gravity of the situation seemed to fade. She forced him to keep eye contact with her. 'I said I would protect you, did I not?'

Those black, murky depths were impossible to look away from. A sense of calm washed through him. His muscles unclenched and he stood, stepping over Argent to get closer to her. 'Yes, that's what you said.'

She smiled, cocking her head abruptly to one side. 'Now you must trust me.'

His hands found her hips while his mind forgot the dead shifter on his floor. 'I do.' It seemed he always had.

'Good,' she whispered, leaning into him. 'I will tell you what we are going to do next.'

And with each word she spoke, his fears drifted away, replaced with little pieces of her will, until Creek no longer understood where she began and he ended.

Chapter Eleven

Lola looked at her watch. Three hours until sundown. All day she'd waited, frustrated by Preacher's refusal to turn her into a vampire. She didn't expect him to understand how becoming a vampire would show the human citizens of Paradise City that there was nothing to fear from their othernatural neighbors. Or how being turned would help her demonstrate to the othernatural citizens that she understood their position. Or how both sides would see she was willing to sacrifice for the sake of the city.

But of all people, he should understand how difficult it was going to be for her to fight the creatures who'd kidnapped her grandchild if she didn't have at least some degree of the ancients' power. Instead he'd insisted she let him handle things. How could he not understand that if he'd turned her, they could handle things together? She was siding with him, after all, and there was strength in numbers.

A quick knock on the half-open door and Valerie stuck her head into the office. 'Madam Mayor?'

Lola set her paperwork aside. 'Yes?'

Valerie came in and handed her a slim manila envelope. 'Here's the report you've been waiting for. If you don't need anything else, I'm headed home for the day.'

Lola took the report, eager to read it. 'No, that's all. Have a good night.'

'Thank you, you too.' Valerie hesitated. John's large form hovered in the open doorway. 'Would you mind if John drove me home? I know he's supposed to be here with you, but—'

'No, it's fine.' Valerie usually rode a scooter. 'Everything all right?'

She shrugged one shoulder. 'Guy in the apartment next to mine has been acting a little hinky since Halloween night. He looks at me like he wants to eat me. Just thought if John walked me up, made a little show of being there . . . '

Lola nodded. 'Sure, no problem.' She looked past Valerie to where John stood behind her. 'Stay as long as you think necessary.'

He nodded. 'Yes, ma'am.'

Lola bent her head slightly until the door shut, smiling to herself. Valerie's neighbor might be acting odd, but there was something going on between Valerie and John that was more than just friendship. She'd seen the way they'd been sneaking looks at one another, the way Valerie touched her hair when John was near, the way John's gruffness seemed to melt away in Valerie's presence. Lola sighed and turned her chair to gaze out the office windows, hugging the envelope to her chest. It was nice that someone could find happiness amid all this chaos.

She wasn't sure it was an emotion she'd ever truly feel again. Not with her daughter dead and her grandchild missing. Which brought her back to the report. She slit open the envelope, pulled out the single sheet of paper, and skimmed the information for the address she needed.

She read it twice before setting it aside. What a strange place to live. But strange probably didn't matter as much as safe did. How safe it would be for her, she wasn't sure. She'd find out as soon as the sun went down.

Her gaze shifted to the windows again. She walked over to them. The setting sun burnished away the ugly bits of the city and gilded the landscape until she could squint and see glimpses of the beauty it had once been. Beyond the buildings, the sea sparkled, throwing back the sun's light in diamond shards.

She planted her hands on the glass, attempting to remember every color and nuance of this moment. The heat of the day seeped into her skin. She tried to embed the experience into her memory.

She'd always loved the moments before twilight, the way the setting sun brought a last brilliant burst of color to the world before night shrouded everything in shades of gray. She crossed herself and said a quick prayer that God would forgive her for reaching so far beyond her place in life and to protect her in the path she was about to travel.

The sun slipped out of sight. Part of her wanted to weep for what she was about to lose. 'Balance,' she whispered. 'Balance and sacrifice.' What did it matter if she never saw another sunset again? She'd have her city, but more important, she'd have her granddaughter. Mariela would be enough.

'I can't believe it.' Chrysabelle leaned her head onto her hand, her elbow propped on the kitchen table.

It's true, Velimai signed. *I saw the blood on you myself when Mal brought you in. He told me everything. He watched a shifter at Bar Nine slice your neck open after you stabbed him, then he carried you up to Doc's office where you came back to life and then passed out right after.*

'Why can't I remember any of this? I remember going to the club, but that's it.' She jerked her head up and pounded her fist on the table. 'It's the Aurelian all over again.'

Velimai got up to start the dinner dishes.

'You shouldn't have let me sleep all day. I need to be out there, looking for Damian and this runaway vampire.'

Velimai shot her a look that said the decision to let Chrysabelle sleep had been in her best interests.

'Well, you shouldn't have.' Chrysabelle ran a finger through the condensation on her water glass. 'Does Doc even know that vampiress might be after him?'

Velimai shrugged.

'You're a lot of help.' She stood and threw her napkin onto the table.

The wysper turned from the sink, soap bubbles dripping off her fingers. Tension creasing her face, she flung the suds off and signed, *Don't take your anger out on me. Deal with what's going on instead of ignoring it, and you might get some answers.*

'Deal with it? How? Acknowledging I've got some kind of power that resurrects me isn't going to help me understand it.'

Find someone to talk to. Someone who can explain what power the ring had.

'You have any suggestions as to who this magical person might be?'

Velimai was wavering between solid and vapor form now, a sign of her upset. Chrysabelle didn't care. She was afraid of what was happening to her, and that fear made her want to lash out, no matter who she hurt.

Talk to Mortalis. With that, the fae stalked out of the room, leaving the dishes, and Chrysabelle, behind.

'What's he going to tell me that I don't already know?' Chrysabelle plopped back down into her chair. She huffed out a few breaths, a little of her anger going with them. She shook her head, disappointed in herself. Velimai didn't deserve her harsh words or crankiness.

She marched up to Velimai's quarters and knocked lightly. 'Vel, I'm sorry. Open the door so I can apologize.'

The wysper opened the door and crossed her arms, waiting expectantly with one brow lifted.

'I'm sorry I snapped.' Chrysabelle sighed. 'Truth is, I'm scared. Scared of what's going on with me, scared I'm not going to find my brother, scared of trying to become something more than comarré even though it feels like learning to walk on legs that don't belong to me. I'm ... well, in Fi's words, freaking out a little. But you don't deserve to take the brunt of that. Forgive me?'

Velimai smiled gently and nodded. *Apology accepted. And I'm serious about talking to Mortalis. He's very well connected. I'm sure he can find someone to explain the ring's powers to you and how having that gold in your skin is affecting you.*

'Okay, I will. I'm going to visit Mal, but first I'll swing by Seven and see if I can get a few words with Mortalis.' She hesitated. 'I know I've never come right out and said this, but I really appreciate that you stayed on after my mother died. You're like family to me and I don't know what I'd do without you. I guess what I'm trying to say is that I love you.'

Velimai's smile got bigger and she swiped at her eyes. *That gold in your skin really is changing you.* She winked. *Now get. I have dishes to do.*

Chrysabelle started toward her rooms to gather a few things before heading out, then stopped. 'Why didn't Mal and Fi just stay here last night? It had to have been close to sunup.'

Velimai pursed her lips. *I told them to stay, but he refused. Said the last time he'd been here when you'd woken up, things hadn't gone well and if you still wanted to apologize to him, you knew where to find him.*

'And he thinks I'm stubborn.'

He did at least let Jerem drive them home, though.

'I guess that's something.' Chrysabelle shook her head as she and Vel went in different directions. Mal would have his apology tonight, and with Mortalis's help, maybe they'd soon have a better understanding of what the ring's power was doing to her.

On the way to Seven, Jerem filled in some details from the previous night, including that Fi had asked Mal why they hadn't just stayed at Chrysabelle's instead of racing the sun home. Mal hadn't answered the question, prompting Fi to denounce him and all other men as pigheaded jerks. Unfortunately, Jerem had no other insight into what had happened at Bar Nine other than what Mal had told him, which was basically the same as what Velimai had told her.

The scene outside Seven was crowded, as usual, but one of the bouncers motioned her forward. She recognized him as Tec, the brother of the dead wolf varcolai Mia.

'You're Doc's friend, right?' he asked.

'Yes, and you're Mia's brother.' How awful to lose a sibling. 'I'm so sorry about what happened to her.'

'Thanks.' Sorrow filled his eyes, then morphed into something else. 'You here to see Dominic?'

'No, Mortalis. Is he here tonight?'

'Sure, I'll take you in.' He unclicked the rope and let her through as he addressed one of the other doormen. 'Back in a few.' He kept pace beside her as they entered. 'Big news about Doc becoming pride leader, huh?'

She nodded as the door swung shut behind them, leaving them alone in the foyer. 'Big news.'

A flicker of wolf blue shifted through his eyes. 'Word on the street is things got pretty exciting at Bar Nine last night.' His gaze said he knew more but was fishing.

'I guess it did. Thanks for your help. I'm sure I can find Mortalis on my own.' She slapped her palm against one of the dragons painted on the interior double doors and pushed through.

Tec went after her, stepping into her path. 'I heard a comarré was killed there last night. And that a noble vampire came out of nowhere, turned into some kind of black-skinned monster, and ripped the heart out of her attacker.'

Scanning the club for Mortalis was impossible with Tec's broad body in her field of vision. 'I'm sure Doc's dealing with the situation.' But why hadn't he controlled it better?

'It's been dealt with according to pride law. Same as pack law, a life for a life.' His eyes narrowed. 'But if one of those deaths wasn't really a death, the situation becomes unbalanced.' He got a little closer. 'A life is still required.'

She stroked the red leather sacre straps crossing her chest. 'Are you warning me or threatening me?'

He backed up. 'Informing you. Do with it what you will, but know that it's going to be dealt with.' He held his hands up. 'Not by me. But Doc's got a lot to prove as the new leader.'

'Shouldn't you be at the front door, Tec?' Mortalis raised his brows in question as he came to a stop at the wolf-shifter's side.

Tec nodded, his eyes on Chrysabelle. 'Headed there now. You have a good night.' He shoved back through the doors.

'What was that all about?' Mortalis asked.

Chrysabelle exhaled a long sigh. The weight on her shoulders never got lighter. 'I'm not even sure where to start.' She tried to smile. 'How are you?'

'Better than you by the looks of it.' He tipped his head into the club. 'You want to talk somewhere private?'

'Love to.'

A few minutes later, he escorted her into a tiny room with a narrow desk and two chairs. 'Welcome to my office. Formerly the broom closet.'

'I didn't even know you had an office.'

'I didn't until a day ago. Luciano, Dominic's nephew, thought I should have my own space. Such as it is.' He pulled the chair from behind the desk and set it beside the other one, motioning her to sit.

When they were both settled, she began. 'I'm going to summarize as best I can. I've died twice in the last few days. The first time was when I last visited the Aurelian, and most recently last night. When this happens, I lose all memory of the event and typically pass out for a day or so. Mal thinks the ring of sorrows never lost its power when it was melted down and stitched into my skin and that its power is the reason death doesn't seem to be a permanent thing for me anymore. Velimai thinks you might be able to connect me to someone who can tell me exactly what power transferred into me.'

He opened his mouth, but she held up a finger. 'There's more. Mal might be in trouble now because he killed the shifter who killed me last night, and as you can see, I am no longer dead. This whole thing apparently happened in front of a crowd at Bar

Nine, so covering it up isn't really an option. Let's see, what else ... oh yes. The vampiress who was being held captive in the freighter's hold? Gone. And she took Damian with her. The kicker to that is, Mal says Damian's name is the last thing I uttered before I woke up after being killed by the Aurelian.'

'Well.' Mortalis sat back slowly. 'I'm not sure where to start.'

'Welcome to my world.'

He steepled his fingers. 'Okay, maybe I do know where to start. First of all, I *can* connect you with someone who can get a read on the new signum and see what power they contain – if he's willing to meet with you. It won't be easy.'

She shrugged. 'Is anything in my life?'

Mortalis continued. 'Second, I'll put out some feelers, see if I can get feedback on where our runaway vamp might be. Third, why do you think you said Damian's name?'

'No idea. There's nothing there but a big blank. The black-outs seem to start a few moments before I actually die.'

Mortalis strummed his fingers on his knees, lost in thought for a few moments. 'With everything you've told me, I can think of only one good reason you'd say his name.'

'Why?' She edged forward, her breath tight in her chest, as she already knew what he was going to say. The same thing Mal had already told her.

Mortalis blew out a breath. 'He's your brother.'

Chapter Twelve

'Nothing in this one either.' Fi tossed another book on the growing pile in the middle of Mal's office. 'You really think we're going to find anything?'

'Yes.' No, but getting Fi to help search for nonexistent information on the ring of sorrows was a great way to keep her away from Doc until he could get his situation figured out. Not that babysitting Fi was really what Mal wanted to be doing either, but there was no point in being around Chrysabelle when she woke up if it was anything like the last time. He'd let her remember she'd wanted to talk to him and come here on her own terms. Better that than arguing with her again. He didn't want to argue. He wanted them to be a team. *How sweet.* However much that was possible. If it even was. *It's not.*

Fi flipped through another book. 'You should sell these. Paper books are worth good money and you could use some of that.'

'No. Keep looking.' Somewhere outside, a car door shut and a new heartbeat announced itself to his senses. 'Someone's here.'

Fi looked up from her pages. 'Chrysabelle?'

'No.' He closed the book he hadn't been reading and stood. 'Get scarce in case it's trouble.'

'I'll be in the galley if you need me. I think there's some pizza left.' She moved out and he followed her, splitting off to head up to the deck. He climbed to the bridge for a better vantage out over the ship.

The sun had set a while ago, leaving a melting blue horizon in its wake. An imported sedan sat at the end of the freighter's gangplank. No heartbeats inside the car, so whoever it was had come alone. Good. Easier to kill if need be. The voices cheered that idea.

He honed in on the pulse. Somewhere to the front of the ship. Trying to find a way in most likely. He dropped down a few levels, landing without making a sound. That's when the perfume hit him. Wasn't strong, but to his nose, it was enough. Why humans doused themselves in scent, he'd never understood. Soap, shampoo, lotion, washing detergent. Everything had an artificial smell. It was almost more than his nose could take at times. Blood, sweat, earth, rain, metal. Those were honest smells. Unlike the fake limey scent that marked his intruder like a flashing neon sign. He settled in among a stack of empty barrels to watch her. When she moved, he followed, always quiet, always a few steps behind. Once close enough to touch. But he didn't.

She finally found an entrance that satisfied her. He leaned against the railing behind her. She knocked, almost making him laugh.

'Slumming, Madam Mayor?'

Pulse bumping a notch higher, she jumped and twisted to look at him. 'You startled me.'

'I'm a vampire. If that's the least I do, you should be thankful.'

Her smile was forced as she straightened her skirt. Nice legs. Not as nice as Chrysabelle's. 'I was wondering if we could talk.'

'Sure. Start with how you found me.'

'I have access to information most people don't.'

He crossed his arms. 'I'm completely off the grid. Have been for centuries.'

'I . . . I hired someone to find you.'

'That someone have a death wish?'

'Please, I'm not here to upset you.' She took a few steps toward him, proving she was either incredibly ballsy or insane. He inhaled, picking up the additional aroma of rum. He added drunk to the list of possibilities. 'I know that my grandchild is in the hands of the ancient ones, as you call them.'

He nodded, the smart remarks dying away. He knew what it was to lose a child. 'That's what we believe, yes.'

'I have to get her back.'

'*You* have to get her back?' His brows lifted a few centimeters. 'You don't understand what you're going up against.'

'Yes, I do.' Her heartbeat calmed slightly. 'They're demons. Fallen angels. Deadly, powerful creatures.'

'That only begins to describe them.'

'I can't let them have her without a fight.'

He pushed away from the railing, causing her to jerk backward. He shook his head. 'If I scare you, how are you going to face them?'

'That's why I'm here.' She held her ground as he took a step closer. 'I'm almost defenseless as a human. I want you to turn me into a vampire. Put me on a more equal playing field. Being turned will help me better serve the city, too. Understand both sides.'

He barked out a laugh, stunned by her idea. 'I thought you were insane to come here; now I know you are.' Why did a damned eternity hold such appeal for humans? He turned to leave. 'Answer's no. Go home.' He wasn't about to offer his or Chrysabelle's assistance until everything with Chrysabelle had been straightened out. The child was half vampire. It was in good company for now.

'I'm siding with you. Don't you understand that? I'm siding with your kind. When the war between varcolai and vampires comes—'

'There won't be a war.' He kept walking. 'Go home.'

She ran after him and snagged his arm, letting it go as soon as he spun to face her. 'Please. I'll do anything you want. Give you blood.' *Blood blood blood*. Her gaze skimmed his body. 'Sleep with you.'

He stared at her. 'Are you for real? Are you truly this clueless about who I am? About what I am?'

'Why do you think I'm here?'

'Because you're crazy.'

She planted her hands on her hips and lifted her chin, tossing her hair. 'I take good care of myself, Mr. Bourreau. A lot of men would find me very desirable.'

'I'm not one of them.' *You're also not a man*. Like he needed to be reminded of that.

With a touch of indignation, she sniffed, her hands dropping from her hips. 'I'd do *anything* you want. Please, just make me like you.'

Faster than he knew she could follow, he grabbed her upper

arms and pulled her close against his body. She gasped and began to tremble. He pressed his cheek to hers so that his mouth was next to her ear, then spoke as distinctly as he could with anger tightening his jaw. 'I am not a man, Madam Mayor. I am a monster. The only part of me I want to stick into you is my fangs. Then I would drink your blood until there wasn't enough left to keep your heart pumping. That's what I'd do with you.' The voices went wild. She was warm against him, but still she shivered. 'And you want to become like me? You are a fool.' He shoved her away. 'I should wipe your mind of this, but I won't because I'm afraid you'd just come back.'

'How dare you,' she whispered. 'I offer myself to you and this is how you treat me.'

'Go home.' He walked toward the ship's entrance. 'Let's both forget this happened.' Footsteps behind him alerted him to her movement. He dodged as she came after him.

Jerking to a stop, she turned, her chest rising and falling. 'Don't walk away from me. This isn't over.'

His human face disappeared. He knew his eyes must be silver by now. 'Get off my ship.'

'Turn me. Or face the consequences.'

The beast within lifted its head in anger. 'Threatening me is a very bad idea.' He spun a little power into his voice. 'Go home. Forget where I live.'

Some of the fire in her eyes died. 'I ... don't ... '

'Forget and go home,' he said again, this time with greater insistence.

She nodded and moved back toward the gangway. 'Home,' she muttered.

As her car pulled away, another pulled up. Chrysabelle. The tension drained from him. If needing her weakened him, so be it, although in truth he felt stronger around her. More complete. And if she didn't want to talk about the ring of sorrows' power, he'd let it go for tonight. After the mayor, Chrysabelle's company would be a welcome change.

She got out, her dark luminescence beckoning in the night's gloom. She waved when she saw him standing on the deck. He lifted his hand to return the gesture. Odd the things he did around her. She jogged up the gangway. 'Was that the mayor I saw driving away?'

'Yes. But I don't want to talk about her.' Screw everything he should or shouldn't do. All he wanted was her.

She stopped a few steps away from him and frowned. 'I know. You want to talk about the ring and the power and all that. I should start by saying you might be right about Damian. At least Mortalis agrees he could be my brother, so if you want to say I told you so, go ahead and—'

'I'll pass.' He took her hand and pulled her against him, then kissed her hard and fast before lifting his head. Her frown turned into an openmouthed gape. 'In fact, I don't want to talk at all. Other than to tell you I'm glad you're still alive.' He closed his eyes as her perfume wrapped around him. Slowly, so did her arms.

'You're in an interesting mood.'

He put a little space between them and held her face in his hands. He was done fighting with the voices in his head. Trying to deny what he felt. 'I have bad news.' He watched her eyes for her reaction. 'I love you.'

Beneath his palms, she tensed. Her breathing and pulse increased and she blinked rapidly.

Love. What a word to come out of his mouth. He shut out the voices' chaos as he dropped his hands from her face. 'Don't expect flowers and candy. I'm telling you because it shades everything I do concerning you. The biggest danger is that you can be used against me now, and trust me, that's the last thing I want. I'll die before I let anything bad happen to you.'

She struggled to nod as he stepped away and gave her some space. 'I know you would. You've proven that.' She gnawed at her lip. 'Except for Maris, no one's told me they love me before. I don't know how to react.'

'There's no reaction needed on your part.' He walked toward the door, letting her breathe air that wasn't tainted with vampire. 'Did you have another memory lapse this time?'

She followed him. 'Mal, you can't just change the subject like that.'

He stepped into the ship. 'Something important must be on your mind if you came all the way out here.'

Her hands gripped the sides of the door, but she came no farther. 'Your declaration is pretty important.'

'No, it's not. It's simply a statement of fact. A warning.'

'A warning? That's romantic.'

'You want romance, look somewhere else.' He loosened one of her hands and closed his around it. Her pulse still raced. He dropped her hand. Maybe she'd had enough of his touch for one night. 'Come inside and tell me what brought you here.'

She opened her mouth, then shut it again and, with a sigh, allowed him to lead her to the galley. Fi sat at the table, eating a slice of cold pizza.

Mal shook his head. 'I don't know how you can eat that.'

She spoke around a mouthful of food. 'And I don't know how you can drink blood.' She swallowed and closed the empty box. 'I'm going to find a Dumpster for this. You two look like you need to be left alone anyway.' She got up from the table and tucked the box beneath her arm. 'Nice to see you're alive again, Chrysabelle.'

'Thanks, Fi.'

Mal gestured toward the kettle. 'You want tea or something?'

'No.' She settled into one of the chairs around the old table and folded her hands on top of it, staring at the signum marking her fingers. 'I feel like I have a million things to tell you and no idea where to start.'

'My apologies if I've discombobulated your thoughts.'

'You tell me you love me and now you're apologizing without prompting? Who are you?' She gave him a crooked little smile. 'Besides, you discombobulate me without trying. Not always in a bad way.'

'Nice to hear.' He took the seat next to her. 'Just tell me what's happening and we'll figure it out together.'

'First of all, I'm sorry about the other night. You didn't deserve that.'

'Also nice to hear.'

'I stopped to see Mortalis on my way over here. Like I said, he thinks the reason I said Damian's name is the same reason you mentioned – because Damian is my brother.' She looked at him, clearly waiting to see his reaction.

'What do you think?'

'I don't know. You pointed out that I haven't seen Damian since he's been here. I barely remember him from life in the Primoris Domus. Could he be my brother? I guess. How do I determine if that's true?' She rubbed the back of her neck.

Fi stuck her head back through the doorway. 'Why not good old-fashioned DNA testing?'

Mal growled softly. 'I thought you were throwing the pizza box away?'

Fi shrugged. 'Sorry.'

'I can't,' Chrysabelle answered. 'Not unless you know someone who could do it with complete confidentiality. I'm not looking to become a government science experiment. Now that othernaturals are out in the open, I'm sure they'd jump on the chance to test more of me than just my blood.'

Mal rested his hand on top of hers. 'I agree, but *if* we can find someone we trust—'

'Big if.' Chrysabelle pulled her hands from under his. She glanced at Fi. 'Could you give us some privacy?'

Fi swiveled back toward the hall. 'Your wish, my command.'

When the sound of her footsteps faded, Chrysabelle spoke again. 'Mortalis is putting feelers out to see if he can get a lead on where the vampiress might have holed up with Damian.' She rolled her bottom lip in, slowly releasing it. 'I also talked to Mortalis, on Velimai's recommendation, about finding someone who could tell me – us – what power the ring of sorrows might have contained.'

Mal kept the surprise off his face. This was a big step for her. 'What did he say?'

She leaned back in the chair and met his gaze. 'Mortalis told me about a very dangerous fae who, if willing, could tell me pretty much everything I want to know.'

'Besides this fae being dangerous, what's the catch?' Because there was always a catch.

'He'll exact a price, but we have to agree to pay it before he helps us, and we won't know what it is until he's done.'

Mal's mood went sour. 'That it?'

'Well, let's see . . . ' She started ticking things off on her fingers. 'He could get here, then decide he doesn't want to return to the fae plane. Then we have to either find a way to persuade him to go home or kill him. Mortalis says no way can he stay on the mortal realm. Of course, he could kill us first. And then again, he might not agree to help us at all.'

'You don't have to do this. We can figure out another way.'

She shook her head. 'No. There won't be another way, or if there is, it'll be harder. You always tell me I run instead of dealing. It's time to deal. I'm doing this, with or without you.'

'There is no without me. Not anymore.'

Smiling, she reached across the table and took his hand. 'That's how I know I'll get through it.' Her smile faded a little. 'Or at least I won't die alone.'

Chapter Thirteen

Fi ditched the pizza box first chance she had, then adjusted her sweatshirt hood so it hid her eyes. The air had the slight nip of what passed for fall in New Florida. Kinda reminded her of her childhood in Colorado, but by this time of year, there'd probably be snow on the ground. Or at least ice on the river. Here, the best you could hope for was a rare frost appearance.

The trek into town wasn't so bad. Gave her time to think, time to figure out her words. She couldn't go without seeing Doc any longer. The separation and the not talking were killing her. They hadn't been apart this long since she'd known him. What kind of a hold did this woman have over him? She had to see his new *wife* for herself. See what the competition was all about.

Wife. What kind of a job came with a wife? That was crazy.

Pride headquarters loomed ahead. She slipped into the alley behind the building but didn't bother with a door, just shifted into her ghost form and floated inside, zipping up through the floors until she reached the penthouse.

She hovered near the ceiling while she searched the place. She found Doc sitting on the sofa, elbows planted on his knees, eyes staring straight ahead. Classic thinking pose. What was on his mind? The incident with Mal and Chrysabelle from the night before? Or was he thinking about her? Missing her?

She drifted down until her feet touched carpeting, then went corporeal. She walked up behind him and slipped her hand over the back of his neck. 'Hi, baby—'

With a snarl, he shifted into his half-form, latched hold of her arms, and dragged her over the back of the sofa until she was pinned beneath him.

She kissed him, just a quick peck, doing her best to avoid the fangs jutting over his lip. 'Hi, kitty cat.'

'Fi.' Her name sighed out of him and he relaxed, going full human again. He sat up, pulling her with him. 'What are you doing here? You're supposed to be with Mal.'

'Nice to see you, too.' Not the welcome she'd imagined, that's for sure.

He rubbed a hand over his scalp. 'Sorry, babe, I wasn't expecting you.'

She sniffed. 'Obviously.'

His gaze shifted to a spot behind her before coming back. 'Look, now might not be the best time.'

'Why? What's happening? I feel like I have no idea what's going on in your life anymore.'

Scooting closer, he took her hands and squeezed them. His voice was low as he spoke. 'What's going on right now is complicated, but you gotta know everything I do, I do for us.'

'Complicated because of your new *wife*?'

He nodded. 'That and what happened last night.'

'Mal killed that guy, huh?'

'Yeah, and it was settled until Chrysabelle showed up alive at Seven earlier tonight.'

'News travels fast. I thought there was a pride rule about feline-shifters going to Seven? As in it's not allowed?'

He dropped her hands and leaned back. 'That was one of the first rules I changed.'

'With your history with Dominic? Did you suddenly become friends with him?'

'I didn't do it for him. I did it for the pride. Seven is a huge joint. Dominic employs a lot of people. I was trying to open up opportunities for the pride, show them ... I don't know ... show them I'm not Sinjin. That I'm looking out for the pride's best interest, not just my own.' He tipped his head back against the couch. 'I never wanted this job.'

She slid closer to him and began to massage the back of his neck. 'I know, baby.'

He bent his head, giving her hand more room. 'Some of the pride members are calling for Mal's death now. It ain't good.'

'Shhh. It's all going to be okay.' She leaned in and kissed the soft spot behind his ear as she dragged her nails over his scalp. Her reward was a soft, growly purr rumbling out of his chest.

'I've missed you something fierce, Fi.' His hand slipped between her knees to massage her leg.

'Me too, you,' she whispered against his skin before nipping his earlobe. 'I hate being away from you.' She kissed his jaw. 'I hate eating alone.' She kissed the bow of his upper lip. 'I hate showering alone.' She ran her tongue over the seam of his mouth. 'I hate sleeping alone.'

He pulled her onto his lap, his fingers digging into her hips as she straddled his legs. 'Fi—'

'I know you want this as much as I do,' she urged him. She

leaned back and yanked her hoodie over her head, revealing a skimpy tank top.

'I can't. Not here. Not now—'

She shut him up with a kiss. Her hands found their way under his shirt.

A hissing noise filtered in through the low purr coming out of him.

'You little *vadia*!' Someone grabbed her by the hair and yanked her onto the floor.

Fi's head smacked the table on the way down. She rubbed the sore spot as she looked up. A leggy brunette stood over her, but the woman's eyes were on Doc.

'And you,' she spat, pointing at Doc. 'Bringing your whore into my home. How dare you? Are you trying to shame me?'

Doc stood. 'Wait just a damn minute.' He held his hand out to Fi, helping her up. The woman backed up a few steps as he tugged Fi behind him. 'Don't you ever call Fi a whore. Ever. So help me Bast, I might actually hit a woman if you do.'

The woman shoved a finger into his chest. 'I am your wife. Any other woman who touches you *is* a whore. You don't like it, don't let them touch you.'

'Heaven, calm down.'

Heaven? Great. Perfect. Doc's new wife was named for paradise. *Fiona* meant 'fair,' but fair didn't compare to perfect bliss.

Heaven hissed at Doc again. 'Don't tell me to calm down. Get her out of here or I swear, I will kill her like I promised.'

Fi stepped out from behind Doc. 'Kill me? Kill *me*? Look, lady, I don't know if you think inheriting my fiancé gave you some kind of special permission, but he was mine first. Got it? Mine first.'

'Fi.' Doc gave a little shake of his head.

'That's right,' Heaven said. 'Tell your whore to close her whore mouth before I do it for her.'

Unable to take any more, Fi launched, catching Heaven by the waist and knocking her off her ridiculous high heels. They hit the floor with a thud. Heaven let out a guttural growl that caused Fi's muscles to contract. The body beneath her shifted and suddenly Fi's hands were full of soft, spotted fur.

She jerked back. Heaven had just become a jaguar.

Doc pulled her away and set her on her feet, his eyes shifter-yellow, his body tensed like a trip wire. 'Get the hell out of here, Fi, and don't come back until I tell you.'

She stumbled away from him, trying not to cry. Those were words she'd never thought he'd say to her. She certainly didn't need to hear them twice.

Morphing to ghost form, she slipped through the wall and out into the night.

Soft knocking woke Lola. She lifted her head from the pillow and turned on the bedside lamp. Squinting toward the door, she called, 'Yes?'

'Sorry to disturb you, ma'am, but there's a visitor,' a voice said from the other side.

'Come in, Hilda.' Lola twisted to look at the clock on the nightstand. Nearly 3:00 a.m. Why could nothing wait until a decent hour? Her maid, Hilda, entered the room a few feet. 'Who is it?' Not many people had the *cojones* to visit her at home, forget at 3:00 a.m., but if they'd gotten past her security, it had to be someone she knew. Or something very urgent. Her only daughter was dead – what pressing news could someone be bringing her?

'He said his name is Thomas Creek, ma'am. Do you want me to send him away? He said you'd want to see him.'

She flipped the covers back and reached for the robe at the foot of the bed. 'No, no. I'll talk to him. Where is he?'

'Foyer.'

'Put him in the living room and tell him I'll be in shortly, then go back to bed.'

'Yes, ma'am.' Hilda left, closing the door.

Looking at the robe in her hands, Lola yawned and changed her mind. Being in her nightgown would make her feel vulnerable. Instead, she dressed in jeans and a sweater, then brushed her teeth and hair and slipped her Walther PPK into her waistband before heading into the living room. She trusted Creek as much as she trusted anyone, which wasn't much.

He stood at the windows, staring into the night. The outside was pitch-black except for the distant glow of the security lights. Somewhere out there, Luke Havoc and the evening security team patrolled the grounds.

'This better be important.'

Creek turned sharply. He tipped his head to one side, eyes gleaming darkly. 'Mayor.'

'Why are you here?' At this hour, her patience was limited.

'I've come to accept the advisory job you offered me.'

She hoped he could read the disbelief on her face. 'Are you serious? At three in the morning?' He deserved a bullet for this, but somehow she managed to keep her hand off the gun resting against her back. 'Go home. We'll pick this up tomorrow in my office.'

He shook his head, blinking rapidly. 'I planned to start tonight since you don't understand the problems plaguing your city.'

'My grandchild is in the hands of demons, the news is full of horrible stories, my inbox overflows daily with complaints, my councilmen are resigning, and you think I don't understand the city's problems? Like hell I don't.'

'Then the time to act is now.'

'What do you think I've been doing? I've already spoken to Malkolm.' Although her memory of their talk was blurred around the edges. 'He's promised that he and the comarré will get Mariela back.' Had he? She couldn't really remember.

Creek's nostrils flared as he snorted out a breath. 'If you're willing to trust your granddaughter's life to a cursed vampire and his blood slave, you may not have what it takes to rescue this city.' He blinked a few more times and stared harder at her. 'Unless they've already gotten to you.'

'What? No.' She looked at him a little closer. He seemed ... not himself. 'No one's gotten to me. I knew Chrysabelle's mother. She was a good woman. Why shouldn't I trust her daughter and Malkolm?'

He came nearer, his steps odd. Mincing. 'Because the comarré work for the vampires and no vampires are to be trusted. Ever. No othernatural of any kind should be trusted. They will all turn against mankind sooner or later.'

'Two of my best security men are othernaturals.' She gestured toward the city. 'So are some of our police, firefighters, and paramedics.'

'And if they decide they'd rather run the city than protect it? Who will guard your streets then?'

Lola settled into the nearest chair, the gun's metal pressing reassuringly into her back. Creek sat on the edge of the coffee table in front of her, waiting. Maybe he was right. Maybe—

'What of the child's father?'

'What of him?'

'Has he offered to go after his daughter?'

She dropped her chin a little. 'He's looking into it.' Not that she knew what that meant.

'You've been to see him, then.' Creek's eyes narrowed.

She sighed. That was information she hadn't intended on sharing. 'Yes. I went to see him.'

'What help *is* he giving you?'

'I'm not sure.' Maybe she should talk to Malkolm about turning her into a vampire. Surely he'd understand the importance of leveling the playing field. The thought was muddled in a cloud of déjà vu. Had she already asked him about turning her? She glanced up at Creek. 'You once told me noble vampires had powers that fringe vampires didn't. What kind of powers?'

He leaned back and squared his shoulders as if preparing to recite something recently learned. 'The power of mind reading, the power of black magic, the power of alchemy, the power—'

'What kind of power does Malkolm have?'

With a burst of rapid blinking, Creek tipped his head to the other side. 'The power of persuasion.'

'What does that mean exactly?'

'He can convince humans to do as he says or cause them to forget things.'

'Forget things? Like conversations?'

Creek leaned in. 'Yes.' He stroked his fingers down her arm, his touch as soft as feathers. The contact drew sparks over her skin, causing her to pull away.

Like a switch being thrown, her memory of the evening returned. She had gone to see Malkolm. She'd begged him to turn her into a vampire, even offered him her body, and still he'd

refused her. The scornful look on his face filled her vision. As
though she were too stupid to understand what becoming such
a powerful creature entailed. And he'd never promised anything
about rescuing Mariela.

That arrogant fool. 'Damn it,' she whispered. Hot tendrils of
anger wormed up her spine. He'd denied her. Then stripped the
memory. She slammed her fist down on the arm of the chair.
'That bastard messed with my mind.'

Creek nodded twice in rapid succession. '*None* of them can
be trusted.'

'So what do I do about it? You want to be my adviser, advise
me.'

Creek stood and planted his hands on his hips. For a split
second, an odd shadow seemed to hang off his arms in the shape
of wings; then he dropped his hands and the shadows were
gone. 'The first step is controlling the othernaturals.'

'How?'

'Hold a press conference tomorrow morning announcing a
curfew with the only exceptions being for law enforcement, fire-
men, and emergency personnel. Your security men may then
continue working for you. Any city employees who disagree
will be showing you which side they've chosen. The human citizens will thank you.'

'I don't think that's a good idea—'

Creek grabbed her arm, his eyes darkening as the protests left
her tongue.

She nodded, a little numb. 'A curfew, yes. The human citizens will thank me.'

He released her.

'What if someone violates the curfew?'

He pressed his fingertips together. 'When they violate the

curfew, they will be made an example of. You will show these othernaturals that you are the one in charge, not them.'

Lola nodded again, the fog lifting slightly from her brain. Maybe she'd get lucky and Malkolm would be the first one to tangle in her net.

Payback was hell.

Chapter Fourteen

Tatiana tipped her face into the evening breeze, lifting Lilith into it as well. 'Isn't that lovely, my darling? Doesn't the night air feel good?'

Lilith cooed, kicking her little legs and reaching out as though trying to grab a star from the sky. Probably she just wanted to be put down. She'd begun to crawl, something the kine doctor had said was far more advanced than an average child of her age, but then Lilith wasn't average. She was a vampire princess and nothing was beyond her grasp.

'Shall we sit by the fountain or shall we walk? Hmm?' Tatiana turned Lilith around, rubbed her nose against her daughter's cheek, and inhaled the sweet smell of her soft skin. Lilith wrapped her hand in one of Tatiana's curls, giving it a tug.

'Silly goose.' Tatiana kissed Lilith's nose. 'Let's go sit by the fountain and wait for Papa.' Octavian had promised to meet them in the garden after he took care of some things, but the sun would be up soon. Not that they were in any danger. The estate's layout had been especially designed so that the gardens remained shaded for almost two hours after the sun rose. Still, she'd expected him to meet them sooner than this. She listened for him but picked up only the distant sound of a car approaching. It was too soon for the Elders and Dominus to be arriving, but if they were, Octavian would deal with them. He knew not to let anyone disturb her time with Lilith this evening.

She set Lilith on a patch of grass between the great tiered fountain and one of the surrounding marble benches, then sat to watch as the child dug her hands into the tufts of green.

Lilith crawled a little, then plopped down onto her backside. The movement made her laugh and Tatiana laughed along with her. She shook her head as she stared at her child in wonderment.

How different things had become since Lilith had entered her life. She pulled the locket loose from her blouse and opened it to study Sophia's face. No one would ever replace her Sophia. No one. Lilith was not a replacement. Lilith was a second chance. She kissed the portrait, then clicked the locket shut and tucked it away.

Tatiana leaned back against the bench as Lilith crawled closer to where the edge of the grass met the pea gravel walkway. She plopped down again, squeeling in delight and showing off her tiny fangs as she looked to Tatiana for approval.

'Such a clever girl, aren't you, my darling?' Tatiana smiled. She'd never had gardens before, but this was the Dominus estate and Ivan had spared no expense. From the night-blooming jasmine to the temperate warmth, layers of magic and wards shielded the gardens from the harsh Romanian winter and kept them evergreen and ever useful.

'Someday, my sweet, this will all be yours.'

Lilith didn't look up from her game of mounding up the pea gravel on the grass.

Footsteps crunched on the gravel path behind them. Tatiana stood, preparing to welcome Octavian.

He wasn't alone.

Her mouth opened and she ran out to meet them. 'Daci. You're back.'

'Tatiana!' Daci met her halfway and fell into her arms with a soft sob. 'It's so good to be home. You have no idea how awful it was.'

Tatiana pushed Daci to arm's length and studied her. Daci's gown was torn and dirty, and her face, although still beautiful, seemed washed in the pallor of stress. 'Whatever happened? I was worried.'

Daci shook her head as if struggling against tears. 'I tried to make my way into the comarré's good graces by telling her I was seeking asylum, but she wasn't home and her friends didn't believe me. They locked me up in the hold of some dirty old ship and left your comar to guard me. It was awful.' She inhaled another sob. 'Awful.'

'But you had the supplies I sent you with, right?'

'Yes.' Daci's eyes brightened a little. 'That's how I escaped. At first I waited for them to come. I figured as soon as they opened the door, I'd make my move. But no one ever came. I heard voices, but never the comarré. Finally, I'd had enough. I used everything you gave me. The blasting cubes took out the metal doors, which knocked out the comar. Then I kept him that way with the sedatives. Made for a much quieter flight home, I assure you.'

Amazed, Tatiana looked at Daci more closely. 'You brought him back with you?'

'Yes, of course.' She straightened. 'He betrayed you. He must be dealt with. And I confess, I was dying of hunger after being held prisoner.'

Tatiana shook her head. 'You are a remarkable woman, Daci. And a good friend.' As the sky above them lightened with the coming dawn, she hesitantly reached out to Daci and squeezed her arm, the gesture alien and yet somehow appropriate. Amazing how much being a mother again had changed her.

Octavian cleared his throat. 'I've put Damian in the sound-proofed rooms in the west wing. He'll be fine there for as long as you wish. I'm sure Daciana would like to rest after her ordeal.'

'I would,' she agreed, stifling a yawn. 'I haven't had a decent daysleep since I left.'

Tatiana felt the need for sleep as well, but she wasn't ready for this moment to end. She reached out to Octavian and Daci, pulling them both to her. She smiled at Octavian. 'Isn't it wonderful that Daci's back with us?'

He nodded and slipped his arm around her waist. 'Absolutely.' His gaze shifted to Daci. 'Tatiana and I were very concerned about you.'

Daci smiled, but it didn't last. 'I have failed you, though, Tatiana. I was unable to capture the comarré.' She dipped her head and backed up a step. The sky behind her was golden with morning sun, but the house's shadow covered them. 'I am fully prepared to return and try again.'

'Nonsense.' Tatiana waved her hand through the air to dismiss the thought. 'We'll deal with the comarré soon enough, but not now. There are too many other things to attend to. After all, the four of us are a family now. We need you here.'

'The four of us?' Daci looked from Octavian to Tatiana. 'I don't understand.'

Tatiana smiled uncontrollably. 'There's someone you must meet. Come.' She walked back to where Lilith was playing, but Lilith was gone. 'Lilith?' Panic bubbled in her gullet like acid.

She searched the garden's shadowed depths. 'Lilith!'

Octavian was at her side instantly. 'Where was she?'

'Right here in the grass.' Tatiana pointed to the stark white pebbles scattered against the green turf.

'She can't have gotten far.'

Daci joined them. 'Who's Lilith?'

'My—' Tatiana stopped cold as she found her child. Lilith crawled toward the far edge of the garden, her little fingers skating the dividing line between shade and bright sun. 'Lilith, no!' She started forward, but Octavian caught her arm.

'Wait.'

She tore out of his grasp, almost snarling. 'My child is in danger.'

'She's not or I wouldn't have stopped you.' A curious expression came over his face. 'Look again.'

Tatiana turned her head. Lilith sat in the sunlight, her face tipped into the killing rays, clapping her hands and laughing. No smoke, no fire, no flames.

The sun had no effect on her.

'How . . . how is that possible?' Tatiana asked. The adrenaline left her in a whoosh, and a new sense of confusion took its place. She leaned against Octavian.

'I don't know, except that with Lilith we should learn to expect the unexpected.'

Daci shook her head. 'I don't understand. Where did the baby come from?'

'The ancient ones gave her to me to rear. She's the first vampire born into this life.'

Daci pointed. 'You mean to tell me that child, sitting in the sun, was born a vampire. *Is* a vampire?'

'Remarkable, isn't she?' Tatiana nodded, unable to take her eyes off the miracle before them.

'Bloody hell,' Daci whispered.

Octavian began to laugh softly. 'Things just got a lot more interesting.'

Tatiana joined him, buoyed by the knowledge that her daughter was even more powerful than she could have imagined. 'Kine or vampire, my child shall rule them all.'

Doc tapped his fingers impatiently on the steering wheel, waiting for the light to change. Where the hell was Fi? He was running out of places to look. He'd gone after her when she'd slipped through the wall, but getting to ground level from the penthouse had taken too long. There'd been no sign of her. Not even in the uptown shopping district, one of her favorite places to walk and look at store windows.

He glanced in the rearview mirror at the entrance to Mephisto Island. No luck there either. He'd thought Fi might have gone to talk to Chrysabelle or Velimai, but Chrysabelle was already in bed and the wysper hadn't seen Fi. The red flipped green and he took off toward Mal's freighter.

The ketamine in his system had kept the flames from bursting off his skin when Heaven attacked Fi and had kept him from striking out even though it went against his upbringing to hit a woman. Protecting Fi was his main concern. Which is why he'd yelled at her to leave. Dammit. It had come out wrong. The anger in his voice had been at Heaven, not Fi, but he knew his woman. She was sensitive. Especially with all that was going on.

He had to find her, explain. Calm her down. Make sure things were okay between them. She was all right, wasn't she? Fi was pretty good at taking care of herself. She was a ghost, after all. If someone threatened her, she could slip away easy. Unless they surprised her. Like Heaven. Nothing had stopped Fi from disappearing when he'd told her to, though.

He growled softly. The whole situation was a complete mess. He loved Fi so much he couldn't fully explain it. What he'd said to her had been spoken in the heat of the moment. In the interest of keeping her safe and away from Heaven. He'd never banish Fi from his life, but he'd bet good money that was what she was thinking. Cripes. Why had she come to the penthouse? She had to have known that was a bad move. He shook his head as he maneuvered the car around a corner. Women could make a man fool crazy, although he could guess why she'd come. He missed Fi so much it hurt.

He couldn't see a clear path for when they'd be together again either. The death of Brutus had complicated things even more. Doc understood why Mal had killed the lion-shifter. Doc would have done the same in that situation. But Chrysabelle's magic resurrection had definitely screwed the pooch.

Speaking of pooches, Tec had promised to let Doc know if Fi showed up at Seven, not that Doc could figure any good reason she'd go there, but then what did he really know anymore? He'd once thought being unable to shift into any form but a house cat was the worst life could get.

Those were the days.

In another hour, the sun would be up. He should just about make it to the freighter before daysleep turned Mal into a comatose lump.

He stomped the gas. The sports car responded instantly,

snapping Doc back into the seat as it leaped forward. At least Sinjin had good taste in cars. This machine was a helluva lot more fun to drive than Mal's old beater. Fi would love the way this car took off.

His joy faded. He had to find her.

Forty-five minutes later, he slammed the door as he got back into the car and cursed into the air as dawn brightened the sky.

He'd been too late to talk to Mal, so he'd searched the freighter. It was the closest thing Fi had to a home, but there'd been no sign of her.

He punched the dashboard. The pride expected him to make a ruling about Brutus's death today. The last thing he wanted to do was stop looking for Fi and go back to the penthouse and Heaven, but he didn't need more problems piled on top of the ones he already had.

Reluctantly he turned the car around and headed home. Such as it was. The responsibility of being pride leader without Fi at his side ... He shook his head as heat built along his tendons. Those kinds of thoughts weren't helping. He reached into his jacket pocket, grabbed the little vial tucked there, popped the top open, then shook out a pill and swallowed it.

Numbing himself was the only way he was going to get through this without killing someone.

Chapter Fifteen

With Creek on the dais behind her, and John and the day-time security team positioned around the room, Lola walked to the podium to address the gathered press. She burned with an unsettled urgency to set the curfew in place. It was the right thing to do and exactly what her citizens needed. Creek had told her that repeatedly last night. Now it was all she could think about.

'Thank you for coming this morning on such short notice. I won't waste your time.' She glanced at the notes Creek had helped her put together. 'As you're all aware, the recent troubles that have plagued this city are unlike anything we have seen before. We can no longer ignore words like *shape-shifter* and *vampire*. The creatures we once thought lived only in our night-mares now walk among us.'

The assembled press before her, a group known for its collective boisterousness, remained steadfastly fixed on her every word, microphones stretched forward to capture each one.

'Unlike many of the other nationalities who have flocked to our shores in hopes of asylum and sanctuary, these newly revealed *othernaturals* present a unique dilemma. Which of them can be trusted? Which of them should we fear?'

A few in the crowd shifted, casting glances at those around them.

'Some have already delineated themselves as friends of Paradise City. As the blogs and dailies have pointed out, my own security team has several varcolai on it. Our police force, our firefighters, and our paramedics all have othernaturals in their ranks. For the service of those men and women, we're thankful.' She paused, watching the faces, trying to read them as she always did in situations like this.

'Among the rest of the population, however, many questions remain. To this end, I am instating a citywide curfew, effective immediately. From sundown to sunup, any othernatural caught breaking that curfew will be subject to disciplinary action.'

A sea of hands shot up before her and the barrage of questions began.

She leaned forward and spoke into the mike to be heard over the ruckus. 'The only exceptions to this will be othernaturals in service to the city as I previously mentioned: our first responders, firefighters, law enforcement, and medical personnel. There will be some leniency for othernaturals employed by humans, but it will be on a case-by-case basis. You'll all be issued a copy of the statement on your way out. Thank you for coming and have a good day.'

The blast of new questions hit her immediately, but she tucked her notes into her jacket pocket and backed away. A sense of calm came over her and the driving desire that had arisen in her last night finally felt sated. Her mission was accomplished. John blocked the crowd so she could exit. Creek jerked into step alongside her.

'Well done.'

'Are you sure? I still don't know if—'

Creek grabbed her wrist as they walked. Again his touch gave her a weird shiver that also somehow calmed her. 'It's what needed to be done.'

She pulled her hand away, unsettled by the contact. 'Yes, you're right. But there will be backlash.' Nothing she said went without critical comment by some newspaper, television station, or website. It was part and parcel of being mayor. The elevator was open and waiting. Creek and John got on with her; then John punched the button for her office's floor. He'd yet to make eye contact with her since the announcement, but it was hard to tell who he was looking at behind those dark shades.

Creek spoke as the doors slid closed. 'Remind them that if this curfew had been in place sooner, your daughter and the two other girls wouldn't have been killed.'

'*Maybe* they wouldn't have.' The memory made her heart ache. 'A curfew isn't going to stop someone intent on killing.'

'It won't,' John said quietly.

Creek canted his head to one side. 'It will. Once an example has been made.'

She leaned against the wall and glanced at him. The smoked mirror interior reflected John's large form and beside him, Creek's slightly smaller one. But there was something odd about Creek's reflection. It was distorted. Like another shadowy figure lay over the top of his. A figure with wings.

She squeezed her eyes shut, then looked again. The distortion was gone.

Creek stared at her, a disconcerting darkness in his eyes. 'Are you all right, Madam Mayor? You don't look like you feel well.'

'I feel fine, thank you. Just stress.' She forced a smile. 'A day without stress is like a day without ... well, I wouldn't know. It's been so long since I had a day without stress.'

The doors opened and John stuck his arm out to keep them from closing. 'You should take some time off, ma'am.'

'I wish I could, John. Maybe when things have calmed down.' She headed for her office.

Creek walked beside her, his hand on her elbow. 'The curfew was a step in that direction.'

Lola nodded. 'Absolutely.' Still, she couldn't shake the sense of foreboding that hung over her like a flock of circling vultures. What was the saying? Darkest before the dawn? If that was true, she hoped dawn came fast.

'Don't worry, we'll find Fi.' Chrysabelle squeezed Doc's arm, slightly amazed at how such a big man could fit into such a small car. 'I know she's got a temper, but she can't stay away from you for long.'

'I don't know about that. After what I said ... ' Doc shook his head, eyes scanning the road as he shifted gears. 'I'm just hoping she'll come out to talk to you.' He exhaled. 'I could really use her company after the day I've had.'

'You want to talk about it? I know all about bad days.'

He snorted a laugh. 'I guess you do.' He turned out of Mephisto Island and headed toward downtown. The late afternoon sun glinted off the bay surrounding the private island. 'I had a council meeting today to discuss ... ' He glanced over at her. 'Maybe I shouldn't talk about this after all.'

'To discuss what happened with Mal and me the other night?'

'Yeah.'

'I'm really sorry about that.'

'Nothing for you to apologize for. Brutus shoulda kept his cool. Nothing would have happened if that cat had just held it together.'

Doc's jaw ticked and she wondered if changing the subject was a better idea, but he kept talking.

'Didn't help that Mal went nuts either.'

Chrysabelle nodded. 'I agree, but if you'd been in his situation, if that had been Fi—'

He held up his hand. 'Trust me, I get it.'

'So what was decided? Or can't you tell me?'

He was quiet for a moment. 'What was decided is that pride law stands and pride law says a life for a life. Technically that was satisfied, until word got out you weren't dead.' His gaze flicked in her direction. 'Not everyone believes it, by the way. Some of the pride thinks the wolves are trying to start things. Some think you've come back as a ghost.'

'What happens when they know I'm alive for sure?'

His mouth hardened into a thin line and he stared straight ahead. 'Shopping district is the best place to start. You know how she loves clothes.'

'Not telling me isn't going to make it go away.'

He stayed silent a few seconds. 'Mal's life will be required.'

She turned away, preferring the blur of the passing landscape to the harsh reality of his words. Her fingers knotted together the same way pain twisted around her heart. 'I can't let that happen.'

'You think it's what I want?' He slammed the heel of his hand against the steering wheel. 'Hell, no. Mal's saved my life more times than I can count. I owe him.'

She twisted to face him. 'Tell the pride that. Explain what happened. They'll understand, won't they?'

'Pride law is pride law. There are no exceptions.'

'Not even on the word of the pride leader?'

He pursed his mouth again. 'I can try. I *will* try. You have my word.'

'Thank you.' It wasn't much, but it was something. She'd hate to make enemies of the entire Paradise City pride, but there was no way she'd let them sign Mal's name to a death warrant for something she'd caused.

Doc parked the car and turned off the engine. He faced her, his eyes earnest. 'Look, if it takes me stepping down from my position, or whatever, I'm going to do everything in my power to keep Mal safe.'

'I appreciate that.' She knew what going against the pride could mean for him. Like being thrown out again. She gave him the best smile she could manage, considering. 'Let's go find Fi. We have only a couple hours before the sun goes down.'

He opened his door and got out as she did the same. 'I plan on looking for her until I find her, sun or no sun.'

'What about the mayor's curfew?'

'Screw that noise. I'm the pride leader. I'm not going to let something like that keep me from the woman I love.'

'You think that's the wisest attitude with everything going on?'

He grinned and held his arms out. 'Wisdom rarely plays a part in my decisions. Why start now?'

She shrugged. It was his skin, but she wasn't going to say it. Doc was a grown man. He could make his own choices.

A couple hours later and there was still no sign of Fi. Chrysabelle glanced at the sky. 'Doc, you should really get back to headquarters or wherever you're staying. I'll keep looking. In fact, I'll go get Mal and—'

'And let him violate the curfew? No, I'm good.'

She'd forgotten Mal was an othernatural, too. How long had she been thinking of him as a man and not a vampire? She checked the sky again. The sun would be down soon and she had no idea how much grace period would be allowed between sundown and full dark. 'Please. Go home. I'll find Fi, I promise.'

He took her arm and pulled her into a narrow alley between two buildings. 'I appreciate your concern, but you're forgetting that I can outrun any mortal alive. Even if some random patrol sees me, they won't be able to catch me or track me.'

The longer they argued, the longer they'd be vulnerable. The street solars had already flickered to life. 'Fine. Let's go back to my house and regroup. We can get Jerem. Technically, as my driver, he gets a pass.'

Doc looked like he was going to say no, but he just shook his head and walked out of the alley. She followed, hoping his response meant he agreed with her plan.

Across the street and down one block, two police officers were getting out of their car.

She shoved Doc toward his little sports car. 'Get us out of here, now.'

With lightning speed, he whipped around. 'I told you—'

'You there!' One of the cops had eyes on Doc and was pointing with his nightstick.

'Hell, no,' Doc snarled. He started toward the officers.

She snagged his arm to hold him back. 'Don't, Doc. Let's just go, please. Fi doesn't need you in jail.'

He hesitated and muttered, 'Dammit,' under his breath. He backed up and pressed his thumb to the biometric lock on the car door. 'Let's get out of here.'

A soft whistle came toward them. A split second later, a tiny orange-furred insect landed on Doc's neck. Except it wasn't an insect. He slapped at the tranquilizer dart, but it was too late. Whatever the cops had been equipped with, it worked fast. Doc slumped against the car, his eyes rolling back in his head. 'Tell . . . '

His mouth moved but no more sound came out. Chrysabelle grabbed his massive form as he slid toward the sidewalk, falling to her knees beside him. 'Tell who? Who do you want me to tell?'

But he was out.

The cops ran up. One held a tranq rifle. 'We'll take it from here, miss. Best you go home where it's safe.'

She stared at them, trying not to hate them for doing their jobs. 'Do you report directly to the mayor?'

The officer with the gun looked at his partner and smiled. 'For taking down the first curfew violator? Absolutely.'

'Give her a message for me. Tell her I said she's an idiot.'

Chapter Sixteen

Mal knew Chrysabelle was on board before he heard her calling out his name. If not for the edge of fear in her voice, he would have met her with a kiss. He rushed to where she stood just inside the door off the aft deck. 'What's wrong?'

She threw up her hands and paced past him. 'Doc's in jail. They're going to chain him in the city square.'

'What? That's barbaric.' *Just like you.*

'The mayor announced a curfew for othernaturals from sundown to sunup. Any othernaturals out during that period are subject to disciplinary action.' She stopped pacing long enough to scowl. 'They shot him with a *tranquilizer* gun. Can you believe that?' She shook her head. 'The mayor's using him as an example to scare the rest into submission.'

'Why wasn't Doc at pride headquarters?'

'He was, but Fi's gone missing – he told her to get lost, but it was for her own safety, and now he can't find her. I was helping him look, but the sun set and he wouldn't go home. Stupid man,' she muttered. 'I went to the police station to get information about how to bail him out when I overheard a couple officers talking about the mayor's plans for the first othernatural caught.' Her hands tightened into fists. 'This is a giant, bloody mess.' She stared toward the glittering line of the city.

'You look like you want to punch something.' He came to stand beside her at the rail, resisting the urge to slip his arms around her. He knew her well enough to understand this mood would not be fixed with his strained attempt at comfort. 'You know when it comes to Doc, I'm in for whatever needs doing.'

She pushed back. 'That's just it. I don't know what to do.' She went quiet, her brows furrowing. She turned, studying him. Unexpectedly, her hands came up to cup his jaw. 'You're bitter cold. You need blood.'

'It can wait.' *Never.* But with her hands on his skin and her wrists so close to his mouth, he was helpless against her delicious perfume. His fangs dropped and his human face shifted away. *Blood blood blood.*

'It can't wait. You need to be strong for whatever happens next.' She took his hand and began leading him into the ship. 'And as much as we need to help Doc, his decisions led him to where he's at, so he can sit tight for a little while longer.'

'Doc can be stubborn.'

She laughed softly. 'Pot, meet kettle.' He was about to respond when she turned a corner and stopped, then glanced back the way they'd come, her eyes questioning.

'You don't know which way to go, do you?'

'Not a clue.'

He smiled gently. 'Where do you want to go?'

'The kitchen, I guess.'

He squeezed her hand. 'The galley it is.' As they walked, she explained in more detail what had happened with Doc and Fi and the mayor's curfew. He shook his head. 'Dominic's going to have something to say about this. She's basically shut down the bulk of his business. Fae and varcolai can come and go during daylight hours, but the fringe who come for his comarré, not so much. She's bitten off more than she can chew.'

'I agree, but Dominic can fight his own battles on this one. I have enough of my own problems to deal with.'

'Then why not let Doc face the punishment that's coming to him? A couple hours in the square isn't the end of the world.'

'Because Doc is our friend and—'

'I agree with that reason completely.' *You don't have friends.*

'It won't look good if the pride leader is put on display like, well, like an animal. Doc will be humiliated. He'll be forced to retaliate. Or the pride will on his behalf. It's just a bad situation all the way around.'

Mal nodded. 'All good points.'

'And' – she took a deep breath – 'if we can get Doc out of this, the pride will owe us. And we need them to owe us.' She came to a stop and faced Mal. 'Pride law says a life for a life. Brutus killed me and you killed Brutus, but word is beginning to spread that I'm alive.' She grabbed his hand and held on. 'They could demand your life. I'm not going to let that happen. Doc won't either. But it would really help if the pride felt indebted to us.'

Mal thought a moment. Solving this problem was easy enough, but Chrysabelle wasn't going to like his solution. Better keep it to himself until the time came. 'I said whatever you needed me to do, I would do. That hasn't changed.'

She smiled, leaned up on her tiptoes, and pressed her mouth to his for the briefest of seconds. 'Thank you.' She tugged him forward again. 'Let's get you some blood.'

Once Mal found a clean glass and they'd settled at the table, she flicked out the tiny blade on her ring and nicked a vein, filling the glass. He held it while the blood level rose, savoring the warmth seeping into his palm. He couldn't stop staring at her, even though he knew it would get him into trouble.

'Stop looking at me,' she whispered without making eye contact.

'I like to look at you. You're beautiful. And you know how I feel.' *Fool.*

'So you've told me.' Her mouth bent in a poorly repressed grin. 'It's just strange.'

He lifted one shoulder. 'I'm a strange guy.'

'That's for sure.' She smiled as she pulled her arm up and pressed two fingers to the tiny cut. She tipped her head toward the glass. 'Drink up.'

'I get to kiss you afterward.'

Her cheeks colored, causing her signum to flare brightly against the rising pink. 'I know.'

'And that embarrasses you?'

'No. But you talking about it so plainly is going to take some getting used to.'

'I'll do my best to contain myself.' He lifted the glass. 'Of course, my best isn't very good, so you should probably just get used to it.' She rolled her eyes, making him chuckle. Torturing her was its own reward. He put the glass to his lips and drank, relishing every swallow of the sweet, rich liquid, but not nearly as much as he was about to enjoy kissing her.

Glass emptied, he set it down, closed his eyes, and tipped his head back to await the rush of power only comarré blood provided. One ... two ... three ... It hit with the force of a full-body blow, first searingly painful as his muscles and tendons tightened with the burst of renewed strength, but then the pain vanished, leaving wakes of heat behind, heat that spread through him and erased his normal chill. He relaxed and blew out a breath as his lungs began to work again and his heart pulsed.

He lifted his head and opened his eyes to find Chrysabelle's gaze fixed on him. He smiled.

She smiled back. 'It's amazing to watch the life come back into you.'

'Is that so?' He shoved the table out of the way, toppling the glass, and pulled her onto his lap. Damnation, but the weight of her body against his brought a maddening pleasure twice as intoxicating as the taste of her blood and the rush of power. 'Feel for yourself.' He put her hand on his chest to feel its rise and fall as he breathed and the beating of his heart.

'I've felt it before,' she protested, but her hand stayed a few beats longer. Then her fingers traveled to his jaw. She narrowed her eyes. Something was on her mind.

That something, it seemed, was him.

'Open your mouth,' she commanded.

'Why?'

'I want to see your teeth.'

'I'm not a horse.'

She traced his bottom lip with her index finger, setting fire to a thousand other parts of his body. 'I want to see your fangs.'

Tremors of pleasure running through him, he parted his lips and tilted his head to give her better access while still being able to watch her.

Her finger moved from his lip to the edge of his front teeth. Slowly she mapped his right fang, stroking the length of it, testing the pad of her finger against the sharp tip. He held absolutely still for fear he'd cut her. Despite the blood in his system, despite the emotion he felt for her, the opportunity to drink directly from her might still overwhelm him. Deep inside, the beast reared its head in agreement.

'They're very sharp,' she whispered, pulling her hand away.

Was she delaying the kiss for a reason? 'You had a patron. You know how sharp fangs are.'

'Yes, but not yours.' She stared straight into his eyes, which he knew must be completely silver with everything boiling inside him. She shifted a little and for a moment, he thought she was getting off his lap, but she only twisted to face him better. Then her hands came to his face again, this time to cup his jaw. She dragged him closer as her lids shuttered. Almost too late, he realized *she* was kissing *him*. Quickly, he forced his fangs away.

His heartbeat revved and he pulled her nearer so that their heat mingled. Too much time had passed since this had last happened. Her mouth was a revelation, a reminder of everything that was right in his world. Of how much he loved her and, even though she hadn't said it, of how much she loved him back.

He was lost to her. Utterly and completely and he'd never been happier.

No matter what else happened in his miserable existence, he would remember the joy of this feeling and bask in the knowledge that it would remain his until the day he turned to ash.

Chapter Seventeen

Tatiana woke an hour before sunset, the urge to check on Lilith overwhelming. After watching her child face down the sun and live, she was ecstatic, but not without worry. She just needed to see Lilith again, to make sure the sun's wicked rays hadn't marred her petal-fine skin, to check her once more for burns or blisters.

The hunger of waking curled at the edge of her consciousness, but she ignored it. There would be time to feed later. She dressed in silence, not wanting to wake Octavian. With the imminent arrival of the Dominus and their Elders, he'd been working so hard getting things ready, always disappearing to handle one chore or another.

Bringing her mouth to his cheek, she kissed him, then slipped next door to the nursery. Oana sat in the rocker near the crib, Lilith on one shoulder, patting her back gently. 'Good evening, my lady.' She nodded her head in deference. 'Lilith woke about half an hour ago. I've just finished feeding her. Would you like to take her?'

'Just for a moment.' She lifted Lilith from Oana's grasp.

Lilith smiled and reached for Tatiana's face. 'Hello, my darling. How are you?'

Lilith's tiny fingers patted Tatiana's cheek. There wasn't a blemish on her. Not a centimeter of skin that showed she'd been touched by the sun. Remarkable. 'She slept well?'

'Yes, my lady.' Oana stood and straightened the crib linens. 'Slept as sound as could be. Not a cry, not a whimper.'

Nothing to indicate Lilith's sun exposure had even registered. Tatiana kissed Lilith's forehead. The scent of blood and milk lingered from her daughter's breakfast. Her own stomach growled. She held Lilith out to Oana. 'Make sure she has her bath.'

'Of course, my lady.' Oana planted Lilith back over her shoulder. 'Any particular outfit you'd like her in tonight?'

The entire household knew the nobility would be arriving throughout the evening. Tatiana shook her head. 'Anything is fine until dinner. Then she's to wear the dress that was made.'

'Very good, my lady.' Oana curtseyed, then turned her face toward Lilith. 'Time for a bath, little one.' Lilith clapped her hands against Oana's back. 'Anything else, my lady?'

'No, you're dismissed.' Tatiana left as Oana carried Lilith in to the tub. Her hunger was now almost a palpable thing.

And a reminder that unfinished business remained. She shut the nursery door and strode down the hall. Servants scurried about, deep in last-minute preparations for her guests. One walked by with a mass of black cherry roses in her arms, no doubt on her way to Lord Syler's suites. Lord Timotheius's suite would get a fragrant mix of lilies. Lord Grigor despised flowers, but Svetla favored white orchids.

Each suite would be supplied with enough personal touches to impress. It was a game the Dominus played with each other, to see who could know more about the others without appearing to care. She'd spent enough time watching Algernon aid Lord Ivan. She hadn't forgotten a thing, right down to Grigor's disgusting combination of blood and vodka.

Deeper into the bowels of the estate, away from the guest suites and common areas, she traversed the corridors of the west wing. She'd kept Daciana confined in a suite here while her late husband, Laurent, and Tatiana had gone to Paradise City.

Now Octavian had secured Damian in this same wing until he could be dealt with. She reached for the door handle, then stopped. Her anger at him would solve nothing. If Daci had gone to the comarré's under the pretense of asylum and ended up captive with Damian as a guard, that meant the comarré trusted Damian, that she'd taken him into her confidence, at least in some small way. What might he now be able to share with Tatiana? What new information could she glean?

This had to be played correctly, no matter how badly she wanted to punish his betrayal.

She schooled her face into a mask of pleasantness and opened the door. The waft of blood scent caused saliva to pool under her tongue. Her fangs punched through her gums. With effort, she retracted them.

He stood near the window but turned at the noise. His expression darkened into something more like anger than the fear she'd expected. 'I've been waiting for you.'

She jerked back in surprise. 'You've been waiting for me?'

He shrugged and turned away, his gaze directed into the growing twilight. 'I must be dealt with. After all, I ran from you.'

This was not how she'd imagined this going. 'Yes, of course, that is not something that can be swept under the rug.'

He said nothing, just continued to stare outside.

'It's well within my rights to have you punished.'

Still nothing. The anger she'd shoved down pressed against her spine along with the surging desire to feed.

'I could have you whipped.' She formed her metal hand into a tapered length of chain.

He shifted to lean against the window frame. Her flesh hand fisted at his insolence. She relaxed it and took a few steps closer, dragging the metal whip over the floor. The succulent perfume of his blood teased the edges of her good sense.

'Or beaten.'

At last he moved, turning his head just enough to make eye contact. He exhaled with what could only be exasperation. 'Or you could sell me or trade me for another or return me to the Primoris Domus and have the blood rights repaid. Which will it be? I don't need a litany of possibilities, just the decision.'

She stared, frozen by the hot rush of rage building inside her.

He shoved away from the window and came toward her, suddenly twice the size she remembered him being. 'Did you expect me to cower? To plead for your forgiveness? To beg to be returned to your good graces and the life I used to have with you?' He snorted. 'I'm not Saraphina.'

His insolence was too much. She snapped her hand forward, the chain hissing through the air. It caught him around the neck. She yanked hard, bringing him to his knees. He clawed at the chain around his throat as she stalked forward. 'How dare you—'

'How dare I,' he gurgled the words out. 'Because you are a contemptible patron. A comar would have to be insane to want to serve you.'

She raised her good hand to strike him just as the door opened.

Octavian stuck his head in. 'Forgive me for interrupting, but Lilith is crying. She wants you.'

Tatiana almost forgot the impudent comar at her feet. She morphed the whip back into a hand. Damian sagged to his knees. 'Be grateful my child needs me or—'

'Grateful for what? For being treated as your chew toy?'

She struck so fast, her hand was a flash of silver light. He fell onto his side, blood trickling from where she'd split his lip. Her stomach knotted in appetite. She grabbed him by his shirtfront and pulled him up until only a narrow slice of blood-scented air separated them. 'I paid your blood rights and that means I own you.'

Without turning away, she spoke to Octavian. 'Tell Oana to feed my child and I'll be along shortly.'

'Oana says she isn't hungry. I think you should—'

She snapped her head toward Octavian, her words little more than a growl. 'Leave us.'

A short nod and he was gone.

She peered into Damian's blue eyes, searching for a hint of regret or fear, but found nothing but contempt. Her anger spiraled higher. 'Owning you means I can do with you whatever I please. And what I please right now is to feed.'

She fell on him, taking him to the ground in one rough stroke. Her fangs descended and she sank them into his neck. The ritual and pleasantries of drinking from his wrist no longer mattered. Not when he'd disrespected her so thoroughly.

She drank deeply and without care, bringing him to the ash-flavored cusp of death before allowing him to fall from her grasp. She rocked back on her heels and wiped the corners of her mouth.

'If the idea of begging for a return to your previous life here appeals to you, let me save you the effort. There is no chance for that.' She stood and brushed herself off. 'You'll be lucky if I let you live, you foolish cow.'

She kicked him in the ribs and, satisfied with the sharp crack of bone and his grunt of pain, marched out.

Her head swirled with questions and disbelief. What had possessed him to act that way? She stopped a few steps toward her quarters, cold shards of realization digging into her brain as her body came alive. She sucked in a breath. Not only had she completely forgotten about trying to get information from him about the comarré, but getting anything out of him now would take vast amounts of torture.

He had played her and she'd fallen for each line of his song like a lovesick *gadje* standing in the crowd, pining after the Roma fiddler. *Fool*. No, not a fool if she didn't fall for it twice.

She tossed her head back. Perhaps the comar had won this round, but the next time they met, she would show him just how much pain his soft human body could endure. That would cure him of his games.

Smiling as the scene unfolded in her head, she went to care for her child. Someday, all this would belong to Lilith. Until that day, Tatiana would do whatever necessary to protect it for her.

When Lola heard who the first othernatural captured was, she knew Malkolm and Chrysabelle wouldn't be far behind, especially since the comarré had been with the shifter. Now the pair stood across from her desk.

Creek's plan had worked out brilliantly. Better than either of them had anticipated. Now she'd not only get to make an example of the varcolai, but she'd also get to punish the vampire for refusing her request. She just wouldn't let him know she'd remembered what he'd done. Not yet.

'I know why you're here.' She spoke without bothering to look up from the nonessential paperwork she was examining intently. Let them think it was about them. Let them think what they wanted.

Mal shifted. 'Good. Then we can dispense with the small talk. We want Doc—'

'So you think I'm an idiot, do you?'

Mal shook his head. 'I never said that.'

'I did,' Chrysabelle answered quietly. 'It was said in the heat of the moment and for that, I apologize. I still believe the curfew is a very bad idea.'

Creek snorted softly from his chair in the far corner.

Lola set the paperwork down. 'Unfortunately, city hall is unequipped with a suggestion box, but I'll make a note of your disapproval.' She stood. 'Unless, of course, you're a registered voter. Then you can express yourself next November.'

'I'm not a—'

'Citizen of this country. I know.' The information Creek had given her made this so much easier. 'Unlike your mother, you've yet to take care of that. Or even make yourself useful to this city in any way.'

'Look here.' Chrysabelle started forward. 'When you needed information on what was happening in this city and what had happened to your daughter, you had no problems talking to me and taking my advice then.' She glanced at Creek. 'You of all people should have explained to her what a mess this curfew is going to make of things.'

He jerked one shoulder. 'You've only been helpful when it suited you, comarré. Why should we help you now?'

'Creek, what is going on with you?' Her face fell. 'I thought we had an understanding.'

He unfolded himself from his chair. 'I *understand* that you have no interest in helping the mayor retrieve her grandchild.'

Angry shadows filled her eyes. She took a few steps forward. 'You told me that was the KM's mission. Not the mayor's.'

Lola looked askance at her. 'Did you think I'd leave my grandchild to rot with those creatures?'

'No, I just' – Chrysabelle glanced back at Malkolm – 'I have some things of my own to deal with before I can take on some-one else's troubles.'

'Just like when my daughter's killer was on the loose.' Lola came around to lean against the front of her desk. 'Sometimes the greater good must come before our own wants and desires, but then you'd know that if you'd spent any time in the real world.'

Chrysabelle's cheek twitched. 'Finding my brother is not a *want* or a *desire*. It's a need. He's my family. And figuring out what's happening to me physically? Also a need. Don't tell me about the greater good. My entire life has been about the greater good.'

Malkolm stepped up beside her and put his hand on the small of her back. She seemed to calm at his touch. A spark of jealousy lit within Lola's bosom. No wonder the vampire had turned down her offer. He didn't need a free-spirited mortal woman when he had his obedient little blood pet. How had Julia lowered herself to that? Deep down, Lola knew. Because the vampire's darkness called to the darkness in her, just as it must have for her daughter. 'As to the reason why you're here, there is no denying Maddoc is guilty of violating the curfew.'

Malkolm nodded. 'You're right. He's guilty. We're not

arguing that. We want to work something out. Doc isn't just any varcolai; he's the leader of the Paradise City pride. Humiliating him like this could buy you more trouble than it's worth.'

She laughed. 'I love that you're so concerned with how I come out in all this. Very touching.'

Creek sat back down in the chair, perching oddly on the edge. 'This conversation is pointless.'

But Malkolm went on. 'What happens in this city affects us all. Putting Doc on display will cause more unrest.'

Lola crossed one ankle over the other. 'And your solution to this? Because I assume if you've come this far, you have a better idea.'

'I do,' Malkolm said. The comarré looked at him as though this was the first she'd heard of his alternative. 'Let Doc go. Take me in his place.'

Chapter Eighteen

Fi sat waiting on the balcony of Chrysabelle's guesthouse, watching the circular drive for the lights of Doc's shiny new sports car. She sighed and kicked her feet onto the railing. By now, Doc and Chrysabelle should have been back. How long would they stay out looking for her?

She thought they would have searched the guesthouse, but not yet. She was tired of hiding. Bored of sneaking around the house, not daring to turn on the lights or holovision in case she got found out. But she was ready to be found now.

It wasn't that she was over being mad at him. She was still mad and probably would be for a good long time. Unless his explanation and apology were world-class, which they'd better be, but she couldn't judge that until she'd heard them.

Which is why she'd decided to show herself when they got back. Not that hiding out in Chrysabelle's guesthouse was such a hardship, other than not being able to turn on the lights or TV. The place was nice. Maybe not as fancy as Doc's new penthouse, but considering the guesthouse didn't have a snooty Brazilian varcolai in it who deserved to be thrown out on her fancy, designer-clad butt, Chrysabelle's digs were plenty nice.

Screw Heaven and her twelve-hundred-dollar shoes. Fi sniffed. Those should be her twelve-hundred-dollar shoes. That should be her in that penthouse with Doc. Not some dead man's wife. She huffed out a breath. Pride law was stupid.

Maybe she should go down and let Velimai know she was here. Velimai was a good listener, and she might have some ideas about what to do with the whole Heaven/Doc situation. Beyond letting Doc do some groveling, because hell yeah, she'd earned some groveling.

Fi stood and peered over the edge of the railing, but from here she couldn't see enough of the house to figure out what Velimai was up to. She inhaled, sniffing for the scent of something cooking, but apparently dinner was over. Too bad. Fi could eat. And unlike the freighter's kitchen, Chrysabelle's was always stocked and her fridge was always full. And not just with blood.

Fi shuddered at the thought as she made her way into the house and downstairs. If she lived to be a thousand, she'd never get how anyone, vampire or otherwise, could stand the taste of the stuff. She shuffled across the yard, wondering if she was setting off the pressure plate sensors installed beneath the sod. She'd arrived in her ghostly form and hadn't touched anything until she was well inside the house.

As if in answer, the security lights flipped on, almost blinding her. She shielded her eyes with her hand and hustled to the front door. She pounded on it a few times with her fist. 'Hey, Vel, it's me, Fi.'

A few seconds later, the wysper opened the door. She took a quick look at Fi; then her eyes roamed the property behind her. *You alone?* she signed.

'Yep, just me.' She shrugged. 'Did I trip the alarm?'

Yes. Velimai tipped her head. *Doc's looking for you.*

'I know. He just wasn't looking hard enough. I've been in your guesthouse.'

Velimai moved out of the way so Fi could come in. *Ready to make up?*

'Maybe. Mostly tired of hiding. And hungry.'

Velimai laughed, a soft wheezing sound. *You always could eat.*

Fi entered and headed toward the kitchen. 'Hey, I like food. Is that such a bad thing?'

Not when it's my cooking. I was just about to get some dinner. It'll be good to have company. Velimai shut the door and walked with her. *Besides that, I'm actually getting a little worried they haven't returned yet.*

'Why?'

About to reach for the fridge handle, Velimai paused to sign, *Because of the curfew.* She opened the door and began taking out leftovers.

Fi got plates down and began to set the table. 'What curfew?'

Velimai closed the fridge. *Haven't you heard? The mayor held a press conference. No othernaturals out from sundown to sunup.*

'What? That's crazy. Othernaturals have rights, too.'

Not as many as we used to. Wait, I'll put the TV on and you can see for yourself. Velimai walked into the living room and picked up the remote, tapping the touch screen. The holovision flared to life, projecting its image into the room, but no sound. Velimai tapped the screen a few more times, changing the channel until she hit the local news station.

A female reporter was standing in the town square. A crowd had gathered and other camera crews were milling about.

'What's going on?' Fi tried to see past the reporter, but the camera lights didn't extend enough into the darkness to show detail. 'Turn it up.'

Velimai tapped the screen again until they could hear the reporter's voice.

'. . . the crowd behind me is only going to get larger as the night wears on, I'm sure. Especially with this new development.' The reporter fiddled with an earpiece. 'Apparently, the varcolai who broke the curfew is being released due to a second othernatural taking his place. Can we zoom in on the action?'

'They caught someone already? Are they serious?' Fi shook her head. This was going to rile people up big-time.

The camera moved off the reporter to focus on the center of the square. Lights, electric lights, had been set up on tripods and aimed toward the area. The sudden brightness caused the camera image to flare; then the scene became clearer as the balance adjusted.

Between two posts set into the ground, a man was chained at his wrists and ankles. A very familiar man.

Fi fell to her knees, her hands at her mouth. 'Oh no. Please no.' A sob caught in her throat. She swallowed it down. 'That's Doc.' She stared blindly for a few seconds more, no longer hearing what the reporter was saying. 'I have to go to him.' She pushed to her feet, her stomach churning.

Wait, Velimai signed frantically. They're releasing him.

'What?' Fi turned. Sure enough, a group of cops, dressed in heavy-duty SWAT gear, were unlocking the manacles on his wrists. Doc kept his head down, but Fi would have known him anywhere. 'How did he let himself get caught? The pride is going to go crazy.'

Transfixed, Velimai just shook her head.

Fi went back to watching. They were leading Doc away now. Where to, she had no idea. 'They better be releasing him and not just putting him in a cell somewhere.' Velimai nodded. Fi wished she wasn't having the thoughts she was having, but the truth was, as much as she wanted Doc free, she didn't want him going back to Heaven.

She rubbed her eyes. They had to get this worked out. She sat on the couch and leaned her head onto her hands. There had to be a solution. She couldn't just walk away from him. Or could she? The ache in her heart and her soul at the very idea said there was no way. Not now, not after all they'd—

A slapping sound lifted her head. Fi looked up. Velimai was smacking the couch's arm. She stopped and pointed at the TV.

Fi glanced at the screen. Doc was gone. The SWAT team was shackling his substitute into place. A new panic filled her as the camera zoomed in on the man's face. 'Oh no. That can't be. Why would he do that?'

The man lifted his head as if he wanted to be seen.

The man was Mal.

Lord Syler and his Elder, Edwin, arrived first at Tatiana's. Lord Grigor and Svetla were the last. 'The last to arrive,' Tatiana spat out. 'Can you believe that? They did it deliberately to show their contempt for me.' She growled from her spot on the raised dressing platform as the servants under Kosmina's watch scurried around with the finishing touches.

Octavian gently nodded. 'They are petty fools, but don't let them upset you. At least they're all here now and in record time.

I'd say word of Lilith has spread. And wait until you tell them what we've discovered about our angel.'

Resplendent in the same unrelieved black they'd all chosen, Daci nodded. 'Octavian's right. There's so much more to concentrate on than their pettiness. Idiots. They have no idea how passé they are about to become.'

Only a few weeks ago, their words would have made Tatiana snap, but now she had to admit they were right. She lifted her chin. 'I suppose watching their faces when I tell them about Lilith's special ability will make it all worthwhile.' The nobility would be rocked to its core with jealousy. 'For that, I cannot wait.'

'Nor I.' Octavian gave her a wink and went back to his valet for his dinner jacket. 'But we must welcome them all, Svetla and Grigor included, with the same good grace. Or at least appear to.'

Stepping off the platform, she frowned as a servant brushed a bit of lint off the side of her gown. 'I know what needs to be done. We can't let them think anything else is afoot.' In the gold-backed cheval mirror, she glanced at him and Daci, catching his gaze upon her as it almost always was.

She turned her head to admire herself. 'What do you think? I don't normally wear my hair up.'

'Beautiful, Tatiana.' Daci nodded. 'You look every inch the Dominus.'

'She's right, you do. The most stunning Dominus.' Octavian took her hand, then extended his arm to Daci. 'Shall we? I think our guests have waited long enough.'

Tatiana held back a little. 'You've taken the potion against Grigor's and Svetla's probing?'

He squeezed her hand. 'Done.'

'Excellent.' Not that she was convinced it would work. She walked with him to Lilith's crib, where he let her hand slide from his. The baby had been dressed in a white lace gown with a matching cap on her head. Tatiana picked her up, cradling her against her own sleek black silk. She kissed Lilith's tiny nose, then nodded at Octavian. 'You and Daci go first. I'll follow with Lilith.'

'As you wish.' He snapped his fingers, Daci still on his arm. 'Kosmina, we're ready.'

Kosmina went ahead of them down the hall to the dining room. 'The staff has prepared a full tasting of twelve different bloods for this evening, animal and kine. I hope my lady finds it to her liking.'

Tatiana couldn't take her eyes off Lilith's sleepy face. 'I'm sure it will be fine.'

They slowed as they approached the dining room. Kosmina swung wide the doors into the space and announced them. 'Your hosts, Dominus Tatiana; her consort Lord Octavian; and Elder of the House of Tepes, Lady Daciana.' After a short bow, she quickly walked to the side of the grand buffet and stood at attention with the other servants in attendance.

Octavian and Daciana entered and stood behind their chairs, one on either side of the head of the table, where Tatiana would sit.

She strolled in and watched, delighted, as the gathered nobility craned to get a glimpse of the child in her arms. Only Syler and Edwin stood. Did the others think she wouldn't notice the slight? She bit back the words souring her tongue and tried to maintain the grace Octavian had stressed. 'Lords and ladies, may I present my daughter, the vampire princess, Lilith.'

'Get up, you fools,' Octavian snapped, warming her dead heart. Grace, it appeared, had its time and place.

Chairs scraped the floor as they were shoved back. All stood. All but Grigor. He lounged in his chair, eyes heavy lidded in certain boredom. 'This child is a vampire princess?' His nostrils flared. 'Who says?'

Svetla sank back into her chair and made a show of studying one of the crystal tasting goblets laid out before her.

Tatiana's body trembled with rage. 'I say it. And the ancient ones say it.' She held Lilith up, her hands firmly on the child's torso. As if sensing her mother's emotion, Lilith whimpered. 'Look at her. She is the first of her kind. *Born* vampire.'

Murmured words of disbelief and doubtful noises echoed off the wood-paneled walls. 'There's no such thing. Poppycock. Well, I never ... '

'You fools,' Daci shouted.

Lilith began to cry in earnest. Tatiana cradled her child in her arms. 'There, there, my darling.' With her first wail, her tiny fangs were visible.

Lord Zephrim fell back into his seat, his mouth gaping at the irrefutable proof. 'The child has fangs.'

'As do we all. I don't see how this proves anything,' Grigor said. 'Any of us could sire an infant. There's no proof this child was born vampire any more than one of us.'

Lord Syler shook his head. 'Would you challenge the ancient ones? Their word on this is enough for me and my house.'

Lord Zephrim nodded. 'I agree. Their word is enough.'

Lord Timotheius cleared his throat. 'So it's true, then. This is quite an amazing occurrence.'

Tatiana hugged Lilith to her, bouncing her gently to soothe her crying. 'I'd say it's more than just an amazing occurrence.

It's the start of a new era. With my daughter, a new race of vampires has begun.'

Kosmina hurried to Tatiana's side. 'Shall I take her, my lady? She sounds hungry.'

'Yes. See that she's fed.' She handed Lilith off. Octavian pulled a chair out for her and she took her place at the head of the table; then he helped Daci into her seat before taking his own. The rest of the Dominus and their Elders sat.

'This new race,' Zephrim began. 'How is it different from our own nobility, other than she was born vampire and we are sired? She is still just a vampire. No disrespect intended.'

'No disrespect? Really?' Tatiana turned to Octavian, savoring the last moment of their shared knowledge. 'Just a vampire,' she mocked.

Octavian sipped his wine. 'She is anything but.'

'Hear, hear,' Daci said, lifting a glass and drinking to her own toast.

'And why is that?' Grigor waved his hand as if trying to hurry her along. 'You must share whatever it is you think is so *special* about this child.'

Tatiana straightened to look down her nose at the Dominus seated at her dinner table, pride rippling through her. 'My child has powers no other noble vampire has.' She paused, savoring their eager anticipation. 'Lilith is a daywalker.'

'You did bravely today,' Yahla cooed against Creek's skin.

'Did I?' He couldn't remember much since last night. 'What exactly did I do?' He moved away from her, trying to clear his head.

'Just what I asked of you.'

She looped her arm through his, but he got off the bed,

walked over to the small flat screen, and turned off the news. That and the small flashes of memories fading in and out were the only way he'd figured out what had happened.

The mayor had put a curfew in place and he was somehow a part of it. He'd gone to her house, been in her office, but beyond that ... there wasn't much. A flash of Chrysabelle. The ever-present urging of Yahla. Mal taking Doc's place. Or had he gotten that part from the news? Not that he'd be watching any more of it. Being with Yahla made it tough to concentrate on anything but her. 'Why is it so hard for me to remember?'

'Perhaps when I am with you, I am all that fills your thoughts.' She slid off the bed and came to him, pressing herself into him and drawing patterns on his chest with her fingers. 'I do not enjoy this place you call home. It is not suitable for you any longer.'

His body was too focused on her touch to remember what he'd been talking about. 'It might be a dump, but that's kind of the point. No one would think anyone living here would have anything worth messing with. Besides, the KM aren't about to fund a new place unless this one is compromised.'

'The KM are not your—'

He shook his head, making a small place in his brain where he could think. 'I know you don't like them. I'm not crazy about them either, but I work for them. You killing Argent doesn't change that.'

She blinked rapidly. 'I said I will free you.'

He kissed her forehead. 'And I don't doubt you. But until then, I have to do the job they got me out of prison to do, or they'll put me back there. And that ain't happening.'

'I would not allow that.' She opened her mouth to say more, but a knocking on the downstairs door interrupted her. He slipped his jeans on, then headed downstairs, crossbow over his shoulder. 'Stay here. Don't make any noise.'

He padded across the space, the concrete floor cool under his bare feet. If he had to guess who his caller was, he'd say Argent's replacement. The KM wouldn't leave him untethered for too long. Bringing the crossbow down, he unlocked the heavy-duty door and slid it back a few inches.

Spiky black hair and wraparound sunglasses greeted him. The woman standing there, dressed in black leather from head to toe, didn't even glance at the crossbow aimed at her heart. Or at least not that he could tell from the dark sunglasses that were ... screwed into her temples. Screwed? Really? And why the shades at all? It had been dark for over two hours.

She nodded at him. 'Creek.'

He held the bow where it was. 'You have me at a disadvantage. You are?'

'Sector Chief Annika.' She spoke with a slight accent. European maybe. 'I'm filling in for Argent.'

Creek dropped the bow to his hip. So they didn't know Argent was dead. 'Filling in?'

'Yes.' She held her arm out, palm up, and pulled her jacket sleeve up. A small brand – the Greek letter W – he'd come to recognize as identifying KM higher-ups, marked the inside of her wrist. 'Are you going to let me in?'

'Sure.' No answer on why Argent needed filling in for, then. More need to know that he didn't need to know. He slid the door back.

Without waiting for it to be opened all the way, she pushed past and came inside. 'When's the last time you saw your sector chief?'

'Couple of days ago. Last time he was here.'

She nodded, studying the interior of the old machine shop.

She glanced briefly at the sleeping loft. 'He hasn't checked in since then. Any idea where he might have been headed when he left you?'

Creek kept a little distance between them. Better that way, at least until he figured out what she was exactly. The screwed on sunglasses didn't exactly inspire warm fuzzies. 'I only get told what I need to know, and with Argent, that isn't much.'

Annika almost matched him in height, and from the muscle filling out her leathers, she could probably hold her own against a man his size. She faced him again. 'I don't run my people that way. I'll tell you what I can, when I can.'

If that was true, she was already a better boss than Argent. 'So I belong to you now?'

'You report to me until you're told otherwise.'

'Yes, ma'am.'

She walked around his V-Rod, not as captivated as Argent had been, but plainly interested in the shiny bits. Another dragon-shifter maybe? Creek used the distraction to sneak a look at the sleeping loft. No sign of Yahla. Maybe she'd have less issue with him working for a woman. He would *not* let her kill another KM agent.

'Bring me up to speed.' Annika trailed her fingers over the bike's seat. The back of her leathers was oddly pleated, the same way Argent's suit had been to accommodate his wings. Another check on the dragon side of things. 'Where are you with getting the comarré to retrieve the vampire child?'

'Not as far along as I'm sure you'd like. She's not interested in going to Corvinestri right now. I can't blame her. Getting the kid means facing off with Tatiana. I don't know if the comarré is ready for that. She's been through a lot and—'

Annika's head came up. 'What she's been through is not as

important as removing that child from the clutches of the ancients.'

'I understand, but I think she feels like there are worse places a vampire baby could be than in the care of other vampires.' He moved toward the kitchen, hoping Annika would follow him to a spot out of sight of Yahla. 'She's more focused on finding her brother. Or at least the comar she thinks might be her brother.' And then there was the whole business of Mal taking Doc's place in the town square. That would keep Chrysabelle occupied for a few more hours. He'd warned her the KM would go after Mal if she didn't do as they asked. Maybe he could find a way to spin this. Damn. He did *not* want to lie to her, but if he didn't get the KM's work done, his family would suffer.

'Damian, right? Tatiana's escaped comar.'

'Yes. He's the one.' Creek leaned against the counter. 'Except he's not exactly escaped anymore. Seems a vampiress by the name of—'

'Daciana, yes, we know. She's gone back to Corvinestri.' Annika shook her head. 'I'm getting ahead of myself.' She unzipped a side pocket in her jacket and retrieved a small flash drive. 'Here.' She walked it over to him. 'Plug that into your phone and you can access everything I'm about to tell you.'

He took it and tucked it into his jeans pocket. Actual info he could hold on to? That was new.

Annika leaned in slightly, her nostrils widening. Creek backed away. Did she smell Yahla on him? Annika returned to the conversation.

'Daciana has returned to Corvinestri with Damian, who's being held prisoner right now. We're unsure what Tatiana's plans are for him, but you can be certain they won't be pleasant. I'm telling you this and giving you the file because we believe this new information will help you convince the comarré to go to Corvinestri on her brother's behalf.'

'So Damian *is* her brother?' That info would definitely get Chrysabelle on a plane.

'We don't know that. Comarré records are sealed beyond our reach. For the purpose of your conversation with her, the answer is yes. It's reflected that way in the file as well.' Annika flattened her palms on the kitchen's worktable. 'While she's there, she *will* retrieve the child. You're to make it clear to her that is the focus of her mission. Anything else is secondary to us.'

'Chrysabelle has no good reason to take a vampire baby from another bunch of vampires. All she's going to care about is getting Damian back.'

She waved her hands. 'It's your job to give her a reason. And that she does it. That is all the Kubai Mata is concerned with.'

'Got it.' So typical. All that mattered was the KM's desires. 'Anything else?' Like maybe what species she was. Knowing that would help him anticipate what kind of boss she might be. Hopefully nothing like Argent, but she was still KM.

'Yes. We obtained blood tests on the vampire child.'

Amazing what the KM could get its hands on. 'From your inside person?'

'From a reliable source.' Above her shades, her brows bent downward. 'You may let the comarré know the cover of night is not critical for this mission. It seems the child's blood contains a UV antibody.'

He canted his head to one side, peering at her more closely. 'Does that mean what I think it means?'

'Yes. The ancients possess a daywalker.'

'Damn, that changes things. But considering the kid's father, that doesn't—'

The bed creaked above them. Annika's head lifted toward the ceiling. Her nostrils flared again, but this time her tongue flicked out of her mouth. Her *forked* tongue. She tasted the air. 'You have a woman here. I smelled her when I came in but couldn't sense her. She is not human.'

They all seemed to figure that out pretty quickly. 'She's not a problem.'

Annika's mouth curved in a not entirely unpleasant smile. 'Good. I'm not unsympathetic to a man's needs. So long as she doesn't keep you from your work.'

'Understood.'

Annika nodded. 'I'll be going.' She walked toward the door. 'Talk to the comarré immediately. I'll expect an update soon.'

Which he took to mean she'd be returning in a day or so. He walked with her. 'Will do.' He hesitated to say more, but curiosity got the best of him. 'So you're a dragon like Argent?'

'No.'

His brow furrowed as they reached the door. 'What are you, then, if you don't mind me asking?'

She pushed the heavy metal back with one hand and turned. 'Basilisk.'

He shook his head. 'What is that again?'

'Like a dragon but with a stone gaze and a few other abilities.'

'A stone gaze?'

She stepped back into his home, her gaze aimed at the ground. 'There.' She pointed at a palmetto bug scurrying toward them along one wall. She stepped into its path and crouched down. 'Watch.' She tapped one of the screws on the side of her glasses, which he now realized was a button. The shades flipped up.

The palmetto bug turned gray and stopped moving. Before facing him, she touched the button again, lowering the shades. With a few steps, she retrieved the bug and tossed it his way.

He caught it, surprised at the weight and smoothness. She'd turned it to stone. He took a step back. 'Stone gaze. Got it.'

With a nod, she exited, unfurled a pair of wings, and took off. Creek watched her disappear into the night sky, hoping like hell that questions about Argent's disappearance never caused her to look at him any closer.

Chapter Nineteen

'Get your hands off me,' Chrysabelle snarled to the SWAT member holding her. The humans around her stared, stepping back as they realized she wasn't one of them.

The man's hands stayed on her biceps, keeping her back while Mal was chained to the posts a few yards away. 'Ma'am, you can't approach the prisoner.'

'He's not a prisoner, you idiot. He volunteered for the job.' She could easily toss the guy aside, but that would just draw more attention to her. Already the confused and troubled citizens surrounding her thrummed with an unwelcome vibe.

Police restrained the murmuring crowds at the square's edges while a few more officers directed a black sedan. The mayor. Wasn't watching this chaos on the holovision enough for her? Rage bloomed in Chrysabelle, causing her muscles to tremble. And this woman wanted help getting her grandchild back? She shook her head at the thought. Not the best way to go about it.

The sedan parked and the mayor got out, escorted by Luke Havoc. How could a shifter work for the mayor after this? He stayed at her side as she walked toward the cluster of cameramen and reporters who'd headed for the sedan the moment it had come into sight.

They held their microphones up as she began to speak. 'As you can see, we've had a change in plans. The varcolai who violated the curfew has been released and his place taken by another othernatural.' She raised a hand toward Mal. 'Before you, citizens of Paradise City, you see a real, live vampire.'

A gasp went through the crowd.

'Fools,' Chrysabelle muttered. Were mortals still so blind? Or had it just been the mayor's confirmation of what they already knew? Either way, it did nothing to endear the masses to her.

The mayor waited for the crowd to hush, then continued. 'The cameras will be granted access all night, until the vampire's release before dawn. If you're not law enforcement or carrying a press card, we ask that you go home and watch from your holovisions.' More noise from the crowd, this time less complimentary. She nodded. 'I understand, but my first concern must be for the safety of my citizens.'

Chrysabelle snorted. 'What does she think, that he's going to break free and start killing people?'

The officer holding her glanced back at Mal. 'Have you seen him? I'm surprised he hasn't snapped someone's head off yet.'

She stared into the officer's eyes, unable to control the anger building up inside her. 'Maybe he'll start with you.'

The officer grimaced. 'You threatening me?'

'I'm done with this.' She yanked her arms free and disappeared into the crowd as much as someone dressed in white could. People stared as she pushed toward the mayor, fear shining in their eyes at the sight of her.

'Othernatural,' one whispered.

'No,' she answered. 'I'm human.' She moved quickly away, pulling her hair down around her face to hide her signum.

Her anger at her own stubbornness boiled up. Why did she hold so tightly to her comarré ways? She'd been disavowed. There was no reason to cling to them. Had she given them up and adopted more ordinary clothing, she could have blended in much better.

Her mother had understood. She'd kept her signum hidden with makeup and had made a normal life for herself.

This life was not normal.

A few more yards and she came as close to the sedan as the police would allow. She pushed to the front of the crowd and stared at Luke, desperate to get his attention.

At last he looked her way. She motioned for him to come over. He nodded slightly, then spoke into his collar. A few seconds later, another security officer took his place while the mayor continued to answer questions.

In a few strides, he was in front of her. 'Chrysabelle, what can I do for you?'

'Can we talk?' She slanted her eyes to the left and right, indicating somewhere out of earshot of the crowd.

'Sure.' He put his hand on her shoulder and guided her through the line of cops. 'She's with me.'

Once they reached the back of the sedan, he stopped. 'What's up?'

'Those idiot cops won't let me get to Mal. The mayor never said anything about me being kept from him.' She glanced at where he was chained. He seemed unfazed by everything going on around him. 'Please, I need to talk to him. I don't even know why he decided to do this. I mean, I have an idea but—'

Luke held his hands up. 'I know you're upset. Let me see what I can do.' He left her standing beside the taillights and went to the mayor's side. After a few moments, Lola leaned toward him and they spoke. She stole a look at Chrysabelle, quickly averting her eyes when Chrysabelle didn't back down. Guilt, maybe? Because the mayor had to know what a screwup this was. How none of this was going to help sway Chrysabelle into helping Lola get her grandchild back.

Chrysabelle crossed her arms and stared the woman down, but Lola never looked her way again. She and Luke exchanged a few more words; then Luke nodded and ambled back to the car.

'Okay, she says you can have all the access you want once the crowd is dispersed.'

She let go of the breath she'd been holding. 'Thank you.'

'You know they're keeping the cameras on him, right? You're going to be broadcast into every household in the city.'

She slumped. She hadn't thought of that. 'Can you get a message to Mal?'

'Sure.'

'Tell him I'll be back when the crowds are gone.'

'Consider it done.'

'Thanks.' She turned and headed down the block to where Jerem was waiting with the car, her entire body buzzing with resolve. She hadn't been a real comarré in almost a month. Any reason she'd had to hang on to those old beliefs was gone. The time had come to make some changes.

As the tasting wound down, Tatiana stood and clicked the nails of her metal hand against her crystal goblet. 'Friends,' *enemies, fools, blighty old ratbags,* 'I'd like to thank you again for coming to celebrate this new joy with me.' She raised her glass and the others did the same, drinking with her.

She put the glass down. 'Now that our tasting is concluded, there is brandy in the library and the baccarat table is set up. I've brought a dealer in from Monaco to further enhance your playing.'

The males looked rather delighted. The pleasure most of them took in gambling was no secret. 'I myself prefer a stroll in the garden. Of course, any of you who wish to join me there are absolutely welcome. The gardens here are quite a sight to behold.'

'That sounds like a marvelous idea, my lady.' Daci smiled broadly, playing her part perfectly. 'Svetla, why don't you join us? We'll make a ladies' escape of it.'

Svetla curled her lip. 'I don't—'

Grigor set his hand upon her arm, stopping her. 'Go. Spend some time with Tatiana and Daciana. It will be a perfect opportunity to get to know them better.'

In other words, try to read their minds. Svetla could try all she wanted, but Tatiana knew she and Daci would give nothing away.

Octavian led the men to the library, where hopefully he'd be able to keep some distance from Grigor. If Kosmina's potion didn't work, Tatiana would kill her.

'Shall we?' Tatiana made for the gardens with Daci at her side and Svetla trailing slightly behind them. She forced herself to slow so that Svetla fell into step.

The pale blonde looked everywhere but at Tatiana. 'Ivan's estate is beautiful.'

Dumb git. She knew well enough that the property belonged to Tatiana now. 'Ivan's estate? You must have forgotten the

noble line of succession. It goes from Dominus to Dominus.'
Tatiana smiled sweetly. 'You do recall that Ivan's dead?'

Frost clouded Svetla's blue gaze. 'Yes, of course. How could
I have forgotten that?'

Kosmina, who'd gone ahead to prepare a few things, met
them at the French doors leading out to the gardens. She bowed.
'My lady, I've brought a bottle of champagne from your private
reserves. Also, Lilith is sleeping peacefully.'

The bottle sat chilling in a stand, three elaborately gilded
flutes nearby. 'Very good,' Tatiana said.

'I'll pass,' Svetla said.

Kosmina lifted the bottle high for Tatiana to examine it.
'Perhaps I should have brought something less expensive ... '

'No, we're celebrating,' Tatiana assured her.

'What a wonderful splurge!' Daci exclaimed. 'I've always
wanted to try a bottle of that.'

As if on cue, Svetla leaned in to get a better look. Her jaw
unhinged slightly. 'Is that Heidsieck?'

'Yes, do you know it?' Tatiana asked. The champagne had
been in Ivan's cellars and, according to the sommelier's logbook,
was the most expensive he'd ever purchased. A little research on
Kosmina's part had discovered why and made it easy for Tatiana
to determine it might be the one glass Svetla couldn't refuse.

Svetla closed her mouth, but only for a moment. 'Yes, I know
it. That's the Heidsieck cuvée Diamant blue vintage 1907.
Those bottles were commissioned by Tsar Nicholas II.'

'But they never made it to his table, did they?' Tatiana
clucked her tongue as if she actually cared about some ridiculous bottle of bubbles. 'Shipwreck and all. Such a shame.'

'Where did you get them?' Svetla looked on the verge of
bursting.

'The wreck was salvaged and about two thousand of the bottles were discovered. Ivan managed to obtain a few when they went to auction.' Actually, he bought all of them for an astonishing two hundred seventy-five thousand apiece, but she wasn't about to tell Svetla that. The woman was jealous enough already.

Svetla just stared, somehow magically unable to speak.

Tatiana took the bottle from Kosmina and began easing the cork out. 'Are you sure you won't change your mind, Svetla? I would love for you to enjoy it with us.'

'You would?'

'I am hoping we can move beyond the difficulties we've had.'

Svetla nodded thoughtfully. 'I am willing to try if you are.' She smiled. It looked almost genuine. 'I would be glad to join you in a glass.'

'Wonderful.' With a loud pop, the cork released. Tatiana handed the bottle back to Kosmina to pour since only she knew which glass had been coated with a tincture of laudanum. Not too much, but just enough to help lower Svetla's resistance to Tatiana's powers of persuasion. If it added any strange taste, hopefully Svetla would just assume it was a side effect of the bottle's time under water. The gilded filigree on the flutes also helped to hide any discoloration. All in all, a perfect plan. So far.

Kosmina handed them each a glass. Tatiana met the servant's eyes for reassurance. She smiled slightly. 'I hope you find it to your liking, my lady.'

'I'm sure I will.' She raised her glass. 'To the future.' She looked directly at Svetla. 'And new beginnings.'

'To new beginnings,' the vampiress repeated.

'To new beginnings,' Daci agreed.

Hades help her, this might actually work. She lifted the glass and sipped, tasting nothing but the champagne's soft, creamy bubbles.

Kosmina opened the door to the gardens. 'Enjoy your evening, my lady.'

Tatiana strolled through with Daci and Svetla on her heels.

Half of Svetla's champagne was already gone. Greedy pig. 'Daci, bring the bottle, will you? Shouldn't let something so delicious go to waste.'

Daci nodded and ducked back inside. Tatiana continued on. 'Do you have gardens like this in St. Petersburg? I saw very little of Grigor's estate when I was there last.' Mostly because they'd kept her waiting outside the council chambers for so bloody long.

'Not quite this grand.' Svetla held out her glass for Daci to top it off. 'Although we do have a skating pond in ours.' She drank a little more.

Tatiana swallowed another small mouthful. 'Skating? How lovely.' If you were too stupid to find other ways to amuse yourself. She glanced back. A little farther from the house and she'd begin.

Daciana chimed in, the bottle swinging in one hand, her glass in the other. 'I loved to skate when I was a girl. Did you learn as a child, Svetla?'

She finished a sip before answering. 'In Russia, all children learn to skate early.' She blinked hard, then lifted her glass. 'This is the best champagne I've ever had. I feel wonderful.'

'I'm so glad,' Tatiana lied. 'I'd be happy to send a bottle home with you.'

Svetla stopped. 'You would?'

'We're starting on new ground, aren't we? I think a gift between friends would be ... a nice way to cement that.' Especially since Svetla wouldn't be going home.

Svetla's mouth curved oddly. A second later, she threw her arms around Tatiana. 'I've been so cruel to you. I am sorry.'

Tatiana stopped herself just in time from thrusting Svetla away. She held still while the intoxicated Russian hugged her. 'There, there. It's all behind us now.'

Daci took both their glasses between her fingers, rolling her eyes and almost causing Tatiana to laugh. 'Let's sit on this bench and enjoy the night, shall we?'

Tatiana pried Svetla off her. 'Brilliant idea.' They were far enough from the house now to be well away from any eaves-dropping guests.

The three of them settled onto the bench, Svetla in the middle. She was on the verge of becoming maudlin, mumbling something about how hard it was to please Grigor and how she longed for other female friends. How much laudanum had Kosmina coated her glass with?

Tatiana patted her on the back. 'You know what you should do?'

Svetla looked at her. 'What?'

Tatiana peered deeply into the other woman's eyes and laced power into her voice. 'You should steal Lilith. Take her for your own.'

Svetla nodded.

So Tatiana continued. 'As everyone is preparing for daysleep, you will remain awake. You will sneak into the nursery and take her.'

'I will sneak into the nursery and take her,' Svetla repeated, her eyes round and glassy.

'If you are caught, you will claim Grigor charged you with committing the act. It was all his idea.'

'All his idea.'

Tatiana laid her hand over Svetla's and smiled. 'We are good friends, you and I. I would never do anything to hurt you. Which is why you won't remember we've had this conversation.'

'I won't remember.' Svetla had barely moved since Tatiana had begun.

Daci glanced over Svetla's shoulder, brows lifted in question. Tatiana nodded.

'Well,' Daci started. 'You look a little tired, Svetla. Shall I help you back to your quarters so you can lie down?'

'What?' Svetla blinked a few times. 'I . . . I am feeling a little odd. Perhaps I drank too much champagne.'

Daci scooped her arm under Svetla's and helped her to her feet. 'I believe I read that the alcohol gets stronger when it sits for so long like that. I feel a bit dizzy myself.' She laughed and made a show of leaning against Svetla, who almost fell over.

'Here, let me help you both,' Tatiana offered. She might as well. It was the last nice thing she'd ever have to pretend to do with Svetla again.

Chapter Twenty

D oc never thought he'd be so happy to see the penthouse. Isaiah met him at the door, his face shifting from fearful to relieved a second after he opened it. 'Good to have you home, sir. We were so worried.'

We were worried? He knew Isaiah couldn't be including Heaven in that. 'I told you not to call me that.'

'Yes, you did. My apologies.' He bowed a little. 'Is there anything I can get you?'

'Dinner.' Not that he had much of an appetite with Fi missing and Mal taking his place in that damned square, but it would occupy Isaiah.

As soon as the man left, Doc popped another K to stifle the heat that had been growing in him since the cops had laid hands on him. Then he settled onto the couch and exhaled a long breath. Damn, it was nice to be somewhere that didn't involve chains. 'TV on.'

The holovision flared to life and there was Mal, hung out for all to see. Doc cursed. He was thankful to Mal, but if given the option, he wouldn't have let Mal take the punishment. Still, he understood. Mal had whispered his reasons as they'd passed in the square. Doc had to give him props for strategy.

'That should be you.'

'Keep it to yourself, Heaven. Now is *not* the time.' He didn't give her the satisfaction of eye contact, although he could see her well enough with his peripheral vision. Hard to miss a woman in a red dress so tight it looked on the verge of exploding.

With a pout, she tottered to the bar in her spike heels and poured a drink, then leaned against the bar and took a sip. 'If you hadn't gone out after that *vac*—'

He whipped his head toward her. 'You want to spend the night somewhere else? Because I *will* put you out.'

'You cannot put me out. I am your wife.'

He pinned her with his gaze. 'I'm the pride leader. I can do whatever the hell I want.' He lifted his finger to point at her. 'Say one more word. One. More. Go ahead, I just need a reason.'

She snorted a breath through her nostrils, flipped her hair over her shoulder, and, drink in hand, sashayed out.

Shaking his head, he settled back against the leather. A soft buzzing interrupted his thoughts. He sat up and looked around but saw nothing that seemed like it might make that sound. A few seconds after he'd gone back to staring at the TV screen, Isaiah came in.

'Pardon the interruption, but the council members would like an audience.'

He rubbed a hand over his scalp. 'Now? Here?'

'As soon as you can meet them in your office, si— Maddoc.'

He needed to talk to them anyway; he'd just figured he'd do it in the morning, once he knew the outcome of tonight's events.

He glanced at the holovision. From what he could see, the crowds were still being turned away. The cameras focused on Mal, and the reporter was now only visible in a small box in the lower corner of the screen. Mal was doing that still-as-a-statue thing old vampires had a real knack for. Must be driving the TV stations nuts that he wasn't thrashing around, trying to break free.

'Tell them ten minutes. I'll head down now.'

Isaiah nodded. 'Very good.'

Doc got up as Isaiah left. What he really wanted was a hot shower, but that would have to wait. He jumped into the elevator and went down to his office. He nodded in greeting to the night-shift guards. One opened the door for him and the lights came on slowly to their preset brightness.

He stopped before going in. 'Council's coming in a few minutes.'

'You want them sent in as they arrive?' the guard asked.

'That's fine.'

'Will do.'

Doc went in and shut the door. Like everything else in his life lately, the place reeked of Sinjin. If this pride leader business turned out to be a permanent thing, something he still had his doubts about, he was definitely going to make some changes.

The light on the e-reader on his desk blinked at him. He turned it on and a message greeted him, telling him the last fourteen editions of the *Paradise City Press* were unread. Headlines from the latest one scrolled across the bottom of the message box. No surprise that the mayor's curfew was mentioned.

He turned the e-reader off and the holovision on, keeping the volume low. He just needed to monitor the situation, in case Mal needed him. No telling what the mayor might try to pull at the last second.

The door opened and two of his three advisers entered.

'Where's Fritz?'

Barasa cleared his throat. 'I'm very sorry, but he's quit.'

Doc furrowed his brow. 'He quit? Why?'

Omur glanced at Barasa. 'He was Sinjin's man, Maddoc. Be glad he's gone.'

Doc nodded. 'In that case, I am.' He gestured to the sofa and chairs in front of his desk. 'Sit, please.'

Omur, a cheetah-shifter, sat last. From what little Doc knew of him, Omur didn't seem like he'd ever been in Sinjin's pocket. His words about Fritz confirmed that. 'First, we want you to know how pleased we are that you were released. We were prepared to break you out.'

'I'm not sure how helpful that would have been to the situation, but thanks.'

Omur nodded. 'We also feel like the time has come to make a statement about the mayor's curfew.'

'Club numbers were almost half tonight.' Barasa was the pride's chief physician. The tiger-shifter sighed, clearly frustrated. 'Folks are afraid to come out.'

Doc leaned his forearms on his desk. 'I hear you. It's not good for business and it's not good for the morale of the pride. Have you put any kind of statement together?'

Omur shrugged. 'We didn't want to overstep our—'

Doc held a hand up. 'It's for the good of the pride, isn't it?'

They nodded.

'Then it's not overstepping any bounds to get something together. I don't know how Sinjin would have looked at it, but

I'm guessing a lot differently. Forget Sinjin. He's gone. And I don't do things like he did. You've got to get that.' He took a breath and made brief eye contact with both of them. 'Things have been tense since I've taken over. Just the circumstances under which I got here have caused cracks in the pride's loyalties. Fritz and Brutus are proof of that.'

Omur steepled his fingers. 'Until *that* situation is resolved, it won't get better.'

Doc leaned back in his chair. 'The vampire Malkolm took my place tonight.' He pointed at the TV. 'If not for him, I'd still be chained in the middle of the square. My final word on the Brutus situation is that Malkolm's act tonight pays his debt. Understood?'

'Understood,' they spoke the word almost in unison.

A new sense of confidence spread through Doc. 'Before we work on this statement, there's another thing I need to talk about.'

Their gazes stayed on him, filled with expectation.

He swallowed and prepared himself for the fight that was sure to come. 'I want to divorce Heaven.'

By the time Lola got home, most of her staff was in bed, the same place she planned to be as soon as she scrubbed off the day's grime. Whatever sleep she could get would have to suffice. In a few hours, she'd have to be up again to deal with the new challenges as they arose. Fallout from the curfew would be a big part of that. She sighed. The job never got easier, but the curfew was a step in the right direction. Both the othernatural and human communities would learn to either get along or pay the price if they wanted to live in her city. They'd also learn she was not afraid of either of them.

As quietly as she could, she made her way to the master suite. She flipped the light on with one hand as she struggled to get out of her suit jacket with the other. Shedding it, she turned around and almost screamed. Her hand went to the gun in her waistband. She brandished it at the intruder. 'Who the hell are you? How did you get in here?'

'Mayor.' The well-dressed vampire sitting in her reading chair nodded in greeting. Behind him, the sheers waved gently where the sliding door was still open a few inches. 'I am Dominic Scarnato.' Even without the name, his accent gave away his nationality. He stood with more than the usual vampire grace. 'I apologize for my intrusion, but we have business to discuss and your *curfew* makes it otherwise impossible for me to meet with you.' He pointed at the gun she currently aimed at him. 'That endangers you far more than it does me.'

She held the gun steady anyway, a triumph considering the adrenaline coursing through her veins. 'What business could we possibly have to discuss?'

'My business. I own the nightclub Seven. You may have heard of it. The tax revenues alone probably pay city hall's electric bill.'

Her hand started to shake. 'You ... you're the one who turned my daughter into a blood whore.' She thrust the gun forward. 'She worked for you. She died because of you.'

He held his hands up. 'Those who choose to become comarré do so of their own free will. I am not responsible for their decisions. And those who work for me are very well cared for, I assure you.' His eyes flashed silver. 'And the comarré are not whores.'

'You don't even know her name, do you?'

He frowned. 'Julia. You have my sincere regrets at her loss.

I know that pain.' He touched his chest. 'It stays with you for the rest of your life.'

'Really,' she snapped. 'Who've you lost? All the victims you've made a meal of?'

'Madam Mayor, I do not kill for my sustenance. That is the whole purpose of the comarré. They provide a valuable service to my kind.' He paused, his face going stony. 'For your information, the pain I feel is for one I loved very deeply. One for whom I gave up everything. One who was once comarré herself. Maris Lapointe.'

Lola held tightly to the gun but let her hand fall to her side. 'Chrysabelle's mother?'

'Sì.'

Her mind immediately went to Preacher's professions of love for Julia. 'Does that happen often? A vampire falling in love with a comarré?'

'Love is its own master. Who can say what is often and what is rare? All that matters is that it happens.' Dominic shrugged. 'You see? We are not so different from humans.'

'Except that you have the power to wipe us out if you so desire.' She couldn't let him distract her from the truth or let herself forget that under his expensive suit and manicured good looks, he was still dangerous.

His jaw tightened and he rolled his eyes. '*Mamma mia*, why would we want to wipe out the human race? What purpose would that serve us? We want to live as you do, to have friends, family, a peaceable existence.' He held his hands out. 'We are not . . . monsters. We are only different.'

'Different.' She exhaled a short, loud breath. 'That's an understatement.'

'You have varcolai on your staff who protect you. There are

fringe vampires who work night shifts on the city's police force. Remnants who care for the sick as doctors and nurses in the hospital. Do you see them as a problem? If you say yes, you are a fool for allowing them to keep their jobs. If you say no, you are a hypocrite for leveling this curfew against them.'

She stared at him, choosing her words carefully. 'Whether human or othernatural, there will always be those who think they are above the law. That sect of the othernatural population is who the human population fears. The curfew is the best defense the city has until both sides find a way to live in peace.' Creek had stressed that. 'So you see, I can't lift the curfew for you and ignore my human constituents. Why should they live in fear so your othernatural patrons can party? The tax revenues can be made up elsewhere.'

'It would be a gesture of good faith. There has been no real reason for the curfew anyway.'

'My daughter's death and the death of the two other women is reason enough.' She blinked, trying to remember what Creek had said that had made the curfew seem like the right decision.

'The killer was caught and dealt with. Would you put a curfew on the human citizens if one of them went on a killing spree?'

'If I thought it would help, yes.' She shook her head. 'I'm not lifting the curfew. Please go.'

But he didn't move. 'There must be something you want. Elections are less than a year away. Perhaps a generous donation to your campaign fund?'

She was about to snap that she couldn't be bought, when she realized there *was* something she wanted very, very much. So much that she rocked back on her heels slightly with the weight of it. This was her chance. Maybe her only chance. She set the useless gun on her dressing table and walked a few steps closer. 'There are two things I want.'

He smiled. 'At last, we see eye to eye.'

She stood as close as she dared, which was still a few feet away. 'First, understand that at the next incident involving any othernatural, the curfew will be back in place and you'll support it.'

His smile faltered. 'I can only control those in my club—'

'Do you agree or not?'

Not a trace of the smile remained. 'I agree. What is the second thing?'

She took a breath. 'I want you to turn me.'

'Turn you?'

'Into a vampire. Like you.'

For a few moments, he just stared blankly at her, as though he couldn't fathom what she'd just asked. 'After setting this curfew in place and everything you've said to me, you would become the very creature you fear? The same creatures who cause your precious city so much trouble?'

'I would not become a monster ruled by my appetites. I would be no different than I am now, just more powerful, more capable of running this city with an understanding for both sides, and better equipped to mediate the wishes of all my citizens.' He didn't need to know about Mariela or her fears that Paradise City would become a ghost town when her citizens fled.

His face shifted the same way the vampire Malkolm's had, leaving all traces of humanity behind for hard angles and jutting bones. His eyes shone silver. 'Foolish, foolish mortal.' He pounded one fist against his chest. 'You think my life is so easy? That I have power and wealth and not a care in the world? Pah.'

He spat. 'You are *stupido*.' He threw his hands up. 'I won't do it.'

She held her ground. 'You will if you want the curfew dropped. Think about how much better things would be if you had me as an ally and not an enemy. Think about how much more compassionate I would be to othernatural issues.'

He leaned in, his fangs gleaming in the room's soft light. 'And if you didn't survive the turning? What then? I would have your death on my hands? I think not.'

His words chilled her. 'What do you mean if I didn't survive?'

He backed away, nodding. '*Sì*, that's right. Death is a possibility. Not this kind of death.' He touched his chest again. 'But real death. Permanent death. Are you willing to risk that?'

She stared at him, trying to wrap her head around what he'd just told her. That wasn't a consequence she'd known about. 'I don't know.'

'That's what I thought.' He made a noise deep in his throat.

His apparent disgust at her weakness galvanized her. 'What if I am willing to risk it?' She stepped toward him. 'Turn me. Right now. And let the consequences fall where they may. If things go poorly, no one will ever know it was you. You'll be perfectly safe. And if things go well, you'll never have to worry about anything interfering with your way of life again.'

'Is that how it will be? I sire you and life becomes wonderful for all of us again?' He stalked toward her, mouth open and fangs fully on display. The urge to retreat scratched at her resolve, but she steeled herself and stayed planted. This was what was best for the city after all, and her only hope of going after Mariela.

'Yes,' she whispered as he grew closer.

His shoulder brushed hers as he circled around behind her. 'And the pain? That won't bother you?'

'No.' Her pulse battered her eardrums as every nerve in her body stretched taut with anxious anticipation. She'd have been calmer lost at sea and surrounded by sharks.

He came around her other side, so close she could count his long, black eyelashes. 'You won't fight me when death takes hold and draws you into the abyss?'

'No, I swear.'

'I think you lie.'

In the next second, he went from standing beside her to pinning her in his arms. His teeth pierced her neck and she cried out, both from the suddenness and the pain. She forced herself not to struggle, to stay calm. She focused on the feel of his mouth on her throat, the coolness of his skin, the strength of his embrace.

Her thoughts blurred into a numb acceptance and a new sensation arose within her, one she'd not felt in many years.

Desire.

His touch sent shivers of pleasure through her. The slight pain that remained sharpened her need for more with every pull of his mouth. She moaned something. Begged for him not to stop. She sank into each throb of her pulse, lost in the decadent haze of being devoured. 'Yes,' she whispered against his cheek. 'Yes.'

He clamped down harder.

Darkness crept under the edges of her pleasure, shattering it into small, jagged pieces. Her fingers and toes went numb. Coldness seeped into her bones, snapping a warning along her nerves. She twitched with the urge to pull away.

A high-pitched whine filled her ears as the darkness drew

closer. She dug her fingers into his arms and pushed, but he held fast. She beat at him as flashes of red pierced her vision. *Run!* her brain screamed. But she couldn't. Her body had gone limp, her bones leaden, her muscles rubber. Panic engulfed her, wrenching her in painful, desperate swells.

Her brain stopped screaming, smothered by the darkness. It was all she saw, eyes open or closed. Suddenly, she fell to the ground.

Her vision returned enough for her to make out Dominic standing over her. He peered down at her with obvious disdain. 'Did you enjoy that? Your taste of death?'

She tried to shake her head but couldn't tell if she managed it or not. Anger at her humiliation overrode all other feeling. Hot tears slid past her temples and into her hair.

'No, of course not, because death scares humans.' He huffed. 'You're not ready. You're too weak. Too frail. Too human.' He leaned down, his lips red with her blood and redolent with the coppery scent of it. 'Don't ask me again, because if you weren't ready this time, you never will be.'

Then he was gone. She clung to the anger growing inside her, held on to it like a buoy and let it lift her up. He was wrong. *Wrong.* She needed the power he had if she was ever going to save her grandchild and her city. She *was* ready. The vampire had just moved too fast. He hadn't let her prepare. But he had made one thing perfectly clear to her.

Becoming a vampire was the only way she was going to survive this new world, but until that happened, she was going to have to act with the same brutal swiftness Dominic just had.

She would show him just how ready she was. She wiped the tears from her face. 'Death doesn't scare me, vampire,' she whispered into the empty room. 'Does it scare you?'

Chapter Twenty-One

Chrysabelle had Jerem park a few blocks from the town square.

He glanced at her through the rearview mirror after he'd turned the engine off, his eyes kind but shaded with worry. 'You sure look different.'

She met his gaze in the mirror, catching a glimpse of herself. The last time she'd covered her signum with makeup, she'd been running from something. This time, she was running to someone. How much things had changed. 'That's the point.' She zipped the big hooded sweatshirt he'd lent her. 'Thanks for this again.' The voluminous black jacket hung past her hips. She'd added a pair of her mother's black yoga pants and simple black flats. The entire disguise made her feel slightly invulnerable. Like an uncatchable thief. She pulled the hood up and slipped on Fi's borrowed sunglasses.

'Be safe,' Jerem said. 'I've got the window cracked. You need me, just yell.'

'I will.' She exited and shut the door behind her. The city was deserted because of the curfew, but also because everyone was now at home in front of their holovisions burning electricity to watch the mayor's show. Fueled by anger, Chrysabelle picked up the pace. Her part in that show would be as minimal as she could make it. Tonight was all about Mal and bearing this punishment with him, as much as she could.

The bright lights set up by the local stations illuminated the square and divided it into patches of brilliance and deep shadow. Police patrolled while the camera crews and reporters hung around drinking coffee. Generators set up to run the media equipment droned like jet engines, destroying any quiet the night might have had. And at the center of it, Mal hung between the two posts as utterly still as he'd been when she left.

She swallowed down her anger, now bitter with sadness. She hated seeing him this way.

The evening breeze shifted, pushing against her back. Mal lifted his head. She smiled. Had he picked up her scent? He might not be able to hear her heartbeat over the incessant buzz of the generators.

Eager to be with him, she cut around the square so she could come in toward him with the cameras at her back. Even with her signum masked with foundation, she had no desire to show her face on television, no desire to do anything that might find its way back to Tatiana and give her new reason to return to Paradise City.

'Chrysabelle?'

She paused near the bumper of a camera truck. Luke Havoc stood just beyond the circle of light. She pulled off the sunglasses and nodded. 'Yes, it's me.'

He came toward her, squinting a little. 'If not for your scent, I wouldn't have recognized you.'

'Good. I'm hoping no one else will either.'

He nodded. 'I understand. I'm here to get you through security. In case they give you a hard time.'

'Shouldn't you be guarding the mayor?'

He shrugged one shoulder. 'I'm the head of the team, not the whole team. Besides, that place is like Fort Knox. No one's getting in there.'

'I don't know how you can work for her given the circumstances.'

He glanced away, his jaw tightening. 'It's a job.'

'Sorry, not my business.' The last thing she wanted to do was alienate the man helping her. 'And I appreciate your assistance with this. Can we?' She tipped her head toward the square. Mal had to know she was here by now.

'Sure. Let me lead.'

As they came out from between two camera trucks, a pair of cops approached them. Luke showed his ID and filled them in on the situation. 'And she's allowed to stay until six a.m. when he's released.'

'I'm taking him home,' she added. But not to the freighter, back to her house, where she'd already told Fi and Velimai to hire a company to helioglaze every window she had. Mal needed to be safe there. Especially since he might be spending a lot more time with her in the future. If things went well. Nervous energy tightened her belly. It *would* go well, wouldn't it?

'We'll make sure the other patrols know,' the older cop said. He moved aside. 'Go on through.'

She touched Luke's arm. 'Thank you.'

'Not a problem.'

With that, she navigated the maze of camera equipment, scaffolding, and power lines. The stench of gasoline and exhaust coming off the generators nearly choked her. Mal's sensitive nose must be overloaded.

As she approached, he lifted his head and squinted. With the harsh lights behind her, he probably couldn't see her glow or make out who she was. Could he even smell her over the reek of the generators?

A few more feet and his expression told her he'd recognized her. 'You came.'

Despite the circumstance, she couldn't help but smile. She wrapped her arms around him and tipped her head back to see him better. 'Of course I did. Did you think I'd let you go through this alone? I know you did this to even the debt the pride wants paid.'

He nodded. 'I got a few words to Doc as we passed. He'd better make this work.'

'He will. I'm sure. The pride has to appreciate what you did for him tonight.'

Mal's gaze pored over her face, his expression softening. 'You look so different. Like the night we first met.' He laughed a little. 'You're not going to stab me again, are you?'

She tightened her embrace. 'Ever? Or just right now?'

He laughed harder. 'I'm really glad you came. It's easier with you here.'

She let go of him long enough to pull her hood down a little more; then she cupped his face, went up on her tiptoes, and pressed a kiss to his mouth. 'We're a team now, right? We stick together.'

'I like you in black.' He leaned as far forward as he could, causing the chains to creak, and kissed her again. 'It makes you much more agreeable.'

She swatted him lightly. 'I see public humiliation has done nothing for your attitude.'

'Did you expect it to?'

She flattened her hand against his chest, feeling the intensity of the moment very strongly. She peered into his dark, silver-speckled eyes. 'Are you okay? Do you need anything?' The chains were enormous. Like something they'd use on a circus elephant, back when circuses had been legal. 'Your shoulders and arms must be killing you.'

He shrugged, or tried to, making the chains sway. 'Another hour and I'm done.'

She checked the watch she'd found in her mother's jewelry box. 'Forty minutes and counting.' Keeping her hood low, she moved behind him and began massaging his shoulders and biceps.

He moaned so softly she knew she alone had heard it. 'Am I hurting you?'

'No. Feels good.'

'Remind you of New Orleans?' The memory of his hands on her swept through her like a wildfire.

'Mmm, yes. I wouldn't mind doing that again.'

She kneaded the heavy muscles of his shoulders. 'Finding the city a new guardian?'

'Being alone in a hotel room with you.'

'Wicked creature.' She massaged his arms a little while longer, then came back around the front of him. His eyes were heavy-lidded with pleasure but sparked with a silvery desire she'd come to recognize long ago. 'I've been thinking . . .'

'Yes?'

'It's time you got off that freighter and found a real place to live.'

Some of the pleasure faded. 'That is a real place to live.'

She glanced down at the cobblestones beneath them. 'You know what I mean.'

He shook his head. 'No, I don't. I'm not exactly flush. It's not like I can buy the house next to you.'

She dug her toe into the space between one of the cobblestones and the large grate covering one of the square's storm drains. 'I'm not very good at this.'

'At what?' He rolled his shoulders like he'd suddenly become uncomfortable.

'I'm going to buy a new boat to replace the one Tatiana torched. I want you to move into it. After it's been helioglazed and everything. Then you wouldn't be so far away. I mean, I have that huge house and it's just Velimai and me. You could, I don't know, train with me sometimes maybe or just hang out in the house if you wanted. There's plenty of room and—'

'Chrysabelle.'

She took a breath. 'If you don't want to, I understand. I know you're not a people person. You've told me that before, so I—'

'*Chrysabelle*.' He said her name a little louder this time.

She glanced up.

'Can I talk now?' His gaze had a glimmer of emotion unlike anything she'd seen before.

'Yes, of course, you can talk.'

'The idea of moving that close to you – and let's be honest, to a wysper – scares me more than anything I've faced in a long time.'

The tenuous joy she'd just felt receded like a fast moving tide. 'I understand.'

'I'm not an easy person to live with, or near, by any stretch of the imagination.'

She nodded, staring at her hands. 'I know.' Maybe she could disappear down that storm drain and away from this embarrassing moment. What had made her think this was a good idea?

'I'm moody—'

'You don't have to tell me.'

'Argumentative—'

'Also not surprising.'

'And there's the issue of the voices and the beast I deal with on a nightly basis.'

She toed a loose stone into the storm drain. 'I'm fully aware how much they like me.'

'But if you're willing, so am I.'

'I knew it was a bad idea when I—' She looked up. 'Did you just say yes?'

He nodded. 'It's not going to be easy having me as your nearest neighbor.'

'And life with you these past few months has been?'

Remembering the cameras were watching, she leaned in to kiss him again, whispering, 'Thank you,' before her ample hood hid both their faces.

'You're welcome,' he answered as they came apart. He flexed his hands, swinging his arms a little. 'This is a hell of a lot better than the last time I was chained up by a woman.'

That he could joke about his past gave her hope, lightening her spirits like the coming dawn lightened the sky. With a start, she stared over his shoulder and into what had once been a very dark sky. 'Something's wrong.'

'What?'

Unwilling to alarm him any more than she already had, she said, 'Actually, I don't think it's anything, but give me just a second, okay?' She held up a finger. 'I'll be right back.'

Without waiting for his response, she ran back through the muddle of wires and equipment. Most of the camera crews seemed to be focused on their reporters now, all of whom were giving updates. Beyond the harsh lights, the sky was even brighter. She searched for Luke but he was nowhere to be found. She checked her watch.

It was ten after six. How had the time gone so fast?

She grabbed a passing police officer. 'What's going on? He was supposed to be released at six a.m.'

'Not anymore. The mayor made a statement about new crimes coming to light and her new zero-tolerance policy. The vampire's not going to be released.'

Unadulterated fear sucked the air from her lungs. Her knees almost buckled. 'What? The sun's coming up. It'll kill him.'

The cop nodded. 'That's the point.'

'She can't do this.' Chrysabelle's entire body trembled uncontrollably. 'Where's Luke Havoc?'

'He's gone back to the mayor's. You want me to call him?'

'No.' There was no time. She shoved past the cop and ran back to Mal. She grabbed the placket of his shirt, holding on to keep herself from collapsing. 'You can scatter, right? Tell me you can scatter.'

'You've asked me that before. The answer hasn't changed.'

'Could you ever scatter? When you were at full power?'

'What does it matter?'

'Answer me,' she snapped, shaking him.

With a look of surprise, he did. 'Not since I stopped drinking from the vein.'

'That's about to change.' She let go of him and unzipped her jacket, pulling it off her shoulders as her hood fell back, panic making her movements jerky.

'What are you doing?' He pulled against the chains. 'What's going on?'

'The mayor isn't releasing you and sunrise is only a few minutes away.'

He glanced skyward. His mouth came open slightly as he saw past the bright lights. 'Dawn,' he said softly. He closed his eyes and turned his head away. 'I'm so sorry,' he muttered. 'Go home. I don't want you to see this.'

'I'm not leaving you.' She grabbed his shirt again. 'Bite me. Drink. You'll get your power back.'

His eyes opened, shining silver. 'And kill you, too? No.'

'You're chained up. I'll get away before you drink too much. Besides, I don't die anymore, remember?' She forced away the tears burning her eyes. 'Mal, you can't leave me like this. Not now.'

'Better one of us than both.' He turned his face away from her. 'I won't do it.'

She grabbed his chin, forcing him to look at her. 'If you die, who will protect me from Tatiana?' It was a weak chance, but she prayed dropping his ex-wife's name would fire him up.

His face shifted, his fangs suddenly visible. 'I guess the mayor's going to get her show after all.' He shook his head. 'Whatever happens, I love you. I want you to know that.'

She wrapped her arms around him and kissed him hard. 'Then stick around so you can remind me.' She bent her head to the side. 'Do it,' she whispered.

He nodded and kissed her neck. Then he struck, fast and deep.

She gasped as he pierced her, the sharp sting long unfelt but still familiar, although she'd never been taken by the throat. Arching into him, she wrapped her arms around his outstretched ones as he drank. His body came to life against hers, warming and expanding with each swallow. Her own body responded in kind, her heart beating in time with his, the freshening of her own power like an intense prickling on her skin. Tears flowed down her face, born of anger and helplessness, but also of joy.

Being bitten was the culmination of a comarré's reason for being. It was their purpose and their reward. But she'd never loved Algernon, and being pierced by Mal was more than a bite. It was a bonding. If he died, so would she. Maybe not physically, but she felt in her soul the need for him like never before.

The thick chains holding him groaned. Tiny fissures split the surface of one massive link.

Darkness invaded her senses and she knew it was time. He'd had enough. She released him and worked her hands up to his jaw. 'No more,' she whispered, putting pressure on him. He nodded, but his fangs stayed in her. She pushed gently at his chest. With him chained and unable to hold on to her, they were separated a moment later.

He panted, openmouthed. Tendrils of black danced above the band of his T-shirt but disappeared as he shook his head, struggling but somehow controlling the beast.

She took a step back. 'How do you feel?'

'*Whole,*' he mouthed. He swallowed and cleared his throat. 'Whole,' he said again.

'So do I,' she said. The camera lights switched off suddenly and in the brief moment it took for her eyes to adjust, she thought maybe she'd been wrong about the sunrise. But she hadn't. The sky was bright enough the lights weren't needed anymore. She turned east. The horizon burned white-orange. Fear punched her in the gut.

'Jerem, bring the car,' she yelled, knowing the shifter would hear her. Then she spun back around. 'Mal, scatter now. You've got to—'

The sun broke the horizon, sending rays of light racing forward.

'I'm trying,' he answered. His face contorted in a mask of concentration, eyes closed, body tense.

On the other side of the square, her black sedan jumped the curb and barreled toward them. The look on Jerem's face said he understood exactly what was happening.

She fell to her knees. 'Holy mother, please don't let Mal die.' The sun kissed his boots, snaking up his legs. Wisps of smoke rose from his body. 'No,' she begged the sun, but nothing would stop it now. She reached for his hand. 'Mal, please, try harder.'

Harsh rays swallowed his lower half. The sedan screeched to a stop inches away. The sun glared off the car in bright flashes as it breached the horizon and enveloped Mal in its light.

With a last guttural cry, he disintegrated into smoke.

Chapter Twenty-Two

The groundwork had been laid and everyone was in their places. All that remained was to wait, something Tatiana had never been good at, but this time was different. This time as she sat in the dark nursery, listening to Lilith's soft breathing, she found new patience. And oddly, a niggling of fear she'd never before experienced.

The fear wasn't for herself but for Lilith. Tatiana was about to put her child in danger, and even if it was ultimately to protect her, that knowledge did not sit well with her. At least she knew Octavian and Daci were in on this plan with her. She felt confident they wouldn't let harm befall Lilith. She'd even come to believe that Kosmina would protect her child for reasons beyond duty.

She tipped her head against the rocker's back. By now Daci would be in place, poised to come running in from where she'd just been 'passing by' to act as another witness. Octavian and the Dominus and Elders who'd not yet turned in were down the hall in the library. As soon as Octavian heard her call out, he'd come running as well, bringing their guests with him.

Hopefully in time to see Svetla's demise at the hands of the Castus.

The nursery door swung open slowly. Tatiana was positioned behind the screen where Oana, the wet nurse, sat to feed Lilith. She could see slivers through where the panels hinged. Svetla would be able to detect the presence of another vampire, but Tatiana hoped she'd attribute it to Lilith. Or perhaps the compulsion to obey would override any other concerns.

She'd soon find out.

Svetla stood silhouetted in the doorway for a second; then she was in and the door shut again, plunging the room back into darkness except for the moonlight filtering through the diaphanous curtains. For a vampire, it was light enough. Without a moment's hesitation, she stole toward the crib and scooped Lilith into her arms. Lilith woke, cooing softly.

Tatiana's heart ached, fearful that Lilith might be scared. She squeezed the arms of the rocker. The one in her metal hand cracked.

Svetla looked up. 'Who's there?'

The time for hiding was gone. Tatiana burst out from behind the screen, throwing the light switch as she did. 'You're kidnapping my child!' she screamed.

'What? No.' Svetla blinked. The compulsion was wearing off, but Tatiana couldn't call the Castus until there were witnesses.

Daci barged in a few moments later. 'What's happening? I heard loud voices.' She turned to Svetla. 'What are you doing with Lilith?'

Octavian skidded to a stop in the open doorway, Lords Timotheius, Syler, and Zephrim following along behind him. 'What's going on? Who's got Lilith?'

Tatiana pointed at Svetla. 'She's trying to kidnap my child.'

The other lords looked appropriately dismayed. That was all the witnessing Tatiana needed.

'Samael,' she bellowed. 'Help me!'

The shadows in the room pulled together into a dark column. A great flash of lightning shattered the space and the jagged sourness of brimstone and unclean flesh cut through the room until the stench was unavoidable. Samael stepped out from the column, the shadows giving way to reveal him in all his fetid glory. From the waist down, his body was hidden by a skirt of shadows shifting with tortured faces and clawing hands. From the waist up, he was nude, his skin the burnished red of dried meat.

Tatiana had never been so pleased to see the monstrosity who'd fathered her kind. The others bowed their heads at his sudden arrival. After a quick bow herself, she took a few calculated steps toward him. 'My lord.' She spoke without waiting for his greeting, something she prayed he'd forgive. 'This one' – she pointed at Svetla – 'is trying to kidnap the child you gave to me to raise.'

His mouth pulled back in a grimace as he twisted toward Svetla. 'How dare you?' His voice grated the air to brittle shards.

Svetla cringed. 'I ...'

Samael charged forward. 'You think you know better than I? That you should be the one to rear this child?'

She shook her head, clearly terrified. Lilith began to cry. Tatiana rushed to Svetla and took Lilith, cradling the child against her body. 'Mama's got you,' she soothed Lilith, bouncing her gently.

Svetla backed away, but Samael followed. The Dominus looked on with mortified interest. He turned to them. 'Which of you is her Dominus?'

The three shook their heads. Only Syler spoke up. 'Her Dominus is Lord Grigor. He has already retired for the day.'

'Get him,' Samael screamed.

As if on cue, Grigor stumbled in. Kosmina had seen to it that his last brandy had been laced with a touch of laudanum as well. He rubbed at his eyes. 'What is the ruckus?'

'The ruckus,' Samael spat, 'is your Elder has defied my command.'

Instantly awake, Grigor assessed the situation. 'Svetla, what is the meaning of this?'

'I am just doing what you told me to.'

An audible gasp went up from the others. Tatiana almost smiled.

'What?' Grigor howled. 'I never told you to do any such thing.'

'Lies. Typical.' Tatiana scowled at him. 'You've never been a friend to the House of Tepes.'

Kosmina entered from the adjoining dressing room. 'My lady, my apologies, but Lord Grigor's car has been brought around front as he requested.'

Tatiana praised the day Octavian had hired the woman. The kine was as good as he had been as her head of staff. This improvisation would earn her a bonus. 'Kosmina, now is not the time.'

'Yes, my lady.' She bowed and ducked out as Samael began to rage again.

'Enough,' he growled. 'I told the council that Tatiana and her family were to be protected. I promised that any harm that came to them would be assuaged with the ashes of those responsible. Did you think me a liar?'

All had gone to their knees but Tatiana and Grigor. They responded as a group. 'No, my lord.'

Grigor stabbed a finger at Tatiana. 'You're to blame for this.'

'Silence or your life will be forfeit as well.' Samael turned toward Svetla, now crouched against the wall, shaking and crying.

'Please,' she begged. 'I meant no harm—'

Samael grabbed her by the waist. His fingers wrapped easily around her body. She pried at his hand, but to no avail. Smoke rose in wisps from her clothing. She swatted at him, terror unlike anything Tatiana had ever seen turning her eyes into glowing silver flares. She wept bodily, screaming, 'No, no, no!'

Then a *whoosh* filled the room and flames swallowed her whole. A few seconds later, they died out. Samael opened his hands and let loose a flurry of ashes to the floor. 'For your part in this transgression, Grigor, your power of mind reading is revoked. As for the rest of you, let this serve as a reminder.' He stomped his foot and a cloud of ash puffed up around it. 'Disobey me at your own risk.'

Another flash of light and he was gone, leaving in his wake a silence so loud, Tatiana's ears burned with it. Somehow, during all of that, Lilith had fallen back asleep. Tatiana turned to Octavian. He came to her, pulling her into his arms. 'It's all right. Lilith is safe.'

She nodded, more upset by the event than she'd have guessed she would be. 'I know. I'm just shaken, that's all.'

Lord Syler joined them. 'It's to be expected.' He turned to the group. 'I want it known that from this day forward, the House of Bathory will always side with the House of Tepes. Cross them and you cross us as well.'

Grigor swore in Russian. 'This is not the end of this, Tatiana. You may align yourself with whoever you choose; it does not change the fact that you are out for your own good and nothing else.'

'If you could read my mind, you'd see that's not true.' She held Lilith tightly, surprised to find those words truer than she could have imagined. Nothing mattered to her so much as protecting Lilith, but that would never be a problem again. No one would dare come against them after word of tonight spread through the families.

Grigor stormed off, shouting for his things to be packed. Timotheius and Zephrim looked like they'd fallen into a state of shock.

Timotheius straightened. 'We should adjourn the council. Grigor's time as Dominus may have come to an end.'

'Yes, perhaps.' Zephrim nodded as both he and Timotheius looked at Tatiana. 'What would you have us do, my lady?'

And for the first time since she'd entered the nursery that night, Tatiana smiled.

When Doc reached Chrysabelle, Jerem was crouched beside her in the square, trying to get her into the car. Jerem stood as Doc approached.

Doc glanced at the chains hanging empty from their posts. 'Tell me what I saw on TV was just a trick. Mal's in the car, right?'

Jerem shook his head. 'I wish.'

As numb as Doc felt, he could only imagine how Chrysabelle was. 'I can't believe this. I didn't believe it when the mayor made the announcement, and I don't believe it now. He can't be gone. He can't be.' How many times had Mal saved his life?

'It was so sudden.' Jerem shook his head. 'Something must have happened to change her mind. Unless she planned it all along.'

'Couldn't be. I was supposed to be there, not Mal. The sun wouldn't have done anything to me.' He never should have let Mal take his place. Dammit. Mal would still be alive now. He lifted his chin toward Chrysabelle. 'How is she?'

'Refuses to leave.'

'Let me talk to her.'

Doc approached her like he might a wounded animal. 'Chrysabelle?' He crouched beside her. She rocked back and forth, arms wrapped around her, tears cutting tracks in the makeup she'd used to hide her signum.

She didn't answer, just stared blankly at the spot where Mal had been.

He wrapped his arm around her. 'Let's go home now.' Gently, he eased her to her feet. Jerem got the car door open. 'Come on now, that's my girl.' She slumped against him, her feet not really moving. Not wanting to make more of a scene for the cameras than they already had, he picked her up and carried her, putting her down again on the backseat. He shut the door and turned to Jerem. 'Get her home. I'll be right behind you.'

Too many minutes later, they'd cleared Mephisto Island security and pulled into Chrysabelle's driveway. As Doc and Jerem got out, a red-eyed Fi opened the door. Behind her stood her the whirling gray storm that was Velimai.

'Tell me it's not true,' Fi cried.

Doc held the car door while Jerem lifted Chrysabelle out and carried her inside. 'I wish it wasn't.'

Fi started crying softly. 'How could the mayor do this?'

'I don't know.' Doc pulled her into his arms and kissed the top of her head. She clung to him and wept. 'Come on, now. Be strong for Chrysabelle.' And Velimai, who couldn't seem to pull herself together enough to stay solid.

'Where should I put her?' Jerem asked.

Fi wiped her eyes. 'Upstairs. In her bedroom. I'll go with you.' She pulled away from Doc and led Jerem up the steps.

As they walked away, Doc shifted uncomfortably. Grief was not something he dealt with easily. Anger, yes. But Chrysabelle needed comfort, and anger wasn't going to do that. 'Uh, Velimai, could you help me make tea?' That's what Chrysabelle had sent him to do the time they'd arrived to find her mother kidnapped by Tatiana. It seemed like a good activity.

Velimai solidified enough to nod. She pointed toward the kitchen, then moved in that direction. He followed.

'I guess you were watching it on the holovision?'

She nodded again and signed something he didn't understand.

'I don't know signing, sorry.'

She shrugged and didn't bother trying to make herself understood.

'I'm surprised you're so upset about a vampire.' He tried to smile a little, to show he'd meant it as a way of lightening the mood.

She just sat at the kitchen table, put her head between her hands, and stared into space.

Without much else to do, he started opening cabinets and looking for supplies. The kettle was already on the stove, so he turned that on, then went back to rummaging. He made a point of knocking a box out of the cabinet.

Velimai caught it before it hit the ground. She rolled her eyes at him and made shooing motions with her hands.

He got out of the way as she went to work. 'Chrysabelle needs us to be strong right now. I don't feel like it any more than you do, but it's what she needs.'

Velimai set the tea canister on the counter, then looked

around for something. Not finding it, she left and came back a few minutes later with an e-tablet in her hands. She scrawled something and held it out for Doc to read.

The mayor's the one who's going to need help when Chrysabelle comes to her senses.

He held his hands up. 'No argument there. I was in a council meeting when the mayor's announcement went down. My council members are plenty concerned about what this means for the rest of us.'

She nodded as she scooped tea into a little silver ball.

'We've got to keep Chrysabelle from doing anything rash. We can't lose her, too.'

Setting the tea aside, Velimai wrote something new. *How could the mayor do this? Doesn't she understand how the city will react?* Her image flickered again.

'I hear you loud and clear. Maybe we should put the TV on? See if there's anything new.'

Yes, Velimai signed. One of the few he understood.

The intercom buzzed. Velimai went over to the panel and pushed a button. The guard from the front gate appeared on the small screen. 'There's a visitor here for Ms. Lapointe. Name's Mortalis.'

Velimai nodded vigorously so the guard could see her.

'Okay, I'll send him through.'

She clicked the screen off, punched a few other buttons, then turned to Doc. She pointed toward the driveway, her eyes questioning.

'Got it.' He walked back to the foyer, opened the front door, and stood waiting. The gate into the estate was already swinging wide. One of Dominic's cars pulled through, looking eerily like no one was driving it.

The driver's door opened, then shut.

'I'm here,' Mortalis called out. 'You'll be able to see me better when I get inside.'

'Better? I can't see you at all.' Doc stepped out of the way, not really sure where the shadeux was.

'How's this?' The voice came from the foyer.

Doc turned. Mortalis was slightly visible now, a faded image that reminded Doc of when Fi had been caught in a death loop. 'You look like a freaking ghost.'

Mortalis smiled unsuccessfully. 'Speaking of ghosts, how's Fi taking it?'

'Not well.'

Apprehension crept into his eyes. 'And Chrysabelle?'

'She's—'

Footsteps interrupted him. Fi padded down the stairs, Jerem behind her. 'She's catatonic.' Fi shook her head. 'I've never seen her like this. I don't know what to do.'

'Maybe we should take turns sitting with her,' Mortalis offered.

Velimai came out from the kitchen, holding a tray with the tea stuff on it. She nodded at Mortalis.

'You want me to go with you? We can sit the first shift.'

She nodded again, moving past him slowly and up toward Chrysabelle's room. He followed without further comment.

Jerem shifted uncomfortably. 'I'm going to crash for a few hours so I can be awake for her later. I'm in the garage apartment if you need me.'

'Thanks, bro.' Doc grabbed Fi's hand and led her into the living room as Jerem left. 'I need to talk to you.' He took a seat on the couch and pulled her into his arms, holding her tight against him.

'Do you need to suffocate me, too?'

He eased up a little. 'Sorry. I just don't ever want to lose you again. Ever. After watching what happened with Mal . . . time is short, baby. We have no idea what tomorrow will bring. I'm sorry for what I said. I meant it to protect you, but I know it didn't come out that way. I'm tired of being separated from you. Tired of wondering every day when I'm going to see you again. When you went missing, it just about killed me.'

She settled into his embrace a little easier. 'That still doesn't fix our problem.'

'I'm working on that. I talked to the council about divorcing Heaven.' He hesitated. There was no way Fi was going to take this well.

Her eyes brightened and she smiled. 'That's awesome!'

'Well, yes and no. There are some . . . stipulations.'

She frowned. 'Like what?'

'In order to keep the alliance between the PC pride and the São Paulo pride, and to allow the São Paulo pride to save face, I must provide them with a bond of allegiance.'

'What's a bond of allegiance?'

He blew out a long, slow breath. 'It means I have to give my firstborn child to the Brazilian pride, to be raised as one of their own.'

'You have to give up a kid?' Her face fell. 'I . . . I don't even know if I can get pregnant. I've been a ghost for so long. I—'

He shook his head. 'The child has to belong to the São Paulo pride as much as to the Paradise City pride.'

She squinted at him. 'What are you saying?'

'I have to get Heaven pregnant.'

Her squint turned into a stare. 'You have to become a sperm donor?'

'Not exactly. It has to happen the old-fashioned way. It's a last-ditch effort to cement the relationship and keep the couple together.'

Fi took a few long, silent breaths, then, just as quietly, got up and stalked away from him. Doc shook his head. The only thing worse than Fi yelling at him was Fi not saying a word.

This was bad. The kind of bad that made the apocalypse seem like a picnic.

Chapter Twenty-Three

C reek parked his V-Rod in Chrysabelle's drive, surprised by the number of cars already there. With an hour left before the sun set, he knew Mal wouldn't be around, which was good. That was one vampire Creek didn't want to run into. Mal would probably have some words about the curfew for him.

Odd that Chrysabelle had yet to revoke Creek's gate privileges. From what he vaguely remembered about the meeting in the mayor's office, he was sure they'd be gone and she'd have put his name on a list of people never to be allowed on her property, but the guy at the guard shack had checked his ID and waved him through.

The door opened as he walked up. Doc, the leopard-shifter, greeted him.

'If you've come to offer your condolences, that's fine, but don't plan on staying long. She's not up for a lot of visitors right now.'

He stopped on the front porch. 'Condolences? For what?'

Doc cocked one brow and stared him down. 'You live under a rock?'

Not a rock, but he had been pretty tied up with Yahla lately. 'Something like that. What happened?'

'Mal's dead.'

For a brief, hard moment, the air left Creek's lungs. His mouth hung open and his heart wrenched with sympathy for Chrysabelle. 'What . . . how?'

'Mayor decided to let him meet the sunrise instead of letting him go at six a.m. as promised.'

'That wasn't the deal.' Or was it? Damn his missing memories. No, he'd never have supported that. He shook his head. 'Mayor wasn't supposed to do that.'

'No kidding.'

'How's Chrysabelle?'

'How do you think she is?' Doc didn't budge from the doorway. 'So why are you here if you didn't know about Mal?'

'I have information for her from the Kubai Mata.'

He crossed his arms. 'You can tell me.'

'No, I can't.' Creek held his position. It took a lot more than three hundred pounds of shifter to scare him.

'You must have a real big pair coming here, seeing as how you're basically responsible for Mal's death.'

Creek jerked back. 'How the hell do you figure that?'

'You work for the mayor now, right? Part of her advisory team? You were at the press conference when she announced the curfew, right there on the platform with her.' He leaned forward a few inches. 'And you didn't do anything to help when I was captured or Mal took my place.'

'Rules are rules,' Creek said.

'Then I have a new one for you. No KM in this house while I'm here.' He started to slam the door.

Creek stuck his foot in it. 'I have information about Chrysabelle's brother.'

Doc pulled the door back open. 'What is it?'

'My instructions are to relay the information to her and no one else.' They weren't, but Doc didn't know that.

'Let him in.'

At the new male voice, Doc looked over his shoulder, turning slightly. 'You sure?'

Behind him stood Mortalis, the shadeux fae. He was transparent, a visual that gave Creek the creeps. 'Yes, I'm sure. Chrysabelle could use a little good news right now.' He glanced at Creek. 'I'm assuming this is good news?'

'It's about where her brother is, so yes. I'd think she'd want to know that.'

Mortalis nodded. 'Okay.'

Doc stepped aside, eyeing Creek hard as he entered. 'Where is she?'

'Out by the pool. Been sitting out there since she woke up an hour ago. Don't expect a big reaction. She's not in good shape.'

Creek nodded. 'Got it.' He started forward.

Mortalis stopped him, his six fingers planted firmly on Creek's chest. He peered intently at Creek. His nostrils flared like he was sniffing for something. 'You smell like black magic.'

Creek shoved his hand away. 'And you reek like the vampire you work for. Get out of my way.'

Mortalis's left eyelid twitched. 'Don't be long.'

Creek stormed past and out to the pool deck. He pulled the slider shut behind him, not that a little glass would keep most of those inside from eavesdropping if they wanted to. Chrysabelle sat on the chaise at the farthest edge, staring out at the water.

He sat beside her on the tumbled marble tile, facing the same direction. If she noticed his arrival, she made no indication. He dipped his head to see her better. 'Hi.'

She blinked but didn't respond.

'I heard what happened. I'm very sorry.'

She pulled her knees up and wrapped her arms around them. 'You did this,' she whispered, her voice raw with emotion.

'No, Chrysabelle. It was never my intention—'

'You told me if I didn't agree to get the vampire baby back, the KM would destroy Mal.'

He swallowed. 'The KM had nothing to do with this.'

She whipped her head around, eyes red-rimmed and bruised with pain. 'You were in the office with the mayor. You sided with her.' A sob stopped her words for a moment. 'And against me.'

He barely remembered being there, but he wasn't going to admit to his memory lapses to her. 'I did what I thought was right.'

'What you thought was *right*?' She lunged toward him. 'I could kill you for what you did. You *and* the mayor. If you think I'm not going to make her pay—'

He grabbed her hands before they found his throat, tried to talk her down. 'But you won't. You're not built like that.' Sorrow made fine lines around her eyes and he wished like hell he knew exactly what had happened in that office. It was so much easier to think when Yahla wasn't around.

'Yes, I am. You just haven't seen that side of me.' She jerked out of his grasp, another sob muffled but audible. 'Why are you here? There's no damage left for you to do.'

'I'm not . . . ' He stopped. What was the point? She was going to think what she wanted to think. 'The KM found out that Daciana has returned to Corvinestri and taken your brother,

Damian, with her. He's back in Tatiana's control now, but being held as a prisoner. She's still using him for blood, though.'

Chrysabelle's breath hitched. 'Damian?'

'Yes.'

A tiny spark of hope lit her eyes. 'They have proof he's my brother?'

'It's in the file they gave me.'

'Is he all right? How does the KM know he's my brother?'

'The KM have been protecting him as best they can. As to how they know, they have inside sources. Ways of finding out this stuff.' Creek took out his phone and pulled up the info he'd been given.

She closed her hand over his to hold the phone steady, her touch colder than he remembered it being. He'd loved her once. Maybe not as much as Mal, but enough that he would have willingly given his life for her. Probably still would. But she'd chosen the vampire and Creek had come to terms with that. Didn't mean he'd ever completely stop caring about her. 'Tatiana will take him to Čachtice, to the Dominus ball.'

She nodded. 'The comarré always travel with their patrons.'

'The KM will give you whatever resources you need to get to Čachtice and get your brother back, so long as—'

'I bring the vampire baby back with me.' She let go of the phone and went back to staring at the water.

'Yes.' There was no point in denying it.

'There's nothing the KM could give me I don't already have access to. Nothing from them I need.'

He reached for the envelope tucked into his waistband beneath his shirt. 'There is one thing.'

She sniffed. 'I doubt it.' But she glanced over anyway. 'What?'

He held out the envelope. 'An invitation to the Dominus ball and maps of the comarré tunnels underneath the estate where the ball will be held.'

'And if I don't bring the vampire baby back with me? If I only rescue my brother?'

He hadn't wanted it to come to this. 'The KM know what you did with the ring of sorrows. They'll come after you and . . . ' The KM's dictates were more than he could stomach at times.

'And what?'

'They'll take it back. By whatever means necessary.'

As soon as Creek left, Chrysabelle loosened her grip on the invitation and let it fall to the side. Despite the news about her brother, her mind had no space for thoughts of going to Čachtice and all that entailed. She couldn't give it room, not with Mal . . . gone.

She swallowed hard and blinked back tears she'd thought long ago used up. Holy mother, how would she survive this? The hole inside her widened with every breath, the pain rippling out in relentless waves. Mal was *gone*. That was the only word she could manage right now, and even it felt much too close to a truth that weighed a thousand pounds.

Sorrow mingled with guilt, scraping her raw every time she managed a breath. Guilt that she hadn't told him how she felt when she'd had the chance. Guilt at her own cowardice.

She closed her eyes. Instantly, his image appeared, playing across the insides of her lids like a horror movie. Her hand reaching up to him. That blinding bright sun off the car that had seared the pictures into her brain and melted away her last shred of hope as he turned to smoke.

How could the mayor have done this? How could she, with

a few words on a written statement, so casually extinguish the one bright spot in her life? What past crimes? An example of what? Of how insane the mayor had become? How cruel? How stupid? Chrysabelle's hands clenched and she imagined them around the mayor's neck. Imagined the mayor's soft flesh and the crunch of bone as her throat gave way. Not since Tatiana had killed Maris had Chrysabelle wanted to take a life with such ferocity. She would *end* Lola for this.

The sun beat down relentlessly on Chrysabelle as it began its descent below the horizon. With a shudder, she bent under its unyielding heat, her anger turning back to sorrow. It burned her skin until she imagined she felt a fragment of the same pain Mal had in his last moments. She tucked her head against her knees and forced herself to breathe when all she really wanted to do was collapse onto the ground and pray for it to swallow her up. If not for the crowd of people inside, who were all friends, all there for her, and all tiptoeing around her like she'd suddenly turned to glass, she'd climb into her bed and stay there for a month, but going inside meant more of the sideways glances and meaningful looks they thought she didn't see.

She saw and understood those looks. They were worried about her. They were right to be worried. She was a little worried herself, about the way she felt, the thoughts building in her head, the revenge fantasies that were the only real comfort she'd felt today. Her friends were here to help her in any way they could, but the help she needed, no one could provide. No one could bring him back.

No one could ease this pain.

Her eyes burned from the deluge of tears she'd cried. Maybe his being ... gone would be easier to take if she'd found the strength to tell him how she felt. Because she *did* love him. Just thinking it caused a sob to snag in her throat. There was no question about it. She'd just been too afraid to say it. She pounded her fist into the chaise and bit back a scream. What had she been so worried about? That he wouldn't say it back? He'd already said it to her.

She rolled her forehead back and forth against her knees. Mal had been right about her. She ran from the things she needed to face the most.

How was she going to go to Čachtice and rescue Damian without Mal? She'd gotten so used to him fighting at her side. They made a great team, no matter how odd a pairing. Her throat closed up again. She cleared it, trying to find a way to breathe that didn't make her soul ache. Maybe she wouldn't live through the visit to Čachtice. Maybe that would be the end of it. Of her. Of this pain.

Anger wormed through the inky black grief suffocating her insides. Anger at herself for not telling Mal how she felt. Anger at the mayor for what she'd done. Anger at Tatiana for being such a thorn in her side. *Their* sides.

Her hands itched for the red leather hilts of her sacres. To spill blood and ash. What did she have to live for anyway? If she was going down, she'd go down big. Unafraid. She'd start with Lola and finish with Tatiana. She'd make Mal proud.

A new quake of grief ripped through her and her fingers found their way to her throat. She touched the skin where Mal had bitten her, the bite now healed, the flesh as smooth and perfect as it had ever been. She pressed her fingers harder, hoping to find a nick or a scab or something, but there wasn't anything to find.

She had nothing left of him. Nothing to prove they'd ever shared that most intimate of moments between a comarré and her patron. She ground her teeth together as the anger surged upward. The sun sank teasingly lower. She shot to her feet, hands fisted at her sides. Maybe she should get Doc or Mortalis to spar with her. If she didn't burn off some of this rage, she was going to do something she might regret.

She almost laughed at that. What would she regret? Certainly not watching the mayor take her last breaths with a sacre stuck in her gut.

The sun disappeared, leaving her in the cooling, sympathetic twilight. Chrysabelle's hands flexed, almost feeling the hum of the sword hilts against her palms. She closed her eyes and tried to inhale with some kind of evenness, the way she'd been taught as a comarré, but the rhythm wouldn't come. Chaos ruled her mind. She needed to focus, to make a plan, not just to run head-first into an unknown situation. Maris had planned for years, taught herself to walk again, built a business, and created a new existence beyond the nobility, all with the hopes that Chrysabelle would one day join her and find a life outside the comarré world. Her mother would not want her to throw that all away. Not after everything she'd sacrificed.

What would Mal do in this situation? What would he say to her?

'Chrysabelle.'

A hard sob racked her body. Holy mother, now she was hearing his voice. She covered her face, unable to bear the madness seeping into her brain.

'Chrysabelle?'

She turned, already knowing it was a trick of her weary, grieving mind.

But it wasn't.

Her lungs heaved against her rib cage, needing more air to

process the rush of emotion threatening to spin her into unconsciousness. 'How?' But it didn't matter how. All that mattered was that Mal was there, standing a few yards from her. Or was he?

'You're real?'

'Don't I look real?' He held his arms out.

With no further hesitation, she threw herself into his embrace, wrapping her arms around his neck and her legs around his waist. 'You're alive.' She was crying again but didn't care. Mal was alive. *Alive*.

He laughed as his arms came around her. 'Of course I'm alive. Why would you think otherwise?'

She pulled away so she could see his face. 'You turned to smoke. The sun hit you and you burned up. I saw it with my own eyes.'

Concern grooved his forehead. 'I got a few burns, but nothing a good daysleep couldn't heal. Don't cry.' He brushed a tear off her cheek with his thumb. 'Your blood saved me.'

'I don't understand. You told me you couldn't scatter.'

He shrugged softly. 'I can't. Never have been able to. Not in the traditional sense anyway. But what I can do is exactly what you saw. Turn to smoke.' He took her by the waist and set her feet back on the pool deck. 'Watch.'

Then he did exactly what he'd done in the square. Vanished into a swirl of black smoke. A second later, the smoke took shape and he was himself again.

She took a step away from him. 'But the sun was out.'

He nodded and stuck a finger through one of several burned holes in his shirt. 'Which is how I got these. I slipped into the storm drain as quickly as I could.'

She shook her head, still staring at him, every horrible feeling she'd had over the past few hours disappearing. 'The sun reflected off the car and nearly blinded me. I must not have seen you go down the storm drain.' She sat on the chaise as a sudden weakness swept over her. 'All this time, I thought you were . . .'

'Dead?'

She nodded.

He kneeled in front of her and took her hands. 'I'm sorry you thought that, but I'm perfectly well.' He glanced at his clothes. 'Except for a few burns and these scorched clothes.'

She tugged her hands out of his to grab his shirt and pull him closer. She kissed him hard until she ran out of air. 'There are two things I have to tell you.'

'I'm listening.'

'One is that I have bad news. I love you, too. I'm sorry I didn't say it to you sooner.'

He nodded a little, like it was something he'd already known. Any other time, that would have earned him a right hook.

'Two is that you smell like a sewer.'

He cocked one brow. 'Considering I spent all day hiding out there—'

'You need a shower.' She grabbed his hand and pulled him up. 'I happen to have one in my bedroom.'

His eyes went silver. 'Are you inviting me up to your room, Ms. Lapointe?'

She was about to respond when a light went on in the kitchen, catching her eye. 'Would you mind if we kept this to ourselves for a little bit? I'm not ready to share you.'

He squeezed her hand. 'I had no intention of inviting anyone to join us.'

'I mean about you not being dead.' She scooped the invitation off the chaise and wiggled it between her fingers. 'There's a lot to be said for the element of surprise.'

Chapter Twenty-Four

Lola stood in her master bath, staring at the ugly red marks on her neck. The reminder of her inability to control what was happening in her city. How was she going to manage it if she couldn't find a vampire willing to turn her? And worse, how would she ever get a chance to get Mariela back from her vampire captors without that kind of power?

Her fingers probed the punctures, testing the soreness. Dominic thought he'd scared her away from her desire to become a vampire. Did he understand now how wrong he'd been? Did he also know he'd caused her to issue the statement that had put Malkolm to death? She knew how harsh an action it was, but the remaining councilmen had supported her. They were as afraid of what was happening in the city as she was. And now both the humans and the othernatural citizens would know she was serious about keeping order.

His death hadn't been the show she'd expected, though. No fire or burst of flames. Not even a shower of ash. Just a disappointing puff of smoke.

Her fingers fell away from her neck. Dominic was also

wrong if he thought her desire to be turned had vanished with his visit. If anything, he'd shown her just how necessary the transformation was. She'd be ready now, stronger. When the dark pull of death came, she'd welcome it, knowing it wasn't the end but a rebirth into the life that would solve all her problems. Being transformed would give her the power she lacked as a human and make it possible for her to raise her grandchild to the fullest of her potential.

A knock sounded at her bedroom door. 'Ma'am?' Hilda.

'Just a moment.' Lola retied the scarf she'd worn around her neck all day to cover what Dominic had done; then she opened the door. 'Yes?'

'Dinner is ready. Also, Mr. Luke and Mr. John have arrived. I took them to your office to wait.'

'Thank you. I'll speak with them, then come to dinner.' After Dominic's visit, she had a few security questions for the shifter brothers. Like how a vampire got into her house without anyone knowing about it. What was she paying them for if not to protect her from situations exactly like that? The more she'd replayed his visit in her mind, the angrier she'd become.

Hilda nodded and left, but Lola kept the door open, pausing to give herself one last glimpse in the entrance mirror before she left. Dark smudges under her eyes betrayed how tired she was, but there would be time for sleep soon enough. Or better yet, less need for sleep once she was turned.

John and Luke rose as she entered her office. Both looked ill at ease. Maybe they already knew someone had been in the house? She waved a hand. 'Sit.' She was going to reprimand them, but no need for them to stand at attention. She took the chair behind her desk, moved a stack of mail to the side, then planted her clasped hands in the center of it. 'Thank you for coming. There's a very serious matter I need to discuss with you.'

The two men looked at each other, both starting to speak at the same time. John gave the floor to his brother.

Luke cleared his throat. 'We have something we need to discuss with you as well.'

She raised her brows and glanced at John, but his eyes were on his brother. Her suspicions that they knew about the security breach grew. They must be here to apologize. She sat back. 'By all means, you go first.'

Again the two varcolai exchanged a look; then Luke continued to speak. 'In light of everything that's happened in the last few days, we can no longer continue working for you.'

Shock coursed through her system. 'What?'

Luke sat forward, glimmers of anger in his eyes. 'Your administration has made it very clear that our kind aren't welcome.'

'That's absolutely not true. I've made special exceptions for those othernaturals who work in any kind of government service.'

He snorted. 'So if the city benefits from us, that's okay, but if we're just ordinary citizens, we're to be treated like enemy number one.'

Indignation straightened her spine. 'My main priority is doing what's best for this city.' She stabbed her finger onto the desktop. 'It always has been and it always will be.'

'Just not for any citizen who's a shade outside of human.' Luke shook his head and stood. 'I'm done.'

'John, certainly you don't feel this way, too? You've worked for me for years.' Kept her alive more than once. Been with her through her divorce. Through the estrangement of her daughter.

Every time the press had hounded her, he'd been there to shield her and protect her when no one else had.

John rose, his mouth a hard line. 'I do, and until the situation changes, that's how it's got to be.'

She exhaled hard as his words sank in. 'That curfew protects both sides.' He couldn't leave her. She needed him. 'You're being ridiculous.'

John pushed his shades up onto his head and leaned over her desk, his hands firmly planted on the wood top. 'You know what's ridiculous? You put a good man to death this morning without cause.'

'A good man?' Did they really think that? Doubt curled through her thoughts, but she forced it away. The time for doubt was past. 'That *good* man was a vampire. And my cause was the protection of the city. I cannot allow things to degrade any more than they already have. That man was a killer by nature. Now the rest of his kind will think twice before they take a life in this city.'

Luke straightened. 'If being a vampire is a death sentence, when do you extend that to varcolai?' He shook his head. 'He wasn't even the one who broke the curfew. Your reasons don't justify your actions.'

'I had the full support of the city councilmen, too.'

'Then they're just as guilty.'

She jumped out of her chair. 'Since the two of you were so busy planning your resignations last night, let me give you one more reason for my actions. Another vampire broke into this house last night and tried to kill me.' She pulled the scarf down on her neck. Their gazes went to the puncture wound. 'I had to make a statement.'

'You made one all right,' Luke started, 'but it doesn't change our decision.'

'Fine.' She fixed the scarf back into place, picked up a pencil off her desk, and squeezed it. It was that or break down from the overwhelming sense of betrayal. She ground her back teeth together, drawing strength from the new anger the situation provided. 'I don't want anyone working for me who doesn't want to be here.'

Without another word, John and Luke left.

She sank into her chair and stared blankly after them. Losing John was like losing a member of her family. She rolled the pencil between her fingers. The sense of being powerless to stop the chaos around her was overwhelming. Her stomach felt like it might rebel at any moment. She had to get control of things again. Had to stanch the bleeding before Paradise City was an empty husk.

The pencil snapped. Lola dropped the pieces. Enough was enough.

Tatiana leaned into the butter-soft leather desk chair and crossed her legs, the sound of her silk trousers like a summer breeze. After all the excitement of Svetla and the heightened sense of power the incident had given her, dealing with Damian should be easy. 'Bring him in.'

Octavian nodded. 'I'll be right back.'

'Thank you, my love.' Tatiana was not about to visit Damian again in his new quarters. He could come to her. In this space, no one would get the best of her.

Lord Ivan's former office was impressive with its black marble, dark wood, and bronze furnishings. Many times she'd sat on the other side of this desk while Ivan held court about some new idea or grand scheme. Many times she'd dreamed of knocking him out of his chair and taking his power for herself. Never had she thought it would taste so sweet.

The new computer Octavian had purchased for her sat on one corner of the desk. A small light on the monitor's frame blinked. Octavian would need a few minutes to bring Damian in, so she tapped the screen to bring it to life. The news site she'd selected as her home page opened up instantly. Keeping an eye on kine activity, especially now that they knew they weren't alone in this world anymore, had proved less interesting than she'd expected.

One particular headline caught her eye. NEW FLORIDA PUTS VAMPIRE TO DEATH. She tapped the article to bring it full screen. Well, this was something. A video was embedded. She tapped the screen again to play it.

The sound was off, but there was no mistaking the vampire suspended by chains between two posts. Malkolm. Her ex-husband. As she watched, a smaller figure dressed in black came into view. Then the video cut away to a reporter. Tatiana dragged her finger along the progress bar to fast-forward through the talking. When Malkolm reappeared, the sky had begun to lighten and the figure in black had pushed her hood back. Blond hair shone with a glow that only one creature possessed. A comarré. *The* comarré. Rapt, Tatiana stared as Malkolm sank his fangs into Chrysabelle's neck. A frisson of joy shook Tatiana. Perhaps they would both die. Knowing Malkolm as she did made her intimately aware of the consequences of him drinking straight from the vein.

The comarré pushed away from him. He strained at the chains as sunlight crept up his legs. A car barreled up behind him, throwing a flash of light into the camera. When the light disappeared, so had Malkolm.

The video cut back to the reporter. Tatiana tapped the screen twice to darken it and sat back. Had she really just seen

Malkolm die? The comarré would have no one to defend her now. If not for the blasted Dominus ball, Tatiana could swoop into Paradise City and take the comarré easily.

Before that fantasy went any further, the office door opened and Octavian shoved Damian through, his hands bound. A fresh bruise marked his cheek. 'Bloody prat took a swipe at me.'

Still thrilled by the possibility of what she'd witnessed, she nodded. 'That's fine.'

'It is?' Octavian cocked one brow.

'No, I mean, it's fine that you hit him back.' She waved her hand, dismissing the unimportant discussion. More than ever, she needed to know the comarré's vulnerabilities. She came around to the front of the desk, leaned against it, and peered into Damian's eyes.

A few moments passed. Wisely, Octavian let the silence go unbroken. At last, when she detected the briefest hint of apprehension in the comar's eyes, she spoke. 'Daciana filled me in on your stay in Paradise City.' She crossed her arms like the whole thing bored her. 'I take it you enjoyed your time with the comarré Chrysabelle?'

'Never met her,' Damian spat.

Her instinct was to strike out, but that had earned her nothing the last time. She lifted her flesh hand and studied her fingernails. 'And yet you stayed at her house? Is she that poor a hostess?'

Damian sneered. 'I'm done talking.'

She nodded. Octavian glanced at her, eyes questioning. *All in good time*, she wanted to tell him. Instead, she walked back behind the desk and sat. 'Help the comar into a chair, will you, darling?'

Damian grunted as Octavian shoved him into one of the seats before the desk.

'Ribs still bothering you?' She smiled. 'We can do this the hard way or the easy way. I prefer the hard way, but you may not.' She tipped her head. 'What will it be?'

He leaned forward as though on the verge of spilling whatever information he had and met her smile with one of his own. 'How about you take a long walk into the sunrise?'

She laughed once, then went stone sober. 'I can think of a thousand ways to kill you that would be far more interesting than you are right now.'

Damian leaned back into the chair. 'But you won't.' He bent his head, displaying the barely visible marks from her last bite. 'You need my blood.'

'You're right that I need blood, but you're mistaken if you think it has to come from you.' She stared at him, wondering how much fear he was capable of hiding. 'As Dominus, I have unlimited funds. Purchasing another comar would not be impossible.'

He shrugged one shoulder. 'There would be questions.'

'And I would answer them by telling the Primoris Domus you ran from me *again*.' She smiled softly. 'But we both know that would just be my way of covering up your death.'

Damian went still for a long moment. 'I'm not going to help you hunt down Chrysabelle.'

This time Tatiana shrugged. 'Then it's a good thing you can provide me with blood or I'd have no need for you at all.' And in truth, she was done dealing with him for more than sustenance. There was little need for this aggravation now.

'I can get information out of him,' Octavian offered.

'Don't bother. The comarré's protector is dead.'

Damian's eyes rounded slightly, but Octavian's jaw dropped. 'Malkolm?'

'Yes.'

'I don't believe it.'

She pointed to the monitor. 'It's all over the kine news.' She rested her hands on the arms of the chair as she looked at her comar. 'The one chance you had just disappeared.'

For the first time, genuine fear played through his gaze.

She nodded to Octavian. 'Take him away.'

Chapter Twenty-Five

Mal came back together on Chrysabelle's balcony, staying in the shadows so none of the security cameras would pick up his form and alert the crew downstairs. He wouldn't hide his presence from them too much longer, but Chrysabelle's desire to keep him to herself for a while gave him an undeniable thrill. Almost as much as her declaration of love, which had caused the voices to gag and retch. Screw them. They'd just have to learn to deal.

He smiled as he opened the French door and went inside. Smiling was such an odd thing for him. It had been centuries since he'd had a reason to. 'Hi,' he whispered.

'Hi,' Chrysabelle whispered back, locking the master suite door behind her as she came in. 'I told everyone I was going to take a long hot shower and not to disturb me. They don't suspect a thing.'

'Are you sure?' He pointed at her clothes. 'Or were you that dirty when you went outside?'

She looked at what she was wearing. It bore the marks of their embrace, remnants of soot and his time in the sewer. 'Well, if they noticed, they didn't say anything. I'll change while you're showering.'

He glanced toward the bathroom. He knew that room well. Last time he'd been in there, she'd opened a portal to the Aurelian and he'd gone through it to save her, only to bring back her dead body. It would be good to replace that memory with something else. 'Turn the water on for me?'

She gave him an odd look. 'Just because I said I love you doesn't mean I'm going to wait on you hand and foot, you know.'

He shook his head. 'I'd never assume that. I'd rather the mirrors steam up before I go in there.' *Coward.*

'Oh.' She grimaced apologetically. 'You don't want to see your true self.'

'After the day I've just had? No.' Seeing his inner monster seemed like overkill after the mayor had just attempted to put him to death for *being* a monster. That was enough of a reminder. *No, it isn't.*

'I understand.' She went in and cranked the water on, the shushing sound allowing them to stop whispering.

He plucked at his T-shirt when she came back out. 'I can't put this stuff back on. There should be a change of clothes in the hurricane shelter.' Unless she'd thrown out his stuff after she'd told him to get out. How far they'd come. *Too bad.*

She nodded and the glimmer in her eyes said she was thinking of that moment, too. 'I can get down there and back without being seen. Not that any of them would question me wanting something of yours right now.' She turned to go, but he grabbed her hand.

'I'm really sorry you had to go through that. If I had known, I would have—'

'Come out during the day?' She smiled. 'It's okay. Now that you're back, none of that matters.' Her face suddenly went solemn. 'Just ... don't do that to me again, okay?'

'I won't. I promise.' He leaned in and kissed her.

Halfway through it, she started to laugh. 'Sorry, but you still smell.' She bit her lip to keep from laughing again. 'I'll kiss you more when you get out of the shower.'

'I'm going to hold you to that.' And hold her against him. The voices could get bent.

She grinned as she slipped out the door. He inhaled, needing to replace the redolence of sewer with her honeyed perfume. Amazing that she was his willingly. Tugging his shirt off, he headed for the bathroom, where clouds of steam already wafted out the door. More steam had fogged the mirrors until all he could see of himself was a rough, dark shape. He dropped his ruined shirt to the floor and shut the door, leaving it unlocked in case his sweet, angelic comarré had other plans.

Chrysabelle had laid out a towel for him, so he shucked the remainder of his disgusting clothes and climbed into her cavernous marble and glass shower.

Hot water sluiced over him, tightening his muscles with an almost painful pleasure. Hot showers were plentiful on the freighter, but something about showering in a space the size of an old-fashioned phone booth sucked the pleasure out of it. Living on her property meant he'd probably get to use this shower whenever he wanted. Preferably with her in it. He leaned into the spray, letting the water beat against his skin and the thrum of it fill his head. The noise almost drowned out the voices.

Almost.

He grabbed the shower gel. The label said *Lapointe Cosmetics*. Thoughts of Maris and all she'd endured for Chrysabelle humbled him. He had no doubts her mother would not approve of their relationship. Mentally, he promised Maris he'd let no harm come to Chrysabelle. Then he squeezed out a palm full of the gel and went to work ridding the sewer's stench from his body.

He emerged from the shower feeling better than he had in centuries. The last time he'd been this happy, freshly bathed, and full of blood from the vein had been . . . never. He snagged the fluffy white towel from the counter and dried off. How many times had this towel dried Chrysabelle? Leaving his hair damp, he wrapped the towel around his waist and walked into the bedroom.

Chrysabelle was curled in a chair near the French doors, reading through what looked like one of her mother's journals. The stereo played softly, probably her attempt to block further conversation from the hypersensitive ears downstairs. Jeans and a black T-shirt waited on the bed for him.

'Checking to see what your mother would think about us?' *She'd hate you. We do.*

She jumped, her head coming up with a snap. 'You startled me. No, I was . . . ' She frowned, peering at him oddly. 'Did the burns leave scars on you?'

'No, why?'

She set the journal down and came to him. 'You have some weird spots on you.'

'Spots?' He bowed forward, trying to see himself without losing his towel.

'Like this.' She touched a place on his forearm above his wrist where there was the smallest area of unmarked skin.

'That's where Fi's name used to be. Remember? It disappeared after Mikkel killed her and never came back even after
she got out of that nightmare loop.'

Her fingers eased to a stop over his right pec. 'What about
this one?'

He worked his jaw to one side, processing how good her
touch felt. Keeping hold of his control while she was this close
and he was this undressed wasn't easy. He bent his head until
he could manage a little better; otherwise the blazing shine of
his eyes would give him away. If his body didn't do that for him
in the next couple of seconds. 'I don't know. That's strange.'

'And this one?' Her fingers coasted toward his abs, stopping
to the left of his navel.

He staggered back slightly and swallowed. Drinking from the
vein after so long had made everything more powerful – his
abilities, his senses, and his reactions. Her fingertips burned into
his flesh, spilling sparks of pleasure across his nerve endings
and muting the voices. Forcing himself to relax, he splayed his
hand against his body, stretched the skin for a better look, then
shook his head. 'I have no idea. Haven't seen my skin without
the names since I escaped the ruins.'

She rubbed her finger across one of the blank spaces, leaving
a trail of heat that burned down to his toes. 'You're missing
three, but we can explain one. Do you know whose names they
were?'

That single question quelled the desire threatening his reserve.
Instead of answering immediately, he studied the blank spaces,
buying time. He knew. He'd had years to do nothing but stare
and remember. Talking about them to the woman he loved was
completely different. He touched the spot on his stomach.
'Margaret.' *The teacher from Berlin.* Then the spot on his chest.

'Helen.' *The flower girl in Gloucester.* Not memories he was proud of. Not now. Not with her.

She peered at him, curiosity brightening her eyes. 'How—'

'Don't.' He gripped her hand, holding her fingers so the contact between them was broken. 'Please.' He loosened his grip. 'That's not a conversation I want to have with you.'

'Okay,' she said softly. 'I understand.' She rubbed her thumb across his hand before sliding her fingers from his grasp.

She seemed saddened by his refusal, so he quickly changed the subject. 'Didn't the Aurelian say the way to undo my curse was to help someone for every name I bear?'

Chrysabelle nodded. 'She did. But who have you helped?'

They looked at each other, each seeing sudden understanding reflected back at them.

'You,' Mal said, the thoughts in his head so wild they were almost impossible to believe. 'Both times you died.'

The Seminole Nation bumper sticker on the truck parked outside of Creek's place meant it belonged to a tribe member. Which tribe member, he wasn't sure, and what they were doing here was another question. A chill shook him. Unless something had happened to his mother or grandmother.

He pulled his motorcycle to a stop beside the passenger door and checked inside. Martin Hoops, one of Mawmaw's neighbors, slouched in the driver's seat, hat tipped down over his eyes. He looked up at the sound of Creek's V-Rod, leaned over, and rolled the window down. He nodded. 'Thomas.'

'Martin. What are you doing here? Everything all right?'

Martin pushed his hat back. 'Everything's fine. Your grandmother just wanted to see you. Made you a pineapple upside-down cake. Asked me to bring her over.'

Mawmaw didn't drive. Never had, but that hadn't kept her from getting where she needed to go. Tribe members had a way of doing whatever their healer needed. 'Good to hear. Was worried something might have happened.'

'Naw, old girl's fit as a fiddle. Just likes to see you now and then.' Martin leaned back, his not-so-subtle hint about Creek's need to visit more as plain as day.

'I was just out there.'

Martin shrugged, closed his eyes, and tugged his hat back down.

Creek got off his bike and walked it to the door. Which wasn't locked. How had Mawmaw opened it? She had her ways, but picking locks wasn't something he'd ever seen her do.

He pushed the big metal door back and got his answer.

Annika, shades firmly in place, sat on the stairs up to the sleeping loft while Mawmaw sat nearby on an empty wooden cable spool. They had obviously been engaged in conversation. On his worktable rested a foil-wrapped plate. The foil was pulled back and the cake beneath it had been cut into. Hell. How long had Mawmaw and Annika been talking? This was not good.

Annika got up to meet him. 'Your grandmother makes the best pineapple upside-down cake I've ever had.' Behind her, Mawmaw smiled. This was worse than not good.

'She's won a few contests with it.' He glanced at his grandmother. 'Do you want me to tell Martin you're ready to go?' Please.

She frowned. 'That's Mr. Hoops to you, and no. When I'm ready to go, I'll tell him myself. You just go about your work. I'll wait.'

Double hell. He raised a brow at Annika. Argent would have

freaked over this. Speaking of which . . .' Any news on Argent yet?'

Annika shook her head. 'No. He's been declared MIA.'

'Sorry to hear that.' Actually, he couldn't care less as long as they didn't figure out what had really happened. He glanced toward the loft. No sign of Yahla. One more thing for him to worry about. If she showed up now . . . No, she wouldn't do that, would she? At least Mawmaw was wearing her feather charm.

'Did you deliver the invitation?'

His attention returned to Annika. 'I did.'

'How did she take it? Is she preparing to leave?'

'I don't think so. She's in mourning over the vampire.' Hard to believe Mal was dead. He'd never been the enemy the KM made him out to be. At least now the Kubai Mata couldn't use him as a threat against Chrysabelle anymore.

Annika's face lost all traces of pleasantness. 'We need her to leave for Čachtice in three days or the window of opportunity will close. She must be at that Dominus ball. It's the best chance to recover the child.'

'I can't force her to do something she doesn't want to. She knows her brother will be there. If that's not enough, nothing will be.'

Annika pulled her phone from her inside jacket pocket and pressed her finger onto the ID scanner. It came to life, and she swiped through a few things, finally pulling up an image. 'Show her this.' She turned the phone so Creek could see it.

The picture was of Damian. One eye was swollen shut and purple with bruises that matched those on his cheek and jaw. Blood trickled from the side of his mouth. Creek cleared his throat. 'Is that real?'

'Of course it's real. You think Tatiana's throwing a parade in his honor?'

Whoever the KM had planted inside Tatiana's, they were in deep if they were able to get shots like that.

Annika turned the phone around and tapped the screen a few more times. A couple seconds later, his phone vibrated. 'There, it's sent to you now. Go back and show her that picture. Make her understand the urgency. If you don't get her to recover that child' – she glanced at his grandmother and lowered her voice – 'your job, and all the benefits that come with it, will be gone. Understand?'

He nodded. That's always how it was. The threats to pull the support of his family were nothing new. 'Yeah, I understand.' For the sake of his grandmother, he said nothing else.

For a brief moment, Annika's face was a stony mask. Then her expression softened. 'I don't make these directives, Creek. They come from higher up. You must know that.' She turned and bowed her head slightly at Mawmaw. 'Pleasure to meet you, Mrs. Jumper.'

Mawmaw nodded back. 'And you, Annika. Thank you for your gift.'

Creek wasn't sure he wanted to know what that meant. He watched Annika leave, then went behind her and locked the door. That hadn't gone as bad as he'd suspected.

His grandmother stood, brushed a few cake crumbs off her lap, and walked toward him. 'That's a rare one there.'

'Annika?'

She nodded. 'Not often you meet a basilisk.'

'You know what she is?'

She laughed softly. 'Child, I know more than you think I do.'

That much he did know. 'What did you mean thanking her for a gift?'

Mawmaw patted the pocket of her patchwork vest. 'She gave me a few scales. You can make some powerful charms with those.' She raised her brows above the heavy rims of her glasses. 'Well, the woman ate some of my cake. Fair is fair.'

Only Mawmaw could accomplish something like that. He shook his head. 'You're amazing.'

'Yes, I am.' She took his hand and led him back toward the stairs, where she sat on the spool again. 'We need to talk.'

'I knew you weren't here just to bring me cake.'

She shook her head, her eyes growing very serious. 'The soulless woman came to see me.'

Chapter Twenty-Six

'How long is she going to shower?' Doc stared at the ceiling. Chrysabelle had come in smelling worse than she had when she'd first gone outside – like smoke and sewage and the faintest hint of vampire. Why, he couldn't guess. Plus she'd been upstairs a long time. Longer than it took to get clean. Something was up.

'Leave her alone,' Fi said. She'd been cranky since he'd told her about the deal with Heaven and having to give her an heir to make her an ex. Couldn't say he blamed Fi, but it wasn't like he'd made the rules either.

'You want to talk about this some more?' He wagged his finger back and forth between them.

Fi planted herself on the couch with a bowl of cheese puffs. 'No.' She answered without looking at him, her eyes straight ahead on the holovision.

Like a movie was going to make them forget that Mal was dead. Doc sat beside her, happy that Velimai, who was also giving him the cold shoulder since the whole Heaven thing, wasn't between them. 'Not talking about it ain't gonna make it go away.'

She glared at him. 'Why not? Taking ketamine seems to be your answer for your fire problem, so why can't I medicate with silence?'

'That's cold. And completely different.'

She went back to watching TV. 'Is it?'

'Maybe I should go outside and hang with Mortalis.' The shadeux had been out there since Creek left, making sure no one else got through security and disturbed Chrysabelle.

'Sure, then you won't have to discuss this with me.' She shook her head and dropped the handful of cheese puffs back into the bowl.

He went still, watching her closely. If Fi had lost her appetite, something was seriously wrong. This was more than her being mad. He grabbed her hand. 'Let's go outside and figure this out.'

She tried to pull away, but he held on. They had to work this out, or they'd both go crazy. Crazier. Reluctantly, she set the bowl of cheese puffs down and followed him.

Mortalis leaned on one of the front porch pillars, facing the entry gate. He turned as they came out. A black cigarette dangled from the corner of his mouth.

'You smoke?' Doc asked.

'Nasty habit,' Mortalis mumbled around the butt. He reached up, took the cigarette between his first two fingers, and exhaled a thin stream of pale red smoke, filling the air with the bittersweet scent of burned fruit. 'Only do it when I'm stressed.' He tapped the ash from the end and studied it. 'It's *nequam*, kind of the fae version of tobacco. Nyssa doesn't like it and Dominic forbids it when I'm working.' He took another drag, tipped his head back, and blew out a series of tight rings. 'You know vampires and smoke.'

And with that, the memory of what had happened to Mal hung heavier than the scent of the *nequam*. Fi whimpered softly and dropped her head.

Mortalis rubbed his eyes with his other hand. 'Damn it. I didn't mean it that way.' He dropped the cigarette and ground out the cherry with the sole of his boot. 'You didn't come out here to talk about my bad habits. I'll leave you alone.' With a nod to Doc, he went back inside.

The *nequam* aroma lingered.

Fi shoved a hand through her long brown hair, but it fell back into place. 'I can't do this. I feel like I'm losing it. First you and this thing with Heaven, now Mal. I'm coming apart from the inside.'

He took hold of her arms. 'I know, baby. I know. Losing Mal is just ...' There weren't words to express how losing the person who'd saved your life made you feel. 'That's why we got to fix this thing with us. And I'm trying to do that.'

She pulled away from him and went to stand by the pillar where Mortalis had been. 'By sleeping with another woman?' She shook her head. 'I don't care if that's what the pride requires. It doesn't work for me. Not in any way.'

'What else am I supposed to do?'

'I don't know, but not that. Not if you want to marry me. If you even still do.'

'Of course I do. Don't say that.' Letting out a breath, he rolled his shoulders to get some of the tension out of his system. Without the ketamine, he'd have been a fireball right about now. 'Look, it sucks hard. I'll give you that. But it's an afternoon at most and then she and I are done and you and I can get on with our lives.'

'What if it takes more than an afternoon to get her pregnant? What if it takes a week? Or a month? Or more?' She wiped at her nose. 'What if you fall in love with her? What if she falls in love with you and decides not to leave? Women get crazy like that.'

Like he didn't know that. 'That won't happen. I won't let it.'

'Maybe I should just show up and beat the daylights out of her like you did with Sinjin.' She held a hand out as if to stop him from arguing. 'Not kill her, just, I don't know, kick her sorry self back to Brazil.'

'Even that wouldn't work. To displace a pride leader or their mate, the challenge has to come from them. Heaven's not foolish enough to challenge you.' He took her hand between his. 'There's no other solution but for me to give her a kid. I know you don't like it, but it's the only way.'

'It can't be.' She turned her head toward the fountain. 'I won't stay if you go through with it. I'll go back to Colorado. Back to my folks. With Mal gone, there's nothing to keep me here anymore.'

If she'd slapped him it would have stung less. 'Nothing to keep you here? Is that what I am? Nothing? What we are? You can throw us away like that? Did you ever really love me or were you just keeping yourself occupied since you were tied to Mal and I was convenient?'

'No.' She looked at him, her eyes clouded with emotions he couldn't read. 'That's not what I meant.'

Reeling from her statement, he stepped toward her. Only the ketamine kept him from jabbing a finger at her in anger. 'You better figure out what you mean and fast, because I'm talking about giving up a child for you.'

She crossed her arms and her brow furrowed. 'Maybe you should just stay with Heaven, then.'

'Maybe I should.' Hell, no, that's not what he wanted at all.

Fi's lower lip quivered. Then she went ghost and disappeared.

The front door of Chrysabelle's house slammed, followed by Doc cursing loudly. Chrysabelle glanced toward the downstairs. Further discussion with Mal about the missing names would have to wait. 'I should see what's going on.'

'Let me get my clothes on and I'll come with you. Seeing me alive might defuse the situation.'

She nodded with hesitation. 'I don't want everyone to know you're alive, though. Velimai, Fi, Doc, and Mortalis are fine, but not Creek. There's something odd with him lately. I think the Kubai Mata are pushing him harder. Making him do things he wouldn't otherwise do.' She lifted one shoulder, trying to play off the seriousness of it. 'Anyway, it would just be better if he continues to think, like the rest of the world, that you're gone.'

'Fine with me.' Mal hitched his thumb beneath the towel covering him from waist to midthigh. 'You might want to turn around while I get dressed.' He grinned wickedly. 'Or you might not.'

She frowned halfheartedly. 'Being dead hasn't changed you one bit.'

'I wasn't dead.'

She cupped her elbow in her hand and turned to give him privacy. 'You were to me. And you can be again if you don't behave.'

He answered her over the sound of a zipper zipping. 'I don't think you missed me nearly as much as you claim to.'

'Please,' she said, spinning back around. 'I probably missed you more than you deserved.' She laughed. Amazing how quickly one's outlook on life could change. She loved this banter between them, the fun of it, the lightheartedness of it. She'd never had that in her comarré life, which had been filled with rules and protocol and ritual. 'I love you,' she whispered, oddly aware of how precious this time was.

His smile softened. 'You okay?'

'Yes. Just thinking how short life can be. Even for people like us.' She sat on the edge of the bed while he pulled his shirt on. There was no better time to tell him what was going on. 'Damian is my brother.'

Mal's brows dipped. 'You're sure?'

'Yes. Creek told me. The Kubai Mata somehow got access to the right records and found out. Creek showed me the file.'

Mal dragged a hand through his damp hair. 'We'll find him, I promise.'

'The KM already have. Tatiana has him.' She traced the pattern woven into the coverlet, trying not to imagine what Tatiana might be doing to him. 'I have to rescue him. I have to try.'

Mal walked around and sat on the bed beside her. 'You mean *we* have to rescue him.' He took her hand. 'We'll go back to Corvinestri just as soon as we see that fae you spoke of.'

She'd told him about Mortalis's offer to help, thinking now that the fae in question might shed some light on the issue of the missing names through his explanation of what the ring of sorrows was doing to her. What she hadn't told him was Creek's message from the KM. 'I also have to bring the mayor's grandchild home. If I don't, the KM have threatened to strip the ring of sorrows gold out of me.'

Mal's eyes silvered. 'Like hell they will. Not with me around.' He squeezed her hand. 'Mortalis downstairs?'

'Yes.'

'Let's go talk to him, then. See how quickly he can arrange for us to meet this fae.'

She smiled, not entirely convinced it would be that easy, but having Mal back had already halved her stress level. 'It's good to have a plan.'

So together they walked into the living room where a distraught Doc paced the floor, muttering to himself, and Velimai stood staring, shaking her head and judging him with her eyes.

'What's going on?' Chrysabelle asked.

Both turned. Their eyes went directly to Mal. Whatever the issue plaguing them, it was forgotten.

Doc stared, as speechless as the wysper fae beside him. Mal slipped his arm around Chrysabelle's shoulders. 'Cat got your tongue?'

Velimai let out a squeal that caused Mal to cringe. 'Watch it, wysper.' But he smiled. 'Nice to see you, too.'

Doc rushed him, pulling him into an uncharacteristic embrace. 'Damn good to see you, bro.' He released him just as quickly. 'What happened? How are you still here?'

Mal gave them the rundown and another demonstration of his scattering ability.

You might have a little wysper in you, Velimai signed, laughing.

After Chrysabelle translated, Mal shook his head. 'Not bloody likely.' He looked farther into the house. 'Where's Fi?'

Doc sighed. 'She got pissed at me and took off.'

'Again?' Chrysabelle took a step forward. 'That's how all this mess got started.'

Doc held his hands up. 'Except this time, I'm not going to look for her. I'm pretty sure we're ... done.'

Chrysabelle's heart sank a little. 'What? How can that be? You love her. And she loves you.'

'And I'm married to another woman.' He shook his head. 'I don't want to talk about it.'

Chrysabelle did. 'Doc, maybe if Velimai and I—'

Mal interrupted. 'Car.'

They all went silent. Then Doc shook his head. 'Motorcycle. Creek's back.'

Chrysabelle pointed toward her room. 'Mal, upstairs and stay there.'

'On my way,' he said, loping toward the stairs.

She turned to Doc and Velimai. 'Not a word to Creek that Mal's still alive. Got it? He's not to know.'

They both nodded. The engine cut off. Doc lifted his chin toward the door. 'What about Mortalis?'

'He can know, but not now.'

A second later, the shadeux opened the door and came in. 'Chrysabelle. Didn't expect to see you down here. Creek's outside, says it's urgent he see you, but I told him you were resting. Do you want me to send him away?'

'No, I'll talk to him. But outside.' Better to keep him out of the house and as distant from Mal as possible. She walked with Mortalis, waiting as he opened the door for her.

Instead, he paused. 'You want the KM out of here at any point, just say the word. I'll take care of it.'

She touched his leather-clad arm. 'Thank you, but I'll be fine.'

His brows drew together above his stormy-sea eyes, but he said nothing. He opened the door and stood aside for her to go ahead of him.

Creek sat on the fountain's edge. He looked less than happy to be back.

'What brings you here again so soon?' She sat on the far side of the fountain, forcing him to look away from the house to see her. She knew Mal well enough to know he'd be lurking on the balcony, listening to what was going on.

'Update on your brother.' Without hesitation, without the normal small talk and nice words, Creek pulled his phone from his pocket and brought it to life. He tapped the screen, then held it out to her. 'An operative just sent this. It was taken less than a day ago.'

The picture didn't register at first as anything more than a splash of colors, blond and gold, purple and red. Then the sick feeling in her stomach and the horror in her brain melded into a crystal-clear understanding of what she was seeing.

Her fingers gripped the edge of the fountain, digging in to keep from pitching forward. 'Damian,' she mumbled. 'I thought the KM were protecting him?'

'They are – otherwise he'd be dead.'

'And if I don't bring back the vampire child, the KM will let Tatiana kill him.'

'I can't say they won't.' Creek tapped the phone again. It went black. 'The Dominus ball is three nights from now. There will be a KM plane waiting for you at the private airfield we've used before. Hangar seven. Be on that plane in two days.'

'I don't need the KM's plane. And you're not giving me much time to prepare for an undertaking of this magnitude.'

He scowled. 'I've been trying to get you to do this for over a week. If time runs out, it's your fault, not mine.' He picked his helmet up from between his feet and stood. 'You want to use your own plane, do it. Just make *sure* you do it.'

She rose, too, his harsh words ringing in her ears. 'That's it? You're leaving?'

'You have everything you need.' He slid the helmet over his Mohawk. 'And I have family of my own to protect.'

Chapter Twenty-Seven

Fi was about to do one of the stupidest things she'd ever done, but it might be the only thing that kept her from losing Doc forever. And time was her enemy. If she didn't do this now, while Doc was still at Chrysabelle's, she might never have the chance again. Despite what she'd said, she loved Doc desperately. The thought of being without him made her sick. She was not about to let him go without a fight.

Which was exactly what she intended to start.

She floated outside the windows of Doc's penthouse, hidden by the night as she peeked in to see if Heaven was home. Fi found her in the master bedroom, sitting on a long padded bench at the end of the bed, buckling on a pair of expensive stilettos. Her hair and makeup were flawless and her dress was on point. No question about it – Heaven was going out. Perfect, because for what Fi was about to do, she needed an audience.

With the mayor's curfew in place, there could be only one hot spot Heaven would be hitting. The one downstairs. Bar Nine.

Trying to get into Bar Nine through the front door was

pointless. The bouncers would never let her in and she'd lose the element of surprise. She might also lose track of Heaven, who undoubtedly would spend most of her night tucked away in the VIP lounge, which in Heaven's case should stand for *very irritating person*.

Heaven stood and took a long look in a mirrored door. She turned, admiring her figure and smiling. Fi rolled her eyes. *Yeah, yeah, you're hot. We get it.*

Finally, Heaven made her way out of the penthouse and into the elevator. Fi floated through the walls and into the elevator shaft, following the car down to the nightclub level. When it stopped, she listened for the doors to open and close, then floated down and materialized inside the car. She hit the STOP button to keep the doors closed, then conjured up the best club gear she could. The dress was something she'd seen in last month's *Modiste* magazine, sleek black leather with grommets that showed hints of skin and a distressed, uneven hem that hit the tops of her thighs. She added sheer black tights and the ultra-high laser-perforated booties from the magazine's 'What to Own Now' section.

She did a little turn in the elevator, trying to see herself in the polished wood paneling. With the blink of an eye, she redid her face with smoky eyes and fixed her hair into an artfully teased mess. Sometimes being a ghost had major perks.

Punching the STOP button again to release the doors, she took a deep breath. It wasn't like her to plan things too much, but this was important. Everything had to go just right. Chances of getting to try this again were slim.

The doors opened and she sauntered into the heavy Latin beat, doing her best to look like she belonged. The place was jumping. Good. Maybe the crowd would give her some coverage. She pushed through to the bar, searching for the VIP section as nonchalantly as she could. It wasn't hard to spot.

The club was two stories, but the second was mostly a wrap-around balcony that overlooked the center dance floor. From what she could see, the upstairs was way plusher and the well-dressed people leaning against the railings looked expensive and snooty. And self-important.

Heaven's kind of crowd.

Fi worked her way into a spot at the bar to see what she could find out. She hadn't brought any money, which didn't matter because she probably couldn't afford the drinks here anyway, so when the bartender asked her what she wanted, she played it off. 'Actually, I'm trying to find my friend Heaven. I came in with some girlfriends but we got separated. Do you know her? Petite, big boobs, likes high heels?'

The bartender smiled. 'Everybody knows Heaven. She's married to the pride leader.'

Not for long if Fi could help it.

'She's usually in the VIP lounge upstairs. If you're with her group, your name should be on the list to get up there.' He pointed across the dance floor. 'Elevator's over there.'

The music changed just in time. 'Oh!' Fi said. 'That's our groove! Any way you could call her and tell her to come down and dance with me?'

'Sure, what's your name?'

Fi squinted like she hadn't quite heard him and started to back away. 'Thanks! I owe you!' Then she turned and made her way toward the elevator he'd pointed at. The bouncer there didn't look like he could be talked into anything. If Fi was getting up there, she was going to have to go ghost again.

She hung on the edge of the dance floor while she waited to

see if Heaven would come down. The longer she waited, the more she thought. Why hadn't Heaven just gotten off on the VIP floor? There was no way there wasn't an exit for the pride leader and his friends.

Fi gave in to the beat a little more, letting it move through her. She knew why Heaven had done what she'd done. Because getting off on the second floor meant all the little people without VIP access wouldn't get to see her. It was the same reason she wouldn't let go of Doc. It meant losing the spotlight.

Doc was just one more trophy she'd won. And Heaven was used to winning. But she was also used to things coming easy to her. She had an important father, all the material things she wanted, and a husband who gave her status.

A hard realization struck Fi, bringing her to standstill. Her approach was all wrong. The panic of time slipping away got her moving again, this time to the ladies' room. She slipped into a stall and from there went ghost and glided through the wall until she was outside. Everything had to change. She pictured it in her head – beat-up kicks, ripped jeans, a favorite rock band tee and a tattered camo jacket. The outfit had been one of her staples during her college days. Then she imagined herself without makeup, her hair stick straight and just the slightest bit dirty.

She had to look beatable. She had to play into Heaven's need to feel superior. She had to give Heaven a way to show off.

She materialized briefly, long enough to glance down to make sure it all looked right. Satisfied, she went back to her ghost form, calculated the spot on the wall above her, then floated up and in.

When she left the VIP ladies' room, those who stared didn't look away except to comment to the person next to them. She needed to find Heaven fast before security came after her.

'Heaven,' she shouted. More VIPs stopped to stare.

Then the soon-to-be-ex – Mrs Maddoc Mays walked out from a secluded alcove, a few girlfriends trailing behind her. Green-gold shimmered in her irises.

Good, Fi thought. *Let her get angry. I can work with that.* 'Hello, Heaven.'

'Look at the filthy little girl who thinks she deserves my husband.' Heaven sneered while her friends laughed. 'You are a joke. He cannot love you.' She walked close enough that Fi could smell her perfume. 'Why have you come here?'

'To tell you Doc's going to leave you for me and that you should prepare yourself. As in, start packing to go home.'

Heaven smiled and glanced back at her friends. 'You hear this?' She shook her head at Fi. 'You are sick in the head, ghost girl. Too bad you didn't stay dead. Maybe you could join your vampire now that he's dead, too, eh?'

Something inside Fi came close to snapping. 'You know what's too bad? That you're too scared of me to settle this once and for all.' She balled her fists. 'See which one of us really is the better woman. Which one is his rightful mate.'

Heaven's eyes went full-on green-gold and her pupils thinned to vertical slits. She leaned in and smiled, showing a set of fangs that would leave pinkie-sized holes in whatever they pierced, but her words held zero trace of humor. 'I could never be scared of you.'

'Prove it. You win, I'll walk away from him forever. You'll never see me again.'

Seconds ticked by. The crowd that had gathered around them stood listening, waiting right along with Fi. She could practically smell the smoke coming out of Heaven's brain.

Then Heaven straightened and a slow, calculated grin lifted

the corners of her mouth. Her eyes went back to human and she tipped her head slightly to one side. 'This is going to be easier than finding the right shoes for my latest couture gown.' She raised one hand like she needed to get the attention of those around her. 'Tomorrow night, here in the arena, I will fight this' – she waggled her fingers at Fi – '*human* to see which one of us is the rightful mate to our pride leader, Maddoc Mays.'

The crowd gasped. Numb nuts. Like they hadn't been listening.

Heaven held up her hand to silence them. 'We fight to death or surrender.' She laughed like she'd just told an inside joke. 'Whichever the ghost girl chooses first.'

'We're packed, my lady, if you'd like to do a final inspection.' Kosmina stood, hands clasped, before Tatiana.

This trip to Čachtice was becoming a monumental undertaking, one Tatiana wished she could throw off in favor of hunting the comarré in New Florida. But that would have to wait. The ball was being held in her honor. Not attending would cause more of a scandal than even she was willing to face. 'Everything from the list packed?' she asked. 'All of Lilith's things? Her toys? Extra changes of clothes? Her gown for the ball?'

'Yes, ma'am. I did her packing myself.'

'Very good. You're dismissed. I'll expect my suite prepared when I arrive.'

Kosmina bowed. 'It will be my first priority, my lady.' With that, she left.

Octavian sat near the cold fireplace, bouncing a giggling Lilith on his knee. Tatiana joined them. 'What of the comar?'

Octavian kept his eyes on Lilith. 'He's healed enough to

travel. I don't anticipate him giving us any more trouble, and you won't have to worry about a blood source for yourself or Lilith while we're away from home.'

'Keep him away from your comarré. I don't want him attempting another escape with her.'

Octavian laughed. 'That girl wouldn't leave if you paid her, I assure you.'

'I wish mine was as docile.' Damian had become the one scar on her otherwise perfect life. If the opportunity came to replace him, she would take it, no matter how it might erode her funds. She smiled. What was she thinking? Her funds were unlimited now that she was Dominus. She nodded to herself. Maybe she would visit the Primoris Domus in Čachtice and see what that house had to offer. Surely for the right amount, they would keep quiet about her *difficulties* with Damian? With a contemplative sigh, she sat across from Octavian and rested her elbow on the sofa's arm, then tipped her head into her hand.

He arched his brows. 'Nervous about the ball?'

She smirked. 'I don't get nervous.'

Lilith reached for the floor, so he set her down to crawl. 'Maybe *nervous* wasn't the right word. It's just that it's the first time the nobility will meet Lilith. There will be such a crowd there. I can see that it might be . . . daunting.'

'Daunting? You think anything daunts me? You seem to have forgotten who I am.' She peered at him curiously for a moment.

'I didn't mean to imply . . . ' He shifted nervously. 'Forgive me and my poor choice of words.'

She reached down to tousle Lilith's dark curls. 'I merely want everything to go off perfectly.'

'I'm sure it will. Lord Syler knows what's at stake for the House of Bathory as the host. He will not disappoint you.'

'No, he won't. Very few people are willing to risk that.' She stared at him pointedly, then shifted her gaze to Lilith, who'd stopped crawling to pet the rug's fringe. 'Things worked out rather well with Svetla, wouldn't you say?'

'Orchestrated genius.' His smile faltered a bit. 'The ancient ones are damn scary, if I dare say so. I don't know how you've dealt with them for so long. You're a brave woman, my love.'

Her own smile faltered as she remembered all she'd been through at the hands of the Castus. 'But now I have Lilith. I wouldn't change anything that's happened, nor will I let anything or anyone take away all that I've worked for. I've earned this life and I'll be damned if I'm going to let it be stripped from me without a fight.'

'After the incident with Svetla, I doubt there's anyone brave enough to try.' He chuckled softly. 'You really have become queen of the vampire nation, haven't you?'

'I said I would and I did.' She lifted her gaze to him. 'Did you ever doubt me?'

'No, never.' He leaned forward, elbows on his knees. 'There's no one more powerful than you. Except for the ancients. No wonder they chose you to be their principal.' He frowned. 'Do you think . . . No, I shouldn't even say such a thing.' He leaned back. 'I suppose we should make our way to the plane, hmm?'

'What were you going to say?'

'It's blasphemous. I shouldn't even think it.'

Her eyes narrowed. 'Octavian, tell me this instant or I'll bite you.'

'That's not a threat, my love. That's foreplay.'

'Tell me,' she demanded.

He paused, hints of silver in his eyes. He was aroused, no question. She knew because the talk of power had done the same to her. 'I was going to say, do you think a time might come when you'll be as powerful or perhaps more so than the ancients?' He laughed nervously. 'See? I told you, blasphemous.'

She stood and put her hands on her hips, the very idea of such power coursing through her with an erotic heat that demanded assuaging. 'Oana,' she called. 'Come take Lilith now.'

The wet nurse ran in from the other room. 'Yes, my lady.' She scooped Lilith up and took her out, shutting the door firmly behind her.

Tatiana stalked across the rug to stand before Octavian. 'You should be punished for even thinking such thoughts.' The need for him was so thick in her blood she could barely get the words out. 'Wicked creature.'

He went to his knees before her, his hands snaking up her skirt to wrap around the backs of her thighs. He leaned his head against her leg. 'Perhaps you should teach me how to behave, my lady.'

'Yes,' she said, her voice husky with the weight of desire. 'That is exactly what I'm about to do.'

Chapter Twenty-Eight

'We have to leave now,' Chrysabelle said a third time.

Mal hated seeing her like this, and nothing he said made things any better. *Did you expect it to?* 'I understand, but we can't go without a plan. It's a suicide mission otherwise.'

She paced the length of the living room, turned, and started back. 'You're right, I know, but I feel like every moment here is a moment wasted.'

Being told he was right, now that was something new. *It won't last.* He slanted his eyes at Mortalis, but the fae just shrugged. Clearly, this was Mal's show.

She twisted her hands together and stopped abruptly in front of him. 'Holy mother, what if Tatiana kills Damian before I get to him? What if he never finds out I'm his sister?'

Mal took her by the shoulders and forced her to look at him. 'Sweetheart, that's not going to happen. We're the ones with the information this time. We have the advantage. But we have to do this right or we'll lose it.'

She nodded. 'You're right.' He raised his brows. Right twice in the space of a few minutes? He could get used to this. *Don't.*

She sighed. 'So what do we do?'

'Come, sit down.' He guided her to the sofa where they sat. 'To start with, we need a way there.'

'Go see Dominic,' Mortalis offered. 'He can supply you with whatever you need.'

'What we need is an idea.' Chrysabelle rubbed at the signum on the back of her hand. 'And I don't want to ask him for his plane again.' She sat a little straighter. 'I should have my own. I certainly have the money.' She looked at Mortalis, eyes hopeful. 'Is that something you could help me with? Buying a plane and finding me a pilot?'

'How soon do you want it? With Luciano here, Dominic isn't in the club as much, so my hours have been lighter.'

'Two days?'

He shook his head. 'Not enough time to buy a plane, but I know one you can charter and a pilot you can trust.'

'Excellent. Get them here as fast as you can.'

Doc came in the front door. He'd taken over keeping watch from Mortalis since they'd started discussing the mission to recover Damian. 'Heads up. Dominic's coming through the gate and I'm out of here before I get into it with him and ruin the happy vibe going on. I should probably get back anyway, seeing as how I have a pride to run and all.'

Mal stood. 'Keep us posted on Fi.'

Doc nodded. 'Will do. Good luck with Damian. You know I'd go if I could.'

'I know,' Mal said. 'And I appreciate it.'

Doc grinned. 'Bro, love has made you all soft and squishy.'

And stupid. Mal wanted to punch Doc in the arm for that. Instead, he shook his head. 'I learned everything I know from you.'

Chrysabelle got up and gave Doc a hug. 'If there's anything I can do to help with Fi, just say the word. Thanks for being here.'

'Sure.' With a nod, he left.

Mortalis went to the door, pausing to catch Mal's gaze before heading out. 'Do you want Dominic to know you're alive?'

'If he's going to help us, he needs to.'

'I agree,' Chrysabelle said. She reached for Mal's hand as Mortalis left to escort Dominic in. 'This isn't going to be easy.'

'Is anything we do?' She was right – it wouldn't be easy – but he had a peace about what needed to be done unlike anything he'd felt before. Peace. *The last thing you deserve.* How odd for him to even use that word, but then everything about his life was odd lately.

Moments after they heard a car door shut, Dominic entered, Mortalis behind him. Dominic was dressed completely in black: suit, shirt, and tie.

Mal raised his brows. 'You weren't in mourning for me, were you?'

'*Mamma Mia*, you are alive!' Dominic raised his hands, palms together like he was praying. 'Now I am only in mourning for my city, my business, and my way of life. This *pazzo* mayor, she is destroying us all!' He went to Chrysabelle first, kissing her on each cheek. 'I came to see you in your time of sorrow, but I am happy to know that time is past, *bella*. I was worried for you.'

Next, he grasped Mal's hand. 'I do not know how you survived, but I am very glad you did.' He smiled. 'Perhaps you have secrets you have not yet shared?'

'Not a secret. Just smoke,' Mal explained. 'When I scatter, I turn to smoke. I hadn't done it in so long, I didn't think I still could, but drinking from the vein restored my full powers and here I am.'

'Very impressive.' Dominic nodded. 'And rare. There was a member of the House of St. Germain who had this power. I never saw him do it, but that was the rumor.' He gestured to the living room. 'May I sit? I have much to discuss with you.'

Velimai stood at the edge of the room, eyeing Dominic like her head was full of murderous thoughts. Mal remembered when she used to look at him that way. *She will again.* Whatever the history was there, it wasn't good.

'Yes, please,' Chrysabelle said. 'We have much to discuss with you, too. Velimai, would you fix me something to eat? I just realized I haven't eaten all day. I'm starving.'

The wysper nodded and headed to the kitchen with one last glare at Dominic.

Mortalis stayed by the door. 'I'll stand guard outside. Call if you need me.'

'Thank you.' Chrysabelle came back to Mal's side and together they followed Dominic and sat down. She stayed close enough to Mal that when they took their places on the couch, the heat of her thigh permeated the fabric of his jeans. The voices whined, but he shut them out. He wasn't about to push her away.

Dominic gestured to her. 'It is your house. You should go first.'

Chrysabelle explained everything that had happened, the information that Creek had given her about Damian, the proof he was her brother, the danger he was in, and the KM's insistence she bring the vampire child back.

Dominic nodded throughout, speaking only when she was finished. 'In truth, I'd hoped I might distract you from your grief by convincing you to accompany me on the very same trip.' He lifted his hands. 'The mayor refuses to remove the curfew that is ruining my business unless I bring her grandchild to her.' He stood and walked to the rear wall of windows. 'How am I supposed to take on the vampire nobility alone? Or worse, the ancients? But she doesn't understand what she asks.' He turned suddenly. 'Do you know she asked me to sire her? Can you imagine?'

Mal snorted. 'She asked me, too.'

'What?' Chrysabelle started. 'That night she came to the freighter?' She shook her head. 'That woman is mad.'

Dominic laughed, a hard, bitter sound. 'Mad is right. You should have seen her when I refused. I confess I let my temper get the best of me. I fear bringing the child back may be my only salvation.'

'So how do we do this? According to what Creek's told me, both Damian and the child will be at the ball, but even with an invitation, they won't let any of us in.'

Dominic tapped a finger against his chin. 'There might be a way.' He made fast eye contact with Chrysabelle before his gaze dropped to a picture of Maris on a side table. 'When your mother and I . . . left the noble life, I created a formula that temporarily changed our appearances. I was still vampire and she was still comarré – I cannot change the core of who someone is – but to the eyes of the nobility, we became someone else, no longer detectable as Dominic and Marissa. I will disguise all of us this way, including my second.'

Mal nodded. 'Excellent.'

'This must be done in Čachtice. I will need nobles to model the images after, blood from them and both of you.' His mouth thinned with uncertainty. 'You trust me? Blood is not to be freely given, as you well know.'

Chrysabelle put her hand on Mal's knee. Did she think he'd balk? He placed his hand on top of hers. 'We're fine with whatever you need.'

'*Bene*. I will have everything with me and begin work on it as soon as we arrive.' He hesitated. 'You should know, I will be taking Katsumi as my second.'

Mal growled deep in his throat. Dominic held a hand up. 'I know you don't like her, but she's an excellent fighter and since the navitas, exceptionally loyal.'

'And your nephew isn't?' Mal asked.

Dominic splayed his hands, lifting his palms up. 'I need Luciano at the club.'

Mal snorted. 'So Katsumi is exceptionally loyal, but not so much that you trust her to run the club alone. Luciano is *caedo*. He's a trained killer. He's *exactly* who we need on this mission.'

Silver edged Dominic's irises. 'Luciano is here because he couldn't complete his last job. He froze. Almost got killed himself. I trust him with my business, but I do not know if I trust him with my life.'

Mal lifted his brows. 'If that's the case, I don't want him at my back or Chrysabelle's either.'

Dominic calmed as Velimai came in with a tray of small sandwiches and set it on the coffee table in front of Chrysabelle, then took a nearby chair.

'*Grazie*. You'll also need clothes for the ball. My formula will change only your facial appearance, not your clothing.' He extended his hand toward Mal. 'If you need, I'm sure my tailor can construct something appropriate for you, but, Chrysabelle, a dress . . . I do not know. A dress fit for a Dominus ball is not something that can be made in a day.'

Velimai tapped her fingernails on the table to get everyone's attention. As soon as Chrysabelle looked her way, she began to sign. For a few minutes, she and Chrysabelle went back and forth, hands moving like pale birds.

At last, Chrysabelle smiled and spoke. 'Velimai says my mother's collection of gowns is extensive and that Nyssa is a wonderful seamstress. She can alter whatever I need.' She looked more confident than when the conversation began.

Dominic knit his fingers together. 'Katsumi and I will leave immediately for Čachtice. It will allow me time to procure everything I need for the disguises and an opportunity to assess the situation. Whatever hangar we are assigned will become our headquarters. You'll just have to look for us when you arrive.'

'Then it's settled,' Mal said. 'We leave tomorrow night.' Once again, he would come face-to-face with the woman who'd been his human wife. The woman who had betrayed him.

Except this time would be the last.

Lola frowned. Chief Vernadetto hadn't touched the good Cuban coffee Hilda had brought in. His visit was a little unusual at this late hour, but nothing she couldn't handle considering every-thing else going on in the city.

'Are you sure you won't reconsider, Madam Mayor?'

'No.' She tapped her spoon before setting it on the saucer. 'Crime is down, isn't it? There have been no other incidents of mischief since the varcolai broke curfew the first night.' She sipped her coffee, the thick black liquid renewing her spirits. 'The curfew is working. In fact, other cities have started curfews of their own. It stays in place.'

Vernadetto sighed. 'The citizens are not happy.'

'You mean the othernaturals? This curfew wasn't set up to punish the othernaturals; it was set up to protect the humans. I know neither side is completely happy, but right now it's the best solution to a difficult—'

'Ma'am, I don't think you understand. The police force alone has lost at least fifty good officers over this.'

She hesitated. 'What do you mean lost?'

'They've quit. The local varcolai groups are urging their members who work for government agencies to resign. The hospital can barely maintain its night staff. One entire ambulance shift has been cut.' A muscle in his jaw twitched. 'Our emergency services are dwindling fast. The city needs these people.'

That explained why Luke and John had left. She smiled anyway. 'If crime is down, we won't need as many emergency services, correct?'

He stood, smoldering like a day old ember. At last, he spoke. 'I'm sorry about your daughter. I'm sorry about your grandchild. But you know what?' He stuck his finger into the air. 'You keep this up and you'll never get re-elected.' He stabbed his finger against her desktop. 'Never.'

'Good night, Chief Vernadetto.' She lifted her cup in his direction. 'Thank you for coming by.'

With a huff, he left, muttering under his breath. *Let him go. Let him be mad. He is the one who is wrong. He is the one who doesn't understand how difficult my job is.* She waited a few minutes to make sure he was gone; then she got up, walked through the house and out the front door.

The new nighttime security officer greeted her. 'Anything I can do for you, ma'am?'

'No, just wanted to make sure the police chief left without incident.' Actually, she wanted another look at him, one of the four new guards she'd hired. He was fringe vampire, but he seemed ... normal enough. Satisfied, she said good night and went back in, but the sense of security she'd had with Luke and John just wasn't there. It would just take some time to get to know the new people, that was all.

She double-checked the locks on the French doors in her bedroom before getting into bed. She lay there, trying to sleep, wondering what was happening with her grandchild, wondering if some other creature would try to get into her room that night, hoping she'd live to see another day and crossing herself against the possibility that she'd never find a vampire willing to give her the power she needed.

Vernadetto was a fool if he thought the curfew wasn't necessary. She sat up in bed. Once again, Vernadetto had stuck his nose into the othernatural problem. She grabbed her cell phone and tapped the last number she'd entered into her speed dial.

It rang twice before the familiar male voice answered. 'Hello?'

'Thomas Creek?'

'Yes, Madam Mayor, that's the number you dialed.'

'I need you to investigate someone for me.'

Chapter Twenty-Nine

'What the hell? Are you sure?' When Doc had arrived at pride headquarters, he'd come straight to his office and called a council meeting to see if there was any way he'd missed a loophole in his mandated marriage.

Omur, the cheetah-shifter, nodded. 'Positive. Your girlfriend was in the club and at least twenty people witnessed the incident. Heaven issued the challenge. There's no getting out of it unless your girlfriend decides not to show.'

Doc slammed his fist onto his desk. 'She can't do this. She'll get killed.'

'As the pride leader's mate, Heaven can do whatever she likes,' Barasa said, his eyes flickering with tiger amber. 'And I doubt your girlfriend will even put a scratch on her. Human-versus-varcolai battles rarely go in favor of the human.'

He stared Barasa down, trying to remember this man was on his side. 'First of all, my girl's name is Fiona. Use it. Second, I was talking about Fi to begin with. And third, I'm well aware of the odds.' He smacked the desk one more time before walking around the side of it. 'Dammit.' What the hell was Fi thinking? Unfortunately, he knew. Once again, she thought she could fix things on her own.

'I'm sorry, Maddoc. I meant no disrespect,' Barasa said.

Doc went back to his desk and collapsed into his seat. 'Fine. Give me the details. I want to know the entire conversation.'

'Neither of us was there, but we have good secondhand knowledge of what went down,' Omur began. 'Basically, Fiona appeared out of nowhere, starting yelling Heaven's name until she appeared, then antagonized Heaven into challenging her. The one upside is that Heaven declared the match would be to death or surrender, so Fiona doesn't necessarily have to die.'

Doc closed his eyes. Things had gone from bad to worse to catastrophic. 'Fiona can't die. Do you understand? I forbid it.'

'Did you have a chance to explain about the divorce allowance to her?' Omur asked.

Doc flicked his gaze to Omur. 'Why do you think this whole thing happened? She's not exactly thrilled about me impregnating Heaven in order to divorce her.'

Omur nodded. 'I can imagine. What do you think Fiona's chances are?'

'I don't know. Not good. She might be a ghost but before she died, she was a grad student. Not exactly a match for a jaguar-shifter who's probably been trained for this kind of combat since birth.' Doc dropped his head back and stared at the ceiling. What a freaking mess this had turned into. There had to be a way to get Fi out of this.

Barasa broke the silence in the office. 'There is a way to give her a better chance.'

Doc picked his head up. 'What's that?'

Barasa glanced at Omur before answering. 'We could train her.'

Creek didn't like being the mayor's personal investigation service, but he liked even less that Yahla had been out to see Mawmaw. He checked the time again. Mawmaw should be well home by now and have had a chance to ward her home against Yahla's return. Warding the whole house meant destroying the feather charm in the process and leaving Mawmaw unprotected, but as long as she stayed inside, she should be fine.

So should he, if everything went according to the plan he and Mawmaw had laid out. He grabbed the feather charm and yanked it off his neck, letting it dangle from his fingers.

His grandmother didn't know much about the Kubai Mata, except what he'd recently told her, but she knew more about the soulless woman than anyone else, except maybe the dead witch Aliza, who had managed to imprison Yahla in her home's structure and tap into Yahla's power to strengthen her own.

He cupped the charm, the feathers cool and silky. He stroked them. Maybe Yahla wasn't so bad. Maybe he was overreacting. Maybe . . . He dropped the feathers onto the kitchen worktable and those thoughts drifted away.

Hell. The soulless woman had bewitched him. His blackouts had all come after contact with her. She'd more than bewitched him. She'd *used* him. He got enough of that from the KM, but at least with them, he got to keep his wits about him.

The talisman taunted him with the blue-black shine of the feathers. The urge to touch the feathers again, to tie it back around his neck, crept over his skin like ants. From here on out, he'd have to rely on the power of the KM to keep him safe. It had kept him alive when attacked by one of the Castus; it should do fine faced with a woman who was more myth and legend than substance and skin.

'Yahla.' He spoke her name without emotion, calling her without tipping her to his anger. She didn't immediately show, so he called again, more sweetly this time. 'Yahla?'

'Hello.'

She was above him, perched on the loft railing. She pushed off and dropped gracefully beside him, the feathers of her hair sailing out around her. 'You've missed me.'

'I have.' He took a step back as she approached. Couldn't let her touch him. Not yet. 'Where have you been?'

She cocked her head abruptly to one side, eyes gleaming and bright. 'You are not the only one who needs me.'

'Should I be jealous?' He came toward her suddenly, testing her.

She startled, flitting backward with a soft cry. 'Jealous? Why?'

'I know how you are with me. What you want from me.' He narrowed his eyes. 'Have you been giving your feathers to other men?'

'No.' Some of the light in her eyes died. 'I have not been with other men.'

He eased up, walking away from her and into the kitchen. He grabbed a water from the fridge to give his hands something to do besides strangle her. 'Then who have you been with?'

She shivered, her feathers rippling around her body. 'Why do you ask so many questions? We should go upstairs.'

'I don't want to go upstairs.' He twisted the cap off the bottle and tossed it onto the worktable. It rolled to a stop beside the discarded charm.

Her eyes followed. 'Why are you not wearing the feathers I

gave you? That your grandmother made?' Her gaze flicked from his bare neck to the charm and back. 'Put it on.'

'I don't think so. Not until you give me some answers.' He took a long drink of water and leaned against the sink. 'Where have you been?'

She jerked her head from side to side. 'I must go.'

Mawmaw had said she'd try to run. And just like she'd told him, he was prepared. He reached next to the sink where he'd set a small dish of salt, scooped up a handful, and tossed it at her. 'Not until I'm done with you.'

She shrieked as the salt touched her, throwing her arms up to shield her face. It bounced off her and scattered, settling into a perfect circle around her. Mawmaw knew her stuff. Yahla quivered with tension. 'Release me.'

'Answer me first. Where have you been?'

'I went to see your grandmother.'

At last, the truth. He slammed the water onto the counter and strode toward her. 'Go near her again and I'll kill you.'

Yahla's eyes went solid, seamless black. 'You cannot kill me. I always come back. There is no death for the woman with no soul.'

'How many times have you possessed me?'

'Twice.' Her gaze flickered to the charm.

That matched the number of blackouts. 'What did you make me do?'

Her mouth took on an ugly shape. 'Made you persuade the mayor to set the curfew. Made you side against the vampire and his whore. All necessary. All to set you free—'

'Shut up.' He grabbed the leather cord off the table and dangled the charm in front of her. 'Why do you want me to wear this so badly?'

'P-protects you,' she stuttered.

He reached back and scooped up another handful of salt. 'I'll ask you one more time. What does this do?'

She cowered as far back as she could within the confines of the circle. 'Opens you up to me and keeps you safe. Otherwise you would die when I left you.'

He had a feeling that wasn't exactly the truth. 'You used me.'

'No more than the Kubai Mata have,' she squawked. 'The othernaturals must be removed. They are polluted with evil. Their blood taints our land.'

'You and I are done. Do you understand? Done. I don't want to see you. No showing up in my bed, no flock of ravens following me on my bike, nothing.'

The whites returned to her eyes and she smiled. 'You cannot be done with me. We are together always. You saved my life.'

'I didn't save your life. You said it yourself – there's no death for the soulless woman. You would have been fine inside the belly of that demon. You trapped me.'

Her smiled stretched farther across her face than was natural, and her hands fluttered at the edge of the circle as if wanting to touch him. 'Let me go and I will show you again how good we are together.'

'I'm going to let you go, but then you're going to leave and never come back. Understand?'

She nodded, the lust in her eyes barely hiding her contempt. He had no doubts she'd try to possess him again as soon as he brushed the salt away. He was counting on it.

He slid his boot out and kicked a hole in the salt circle.

She gathered like a rising storm cloud and thrust forward, plowing into him with the intensity of a hurricane gust. He staggered back with the force, feeling her struggle inside him. He knew instantly this was why she hadn't tried to possess him until he'd worn the charm. Whatever the KM had done to him didn't agree with her; that much was painfully clear.

His ears rang from the inside with her screeching. Out of reflex, he clamped his hands over his ears as he fell to his knees. She was trying to seat herself in him and tearing him apart in the process. Raking his bones with her talons, shredding muscle and sinew as she fought against the power sealed into his flesh.

At last she burst free of him. She hovered before him, barely resembling the Yahla he knew. Smoke trailed off the singed remnants of her feathers; blood dripped from the hooked black beak of her mouth. Her body was a shifting mass of bird flesh and human limbs. She opened her beak once to caw at him, then dissolved into a flock of ravens. They shot straight up, shattering the dirty skylight and raining broken glass over him.

He collapsed as the shards bit into his skin, knowing he was about to pass out but unable to stop it. His last thought was for Mawmaw's safety, his last sight the dirty concrete floor sparkling with broken glass and black feathers.

Chapter Thirty

Chrysabelle closed the door to the hurricane shelter where Mal was catching up on his daysleep, his last kiss still cool on her lips. Calm filled her, despite the situation they were preparing for. Whatever happened, they would face it together, and she had faith that the holy mother would bring them safely back, Damian included.

Velimai met her halfway to the living room. *Mortalis just dropped Nyssa off and is on his way to Dominic's tailor with Mal's measurements. She's having a cup of tea and a muffin in the kitchen. You should eat. It's going to be a long couple of days.*

'I'll eat a big lunch. I'm too wound up to eat right now. I'd rather go upstairs and start looking through the dresses. Which room?'

Last room in the east hall, right next to the gym. The key is in your mother's jewelry box in the bottom drawer.

'I thought that door was another entrance into the gym.'

Velimai smiled wryly and shook her head. *See you in a few minutes.*

Chrysabelle headed upstairs and retrieved the key. It was just where Velimai had said it would be, tucked into the bottom drawer of the jewelry box Chrysabelle hadn't paid much attention to. She hadn't had a reason to, but maybe for this ball she would borrow a few pieces to make her outfit convincing.

Key in hand, she headed down the hall, passing the same rooms she walked by every time she went to train. When things calmed down, she'd investigate the rest of the house. Would Damian want to live here with her? It was as much his house as it was hers. The whole property was. She'd have to talk to the Lapointe Cosmetics board of directors, let them know that the company was half Damian's. Surely the corporate lawyers could take care of that paperwork.

Making plans like that filled her with happiness. Damian would be pleased to know there was something waiting for him when he returned to Paradise City. She smiled wistfully. It might take him a while to come to terms with having a sister. Comarré education gave no place for such intimately connected family. Hopefully he'd be as happy about the news as she was.

If only Maris had lived to know all of this. Chrysabelle's smiled disappeared. No doubt if Maris were still alive, things would be different. She couldn't picture her mother allowing a vampire, Mal or otherwise, into the house or approving of her daughter's relationship with one. Would Chrysabelle be living at Mal's? On her own? Or would things between her and Mal never even have developed?

That thought saddened her more than she expected. No matter how she'd fought her feelings for him, now that she'd accepted them, she couldn't imagine not caring for him. It seemed as natural as breathing. She was still scared of what it meant for both their futures, still learning not to run from the difficult times, still coming to grips with what it meant to make decisions based on two people instead of one, but that's what love was, wasn't it? Compromise? Growth? Finding new ways to do old things?

If not, someone else would have to teach her, because nothing in her background had prepared her for this. The only relationship rules she knew involved the care and feeding of one's patron.

Was that what had come between her mother and Dominic? Chrysabelle expected she'd read the full story in her mother's journals at some point but had found nothing yet, and Dominic didn't seem inclined to talk about it. Whatever had happened between them had left them both scarred and bruised.

Would that ... could that happen to her and Mal? How would she know what to watch out for if she didn't know what she was looking for? Maybe Dominic would give her a few clues. Or maybe she was being silly. Maybe whatever had happened with them would never even be an issue.

She trailed her fingers across the doors into the training room. With the time she'd lost to recovering after being dead and everything else that had been going on, she hadn't sparred in days. She missed it, but when Damian was here, she'd have a permanent training partner. That would be wonderful.

Pausing in front of the storage room door, she fit the key into the lock and turned. After the soft click, she twisted the handle and pushed. The door opened with a soft hiss and a rush of air as the rubber sealing around the frame released. Leave it to Maris to preserve her things with an airtight closet. Chrysabelle felt the wall for the light panel, tapping the softly glowing green button.

The overheads flooded the space with cool light.

Racks of garments lined each side of the long room. At the end, ceiling-high shelves held handbags of every description, shoe boxes, jewelry rolls, and other accessories. Judging by the lack of color present in the clothing, Maris's early days had been a struggle to wear anything that wasn't white just as Chrysabelle's were now.

She walked in, the scent of her mother's perfume almost bringing tears to her eyes. There was no doubt to whom these things had belonged. Chrysabelle caressed the sleeve of one gown, the silk slipping out of her fingers like a whisper.

Behind her, a throat cleared. Chrysabelle turned to see Velimai and Nyssa standing there. She waved at the remnant. 'Hi, Nyssa. Thanks for coming over so early.'

Nyssa nodded and signed, *Happy to help.*

Chrysabelle's hand strayed back to the silk dress, her fingers rubbing the soft fabric. 'Velimai, why are these things in here? They're all beautiful. Why not keep them in the closet in her quarters? She didn't give up wearing white entirely. She wore it much of the time she was here with me.'

Velimai smiled a little sadly and her gaze drifted through the room. Slowly, her hands began to move. *These things ... she loved them very much, but they were a reminder of ...* Velimai's words faded along with her smile. *This is everything Dominic ever bought her.*

The declaration weighted the air with a heartbreaking poignancy. Chrysabelle nodded, not knowing quite what to say but feeling very much as if she'd just entered a shrine. The room held a fortune of things, but the cost wasn't what staggered her. It was the effort that had been made on Dominic's part. The pure display of love and affection that the items represented. And how her mother had packed them away, carefully preserving them but wanting nothing to do with them either. 'He must have truly loved her to buy her all of this.'

Velimai shook her head. *It wasn't just that. Your mother had a hard time leaving the comarré life behind. Perhaps it was the injuries she sustained during libertas or the friends she left behind or knowing that her children were still trapped in that life. Neither Dominic nor I could figure it out, but he did his best to surround her with the things she'd left behind. Beautiful clothes, fine jewels . . . she wanted for nothing. And yet, she was never really happy.*

Imagining her mother longing for something unknown broke Chrysabelle's heart a little. What was it that her mother had missed? Her daughter? Her head suddenly came up. 'Wait, you said neither Dominic nor I. Exactly how long did you work for my mother?'

Long enough. Velimai's gaze hardened, and she gestured toward the racks. *We should pick a dress so that Nyssa can get started with the alterations.*

'Yes, we should. There are so many to go through.' Chrysabelle let the conversation drop. Velimai was a tough nut to crack when she wanted to be. There was no point in pursuing what had happened between Dominic and Maris now, but certainly Velimai knew. Soon, Chrysabelle would get the wysper to explain. Then maybe Chrysabelle would understand better how to be with Mal.

Nyssa helped Chrysabelle go through the racks while Velimai, unable to touch most of the delicate fabrics due to her sandpapery skin, explained the last place Maris had worn each gown or in many cases, pointed out that it had never been worn at all. Indeed, tags dangled off much of what the closet held. Dress after beautiful dress was examined, but nothing quite fit what they were looking for. The dress had to be white and cover a good portion of Chrysabelle's signum in keeping with comarré custom, and it had to be lightweight enough for fighting, with a skirt full enough to hide the slits Nyssa would add so Chrysabelle could easily access the daggers she'd be strapping to her thighs, yet not so full that Chrysabelle would get tangled in the fabric.

'How can there be so many dresses and still not one that works?' Chrysabelle hung yet another gown back on the rack. 'I wish that pale blue gown was white. It comes pretty close.'

Wait, Velimai signed. She walked the racks, peering intently at the garments as she passed. Near the end of the long room, she pointed to a large white box on a shelf near the ceiling. *Get that down.*

Chrysabelle unfolded the stepladder tucked between two rack supports and climbed up. Carefully, she balanced the large box in one hand and came back down. 'What is this?'

A dress that might work. Velimai took the box and set it on the floor, then eased the lid off.

Precisely folded tissue paper covered the garment. Chrysabelle pulled back the first layer of snowy white wrapping. 'Oh.' The word left her like a sigh.

Velimai nodded, waving her hand and urging Chrysabelle on.

She lifted the dress out of the box. The fabric fell loosely, unfolding to reveal a swath of white silk and shimmering lace. 'This is . . . gorgeous.'

Try it on, Nyssa signed, smiling. *Let's see it.*

Chrysabelle shed her loose tunic, pants, and half-cami, then stepped into the dress and eased it over her body. She moved so that Nyssa could zip it and tic the sash around her waist. Then she turned to face the mirror on the back of the door.

And let out the breath she'd been holding.

The skirt was full enough to take the necessary slits, descending from a narrow waist defined by a gold-embroidered sash that looked as if it might have once belonged to a Medici countess. Lace flowed from the straight strapless neckline to hug her upper chest and arms, sheer enough to show off her signum, except that they blended with the design and luster of the lace so well it was hard to tell what was gold and what was lace. It revealed her and hid her at the same time.

'This dress was made for my mother, wasn't it?' Even the gold embroidery on the sash mimicked the curves and swirls of signum. 'It's amazing. Did she ever wear this?'

It was *custom made and it's stunning on you*, Velimai signed. *No, she never wore it.*

'Why not?' Chrysabelle twirled. The skirt flared softly. It would hide the daggers perfectly.

Because she changed her mind about marrying Dominic.

'This was her wedding dress?' Chrysabelle went still. The skirt swished to a stop. She let the significance of the words settle over her as she nodded slowly. 'Then it's the perfect dress to wear to kill Tatiana.'

'Syler's outdone himself, don't you think?' Tatiana cupped the Casablanca lily to her nose and inhaled.

'I do.' Octavian relaxed in an overstuffed chair before a crackling electric fire and sipped from a crystal goblet of blood, fresh from the suite's well-stocked chiller. Lilith played with a doll at his feet. Over and over she bit the doll's neck and laughed.

The suite of rooms Lord Syler had prepared for them was exceptional. Most definitely the best he had. The apartment also adjoined the quarters reserved for Daciana. The staff that they'd brought with them, just Kosmina, Oana, and Daci's dressing maid, scurried about unpacking, putting things away, steaming their party clothes and setting their personal things around. Oana was making up the crib Syler had provided and preparing to put Lilith down for a nap. Poor child hadn't slept at all on the plane.

'I'll be back in a bit. Keep an eye on Lilith?'

Octavian nodded. 'With pleasure.'

Tatiana walked through the suite to Daciana's side. 'Settling in?'

Daci turned from directing her maid and smiled. 'I was just coming to see you. Lovely rooms, don't you agree?'

'I do. Care to walk down to inspect the comar's quarters with me? I'd like to make sure he's properly secured. I will not abide any stupidity on his part. Not here.'

Daci clapped her hands. 'I'd love to. You know, it's so good of you to share him with me the way you have been. Now that I'm Elder, I've decided it's time to get my own. Maybe while we're here in Čachtice.'

Tatiana nodded. 'I can't think of a better souvenir.'

They laughed as they made their way toward the comar's space. Alone in the hall, Tatiana hooked her arm in Daci's and pulled her closer. With a quiet voice, she said, 'There are eyes and ears everywhere. We must be vigilant.'

Daci's pale brows lifted. 'You think someone would make another attempt on Lilith after what happened with Svetla?'

'No. I fear now that they will come after you or Octavian in an effort to weaken what we have created. I just need you to be vigilant at all times.'

With a sincere nod, Daci answered, 'Absolutely.'

'That's all I ask.' Tatiana hesitated as the hall forked. A servant came toward them from the left. 'You there. Which way to the rooms where the comarré are being kept?'

'Back that way, my lady.' He pointed in the direction from which he'd come. 'You'll come to a set of locked double doors. The guard will let you through.'

The servant passed and Tatiana and Daci exchanged a look.

'Locked doors and a guard?' Tatiana laughed softly. 'Syler really isn't taking any chances, is he? I think it's safe to say Damian won't have an opportunity to misbehave.' She tipped her head at Daci. 'Were you serious about buying your own comar?'

'Completely.'

'How about a trip to the Primoris Domus right now?'

Silver brightened Daci's eyes. 'I'd love that.'

'Wonderful. Let's find Syler and have him arrange it this instant.' Tatiana stifled the laugh building inside her. How perfect. Acquiring a comar for Daci would give Tatiana an alternate blood supply should something *unfortunate* befall Damian here in Čachtice.

Chapter Thirty-One

As Doc zipped up his jeans, Fi floated through the bedroom wall of the penthouse. He jumped back. 'Holy hell, you scared the devil out of me.'

She materialized, dropped to the floor, and crossed her arms. 'Somehow I doubt that.' She looked around the room like it was the first time she'd seen it. Something told him that wasn't the case.

He'd thought finding Fi would be the hard part of getting her ready for the fight with Heaven, but apparently he was wrong. Seemed his ability to predict her actions was getting less accurate every day. 'I'm sure you're here because you know Heaven isn't.'

She shrugged, still not making eye contact. 'Yeah, I know. I saw her get into that big limo downstairs. Must be a shoe sale somewhere.' She frowned at the bed and finally glanced at him. 'I need to tell you something.'

'I already know what it is.' He sat on the bed and picked his words carefully. Doing something to send Fi running again would be a bad thing.

She shoved a bunch of Heaven's stuff to one side of the dressing table and plopped down on it. 'I kinda figured. I was hoping to tell you myself.'

'Council filled me in as soon as I got here.'

Her face screwed up into a question. 'The council told you I was sorry about what I said to you at Chrysabelle's?'

'No, they—'

'Because I am really sorry.' She hopped off the dressing table. 'You know I have a little temper sometimes and this whole thing with Heaven is making me crazy.' She walked to the windows and stared out. 'Doesn't change the way I feel about you sleeping with her.' She turned back to him. 'I can't get past that. I just can't.'

'I'm not sleeping with her.'

'I mean to get her pregnant.'

'That why you got her to challenge you to a fight?'

Fi rubbed her nose, then scratched a spot on her head. 'Yes.' She sighed. 'It was a stupid thing to do.'

He nodded. 'At last, something we both agree on.'

'Well, what was I supposed to do? Let her have you?'

'Dammit, Fi, she's not going to—' He stopped, forced himself to lower his voice. 'She's never going to have me, baby.'

Fi looked away, her eyes suddenly big and liquid. 'She's going to kill me, isn't she?'

'No.' He stood up. 'Hell no.' He went over and grabbed her hand. 'Let's go.'

'Where?'

'You'll see.' He pulled her along into the living room. 'Isaiah!'

The butler hurried out from the kitchen. 'Yes, Maddoc?'

'Get Omur and Barasa to the arena, then tell security no one else is allowed in.'

'Yes, sir.' Isaiah went for the phone as Doc punched the elevator button.

He was too hyped to care if Isaiah called him sir or not. They only had a few hours to give Fi some kind of fighting chance. The doors opened and he guided Fi in, then hit nine.

As the doors closed, she asked again, 'Where are we going?'

'To turn you into a fighting machine.'

She frowned. 'Are you making a joke? Because now is not the time.'

'No joke.' The elevator slowed to a stop and the doors opened. Security hadn't arrived yet. Good. He held his hand out. 'This is where all sanctioned challenge battles take place. The arena.'

They stepped out and walked toward the double doors, each side guarded by a towering Bast statue. As they passed, Doc brushed his fingers over the chest of one statue, then touched his heart. Fi needed all the help she could get.

He pushed a door open and let Fi in ahead of him.

'This place is huge,' she whispered. The cavernous space swallowed her words.

'It's meant to hold two prides.' He took her hand, gentler this time, and held it as they made their way to the center of the arena.

She kicked her feet through the layer of sand on the floor. 'Hey, it's like a giant cat box.' She laughed nervously.

'Sand makes the blood easier to clean up.'

'Oh,' she answered. In the great oval space, surrounded by rows and rows of stadium seating, she looked very small to Doc. She pulled her hand out of his and wrapped her arms around her body. 'I can't do this.'

Voices rang out from behind them. 'Maddoc, we're here.'

Fi spun. 'Who are they?'

From behind her, Doc clasped his hands on her shoulders. She was trembling. 'My council members. They've offered to train you.'

She tilted her head to look at him. 'Really?' She glanced at the approaching shifters and smiled a little. 'Guess I'm not the only one who thinks Heaven's the wrong woman for you.'

Omur stuck his hand out in greeting. 'So you're Fiona.'

She shook his hand. 'Yep.'

Barasa offered his next. 'You're a brave woman to fight Heaven.'

'I don't know about brave. Stupid maybe.' She frowned at Doc. 'Love does that to you.'

Both men smiled. Omur nodded. 'Love is a good reason to fight.'

'But now you need to know how,' Barasa said. 'We're going to help you as best we can.'

'How does this' – Fi waved her hands over the arena floor – 'work exactly? Are there rules?'

Omur nodded. 'Very few, but yes. Once a match begins, the first one out of the ring before the other opponent is beaten loses. In the case of a ... a ... ' He trailed off and looked at Doc.

Doc's jaw tightened. 'This isn't a death match. It's a mercy match.'

'Are you sure Heaven knows that?' Fi asked.

'She knows.' Doc motioned toward Barasa. 'Time's wasting.'

'Wait.' Fi put her hand up. 'Doc, can I talk to you alone for a minute?'

'Sure.' He shot a look at Omur and Barasa, but they were already headed for the door. 'Back in five.'

They nodded as they left. He looked at Fi. 'What's up, baby?'

'What Omur said about the first person to step out of the ring. I was thinking . . . ' She bit her lip and flickered a little. 'I might have a plan.'

'Tell me.'

'If I can get her close to me—'

He scowled. 'I don't like this already.'

'But if I go ghost at the right time . . . '

He nodded. 'I see where you going.' He studied the arena. 'You'll have to be positioned just right.'

'I can do that.'

'You'll only get one shot.'

'That's the part that worries me.'

'Then you still need to train.'

'Agreed.'

He whistled loud and long.

Barasa stuck his head through the door. 'You ready for us?'

Doc clapped his hands. 'Let's give her everything we've got.'

For the next few hours, Doc, Omur, and Barasa showed her every trick they could think of, patiently correcting Fi until she got each move right. She was a good student. Not surprising since that's what she'd been when Mal had sunk his fangs into her.

Panting and dripping with sweat, Fi held her hand up. 'One more round and I think I'm done. I won't have anything left for tonight.'

'Enough, then. I'm proud of you. You did great,' Doc said. He didn't want her worn out for what was to come.

Omur nodded. 'You did very well.' He turned to Doc. 'Where is she going to stay until—'

Shouting from outside the arena interrupted him. 'What do you mean no one's allowed in? I'm not no one, you stupid *bunda*.'

Doc rolled his eyes. 'Heaven.' Like the rest of them couldn't tell. 'I'll deal with her.' He kissed Fi, tasting salt on her upper lip. 'One of you take Fi out the back and let her stay at your place until it's time.'

'I was just about to offer,' Barasa said.

Doc squeezed Fi's hand. 'They'll take good care of you, baby. And don't worry about tonight. No matter what happens, you're going to live through it.'

Fi didn't look convinced. 'What if Heaven changes her mind about letting me claim mercy?'

Doc stared into her eyes a long, hard second, trying to see past the scared college student and find the ghost girl who'd lived with Mal's demons long enough to know how to handle herself. 'I'll kill her before that happens.' And in his heart, he knew that's exactly what would happen before he let harm come to Fi.

Barasa stepped forward. 'Omur and I won't let you do that.'

Doc snorted. 'I thought you were here to help.'

Omur nodded. 'We are. What Barasa meant is that we'd do it for you. That way you can remain pride leader.'

Without a word, Doc clasped the other varcolai's hand. 'To victory, then.'

'To victory,' they both responded.

Or death, Doc thought. If a woman had to die in this arena tonight, he prayed to Bast it wasn't Fi.

Lola hung the phone up and pinched the bridge of her nose, but the hospital administrator's voice still rang in her ears. He'd called to complain about losing ten of his night-shift nurses and demanded she lift the curfew.

As angry as his words had left her, she wondered if maybe it wasn't time to do exactly that. She'd have to lift the curfew anyway if she ever managed to become a vampire herself. She drummed her nails on the desk. Why couldn't Dominic have been more cooperative? Surely by now his pocket must be hurting.

She checked the time on her desk clock. An hour until sunset. Her finger tapped the intercom. 'Have the car brought around, please.'

'Yes, ma'am.' Since John had quit, Valerie had cooled toward her. Still doing her job with efficiency, but without the warmth and friendship that had once been there. Yet another casualty of protecting the city.

Lola shook her head as she buttoned up her desk, grabbed her briefcase, and headed out. 'Good night, Valerie.'

Her administrative assistant nodded without looking up from the filing she was doing. 'Good night, Madam Mayor.'

Lola sighed. 'I know you're upset over the curfew and I'm sure your affection for John has—'

'I would prefer not to discuss my private life.' Valerie shut the filing cabinet firmly. 'And yes, like most of the people in this city, I don't care for the curfew, but my opinion isn't going to change it, so I see little point in discussing that either. Is there anything else you need today?'

'No.' Lola walked to the elevator without further comment, her mind made up. In the course of the hour, she went home, changed into more appropriate evening attire, and had her driver take her to Dominic's nightclub, Seven.

As she suspected, there was no crowd outside the velvet

ropes, just two bored doormen. She exited the car and strode forward, refusing to allow herself to be fearful. She was the mayor. Her security team knew where she was. No one would harm her. At least they wouldn't get away with it if they did.

The closer she came to the front door, the more familiar one of the doormen looked. 'John?'

He lifted his chin slightly. 'Madam Mayor.'

'I didn't expect to see you here.' She supposed he had to work, but to take a job that blatantly flaunted the curfew cut her.

'I was thinking the same thing about you.' He tipped his head to look around her. 'You should have security with you.'

'Do I have something to fear?'

'You must. Otherwise there'd be no need for that curfew.'

Touché. 'I'm here to discuss that very thing with Dominic.'

He unclipped the velvet rope separating them. 'I'll lead.'

She gave him a little insincere half-smile. 'How very kind of you.'

He didn't answer, just walked toward the doors, so she sailed after him with a confidence she didn't feel. Inside she was greeted with a second set of red doors painted with gleaming gold dragons. John pushed one open, holding it behind him as he went. A wave of music hit her like a blast of hot air. She blinked, trying to adjust her eyes to the darkness. She'd never been in a club so dark, but then better-than-human night vision was part of being an othernatural, wasn't it? That would be a nice perk.

She shuffled her feet as she eased forward, trying not to run into John. As her inadequate vision adapted to the low light, she realized the club was essentially deserted. Servers milled aimlessly about while go-go dancers leaned against their cages or dangled from their swings. She squinted, trying to find John.

Instead, her gaze hung up on the blond-haired, gold-tattooed men and women sitting around chatting with each other. Her heart clenched. Those were the comarré. Just like her daughter had been. Had any of them known Julia? Maybe she'd talk to a few of them, see if—

'Humans aren't allowed in here. Not without an othernatural.' A server with gray skin and six fingers blocked her path. 'You here with someone?'

'With me.' John stepped between them and took her arm. 'Stay close.' He started off again, pulling her along.

'I was trying to. It's a little dark in here for human eyes.'

He slowed but said nothing. They walked for quite a ways, diverting from the main floor to head through a series of impossibly descending concrete halls lit by phosphorescent paint. After a maze of turns, they stopped outside a door. John knocked. A voice called, '*Sì*, come in.'

John stuck his hand toward the door. 'All you.' Then he walked away.

She swallowed down the fear that had taken hold of her throat again. She could do this. His business was obviously suffering. He needed the curfew lifted much more than she did. Straightening herself, she opened the door and walked into Dominic's office.

Except Dominic wasn't there.

'*Ciao, bella*. What can I do for you?' If not for the fangs he proudly displayed, she wouldn't have been sure the man who'd greeted her was actually a vampire. Something about him just didn't read that way. He was lean and ropey like a long-distance runner, his dark complexion reminding her of Dominic, but with an edge. Despite their one encounter, Dominic had struck her as a smooth character, a man used to getting his way. 'I'm looking for Dominic.'

'Ah, I am so sorry, but Dominic is not available. I am his nephew, Luciano. And you are?'

'I am the mayor of Paradise City, but you can call me Lola.'

'Lola, *cara mia*, it is my great pleasure to meet you.' He took her hand and lifted it to his mouth, brushing his cool lips across her knuckles. She shivered. 'You are a very important mortal, no? Perhaps I can help you with something?'

Being referred to as mortal, important or otherwise, reminded her of her mission. She eased her hand from his grasp as wheels in her head began to turn. She smiled at the plan forming in her thoughts. He smiled back and she had a good feeling this evening was going to go exactly the way she wanted it to. 'You can help me. May I sit?'

'*Mi scusi! Sì*, come in, sit down.' He moved out of her way and held his hand toward a pair of beautiful antique chairs.

'Thank you.' A wealth of antiques filled the office, but the centerpiece was an impressive marble-topped desk. Dominic had expensive taste. He had to be hurting. She took one of the chairs.

Luciano sat across from her, not behind the desk as she'd expected. He pinched the knife-edge crease of his trousers to straighten it. When he looked at her, his eyes held one of the most calculating stares she'd ever seen. It was as though he were sizing her up, measuring how fast she could run, how quickly she'd react. How loud she'd scream. 'My uncle tells me you are the one responsible for the curfew.'

'Yes, I am. That's why I'm here, actually.' How much had Dominic told him? Not too much, hopefully. 'Your uncle and I had discussed the possibility of ending the curfew. Did he mention that to you?'

'No, I am afraid not. You would be so kind as to fill me in?'

Luciano blinked far too little for her liking. She swallowed and prayed that he was telling the truth and that her lies came off sincerely. She crossed her legs. His gaze drifted from her face to watch. The little black dress had been the right choice. 'The matter is simple. I am willing to drop the curfew so that your uncle's business may resume and the lives of all other-naturals will return to their normal routines. However—'

'You want something in exchange.'

She laughed, her nerves showing through more than she liked. 'Isn't that the way of the world?' She rested her elbow on the arm of the chair and stroked the underside of her jaw. Again, his gaze followed. 'I would ask that men of power like your uncle and yourself urge the othernatural community to be patient with the mortal citizens of the city.'

'That is not such a difficult thing.' He sucked his bottom lip between his tongue and teeth, his fangs scraping the skin almost audibly. Then he smiled and this time, it reached his eyes, lighting his entire face with a wickedness that sparked something deep in her belly. Did all vampires cause weakness in mortal women? He leaned forward, elbows on his knees. 'But that is not all you desire, is it, Lola?'

Again, she swallowed, but this time it was to rid her mouth of the saliva pooling there, not to control her fear. If he was using some sort of power over her, it was working. Very well. 'No,' she breathed. Her fingers traced the wide neckline of her dress. If he rejected her ... 'I want to be turned.'

He sat back and squinted as if he didn't understand. 'Turned?'

Her hands dropped to her lap and she twisted the gold and onyx ring on her pinkie. 'I want to be made vampire.' She waited for him to laugh or yell or throw her out. When he did none of those things, she glanced up.

His intense stare met her. 'Why?'

There was no derision in his question, just honest curiosity. It emboldened her to tell him the truth. 'My daughter was one of Dominic's comarré, but she was murdered – maybe you heard about that?'

He nodded ever so slightly.

'Before she died, she had a baby with a vampire named Preacher.'

'I have also heard of him. He is not like the rest of us.'

'No, he isn't.' Except that he wouldn't turn her either. 'The baby is half vampire. And while I have plenty of experience being human, I don't think I can raise a child like that without personally understanding what it means to be a vampire. '

He nodded. 'That seems . . . reasonable.'

'That's not my only reason. I believe being vampire would enable me to be the best mayor possible for Paradise City. I could serve both the mortals and othernaturals equally well. Understand each side and their needs. And ultimately, by becoming a vampire, I would be siding with your kind should any difficulties with the varcolai or fae arise.' She smiled, hoping he saw the logic in her argument.

He tapped his long fingers on his knee. 'You would have no choice but to lift the curfew if you were vampire.'

Light filled her vision. 'That's right.'

'Being sired is painful. Frightening.' His voice became quieter, more serious. 'Some do not survive.'

'I know and I am prepared. Pain does not frighten me. I have lost a child. What greater pain can there be? And I know I will survive because I want it so badly.'

He stood and held his hand out to her. 'Come. This is not the place. And I have . . . requirements of you before we undertake this thing, yes?'

She hesitated in taking his hand. 'Are you saying you'll turn me?'

'I am, *cara mia*.' He laughed softly. 'But not until I am satisfied.'

Chapter Thirty-Two

The chartered jet was in the hangar just as planned when Mal and Chrysabelle arrived that evening. The plane wasn't as large as Dominic's but it would do. Mal had to hand it to Mortalis. When the fae said he'd do something, he did it. Jerem pulled Chrysabelle's car inside and popped the trunk to unload their things while she and Mal got out.

'You're late,' Mortalis called out as he jogged down the jet's steps.

'Dominic's tailor had to make a few adjustments to my suit,' Mal answered. 'Plus we stopped at the freighter on the way.'

Mortalis nodded. 'That's fine. We're fueled and ready to go. I'll help with the bags.'

'Thanks.' Chrysabelle went around to the trunk, pulled her sacres out, and slung them over her shoulder. Even though she couldn't bring the swords into the ball, she'd brought them anyway. Mal couldn't say as he blamed her. There was comfort in being well armed. She took one small bag from the trunk while Jerem got the rest. 'Where's the pilot? I'd like to meet him.'

'I'm right here.' A familiar gray-skinned figure waved from the jet door.

'Amery!' Chrysabelle waved back as she walked toward the jet. 'I didn't know you flew.'

'One of my many talents.' He came down a few steps. 'Malkolm, nice to see you.'

Mal grabbed the handle of his worn leather satchel. 'You too, kid.' Having another fae on board wasn't a bad thing. Amery had been helpful enough when they'd been in New Orleans. If the need came to defend the plane against vampires, the shadeux and their ability to possess soulless creatures would come in very handy.

A few minutes later, they were on board. Mortalis secured the door. 'I'll be in the cockpit with Amery if you need me.'

'Thank you.' Chrysabelle took the seat next to Mal and fastened her safety belt. Her arm pushed against his as she got comfortable. The movement stirred a fresh waft of her enticing perfume around him.

He growled softly, opening his mouth to let that velvet scent tease across his tongue.

She smiled shyly. 'You need to feed. We'll take care of that as soon as we're up, okay?'

'I'm . . .' He was about to say *fine*, but that wasn't the truth. He *did* need to feed. *Drink her, drain her, all of her.* 'When we're up.' He tipped his head back against the seat as the jet taxied out of the hangar. How was he going to go back to drinking her blood out of a glass after tasting it from her vein?

He closed his eyes, lost in the thought of being able to pull her into his arms and hold her as he sank his teeth into the pale expanse of her gilded throat, the way she'd clutch him and inhale, the way their bodies— He abruptly opened his eyes and shifted in his seat. That line of thought was going to make for a very long plane ride.

Chrysabelle laid her hand on his arm as the plane shot forward and the g-force of liftoff pushed them into their seats. 'You okay?'

He nodded. 'Just thinking.'

'About how you'd rather bite me again than drink from a glass?' She laughed. 'No, I can't read minds, but your eyes are about as silver as a new coin and if your face shifts any further, you might break a bone.'

He forced his human features back into place. 'Sorry.'

'Don't apologize.' Her lids lowered and one side of her mouth tipped up. 'I was thinking about it, too.'

Her words sent a bolt of heat into his belly. He squelched it. 'No point in thinking about it. Can't happen. I won't risk killing you.'

'Are you sure?' Her hands gripped the armrests. 'We did it once and I'm still alive.' The plane started to level out. 'Besides, even if you do accidentally drink too much, you can't kill me. You might knock me out for a day or two, but then I'll be as good as new.'

He twisted to face her. 'I was chained up. That's not the same as being in a confined space with me. And we don't know that you'll survive dying again. You're assuming that.' He glared at her. 'If you're going into this confrontation with Tatiana thinking it's okay to die, you'd better get your head on straight. You take one foolish chance and I will pull you out of there so fast—'

She clamped her hand over his mouth until he stopped talking. 'There's the Mal I'm used to. Bossing me around, telling me what to do. You must have been chomping at the bit, huh? Feel better now that you've gotten that out?'

'I'm serious.'

Her eyelids fluttered as she inhaled. 'Yes, I know you are. I don't plan on taking any unnecessary chances, but this isn't just Tatiana we're about to face. It's the upper crust of vampire nobility. Something goes wrong and neither of us is getting out of there alive, which is why you need to keep your strength up. You need to be able to scatter in case that's the only option you have left.'

'I won't leave you behind.' *Too bad.*

'You won't have to.' She reached up and cupped her hand against his cheek. 'I kind of missed bossy Mal.'

'I'm not biting you.' *Do. Drain her.*

She patted his cheek. 'Yes, you are. If things go poorly, Mortalis can slip inside you and pull you off me. It'll be fine, you'll see.' She unlocked her safety belt and got up. 'I'll be right back.'

'Chrysabelle.' But she kept walking until she reached the cockpit. Fresh fear rose up like bile in his throat. He agreed that being at full power for what they were about to face was important, but not at her expense. What if the beast took over? Could Mortalis wrest control of that much darkness? He looked out the window into the pitch-black night. The face reflected back was the ugly reminder of just how much of a monster he was. He turned away. Laughter rang in his head.

Doing this was a very bad idea. *Do it do it do it.* The voices were proof of that.

Chrysabelle came out of the cockpit, Mortalis behind her. Mal shook his head slowly and stared at the tan carpeting covering the walkway, his jaw popping to one side.

She sat beside him, reaching for his hand. 'Ready?'

He pulled away. 'No.'

Mortalis took the seat opposite them. 'It would be better to try this now before you need the blood so badly your control is undermined.'

'It would be better not to do this at all.'

'I won't let you hurt her.'

Mal got out of his seat. 'You think you can control what's inside me?'

Mortalis scratched one of his horns. 'There's only one way to find out, isn't there?'

Something nudged Creek's side. He opened his eyes, wondering if his lids were the only part of him that didn't hurt.

'What the hell happened to you?' A black shadow stood over him. Annika.

Slowly, he pushed to his knees. Shards of glass pinged to the concrete. He blew out a slow breath, his insides aching like they were sunburned. Yahla had done a number on him when she'd been in there. 'Damn it. What time is it?'

'Couple hours after sunset. Why?'

He'd been out too long. Hopefully Yahla was still recovering from her last attempt to possess him. That would buy him some time. Whether or not it would be enough time remained to be seen. He got to his feet and brushed his hand over his head, loosening one last splinter of glass from his Mohawk. 'I gotta go.'

'Not until you answer some questions.'

A little ambient light spilled through the broken skylight, turning the floor of the old mechanics shop into diamonds. 'My grandmother's in trouble. I have to go help her.'

'Spent the grocery money on bingo again?' Annika smiled.

He narrowed his eyes at her. Up until that point, he'd almost started to like Annika. 'I'm going to pretend you didn't just insult my grandmother, because I have a thing about not hitting women.'

Her smile disappeared. 'Sorry. I didn't – I like your grand-mother. What kind of trouble could she be in?'

There was no point in hiding what had happened. 'Yahla.'

'What's that?'

'The woman you smelled on me the first time you visited.' He snagged his motorcycle helmet off the work-table. 'I'm pretty sure she's going after my grandmother to get revenge on me.'

'Why?'

'Long story I don't have time for.' He grabbed his crossbow and his halm.

'A fight? I like a good fight.' Annika's smile returned. 'When do we leave?'

'Sure, you can come, thanks for asking.' He rolled his eyes as he went to open the door. Pushy women plagued his life. Hopefully after tonight, there'd be one less.

'This Yahla, is she really that dangerous?'

He stopped, hand poised above the door's locks, and turned to look at her. 'Argent killed her once. It didn't take.'

Annika's brows lifted above her permanent shades. 'Argent was here? We were starting to think he was dead.'

'Oh, he's dead all right.' Creek shoved the metal door back. 'Yahla made sure of that.'

Annika followed after him. 'Explain.'

He went back for the second helmet, glad for the wireless comms that would let them chat. 'Ride with me. I'll tell you on the way.'

By the time they got to his grandmother's road, Annika knew everything that had happened with Yahla from the first time Creek had met her. He slowed the bike as they approached the little house. Annika's arms loosened from his waist. Up ahead, his grandmother's metal roof came into view above the mangroves and pepper trees lining the dirt road. The metal gleamed in the starlight and a soft curl of smoke drifted from the chimney pipe. Everything appeared normal, but he knew with Yahla, normal meant nothing.

He parked the V-Rod at the end of the long driveway and slipped his helmet off, then leaned back to Annika. 'Stay quiet.'

She nodded, removed her helmet, and got off the bike. He did the same, then motioned for her to follow him. Mawmaw's porch light brightened the night enough that he could see perfectly. He hugged the line of sawgrass and pines that bordered the property line. After that, it dropped off into impassable swampland. He kept an eye out for gators, pythons, and anything else he didn't want to step on.

Together they crept toward the back of the house. It was too quiet. The glades at night should be loud with buzzing insects, croaking frogs, and gator calls, but all he could hear was Annika's breathing. Even Pip hadn't barked to announce their arrival.

A yell pierced the quiet. Mawmaw's voice. He ran for the back porch, Annika behind him. No longer caring about being quiet, he sprinted up the steps and skidded to a stop.

The sliding door was open and half off its track. Just in front of it, like she'd almost gotten inside, Mawmaw sprawled on her stomach, one arm stretched toward the sawed-off pool cue his grandfather used to carry around in his pickup truck.

'Mawmaw, what happened?' He started forward, but the air above her smudged with smoke and feathers.

Yahla stepped out of the house, cocked her head at him, and frowned. 'You are late.'

Chapter Thirty-Three

From what Tatiana could see, Čachtice's Primoris Domus occupied a slightly smaller estate than Corvinestri's but was no less grandly appointed. The center hall of the main building, the only one she and Daci would be allowed entrance to, dripped with crystal, artwork, and gilding just as the comarré estate in Corvinestri did. Obscene, really.

The woman in charge here, Madame Vilma or Velma or something, was just as uptight, just as militant about them not stepping a foot beyond the center hall. Apparently, Syler's insistence that Daci be allowed to purchase a comar despite there being no prior appointment had flustered her. As if Tatiana and Daci would even want to see more of the place. Tatiana had been down the halls of the Corvinestri house. Those dull little cells held no attraction.

She snorted softly.

'What is it?' Daci asked.

'How these comarré live and the way they act considering how well they're paid.' She shook her head. 'Look at this luxury. And for what? A little blood? A little power?' She leaned into the brocade sofa and crossed her arms. 'And they call us parasites.'

'Ladies.' The voice came from behind them. Daci twisted in her seat. Tatiana merely lifted enough to look over the back of the sofa. The comarré housemother stood waiting. Had she heard what Tatiana had said? Not that it mattered, except she might further inflate the comar's blood rights. 'My available comars will be out shortly. Is there anything else you need?'

'No, thank you,' Daci answered. 'Just the comars.'

The woman nodded her blond head and disappeared down a hall. Daci leaned in. 'How much do you think this is going to cost me?'

'As much as they can get out of you. Primoris Domus comarré are the most expensive and the best quality.'

'Which is why they're the only house allowed within vampire city limits. I know that, but no one ever really talks about how much it takes to purchase blood rights.'

'That's a requirement of the paperwork you'll sign. You agree not to reveal what you've spent.' Tatiana rolled her eyes. 'That's part of their *mystique*.' She thought for a moment. 'We could always go outside the city to one of the lesser houses, but I'm not sure we have that kind of time here in Čachtice. Maybe when we get home to Corvinestri?'

'No, no.' Daci shook her head. 'I want a Primoris Domus comar and I want one now. I want to show him off at the ball. I am the House of Tepes Elder, after all. I just hope I pick the right one.'

'Ask the questions I told you to ask and you'll be fine.' Not that she'd fared that well with Damian, but how was she to know he'd turn into such a problem? At the time, he'd been the cream of the comar available, and there had been no question of whether or not she'd purchase his blood rights, just the negotiation as to how much she'd pay.

The sudden rush of blood scent filled the room, causing both women to gasp softly.

'Here we are,' the headmistress announced as she walked into the hall's open space. Behind her followed four comars. All blond, all blue eyed, all dressed in white, and tattooed in gold. Each one a perfect specimen of their breed.

Tatiana watched as Daci scrutinized the men standing before her, although calling two of them men was a fair stretch considering they probably weren't more than seventeen. She sat back to see how Daci would do.

Daci strolled both sides of the row of comars with a practiced nonchalance, getting a good look at each one. Then, without the slightest indication of her feelings upon her face, she stopped in front of Madame Vilma. 'Have any had their blood rights purchased before?'

Madame Vilma nodded at the last one, also the oldest by his looks. 'Daniel has. Unfortunately, his patron passed on but Daniel's returned to us, eager to serve another.'

'He's dismissed.' Daci waved her hand like she was pushing him away.

Tatiana smiled. Her Elder was doing well.

As that comar left, Daci asked her second question. 'Which one is the youngest?'

'Jonah,' Vilma commanded. 'Step forward.'

'His age?' Daci asked.

'Sixteen.'

Daci went to stand before the boy. He was easily a head taller than her and his broad body eclipsed her slim build. She leaned in and inhaled. He stood motionless under her scrutiny. She shifted her face and dropped her fangs, opening her mouth to breathe in his scent. He didn't flinch, but his cheeks flushed the deep red of strong blood. The sight made Tatiana's gums ache. This was the one.

'My lady,' he murmured, dropping his head a few centimeters.

Daci smiled and pulled back. She nodded, casting a glance at Tatiana before speaking to the housemother. 'He'll do.'

Tatiana covered her mouth to hide her prideful smile. The slightest twinge of jealousy bit at her, knowing that Daci would be the first to break that boy's tender skin and taste the life that flowed in his veins.

She'd never wanted to rid herself of Damian so badly.

Fi couldn't stop trembling. Beyond the ready room, the noise of the gathering crowd in the arena filtered through. The crowd that was going to watch this madness unfold. The crowd that would cheer Heaven on, because Heaven was one of their own.

All of them varcolai. All of them, save Doc, Omur, and Barasa, here to watch Heaven destroy her.

Heat built at the back of Fi's eyes. Heat that meant tears. Why had she done this? She tipped her head back. She would not cry. No way in hell. She might be scared. And stupid. But she wasn't going out there looking like a crybaby who'd suddenly realized what a jack-witted thing she'd done. Besides, she knew what she needed to do when she got out there.

She breathed a few steadying breaths and forced herself to run through the moves Omur and Barasa had taught her. Just in case. The way to move when Heaven lunged, how to anticipate a punch, how to take a punch.

How not to die.

'Mercy,' Fi whispered, tasting the word to see how bitter it was. She didn't plan to use it, because using it meant losing Doc, but if not using it meant dying, she might. Dying would give Heaven complete access to Doc. Unless . . . Fi sat down on the narrow bench attached to the wall. Would she actually die? Or would she just be unable to return to a solid form? Or worse. Fi shuddered. If she died and got stuck in that nightmarish loop of repeating the day Mal had killed her . . .

She got to her feet. That wasn't a chance she was willing to take. Not with the old witch Aliza dead. Who would cast the spell to get her out of the loop if it happened again? She shook her head and began to walk the perimeter of the room.

Doc burst in. 'Fi.'

The tears she'd been holding back rose up fresh, spilling down her cheeks. She ran to him, buried herself against his hard body. 'This has got to be the stupidest thing I've ever done.'

'Hey now.' He petted her hair as she sniffled into his chest, then gently pulled her back. 'I think we both know falling in love with me was the stupidest thing you ever did.' He smiled and winked, but his eyes mirrored the fear she was feeling.

She smiled back anyway, knowing that was what he wanted. 'I'm afraid.'

He frowned. 'Your plan's going to work. I know it will. And don't be afraid of Heaven. Please, baby, you've already been through worse than anything that woman can dish out. You died twice, for Bast's sake. You've lived with all the crap that goes on in Mal's head. Heaven can't be scarier than that.'

'She's not. I'm afraid of losing you.' She sniffed and wiped her nose on the sleeve of the oversized jumpsuit she'd been issued. At least the boots they'd given her fit. Didn't hurt that fashionista Heaven would have to wear one of these getups too. It was supposed to help even the playing field. 'And you're right.' She nodded. 'I can do this.' But those words were for him. Inside, doubt raged. Would Heaven really let her cry mercy if something went wrong? Somehow she didn't think so. 'It's going to be fine.'

His smile returned. 'That's the spirit.' He kissed her, too briefly. 'I have to go. I gotta visit Heaven. Not supposed to even be here, actually.' He shrugged, looking embarrassed about what he'd just admitted. 'That'll all change soon enough.'

'It's okay. I understand.'

He backed toward the door. 'One move and this is all behind us.'

She nodded. 'One move.'

His smile broke down. 'See you when it's over.'

She just nodded again, unable to find words. He shut the door. She went back to the bench, bent her head into her hands, and began running through the training once again just in case her plan didn't work.

The door opened a second time. Barasa slipped in, closing the door quickly behind him. 'I just have a second; they're coming to get you. Draw the fight out as long as you can. Understand?'

'I understand, but I don't think it'll be necessary.'

Barasa hesitated, then patted her arm. 'I hope you're right, but if not, tire her out. And remember what we showed you.' He turned toward the door like he'd heard something. 'Best of luck. Must go.'

And then he was gone.

Odd, but she didn't have time to think about his strangeness, because seconds later, two big varcolai showed up to take her to the arena. They walked her down the hall and when the doors opened before her, the noise of the crowd rolled over her like a tsunami.

The guards stopped her at the edge of the arena. 'Whoever leaves the ring alive, leaves victorious.'

Fi twisted sharply. 'This isn't a death match. Death *or* mercy.' Unless something had changed. Wouldn't Doc or Barasa have told her? Panic scratched at her throat. 'Right?'

The guard shrugged, then grunted, 'Forward.'

She didn't move. 'Not until you answer me.'

The second guard laughed. 'It's death or mercy. But a human against one of us? Death would be mercy.'

She opened her mouth to argue, but he shoved her toward the arena. 'Get in the ring or forfeit. Now.'

She stumbled forward, fear making her feet leaden and her muscles loose and rebellious. The varcolai stayed behind as she stepped over a raised lip that separated the grated metal from the sand. A light flared above her, trapping her in a blinding circle. The crowd exploded, chanting words she was glad she couldn't understand. The impact of what was about to happen crushed her chest like a falling building. She focused on the only thing she could see, the sand, and tried to shut everything else out. The sand was soft and white as sugar. The tiny grains sparkled like little stars. Like diamonds.

Like Mal's eyes when he was angry.

She closed her eyes. What would Mal do in this situation? He'd fight until he dropped. Until he had nothing left. Just like when he'd been in the Pits. She nodded to herself. That's what she'd do, too, if her plan didn't work. No one would be able to say she hadn't given it her best shot.

And Doc would know that she'd died loving him enough to lay it all on the line.

With a fresh boom of noise, the crowd's chanting broke through her thoughts. She looked up, peering through the light.

Heaven walked toward her from the far side of the arena. Even from a hundred feet away, Fi could see her jumpsuit fit like haute couture, her hair and makeup flawless, her combat boots shiny. As the spotlight above her came to life, she stopped, raised her hands, and waved to the crowd. They cheered back.

Fi felt like the girl who hadn't made the pep squad all over again. Not that she'd ever really wanted to be a cheerleader. They were all so shallow. And slutty. Anger overtook fear. Why was she scared of this prissy little Brazilian chick? So what if she had the wardrobe that Fi had always wanted. That was *all* she was going to have because no way was Fi letting Heaven take her man. No girly-girl who'd had life handed to her on a silver platter was going to beat Fi; that was for damn sure.

Fi dug her feet into the sand, planted her hands on her hips, and lifted her chin to survey the crowd for Doc. Row after row of varcolai eyes met hers, some golden, some gleaming, all filled with anticipation. Except Doc's. She found him in the pride leader's box, the chair beside him empty. And waiting. Fi nodded. That was her chair and she'd take her place there, just as soon as she showed Heaven what she was made of.

She looked back at Heaven, still standing at the opposite end. Heaven made eye contact with her and a slow smile upended the corners of her mouth. She started forward again with a weird, loping gait.

Fi just watched, slightly puzzled. Talk about running like a girl. She hunkered down, digging her feet in a little more and lowering her center of gravity in preparation. She'd expected a bell to ring or someone to shout, 'Go' or *something* to let her know the fight had started, but whatever. This was going to be so freakin' easy—

Suddenly, Heaven leaped. Midair, she shifted into her jaguar form. She landed and kept running. Straight at Fi.

The crowd yowled in approval.

Fi held her ground. Only yards separated them now. Her heart pounded louder. This would work, wouldn't it? It would. If she timed it right. If she didn't—

With a snarl, Heaven leaped again.

Chapter Thirty-Four

When Luciano had told Lola he'd wanted to be satisfied before he'd turn her, this was not what she'd expected. For several hours they'd sat in his apartment, a beautifully decorated suite of rooms so deep within the bowels of the building that they physically shouldn't exist, and done nothing but talk. Or rather she had.

He'd wanted her to recount in detail her favorite sunny days. And so she had. Days spent at the beach, days with family, when Julia had been young and still her sweet little girl, busy spring days working in the garden, lazy fall days swinging in the hammock with a drink and a good book, stormy days that ended with rainbows and air that sparkled in the sun.

He'd sat in a dark corner far away from her, and although her eyesight and her hearing couldn't compare to his, she was pretty sure he'd wept during her descriptions. If he'd meant to make her doubt her decision, he hadn't. He'd only strengthened her convictions. Made her impatient for the change.

He rolled his hand through the air. 'Tell me more.'

'I have nothing left to tell you.' She pushed to her feet. 'Please. Time is running out.'

'Soon you'll have nothing but time.' He stood and in an instant was in front of her. What would it feel like to move that fast? He held out his hand. 'Come.'

She took it and he led her to the bed. At last, he was going to sleep with her as she'd originally thought. She was ready and willing. It wouldn't be such a sacrifice. He was handsome and charming and possessed the same dark allure all vampires seemed to. Her body would welcome the use after the years she'd gone without. Not since her divorce if she counted the time. Being mayor made dating difficult. Few men wanted the scrutiny.

'Lie down,' he told her. 'Make yourself comfortable.'

She did as he asked. 'Do you want me to take my clothes off?'

'What?' His mouth opened quizzically. 'Why would I want you to do that?'

'I thought . . . Don't you want to sleep with me?'

His face stayed blank for a moment; then he burst into laughter. '*Cara mia*, you are *human*. Perhaps when you are turned, but now?' He shook his head. 'You will understand soon enough. There are some of us who have sex with humans, but' – he raised his brows and tilted his head as he lifted one shoulder – 'they do not plan to let them live anyway. Do you understand what I am telling you?'

'Yes.' She swallowed the wave of fear. This was what she'd asked for. And once she was turned, nothing else would matter. 'I also understand I have a lot to learn.'

He sat beside her on the bed, their hips touching. 'And I will teach you.' He placed his hand on her rib cage, just beneath her breast. 'Calm your breathing. Your heart beats like a hummingbird's wings. The change will be easier if you relax.'

'As much as I want it, it's still a hard thing to relax for.' She blew out a long slow breath and stared up at the intricately painted ceiling. The blue sky and darting birds seemed very unvampire like. 'How many others have you turned?'

'Sired,' he corrected her. 'And I have sired ... enough. When they were needed. My house – you understand what this means? All noble vampires come from one of five houses or families. I am House of Paole. It is a small one. Many think we are not so powerful, but we are.' He shrugged again. 'We can be.'

'And because you're my sire, I'll be that house as well?'

'Yes.' He smiled. 'You are quick.'

'You don't get to be mayor by being slow.'

He laughed. 'I suppose not.' He squeezed her side where his hand still rested. 'And now you are more relaxed, yes?'

'Yes. I feel ready.' Or as ready as she was going to be.

'Good.' His face shifted into the jutting mask of bones she'd seen before on Malkolm and Dominic. The face she'd soon wear herself. He bent over her.

She flinched, then laughed. 'I'm sorry. I'm not afraid. I'm really not. I'm just ... human.'

He leaned on his forearm, his upper body resting lightly on hers. With a gentle look that seemed misplaced on the monstrous face before her, he brushed his fingers down her cheek. 'I understand.' He placed a kiss on her jaw.

His cool mouth on her skin sent a shiver through her, alighting every nerve that had been poised to snap at the first instance of pain. His mouth went lower, down her neck. Goose bumps rose across her body and she arched into him, tipping her head back to give him greater access. She closed her eyes and murmured her approval.

The bite came immediately. The pain blossomed out from where his teeth were buried in her neck. She swallowed and clung to him, forcing herself not to cry out or pull away. But a few moments later, the pain faded and pleasure verging on the edge of orgasmic spiraled through her. She was on the bed, but falling, spinning through blissful waves of heat and pressure.

Air shuddered through her lungs, catching in her throat. Faster and faster she plummeted downward. Shadows rose up to meet her, a silky drift of murky longing. The longing grew sharper, the pleasure dissipated, and alarm took its place.

Death had come for her.

The urge to fight pressed hard, heating the air in her throat to a blazing furnace. Her lungs burned, but relief was gone, lost in the sharp spines of pain that held her in place. She dug her fingers into Luciano, clawing at him but all the while willing herself to accept.

He clamped down harder and then ... blackness.

The pain was gone, and along with it the need to breathe and the desire to live. A tiny pinpoint of light beckoned to her, so distant it could have been a star. She floated, no way to move toward it, no body to command. The light shifted into the shape of her *abuela*'s face. She reached out, tried to speak, but she was nothing.

Abuela's face disappeared.

Bittersweet liquid coated her tongue. She turned away from the foul taste, but it clung to her. The wetness clogged her mouth and ran down her chin.

'Drink.' The command was hollow and distant, as if spoken through a tube miles away.

Her throat convulsed, but the convulsions didn't stop there. They echoed through her, lighting an icy spark that fired a hunger unlike anything she'd ever felt. She sucked at the source of the liquid. Blood, her new brain told her. *Blood that is now life*.

Her body came back to her, weakly at first and hard to control, like a toddler's. Shaking, her hands reached up for the limb that pressed against her mouth. Her eyes opened.

As crystalline as if cut from glass, Luciano smiled down upon her. It was his wrist she clung to, his blood she swallowed. 'That's it.' He nodded. 'Drink.'

She did, trying to ignore the sounds drilling into her head. The tick of the clock on the bedside table, the soft gurgle of water through pipes, the scurry of tiny feet somewhere very far away. She inhaled out of habit and a thousand scents filled her nose. Dust, fabric, cleaning chemicals, cosmetics, water, but above all . . . blood.

'That's enough, *cara mia*.' Luciano pulled his wrist out of her fingers with a small struggle. He nodded. 'Already your strength grows.' He licked clean the blood left behind, the twin puncture wounds healing before her eyes.

'I need more.' Need did not begin to describe the craving in her belly.

'I know. Your hunger will be overpowering for a few days.' He patted her leg. 'I'll get you some more right now. Stay in this room, understand?'

'Yes.'

'*Bene*. I shall return shortly.'

As soon as he left, she jumped off the bed. Literally. The small amount of effort she exerted landed her several feet away. She walked to an overstuffed club chair taking up a corner of the room, reached down, grasped one of its bun feet, and lifted. Single-handed, she brought it above her head.

Amazing.

She dropped the chair and her hands went to her face, feeling for the strange angles of her new nature. The hard ridges rose over her cheekbones and brow. A mirror. She tried the door on the right side of the room. It opened into a large bath.

She flicked the light switch and blinked as the illumination flooded the space. The grains of sand in the tile's grout lines were visible. How was that even possible? She turned toward the gold-hued mirror.

The monstrous face she'd expected to see stared back at her with the same silvery gaze the rest of the nobles had. She ran her fingers over her skin, studying each new slope and rise. Peered closer at her luminous eyes. Not monstrous. Powerful. Intimidating. Noble.

Human face. But the thought only caused her human face to flicker over her skin. She concentrated and it came back. She leaned in. The fine lines around her eyes and mouth were gone, her forehead smooth. Not a strand of gray showed through the root line where her color was growing out. In fact, there was no root line anymore, just a head full of silky, bouncy brunette hair. And her eyes . . . her eyes had never been anything special, but their ordinary brown was gone, replaced by a hundred shades of the same color. Her eyes were spectacular.

The moment she stopped concentrating on her human face, it disappeared and her vampire one returned.

Curling her lips back, she turned her head side to side to see the fangs that now jutted from her upper jaw. Also intimidating. She growled at herself, then laughed at her childishness. Her tongue tested the fangs' sharpness. The jagged tip of one pricked the surface and caused a small drop of blood to well up.

Saliva pooled in her mouth and her stomach clenched. She swallowed and looked back toward the door. If Luciano didn't return soon, she'd have to head out on her own. She couldn't go much longer without—

The suite door opened. 'Lola? I've brought you a decent meal.'

She stepped out of the bathroom and a new emotion swelled alongside her hunger.

Luciano had brought one of Dominic's comarré with him. The slim young man smiled at her, his eagerness spilling off him like a delicious perfume, but everything about him – his gold marks, his bleached blond hair, his age – reminded her of the last time she'd seen Julia.

'Bloody hell,' Mal snarled. 'This isn't a game.' He was fully aware that his anger came from fear. The fear that he'd hurt Chrysabelle. Or worse. The voices applauded.

Chrysabelle exhaled slowly. 'So you acquiescing to my every desire over the past few days was due to some fugue state born out of your joy at still being alive?'

'Life with me is never going to be easy. I told you that.'

She nodded. 'Yes, you did.' She hesitated like she was looking for the right words. 'I know this isn't a game. It's your life. It's *our* life. For what we're about to go up against, you need to be at your most powerful. Drinking my blood out of a plastic cup isn't going to get you there.'

'I've made it through worse with less.' *What you deserved.*

'But you don't have to this time.' She grabbed the hand he'd pulled away from her. 'Stop fighting me. We've done this once already without Mortalis there to protect me. It's going to be fine.'

He glared at her. 'The last time we did this, I had chains the size of tree trunks holding me back. And they were starting to give.'

'But they didn't.' Mortalis gave Mal a stare that had frustration written all over. 'And she's right. You need to go in strong. The numbers are not on our side this time.'

Mal leaned back, casting his gaze at the twin strips of overhead lighting. Chrysabelle's fingers caressed the palm of his hand. He closed his fingers over hers. 'You're asking a lot of me.'

'I know,' she said. 'But if I'm willing, you should be, too.'

He tipped his head to look at Mortalis. 'You're sure you can do this? Sure you can manage the beast if I can't?'

Mortalis nodded. 'If I can't, Amery will step in to help, too.'

'Great,' Mal cracked. 'Two shadeux inside me. Sounds like a freaking picnic.'

'Mal.' Chrysabelle's voice went soft and breathy, and she leaned into him, her warm body pressed against his. The small contact was enough to amp up his hunger and spin the voices into an unbearable whine. She blinked, her blue eyes pleading. 'Do this for us.'

He dropped his chin, and after a moment stared up at her from his lowered lids. 'You and I are going to talk later.'

She canted her head to one side. 'About what?'

'About the inappropriate use of feminine wiles.'

She smiled and, damn it, he liked it. 'That's a yes, then?'

He nodded. Doc was right. Love had made him soft. *And stupid.*

'Do you want me to sit on your lap?'

'No.' The word came out louder and sharper than he'd intended, but her question had driven home just how intimate an act they were about to partake of in front of Mortalis. Mal had never been an exhibitionist, and he wasn't about to start now. 'Just sit where you are. Give me your wrist.'

Her frown morphed into a more understanding look, and she extended her arm. Without another glance at Mortalis, Mal rested his hands beneath her wrist. The flesh there was unadorned, the signum scrolling away from the spot where the veins showed through her pale skin. He closed his eyes as he took her scent into his body. Son of a priest, she undid him, and despite the fae's presence, Mal let out a soft sigh of pleasure.

Her heat traveled through his fingertips, urging him on. His face shifted and his fangs dropped. Lifting her wrist higher, he pressed his mouth to her skin and bit down.

She inhaled, a half gasp, half laugh that shot straight to his remaining humanity and reminded him what it felt like to be a breathing, daywalking, warm-blooded man who had once known the pleasure of a woman.

The voices drowned that feeling in seconds, their cries and whimpers filling his head until the chaos scratched at his skull. He sucked at the bloodstream harder, wanting this over before the inability to stop overpowered him.

As if called, the beast lifted its head. The names scrambled across his skin like rats, colliding and gnashing their teeth. Still drinking, he focused less on the blood and more on his control, but the voices began to fade and the beast's raging grew no worse.

Before any of that changed, he released Chrysabelle. He wasn't quite sated, but the victory of being able to stop was satisfaction enough.

He dropped her arm and pressed back into the seat as the hot-cold power of her blood struck him, shooting jolts of pain through his bones and tightening his muscles. The pain vanished seconds later, leaving him with a euphoric sense of well-being, a beating heart, and the need to breathe.

He let out a long breath. 'I can't believe I just did that.' He straightened, the pounding of his heart exaggerated by the rush of what had just happened. 'How was that even possible? Could my curse be broken?'

'I don't think so.' Chrysabelle cradled her arm to her chest. 'More like it's the ring's power, protecting me.' She glanced at Mortalis. 'As soon as we get back, you're going to make that meeting happen, right?'

He nodded. 'Amery has already agreed to help me.'

Barely listening to anything but the rush of blood in his ears, Mal rolled his shoulders as a fresh charge of power coursed through him, buoyed by the release of no longer being enslaved by the curse. The voices had gone oddly quiet. Not silent so much as hushed. As if they were trying not to be heard.

Slowly, the whispers filtered through the sound of his breathing and his pulse. He stood as comprehension struck him. He grabbed hold of the bulkhead. 'I need to go lie down.' Without waiting for a response, he made his way toward the back of the jet.

He shut the bedroom door, locked it, and dropped onto the bed. The voices grew louder. He squeezed his head between his hands, trying to shut them up, but still they raged. The beast joined them and the maelstrom of mental pressure increased tenfold.

The torture seared his brain. He rocked back and forth, still holding his head, wondering if it would split in his hands from the pain.

Chrysabelle might be safe, but the next human to cross his path wouldn't be. Drinking from her had reignited a fury in the voices unlike anything he'd experienced before. They sank their teeth into him, chewing through his resolve, weakening his control.

The question was not if he'd ever kill again, but when.

Chapter Thirty-Five

'Let her go,' Creek snarled as he lunged for his grandmother. Yahla was closer, grabbing Mawmaw up and using her like a shield. Now she hung limp in Yahla's arms, only the rise and fall of her chest an indicator that his grandmother still lived. And somewhere in the night, Annika was out there, hopefully coming up with a better plan.

'You tried to kill me.' Yahla's eyes narrowed to slits of bottomless black.

'You used me. Took control of me. I think we're even.' He took a step forward. 'Put my grandmother down and I won't try to kill you again.'

'You lie.' Yahla slanted her head back and coughed, expelling a raven that flew at Creek.

He grabbed the bird as it dove toward him, wrung its neck, and tossed it off the porch. In his peripheral vision, it disappeared in a cloud of dust before it touched the ground.

In the distance, a dog barked. Creek hoped it was Pip. If Yahla had done anything to that dog, Mawmaw would kill her, then find a way to bring her back from the dead just so she could kill her a second time. Yahla's feathers flew out around her, lifted by an unseen wind. 'You have no respect.'

'You've given me no reason to respect you.' A tiny movement near the back of the porch caught his attention. Annika. What was she planning?

Yahla tossed her feather hair. 'I am done speaking to you. I only waited until you arrived to take this woman's soul. To let you see what you had caused.' She squatted, taking Mawmaw to the porch floor; then Yahla opened her mouth in the same unnaturally wide way she had when she'd killed Argent.

With no idea what Annika was up to, Creek couldn't wait any longer. He leaped forward, grabbing fistfuls of Yahla's feathers and hurtling them both through the side railing. Splinters flew as wood cracked and they hit the ground.

Squawking with fury, Yahla swiped at him, slicing his cheek and forehead with a handful of talons. Blood trickled into his eye. He pulled her close enough to pin her arms and caught sight of Annika crouched against the lattice that covered the house's stilts.

'Face her to me and shut your eyes,' Annika yelled over Yahla's cawing.

Creek rolled onto his side, hugging the squirming Yahla tight. She was half woman, half bird now and pecking furiously at his face and chest. Each time she connected, she took a hunk of flesh. Shutting off the pain as best he could, Creek flipped over, landing hard on Yahla.

The move had the desired effect. She gasped, stunned. He quickly turned her in his arms so she faced Annika.

'Close your eyes,' Annika called again, her fingers hovering near her temple.

He squeezed them shut, forcing more blood into his field of vision, and waited for the struggling woman in his grasp to go to stone.

Annika swore softly and he opened his eyes. Yahla's beak pierced his forearm. He glared at Annika, her shades firmly in place. 'What the hell?'

'She won't look at me!'

Yahla smashed her head back and broke his nose. 'Let go of me,' she squawked.

With a curse, he angled his arms across her body so he could grab a handful of feathers and keep her head still; then he wrapped his legs around hers and immobilized her.

A small figure rose behind the porch's broken railing. Mawmaw. She hugged the closest four-by-four, using it for support. 'Squeeze her tighter, Tommy.'

Creek did as he grandmother asked. Yahla screeched like a banshee, almost drowning the sound of an approaching truck engine.

'Tighter,' Mawmaw said.

Creek squeezed as hard as he could. The woman in his arms gave way to a cawing, scratching flock of ravens. They burst out of his grasp and flew into formation above him like they might dive at any moment.

'Now, basilisk, now.' Mawmaw pointed at the ravens, then threw her arm over her face. 'Creek, your eyes.'

He closed them again. A few seconds later, heavy objects began pelting him. Eyes still closed, he got to his feet and ran out of the shower of stone ravens. He collided with someone, knocking them down. He opened his eyes to see his grandmother's neighbor lying on the ground. 'Martin.'

The man picked his hat up and stuck it back on his head.

'Thomas.' He looked past Creek. 'Looks like one's getting away.'

Creek turned to see the side yard littered with frozen birds. A solitary raven flew toward them. The whoosh of air beneath its wings beat defeat into Creek's soul. One bird would be enough to bring Yahla back.

'Pip,' Mawmaw yelled, pointing beyond where Creek and Martin lay.

Creek followed the line of her finger. Pip stood in the back of Martin's truck, his pink tongue lolling out of his mouth. At Mawmaw's command, Pip jumped into the air and caught the raven, landing with a thunk and disappearing behind the truck bed walls.

On his feet and running before another command came, Creek raced to the truck. Pip yelped as Creek got there. Blood covered the dog's nose. He grabbed the raven, which instantly turned on him, striking hard. Creek grabbed Pip's collar with his free hand and held the dog down behind the truck bed, then lifted the bird and closed his eyes. 'Annika!'

'Eyes,' she yelled back. A moment later, the raven in Creek's hand stopped fluttering.

Yahla was dead.

The plan hadn't worked. With a spray of sand, Heaven, in jaguar form, had turned in time to keep from tumbling through Fi's ghost form and out of the ring. Fi couldn't tell how long the fight had been going on; neither she nor Heaven, still in jaguar form, had landed a blow. As long as Fi stayed in ghost form, Heaven never would either. They circled each other, like they'd been doing continuously. Once in a while, when they were near the center of the ring, Heaven would make a move, but every time she leaped, she passed straight through Fi just like she had the first time. The crowd hated it, but as far as Fi was concerned, they could all get stuffed.

Finally, Fi sat down cross-legged in the sand. What was the point of pretending to fight? Heaven couldn't touch her.

Across the arena, the jaguar snarled. Fi stuck her tongue out at the animal. 'What's the matter? Rather be shopping?'

With another, weaker snarl, the jaguar sat.

Maybe they'd call it a draw and have to decide this marriage thing another way. Fi almost laughed at how it was turning out. She'd freaked out for nothing. No one was going to get hurt or even—

An ominous clanging rang out, silencing the boos and jeers of the crowd. Both she and the jaguar looked toward the sound.

A voice boomed from the overhead speakers. 'Due to the nature of the combatants, only human forms will be allowed. The first combatant to shift out of human form will be declared the loser.'

Fi stood as the jaguar across from her became Heaven once again. 'What? That's not fair.'

Heaven laughed. 'What's not fair is how short this fight is going to be.'

Fi materialized and started backing away. Every move she'd learned from Omur and Barasa tumbled through her head in a mishmash sequence that no longer made sense. Crap. Think, *think*. She wished Mal were here, fighting for her. With all that time he'd spent in the Pits, he'd know exactly what to do, how to find Heaven's weaknesses and exploit them.

She tried to think like him. What would his first move be? She knew it wouldn't be to let Heaven make the first move.

Gathering her courage, Fi launched at the other woman. She knocked Heaven into the sand and began whaling on her.

Heaven dodged the first blow, but the second caught her cheek and split her lip. At the taste of blood, Heaven's eyes went green-gold.

'Now, now,' Fi said. 'First to shift loses.'

Heaven's eyes went back to human. She bucked Fi off with enough power to throw her several feet away. Fi landed hard but rolled to her feet immediately and faced her challenger once again.

Drawing first blood felt good. Fi grinned. Now she wanted second blood as well. And if she'd learned anything from Mal, it was to never back down. She threw herself at Heaven again, grabbing Heaven's wrists as she raised her fists. Together they went into the sand.

Fi's jumpsuit was full of it by now, so Heaven's must be, too. Sand might make the blood easier to clean up, but it also aggravated the crap out of the fighters. Maybe that was part of the point.

Heaven slapped Fi across the face and Fi tasted blood. She smashed her head into Heaven's chin and was rewarded with a loud cry.

'*Vaca.*' Heaven dropped her and spat out a mouthful of blood, sand, and possibly a small piece of tongue. 'You're going to pay for that, human.'

'*Blah, blah, blah,*' Fi mouthed back. 'Empty words, fleabag.'

They began circling each other, arms out, ready to strike. Heaven stumbled once as her ankle twisted, but she quickly righted herself. She shook herself and blinked a couple of times.

With a frustrated yell, Heaven attacked, her petite figure

charging with all the power of her varcolai heritage. She took Fi to the sand hard enough that she lost her breath for a few frightening seconds. In that brief span, her eyes connected with Doc's in the audience. She'd never seen him so afraid. Did he think she was going to lose? What little confidence she had drained into the sand beneath her.

Heaven jumped on top of Fi and punched her in the side of the head. Stars shot through Fi's vision and the world wobbled. If she hadn't already been down, she would have fallen over.

Shot after shot to Fi's head and body pushed her deeper into the sand. She twisted away, earning herself a couple whacks to the ribs. Something cracked and pain radiated through her body with every breath. She clawed at the sand, trying to find purchase, trying to pull herself out of Heaven's reach. Desperate to stop the punishment, she flung handfuls of sand at Heaven.

The shifter caught the first one square in the mouth. She coughed out the sand she'd inhaled, gagging and spitting. Fi dug her elbows in and dragged her aching body a few inches away.

The sand clung to Heaven's sweaty face. She wiped a forearm across her eyes but only made it worse. Blinking hard, she crawled after Fi. Barely an inch remained on either of them that wasn't caked with sand or sweat. Under the intense lighting, their crusted skin glittered.

Fi kicked, catching Heaven in the collarbone. Something snapped and Heaven howled, the sound eerily unhuman. Her eyes yellowed and she flung herself on top of Fi.

Panting and growling, she landed multiple shots. Fi curled into a ball. The stars swimming across her field of vision became black spots. Swelling shut her left eye almost entirely and her body burned with pain.

She shoved both feet out with what little strength she had left, but Heaven dodged the effort. The shifter grabbed Fi by the hair and yanked back, then shoved Fi's face into the sand.

Fi jabbed an elbow back, catching Heaven hard, but the varcolai didn't let up. Grit clogged Fi's nose and throat with each hopeless breath. Heaven was going to kill her. The only way out was . . .

'Mercy,' Fi whispered.

Heaven tugged Fi's head out of the sand and leaned in close enough that their cheeks touched. 'What did you say, human?'

'Mercy.' The word tasted worse than the metallic tang coating her tongue.

'Hah!' Heaven flung Fi's head back down.

Fi twisted enough to breathe clean air. Somewhat unsteady, Heaven pushed to her feet and slogged toward the edge of the arena. She brushed herself off, then raised her hands. The crowd went nuts, whether or not they understood what had just happened.

A sob tore through Fi's chest. She couldn't look at Doc. Couldn't stand to see the disappointment in his eyes. Tears spilled down her face and she let them. At least they washed the sand from her eyes.

Heaven fell onto one knee, then tumbled onto her side. She rose slowly, leaning on her hands. She shook her head like she was clearing cobwebs and struggled to get up. Again, she fell.

This time she shifted to her jaguar form.

The crowd went still. Omur and Barasa ran into the arena and kneeled beside Heaven. Omur put a hand to her throat as he bent over her, his ear to her muzzle. He righted himself and gave Barasa a serious look. With a nod, Barasa jumped up and ran to Fi.

He brought her to a sitting position, then pulled her arm around his neck and lifted her to her feet. 'Raise your hand.'

She bit down to keep from crying out in pain. Through gritted teeth, she asked, 'Why? What happened?'

He reached around, grabbed her elbow, and forced her arm into the air, all the while walking her toward the exit. The crowd stayed silent, their stares amplifying her discomfort. Then he answered. 'You won. Heaven's dead.'

Chapter Thirty-Six

Lola hesitated. Her body wanted to lunge forward, to grab the comar before her and sink her teeth into his flesh without a second thought, but what was left of her heart and humanity kept her feet planted. She'd sworn she wouldn't become a monster. 'I don't know if I can do this.'

Luciano frowned. 'You can and you will or you will die. Permanently this time.'

The comar stepped forward. 'It's okay, my lady. My purpose is to provide you blood.'

Luciano nodded. 'Listen to the pulse of his heart. It beats with excitement, not fear. He is here to serve. He wants to do this.'

A refocusing of her senses and she actually could hear the comar's heart. The sound was vaguely reassuring. Her mouth watered and the muscles in her thighs twitched, trying to move her forward. 'Maybe . . . I should do this alone.' She glanced at Luciano.

He settled into the club chair. 'No, *cara mia*. You are a vampling. The chance that you would drink too much and harm the comar is too great. I stay.'

'Oh.' That possibility had never occurred to her. 'That's a good idea, then.' She sat on the bench at the end of the bed and patted the spot next to her. 'Please,' she said to the comar. 'Come sit.'

With a smile, the comar joined her. His scent was intoxicating. She closed her eyes slightly as she inhaled. The fragrance was rich and heady, like the finest rum. 'You smell delicious.'

The word slipped out before she realized how it sounded. 'I didn't mean—'

The comar laughed. 'Please, my lady. I'm supposed to smell delicious.' He held his arm out to her.

She stared at it, unsure.

'To bite,' Luciano said. 'The wrist is less intimate.'

She nodded and took the comar's arm, then stopped. 'What's your name? I feel like I should at least know your name.'

'I am Hector.' His slight accent recalled her childhood.

'Are you Cuban?' No wonder he'd reminded her so much of Julia.

'Sí.' He laughed. 'And I know who you are.' He tipped his head. 'I am honored to be your first blood.'

The realization that what she'd become would soon be public knowledge struck her. Despite her growing hunger, she let her hands drop to her lap. Hector's arm rested lightly in her grip, his warm flesh teasing her fingertips.

'Something wrong, Lola?' Luciano raised a brow, the displeasure on his face evident.

There was no turning back. She must embrace this new life that would allow her to govern Paradise City with the necessary power and rescue her grandchild. 'No. Nothing is wrong.' She forced herself to smile at Hector. 'I am pleased you are my first as well.'

She lifted his wrist, breathing in his luscious scent again, then closed her eyes, opened her mouth, and sank her fangs into him.

Hector's only sound was one of pleasure. As blood surged into her mouth, she opened her eyes. Luciano had moved to the edge of the chair. He nodded at her. She closed her eyes and returned to drinking the life spilling out of Hector. Her body seemed to expand with every swallow, the sense of power increasing as her hunger waned.

Not wanting to disappoint Luciano or harm Hector, she stopped when the urgency to drink narrowed from the raging river it had first been to a small trickle of desire. She pulled her mouth away from his arm reluctantly.

'You're done?' Luciano asked.

'Yes.'

With a look that said he didn't quite believe her, Luciano stood. 'Very well. You will be hungry again – not just hungry but ravenous – when you wake from daysleep this next week or so. It would be best if you stay here. There are plenty of rooms—'

'No.' She rose. 'I have a city to run. I can't take up residence in a nightclub. And I can't sleep during the day.'

'I have a potion that will shorten the hours of daysleep you require, but I do not think you understand how much you'll need blood.'

Hector jumped up. 'I'll go with her.' Uncertainty in his eyes, he paused, his hand clamped over his punctured wrist. 'If the mayor wishes.'

'You cannot just go. A comar's blood rights are not free.'

'How much?' Lola asked, suddenly willing to pay whatever it took to keep Hector with her.

'I must check with Jacqueline. She is our comarré house-mother. She keeps their records.'

Lola rested her hand on Hector's shoulder. 'You know where I live. Send me the bill.'

Now was not the time to worry about Mal, but Chrysabelle couldn't help but let a small amount of concern filter through her preparations for the ball. She didn't like that he'd isolated himself after drinking from her, didn't like how quiet he'd become. How purposefully distant. She hated it, actually.

Hated that *something* had happened and he wasn't talking about it. But then expecting him to change overnight was a fool's game. She crossed her arms and returned her focus to what was happening in the hangar.

The comarré Dominic and Katsumi had captured, the comarré who would provide the blood for Chrysabelle's dis-guise, stood huddled near her patron. Chrysabelle felt for the girl, knowing she was an innocent participant in all this. Her patron would provide the blood for Mal's disguise and the two vampires beside him, the blood for Dominic and Katsumi. Maybe before they returned home, Chrysabelle would give the comarré the chance to go with them.

Maybe.

The four hostages were bound with silver-core rope and blindfolded. The silver – and a shot of laudanum when Dominic was finished with them – would keep the vampires from escap-ing, but the comarré would have to be watched. That job fell to Amery, along with guarding the two planes now parked side by side in the secured hangar. The comarré's behavior would deter-mine what Chrysabelle offered.

Dominic came out of his plane, a tray of tools in one hand.

Mal followed. Helping Dominic was a great way to keep his distance from her. She spoke to Dominic as he approached. 'Do you need me for this?

'No, Malkolm will assist me. Katsumi is changing. You probably should as well.'

'All right.' Her gown would take a little time to get into anyway.

Mal grabbed the first vampire, a female, and held her in place while Dominic picked up the first syringe. Chrysabelle turned away and walked back to the jet. As she stepped inside, the vampiress let out a curse that rattled the hangar walls.

'Solomon, bring four gags,' Dominic called to the cypher fae he'd brought along. Solomon would get them through Čachtice's warded gates, but then he'd return to the protection of the hangar. Cyphers were extraordinarily useful except when it came to fighting. Then they were pretty much helpless.

Dominic's pilot, a fringe vamp, would drive them to the estate; then he'd stay outside with the other drivers, keeping to himself and sticking to his story of being a new hire. Once inside the ball, they couldn't afford a single loose piece in the very complex puzzle they were creating.

Mortalis would wait in the second car at the end of the tunnels, where hopefully she, Mal, and the vampire baby would end up.

Chrysabelle retrieved her garment bag from the plane's storage closet and carried it to the bedroom. There, she stripped down to her underwear, taking off the sheaths that held her wrist daggers and laying them on the bed. Her sacres were currently stored in the front closet where her dress had been. The small Golgotha blade normally tucked in the back of her waistband had stayed home. Going into this ball with only a pair of daggers strapped to her thighs was almost the equivalent of going in unarmed. Two short blades against Tatiana, who could transform her metal hand into any weapon of her choosing, was ludicrous. It meant the only effective fighting Chrysabelle could do was up close. Not really where she wanted to be when dealing with an aged, noble vampire.

With a resigned sigh, she clipped on the garter belt Nyssa had altered to serve as the sheath for the daggers and aligned it, then attached the stays around her lower thighs and inserted her wrist daggers into place.

The dress went on next, carefully so as not to damage the delicate lace. For a moment, Chrysabelle wished Velimai and Nyssa were with her, but it passed quickly. She wouldn't want them in harm's way. Not that Velimai's vocals wouldn't come in handy against Tatiana. Chrysabelle zipped the dress as best she could. Someone would have to finish the job for her.

She slipped her hands through the slits designed to look like pockets. Her hands connected immediately with the hilts of her daggers, their smooth surface offering some comfort to the anxious prickling running the length of her spine.

At last, she pulled the sides of her hair back with diamond combs and let the rest of it fall loose. She did a quick turn in the full-length mirror on the back of the bedroom door to make sure everything was okay. Except for not being completely zipped up, she was ready to go. She opened the door and found Mal waiting.

Her heart caught in her chest at the sight of him wearing the outfit Dominic's tailor had prepared. From the snowy cravat to the velvet frock coat and soft wool trousers, it was like getting a glimpse of him as he might have been so many centuries ago. Just seeing him dressed as befit his true noble status washed a curious sense of weakness through her. As if he were suddenly some distant, untouchable patron and she, his submissive comarré, awaiting his command. She glanced away and gathered her composure around her like a screen, but he'd already have heard the uptick in her pulse.

He shook his head, his gaze running the length of her. 'Bloody hell.'

Her spirits sank and she glanced at him. 'You don't like it?'

'I *like* it. I *don't* like the thought of other men looking at you in it.' His eyes silvered. 'Come here.'

She did as he asked, the feeling of being possessed by this wicked creature coiling through her in a way that tripped the darkest pleasure centers of her brain. When she stopped before him, she lifted her chin. 'You don't own me, you know.'

He slipped his hand around her waist and drew her in until the space between them disappeared; then his lids dropped a little lower and he smiled, his mouth closed and assessing. 'I'm well aware of who owns who in this relationship.'

'Then tell me why you've been avoiding me since you fed.'

His smile disappeared. He released her and stepped away, turning so that he no longer faced her. 'The voices, the beast . . . they're pushing me to kill. To make up for not killing you. It's like they know I've gained the ability to protect you and they want to punish me for that.' He rolled his head to one side, closed his eyes, and sighed. 'My head aches with their efforts.'

'I'm so sorry,' she whispered, wanting to go to him, but not sure if he would welcome the touch since he'd moved away from her.

He tilted his head to look at her. 'I'll be okay.'

'You look very handsome, by the way.'

His smile deepened and he laughed softly. 'I don't think

anyone will be looking at me this evening, but thank you. That dress is really something.'

She smoothed the skirt. 'It was supposed to be my mother's wedding dress.'

His brows rose. 'Has Dominic seen it yet?'

'No, but I don't think he knows that's what it is.' She held out her hand. 'Shall we go?'

'Wait. I have something for you.' He went to the closet her dress had been in, took his bag off the top shelf, and rummaged through it, finally pulling out a long, cloth-wrapped parcel. He handed it to her. 'I want you to have these.'

She untied the leather cord securing the cloth and unfurled it into her hand, already recognizing the shapes within. When the matched set of daggers fell into her palm, she let out a soft, 'Oh.' She set the cloth aside and inspected the weapons. Tiny rose-covered vines curled down the slim blades. Just before the blades met the rosewood hilts, their edge gave away to about an inch of serration, making them deadlier than the daggers she'd planned to use. 'They're beautiful.'

'More important, they're as sharp as the devil's tongue.'

'I love them. Thank you.' She leaned up and kissed him. 'These are from your personal collection?'

'Yes. They were one of the first pairs I ever ... acquired.'

She frowned, knowing that most likely meant he'd killed their owner.

'Don't look so upset. He was a highwayman who attempted to rob the carriage I was traveling in. He killed my driver before he got what he deserved.'

She tilted the blades so they caught the light. 'All that matters is that you wanted me to have something of yours.' She smiled at him. 'I like that.'

'So do I.'

'Here, hold them while I take the old ones out.' She handed them over, then balanced her foot on one of the seats, pulled her skirt up, and slid the first dagger out. She held her hand out to Mal for the replacement.

Nothing filled her open palm. She glanced up. Mal was holding the dagger out to her, but his gaze was on her bare leg. She cleared her throat. 'A little to the left.'

'What?' He looked at her and readjusted his aim. 'Don't show that much skin if you don't want me to look.'

She slipped the new dagger home. 'I never said I didn't want you to look.' She switched legs and repeated the process, enjoying the ability to turn him into vampire mush. Finally, she adjusted her skirts. 'Let's go find Dominic.'

He stood to one side and gestured toward the exit. 'After you.'

But as she started by, he caught her and pulled her close to kiss the tender spot below her ear. 'Be careful tonight. I will *not* lose you.'

She splayed her hands against his chest. 'We have the element of surprise, remember? The upper hand.' She gave him a smile she didn't fully feel. 'Tatiana's the one who should be worried.'

He didn't answer, just pushed her gently toward the exit again. She dropped her smile as soon as he was behind her. There was no question death would be woven through the hours that lay ahead of them, only which one of them would be ensnared by it first.

Chapter Thirty-Seven

Tatiana looked up as Octavian entered the suite. 'The nobles have begun to arrive.' He came to where Tatiana sat rocking Lilith and kissed both their cheeks. He'd been ever so amenable lately. Almost careful. It was enough to make her wonder if he was up to something. 'Where's Daciana?'

'I imagine breaking in her new comar.'

'Ah, yes, Lord Syler asked me how that had gone. I assured him everything was fine. I hope that was the case?'

'It was.' She kept her eyes on him until he seemed uneasy. 'What have you been up to?'

'Up to? Nothing, just making sure this evening will go as smoothly as possible.' He smiled unconvincingly. 'Your needs are always my first concern.'

She raised one brow. 'You're planning something.'

'What? No.' He swallowed.

She shook her head. 'Don't lie to me. I can sense it.' She shook her finger at him. 'I hate surprises. *Hate* them. I want no grand gesture this evening, understood? If anything happens outside of what's been scripted, I will hold you personally accountable.'

He nodded vigorously. 'Yes, absolutely, nothing outside what's planned.' He exhaled unnecessarily and relaxed a bit. 'Back to the subject of comars – have you seen Damian recently?'

She bounced Lilith lightly, causing her to giggle. 'I've been sharing Daci's comar, but I did look in on Damian. His bruises are completely healed. He'll be in fine shape for the ball.' Especially since she'd taken care of adding a little sedative to his evening meal.

Octavian nodded. 'Excellent. I'll be sure he's dressed and ready.' He tapped a finger on the arm of the chair. 'Lord Syler also mentioned you'd spoken to him about when you're to be announced?'

'I did.' She brushed the soft cotton of Lilith's day gown. 'I don't want us to enter until the majority of the nobles are here. At least two hours in should do it, don't you think?'

He took the chair across from her and wiggled his fingers at Lilith. 'Two hours from now they'll be chomping at the bit to see you.'

She laughed. 'We both know they're here to see my daughter.'

He looked at her. 'Yes, but I promise you that's not the only reason. Word of Svetla's death and the ancient one's declaration have spread. Besides that, you are the first female Dominus. The nobility know your name but not your face, and with your reputation, they very much want to know who you are. The crowd will be thick this evening. I imagine you'll be inundated with gifts, offers of assistance . . . a great number of things I'll have no control to stop.' He sat back, his eyes worried. 'Prepare yourself.'

'I won't hold you accountable for those things.' He was definitely planning something. Or had been.

'Thank you. Still, you and Lilith are my primary concerns. It's my job to make sure every possibility has been examined.'

She set Lilith on the floor to play with her blocks. 'How is security?'

'Tight. I've walked the perimeters and watched some of the nobility being checked in. No one who doesn't belong will get through.' He snorted. 'Not that anyone will try. Who would be foolish enough to invade a large gathering of powerful vampires? No one I can think of.'

She nodded, listening but watching Lilith more intently. 'That's very true. I'm sure the comarré is busy mourning Malkolm.' She glanced up. 'Which reminds me, pay attention to those you speak with tonight. My first project after we return home is to put a tcam together to go to Paradise City and retrieve the ring of sorrows and the comarré once and for all. I've decided I will not set foot in that city again, but with the position and power I now hold, I don't need to, nor do I wish to be separated from Lilith. I want a good group, ten or twelve strong, loyal nobles who will put this matter to rest for me. We can handpick them from the crowd this evening.'

'I will pay close attention. I'm sure you'll have many volunteers.' He offered a hand to Lilith, who was trying to pull herself up using the edge of the small table next to his chair. 'There you go, my darling.' He smiled at Tatiana. 'Amazing how fast she's growing. I expect she'll be talking before long.'

'I can't wait for that.' She smiled down at Lilith. 'Are you going to talk to Mama, my darling? Can you say *Mama*, sweetheart? Mama?'

Lilith laughed and waved bye-bye.

Octavian stood. 'I believe I'll go makc sure Damian is ready, then come back and get dressed myself. That way I can watch Lilith while you're occupied.'

'Excellent.' She smiled as he left, then kneeled on the floor beside Lilith. 'We are lucky to have Octavian, aren't we, my sweet? So long as he doesn't do something foolish.' She kissed Lilith's fingers, then sat and began stacking the blocks Lilith had been ignoring.

When they were five high, Lilith clapped her hands, then shoved them down and giggled as they crashed to the ground. Twice more, Tatiana built the tower and twice more, Lilith toppled it.

Tatiana sat back and tried to ignore the buried remnants of her Roma soul. This was *not* an omen. *Not* a sign of things to come. Lilith was just a child and all children liked to destroy things.

Didn't they?

'I can't believe it's over.' Fi, freshly showered, sat on the padded table while Barasa did his doctor thing and wrapped her torso into a compression garment. She'd told him a pain shot wasn't necessary, but he'd insisted. Good thing, too, because the cuts on her face had stung like a mother when he'd cleaned them. Now, though, the meds had kicked in and she barely noticed her cracked ribs anymore. In fact, she felt about as good as she remembered feeling in a long time.

'Well, believe it. You're the pride leader's mate fair and square.' He didn't look at her while he spoke, just kept his eyes fixed to his work.

'How did I do it, though? I barely touched her.' Fi closed her eyes to help her brain work and started tilting backward.

'Whoa, there.' Barasa righted her. 'You need to sleep for a while, let your body heal.'

'I told you, I can go ghost and do that.'

He caught her gaze and shook his head. 'How can your physical body heal while you're a ghost? I don't think it works that way.'

'What do you know about ghosts?' The urge to sleep was pretty freaking strong. Maybe she'd just lie down right here. 'What kind of a cat are you?'

'I know about ghosts because – I'm a tiger. I did a year of residency at a hospital that specialized in othernatural patients and—'

'A tiger? That's so cool. Lemme see.'

A knock interrupted them and the door opened. Doc stuck his head in. 'How's my girl?'

'Pretty looped on pain meds,' Barasa answered.

Fi heard a squeal, then realized the noise had come out of her. 'Hiya, baby! Hey, did you know Barasa's a tiger?'

Doc laughed. 'Yeah, I know that.' He looked at Barasa again. 'She going to be okay?'

'A hundred percent. Just get her into bed and make her stay there for a few days. She'll be sore and bruised for at least a week. Her ribs are only cracked, not broken, but they'll take a good four to six weeks to heal completely.' He smiled sheepishly. 'So no unnecessary activity.'

'He means no sex,' Fi whispered loudly.

'Yeah,' Doc said. 'I knew that, too.'

Fi pointed at him and kept whispering. 'You should tell Barasa about your fire problem. He worked at a ghost hospital. He might know how to fix that.'

Doc's expression froze; then he covered with a laugh. 'Cripes, those drugs sure are doing a number on her, huh? Better get her to bed. I'll just—'

'So it's true?' Barasa asked.

Doc's eyes glittered gold. 'I don't know what you're talking about.'

Barasa put his hands up. 'You think you can't trust me? I've been on your side since you got here. I helped train Fiona.' He muttered something else Fi couldn't make out.

'What?' Fi asked, but the two men didn't seem to be paying attention to her anymore. 'What did you say?' she asked again. Maybe he'd said something about Heaven. Wait, Heaven was dead. How exactly had a human defeated a varcolai? Fi couldn't make it work in her head.

Doc's jaw popped to one side. 'Yes, it's true. But as long as I keep a small dose of K in my system, it seems to hold the flames at bay.'

'K?' Barasa's mouth dropped. 'Ketamine is one of the most dangerous things our kind can ingest.'

'You don't have to tell me that,' Doc said. 'One bad experience with it was enough, but I didn't know what else to do. I don't want to hurt anyone, especially not Fi. Who was I going to turn to for help? The witch responsible is dead.'

Barasa leaned against the exam table. Fi leaned over and sniffed him. He slanted his eyes at her, one brow raised in question.

'I just wanted to see if you smelled like a tiger.'

With a shake of his head, Barasa turned back to Doc. 'The witch is dead, but the power of her spell remains? When's the last time you saw the fire?'

'The night Sinjin died.'

Fi leaned over again, resting against Barasa's shoulder. 'He went up like a marshmallow on a camp fire.'

'Fi.' Doc shot her a look she knew well. It meant zip it.

'The men in my family tend to be shamans. I took it a little further, but I can tell you there's a good chance her spell's worn off and you aren't even aware of it. Stop taking the ketamine immediately. Then let's see—'

Fi yawned loudly. Any minute now she was going to pass out; she could feel it. She sat up and tapped Barasa on the shoulder. 'Will you turn into a tiger now? I really need to go to sleep.'

Barasa sighed and handed Doc a prescription bottle. 'For pain, if she needs them. By the time she wakes up, the ketamine should be out of your system. Both of you come back then.'

Chapter Thirty-Eight

Creek wasn't sure what surprised him more – Annika's willingness to sit with his grandmother or his willingness to let her. Martin was there, too, not that the old man was any protection against the basilisk's power. Creek should have pushed harder for Mawmaw to see a doctor, but she'd insisted that was a waste of money over a few bruises. She could take care of herself.

Stubborn woman.

Well, he'd be done with his errand soon enough and then Annika could go back to KM headquarters or wherever it was she lived, and the rest of them could get on with their lives. And he could shower. And sleep. His body ached in a thousand different spots from Yahla pecking at him, but at least he'd been able to change into a clean, undamaged T-shirt at Mawmaw's.

Couldn't exactly visit the mayor in a holey shirt covered in blood. He rolled the V-Rod up to her gate. Especially when she was probably still in bed. He knew the mayor wasn't a late sleeper, but the sun had only been up a few minutes. Even Lola probably didn't start her day that early.

He killed the engine, pulled his helmet off, and stood where the security camera could see him. The intercom crackled to life. 'What's your business?'

'I'm Thomas Creek, special adviser to the mayor. I have an urgent, private matter to speak to her about.' Like how he'd been possessed by a mythological woman and how the curfew was a really bad idea. The intercom went silent and he dropped his head. How was he going to explain to Chrysabelle that he was partially responsible for Mal's death? If she'd even see him. After his last visit there, he couldn't blame her if she never spoke to him again.

He had to find a way to end his service to the KM. Annika wasn't such a bad boss, but she only delivered his directives. Whoever was making the orders was also making his life hell. And he was about damn done with that.

The gates swung open. He hopped on the bike, started it up, and drove through. Maybe the mayor was awake after all. He parked in the drive in front of her house and walked to the door. He didn't recognize the security guard. 'Thomas Creek to see the mayor.'

The security guard tapped the radio at his hip. 'They cleared you.' He knocked on the front door and a staff member opened it.

'Good morning, Mr. Creek.'

'Hilda. You're up early.'

'So are you. The mayor isn't awake yet, but I'll get her. I've already told the kitchen staff to set breakfast out early. They'll have coffee in the dining room if you want to wait in there.'

'Coffee sounds exactly like where I want to wait. Thank you.'

She pointed. 'You know the way. I'll have her in soon.'

He kept going as Hilda veered toward the mayor's private wing. Lola might not be happy about being woken up early, but she really wasn't going to be happy when he resigned and told her exactly what had happened. That curfew had to end.

He'd had one sip of coffee when Hilda came running in. 'Help me, Mr. Creek. Something's wrong with the mayor.' Her face crumpled. 'I think she's dead.'

'What?' He jumped out of his chair and ran down the hall to Lola's bedroom. Her bed was empty. 'Where is she?'

Hilda ran in behind him. 'In the bathtub. I couldn't wake her.'

He found her there in silk pajamas and wrapped in a comforter. She looked . . . different. Like she'd had a makeover. His fingers went to her throat. Ice cold and no pulse. 'Damn it.' He leaned down and listened but even his heightened senses detected no breathing.

Hilda crossed herself and moaned. 'Is she dead?'

Creek pushed one of Lola's lids up. Her eye was silver. 'Son of a—'

'What's going on?'

Creek dropped her lid and stood to see who was talking. A young man in white pajama pants had wandered in behind Hilda. A few gold tattoos marked his skin and his blond hair showed dark roots. Double hell.

'Please, Mr. Creek. Is she dead?'

He frowned at the comar, then nodded at Hilda. 'Yes. She is.'

Dominic handed them each a small metal plunger, then tapped the side of his neck. 'Right into the aorta. The change will be fairly rapid and somewhat painful.'

'How painful is somewhat?' Mal asked. He didn't care personally, but he wanted to know how much Chrysabelle would have to endure. *Sucker*.

'It's okay,' she said.

Was she reading his mind now?

'Let's go,' Katsumi said. 'We can't leave the hangar until we've transformed.'

'She's right.' Dominic stuck the plunger to his neck and pushed the button on the end. It made a small *whooshing* sound. He grimaced a second later but the expression didn't last long. 'There. How do I look?'

'The same damn way.' Mal frowned. 'If this doesn't work—'

'Look.' Chrysabelle pointed.

Dominic's face began to shift as they watched. He looked like he was underwater. The strangeness passed, leaving behind the blended characteristics of both Dominic and the vampire he'd taken blood from.

Katsumi stuck the plunger to her neck. Within a minute, she, too, was transformed.

Mal pressed his plunger against his skin as Chrysabelle did the same. He watched as her familiar beauty faded into something much more pedestrian. Her gaze skimmed his face. 'How do I look?' he asked.

Katsumi snorted indelicately. 'I'd say it's an improvement.'

'You look fine,' Chrysabelle said. 'Tatiana will never know it's you.'

'Unless she hears you speaking too much,' Dominic corrected. 'If you talk to her, modulate your voice. And be careful that neither of you shows affection to each other. You are patron and comarré, not . . . whatever it is you have become.'

The words angered Mal for some reason. He knew Dominic

wasn't belittling his relationship with Chrysabelle, just warning them, but it still rankled. 'We understand that.'

'*Bene*.' Dominic rapped his knuckles on the limo's partition. 'Let's go.'

The fringe driver waved his hand, then gave a thumbs-up to Amery, who rolled the hangar doors back so both cars could head out. Solomon was in their car, but he sat up front with the driver. The cypher was as quiet as Mal remembered him. How Dominic had the fae in his employ was a mystery, just like how Mortalis had come to work for the vampire.

Chrysabelle squeezed his hand and Mal smiled at her, forgetting his insignificant concerns. They had enough to worry about as it was. 'Ready?'

'Yes,' she answered. 'We mingle, locate Damian and the baby. I talk to Damian and let him know his part. Then we regroup, make sure the plan still works, and revise as needed. Right now, Katsumi will be taking Damian out disguised as her comar.' She pointed at Katsumi and Dominic. 'In theory, you three will be able to walk out the front door. You'll fly out as soon as you return to the hangar. Mortalis will wait for us at the end of the tunnels.' She smiled. 'Then he and Amery will fly us home.'

It sounded so easy. He knew it wouldn't be.

Katsumi stared out the window into the night. Or maybe she was studying her new face. 'How long will these disguises last?'

'Five hours. A little more, a little less.' Dominic tipped his hand back and forth like a scale. 'Longer if you don't drink any blood.'

'Not a problem.' Chrysabelle laughed. 'You have the vial for Damian?'

Dominic patted his suit coat. 'In my pocket. Hopefully your

blood is similar enough to his that it works.' Lines framed his mouth. 'You might be his sister, but you and the other comarré are female. I'm not entirely sure what he'll end up looking like.'

Chrysabelle nodded. 'I thought about that, too, but all you have to do is get him out the door and into the car.'

'We will,' Dominic assured her.

After that they settled into a tense silence. At last, they approached the gates. The driver stopped the car and Solomon got out, held the wards open long enough for both cars to get through, and then they were in the city.

It wasn't so different from Corvinestri. Narrow cobblestone streets, buildings that looked like they'd been new a couple hundred centuries ago – some still bearing gas lamps – human inhabitants bent over by the fear of serving creatures that could kill them in the blink of an eye. And just like in Corvinestri, the landscape changed as they broke away from the human village and into the vampire estates. Open space was abundant, the well-lit buildings glimpsed behind high masonry walls and gated entrances were in pristine condition, the grounds impeccable.

The car slowed and drove through an enormous gate, already open, the word BATHORY scrolled in iron at the top. At the end of the long drive, they joined a line of cars waiting to be attended to.

Dominic watched as liveried servants came toward the limo. He turned back to them, lifted his chin, and said, '*In bocca al lupo*.'

'Exactly,' Mal replied. He knew Dominic meant to wish them good luck, but the words' literal translation settled over him like a dark shroud. They were indeed about to be in the mouth of the wolf.

'No, no.' Dominic shook his head. 'You must respond *crepi lupo.*' His brows arched and his gaze slanted toward the house. 'For the wolf is about to die.'

Before Mal could say anything further, the doors were opened. The four of them got out and, with Dominic and Katsumi leading, made their way with a few other nobles to the mansion's entrance.

A fringe vampire checked their invitation. Dominic had duplicated the one Creek had given to Chrysabelle so that each pair had one. The fringe scanned the invites and nodded. 'Welcome to the House of Bathory's Dominus ball. Enjoy your evening.'

And just like that, they were in.

From here on, he was Lord Moreau and Chrysabelle was Carissa. Dominic was Lord Santoro and Katsumi was Lady Kobayashi. Once they were through the main doors, they were directed through the house to the ballroom. The space was enormous, and in typical noble fashion, it was disgustingly overdone. Apparently the theme was the Garden of Eden. Mal tried not to roll his eyes, but it was hard.

Dominic stopped them near an enormous gilded cage filled with brilliantly colored macaws, most likely cloned. 'Lord Moreau, if you'll excuse Lady Kobayashi and me, there's someone on the other side I must speak with.'

Mal nodded and tucked himself a little deeper into the surrounding jungle of potted palms and overwhelmingly fragrant tropical flowers. 'Smells like a whorehouse in here.'

Beside and slightly behind him, Chrysabelle whispered, 'And you would know that how?'

He ducked his head and forced himself not to smile. 'Jealous already?'

'Just remember, I'm the only one of us adequately armed.'

That much was true. Dominic had a narrow blade hidden in his cane, and Katsumi's hair was held up with a double-pronged six-inch *kanzashi* that looked like nothing more than an elaborate hairpin. All Mal had was a good length of garrote wire sewn into the lining of his coat. Chrysabelle's pair of blades made her twice as armed as the rest of them. 'Duly noted.'

They stood in silence for a while, observing, trying to determine where either of their targets might be.

'Maybe you should get a glass of blood,' Chrysabelle said. 'Most of the nobles have one.'

'Dominic said drinking blood would shorten the life span of the injection.'

'Don't drink it. Just hold it for effect.'

He nodded. 'Fine, but not yet. This is a good spot.'

'I can get it for you. That would be my job anyway as your comarré.'

He hesitated, choosing his words carefully. 'How does it feel to be back here? You miss any of this?'

'Not in the slightest.' He felt her eyes on him. 'Have I ever given you the impression that I had?'

'No. Not lately anyway. Maybe in the first few days after you'd left.'

Out of the corner of his eye, he saw her give a tiny shake of her head. 'When this is over' – her voice lowered – 'I will put this life behind me once and for all.'

He tipped his head to see her better. The face wasn't hers, but the expressions rang true and the look in her eyes held the strength of will he'd come to love about her. 'You have plans?'

She smiled slightly and looked up from beneath her lashes at him. 'Oh yes.' Her smile broadened for just a second. 'And they include you.'

Chapter Thirty-Nine

With Lilith cradled in her arms, Tatiana stood beside Octavian and Daciana outside the closed ballroom doors. She turned to take one last look and make sure everything was as it should be. Their comarré, Damian, Saraphina, and the newly purchased Jonah stood a few feet behind them. Since Damian had been here at Lord Syler's, his spirit seemed broken. Like he'd resigned himself to his position once again. Or maybe it was the sedatives she'd put into his food. She'd have to determine if he was worth keeping soon. She couldn't very well drink his blood while he was doped up.

The doors opened a sliver and Lord Syler joined them. 'It's time to announce you. The ball has been under way for nearly two hours. Lady Tatiana, you'll be pleased to know Lord Grigor is not in attendance.'

'That does please me.'

Lord Syler held his hand out toward the ballroom. 'Are you ready for the nobility to meet Lilith and greet the newest member of the House of Tepes?'

She kissed Lilith's head, now crowned with the diamond and

amethyst band that perfectly complemented Tatiana's gown. 'I am.'

Somewhat pensively, he moved a step closer. 'It's my great pleasure to do this for you and the House of Tepes. I hope you know you can come to me, should you need anything.'

She dipped her head graciously. He was not nearly the over-bearing bore Ivan had been. 'Most gracious of you.'

He smiled. 'Let us proceed, then.' At the nod of his head, the servants threw the doors wide and he entered the ballroom. Tatiana followed with Octavian at her side as consort, then Daciana as Elder and lastly, their comarré. Kosmina was inside already and would be nearby to take Lilith when Tatiana gave her the sign. She had no intention of keeping her daughter in front of the ogling nobility all evening.

The noise from the assembled crowd fell to a whispered hush as they walked through. The ballroom was enormous, as was the ballroom in her own estate, and tonight it was at capacity. Perhaps a thousand vampires. Perhaps more. She lifted her chin a little higher and kept a firm grip on Lilith, one hand curled around her body, the other on her head.

The dais had been set with a long banquet table. Syler's elder, Edwin, was already in the chair to Syler's left. He rose as they approached and greeted Tatiana with a short bow. She nodded in return. She didn't know much about Edwin, but he seemed a levelheaded sort.

Lord Syler stood beside Edwin at the first of the large center chairs, while Tatiana stood beside the second. Octavian and Daciana filled in the next two spaces. The comarré settled into a row of seats at the very back of the dais where Syler's and Edwin's were already in attendance.

The ballroom was beautifully decorated with an abundance

of live plants and animals and lighting that made it seem like a warm spring day. The Garden of Eden theme was something she'd personally approved. She sniffed once, reminded of her late Nehebkau. The albino cobra would have loved what Syler had done.

When they were all in place, Syler raised his hand. 'Good nobles of the five families, welcome to my home and to the Dominus ball in honor of Lady Tatiana, newly appointed Dominus of the House of Tepes, and her consort, Lord Octavian.'

Polite clapping answered him. Tatiana merely gazed out across the crowd, recognizing some faces and others not at all. It mattered little. They needed to know her; she didn't need to know them.

Syler continued, his voice carrying effortlessly across the vast space. 'I am also honored to introduce the newest member of the nobility. She is a gift from the ancient ones to Lady Tatiana, the first of our kind to be born vampire.' He held his hand out toward Tatiana. 'I present to you Princess Lilith.'

At the end of Syler's prearranged introduction, Tatiana turned Lilith to face the crowd and raised her overhead. Lilith laughed and kicked her feet, no doubt thinking it was playtime. A few of the faces in the crowd softened, fear edged a few more, but the bulk of the nobility stared stone-faced, no doubt purposefully hiding their true feelings of jealousy or intimidation.

To turn the knife a little deeper, Tatiana smiled sweetly back at them and, bringing Lilith back into her safe embrace, calmly spoke. 'Thank you for your abundant generosity, Lord Syler. My family and I are in your debt.' She moved from face to face. 'I'm sure many of you are curious about Lilith. I cannot blame you. She is an extraordinary child. As Lord Syler indicated, she is the first of us to be born vampire.' She paused for effect. 'And the first of us to be immune to the sun.'

The stoniness dropped away from all but a few faces. Yes, let them soak in that astonishing bit of news.

'She is truly the arrival of our next generation,' Lord Syler proclaimed. 'Thank you all for coming. Now, please, enjoy the rest of your evening.' He snapped his fingers and servants came forward to pull out Tatiana's and Daciana's chairs. The music swelled again and the crowd returned to mingling, their topic of conversation no doubt what they'd just witnessed.

Tatiana sat and positioned Lilith on her lap facing the audience as everyone else on the dais took their chairs. A servant appeared at her right-hand side and filled her goblet with blood, but she paid him little attention. The crowd was far too interesting. All across the ballroom, nobles formed small circles, exchanged a few words, then glanced her way. She stared back imperiously at each prattling cluster.

Until she found one solitary noble tucked into a pocket of greenery. A highly gilded comarré hovered behind him. That combined with his exquisitely tailored clothing confirmed he had means. He spoke with no one, his gaze simply fixed on her. His face meant nothing to her, but something about him – the breadth of his shoulders, his loosely dangerous stance – felt familiar in a not unpleasant way. Perhaps they'd met at a previous engagement. A vampire of that size and bank account would be an invaluable addition to the team she planned to send to Paradise City. She would seek him out, find out who he was. Then make him an offer he couldn't refuse.

Doc stared blankly at his office door, his mind upstairs where Fi was asleep in the bed Heaven had once occupied. He should be there with her, but Heaven's death had frayed into a thousand loose ends that only he could tie up. Most important, her father had to be called. Doc exhaled. Of all the things on his list, that was the one he dreaded the most.

Barasa was preparing her body for transportation back to Brazil and Omur was overseeing the cleanup of the arena. That was one thing he knew about. Back in the day before Sinjin had thrown him out for his curse, he'd been on a few cleanup crews. The arena was pretty sophisticated and the mechanics built in did most of the work of funneling the sand through a series of drains where it was steam cleaned and then pumped back in. The hard work was sweeping all that sand into the drains.

Maybe some hard work would be good. Being pride leader was a lot of sitting around and he wasn't a sitting around kind of brother.

He shoved his chair back and headed out. A few minutes later, his fingers trailed across the Bast statue outside the arena, then he pushed through the doors.

A very startled Omur looked up from where he was sweeping. 'Maddoc, I didn't expect to see you here.' He dropped the push broom and hustled to the entrance, blocking Doc's path. 'How's Fiona? She seemed pretty banged up. Is someone with her?'

Doc narrowed his eyes. 'Isaiah's with her and I don't like that you're implying I left her alone.'

'No, of course not. My apologies.' He shifted from one foot to the other. 'I should probably get back to work. Thank you for stopping by.'

Doc looked past him. 'Where's your crew? This isn't a one-man job.'

'They're on break.'

Letting a few uncomfortable seconds tick by, Doc finally spoke. 'Where are their brooms?'

Omur looked behind him, his gloved hands opening and closing. 'They must have taken them with them.'

Doc crossed his arms. Enough was enough. 'Lie to me again and I will remove you from my council.'

Omur's eyes yellowed. 'I would never ...' He sighed and glanced behind him again, his shoulders bowing slightly. 'Something has happened.'

Doc's sixth sense triggered, icing his spine. 'This has to do with Heaven's death, doesn't it?'

Omur nodded, his eyes shifting back to human and his body sagging. He ran to lock the arena doors, then motioned for Doc to follow him. 'Come with me.'

He led Doc to the edge of the arena where the metal floor stopped and the lip that outlined the sand-filled area began. Omur scooped up a small handful of the sand and held it out to Doc. 'Someone put powdered silver in the sand.'

The ice spread from Doc's spine to his bloodstream. 'You're positive.'

Omur nodded. 'I'm sure Barasa will find evidence of it on the body.'

Doc rested his hand against his forehead for a moment, then dropped it and walked a few steps away. 'That's how Fi barely touched Heaven but still managed to kill her.'

Omur tipped his hand and dumped the sand back onto the floor. 'Fiona cut Heaven's lip, so it could have easily gotten into her bloodstream that way, and they were both covered with sand by the end of the fight. Because the silver was powdered, the concentration would have been fairly low. Probably only meant to weaken Heaven, but once it got into her system and made its way to her heart . . . ' He frowned. 'Heaven was a small person. It wouldn't have taken too great a quantity. The amount wasn't figured properly.' He glanced at Doc. 'Whoever did it.'

'If this gets out – dammit, it can't get out. I can't have pride members saying Fi didn't win fairly. She's been through enough. Heaven almost killed her.'

Omur raised his hands. 'Barasa and I won't say a word, I promise you. I don't think it's wise to tip off the person who actually did it anyway. We'll find out more if they don't know we're investigating.'

Doc canted his head back and put his hands on his hips. 'This isn't good. I don't like the idea of keeping a secret this big.' One secret was enough, but if Barasa was right about Aliza's spell, keeping the fire secret might not be a concern anymore.

'Look, we hold this to ourselves, find out who did it, then deal with them and it's done. It doesn't need to become an issue.'

'It *can't* become an issue.' This had the potential to blow up big-time, but at least whoever had done it had tipped the scales in Fi's direction. If they'd laced something into the sand that had caused her to die instead, things would be very, very different. 'What if there are marks on Heaven's body? How am I supposed to explain that to her father when he comes to get her body?'

Omur's posture relaxed. 'Chances are Heaven's father will send an emissary in his place. The fact that she lost a challenge to a human and disgraced her pride will most likely mean his disappointment in her will override his parental duty.'

'Damn. Tough family.'

Omur whistled softly. 'You have no idea.'

Doc sighed and stared out at the vast field of sparkling, deadly sand. 'Get me some gloves and a broom.'

Chapter Forty

The sense of pressure registered against Lola's body, but she wasn't ready to turn her back on the deep, beautiful sleep cocooning her. She pushed at whoever was shaking her, trying to connect and finding only empty air. 'Stop,' she muttered.

'Get up,' a familiar voice snarled.

So hungry. Maybe it was time to feed.

Hot breath teased her ear. 'Get the hell up now or I'll find a way to let sunlight in here.'

A sudden panicky rush snapped her into awareness. She bolted upright in the tub. Thomas Creek stood beside her with the comar, Hector, just a few feet away. Hilda, one hand covering her mouth, hugged the bedroom door.

Hilda crossed herself, eyes fearful. 'What's happening? I thought you said she was dead.'

'She is,' Creek answered, his lip curled in disgust. 'She's become a vampire.' He grabbed Lola by the arm and yanked her to her feet. 'Who did this to you? Tell me and I'll go after them.'

Instinct kicked in and she snapped at him. The bathroom

mirror reflected the shifting of her bones and the gleam of her fangs. 'No one did this to me. I wanted this.'

Hilda fainted.

Hector stepped into the bathroom. 'Take your hands off her.'

Creek didn't look at him. 'Kid, you better go while you still can.'

'He stays,' Lola spat. No one told her comar what to do but her. 'I've already purchased his blood rights.'

'The change comes fast, doesn't it? What a piece of work you are.' Creek released her.

All she wanted was to return to the numbing sleep she'd been ripped out of. She needed some of Luciano's potion as soon as possible. Until then, she tried to ignore the fact that the sun currently ruled the sky. It scratched at her skin like a rash and she wasn't anywhere near the light. She needed to arrange for the helioglazing Luciano had told her about. 'My business is just that. Mine. Save your concern for someone who wants it.'

'How could you do this? Especially after everything that happened with Julia?'

The mention of her daughter's name stripped the last shreds of sleep from Lola. 'Don't talk about my daughter like you knew her. I did this for my city and for my grandchild.'

He snorted. 'Doesn't make it right. And after what you did to Mal?' He stared her up and down. 'Hypocrite. Drop that curfew immediately or I will rain the full power of the Kubai Mata down on you so hard, you'll wish you'd never been born. Do I make myself clear?'

'*Ai yi yi*, you're the one who told me to put the curfew in place to begin with! If anyone's a hypocrite, it's you.'

'I was under the spell of an evil woman. She used me to

persuade you. I didn't do it willingly. Now I'm here to tell you to lift it once and for all.'

She tapped her chest with her finger. 'I will, but only because being sired has given me the power to run this town properly.'

He shook his head and backed out of the bathroom, past the comar and away from her. 'You think the human citizens of Paradise City are going to stand for this? As of today, I'm making it my number-one job to watch every move you make.'

'Go ahead and watch. You'll see the citizens understand my sacrifice.' She scowled at him. 'Cross me and I'll put you back behind bars where you belong.'

'No,' Creek answered. 'You won't. The KM are bigger than you. We're here to protect humans from monsters like you.' He narrowed his eyes. 'Your threats are as powerless as you are. Becoming a vampire hasn't made you stronger; it's made you more vulnerable.'

She hissed at him again as he helped Hilda to her feet. 'Get out of my house.'

'Gladly.' He started to go, then turned. 'I'll make you one more promise. As long as there is breath in my body, you will never get your hands on that child.' With that, he stormed out. Hilda ran after him.

Lola planted her hands on her hips. It wasn't worth her energy to respond. She knew how wrong he was and had no doubts that he did, too. Her stomach growled. Luciano had told her she'd wake up ravenous. She held her hand out to her comar. Everything else could wait until she'd fed. 'Hector, if you please, I'm starving.'

'She's coming toward us.' Chrysabelle's throat narrowed a little more with every step Tatiana took. Her hands dipped into her pockets, easing through the slits to grasp the hilts of her daggers. Just the feel of them in her palms gave her comfort.

Mal kept his eyes on his ex-wife. 'I can handle this.'

Her fingers twitched. 'Really? Because all I can think about is sinking one of these blades into her chest.'

He turned and frowned at Chrysabelle. 'Go. Take this opportunity to talk to Damian and get him into position.'

She opened her mouth to argue, but shut it a second later. At least one of them was keeping their wits about them. How it became Mal, she wasn't sure, but he was right. This might be the only chance she had to let Damian know their plans. She nodded and slipped away in the opposite direction of Tatiana's approach.

As she skirted the ballroom and the groups of nobles, she absorbed every snippet of overheard conversation. To a person, they spoke of the child, Lilith, and what it would mean for the future of the vampire nation. Few seemed happy that Tatiana had been chosen as Lilith's guardian, but no one seemed willing to say it to Tatiana's face.

Chrysabelle sincerely wished this started a great many rifts that would grow and fracture the families, weakening them until they were as powerless as they had been so many centuries ago. In those days, the squabbling and infighting had made organization nearly impossible and the comarré had been able to manipulate things from behind the scenes with tremendous ease.

Now the comarré were relegated to their surface abilities, unable to do much more than serve and provide blood, a situation that would only worsen if the nobility's sense of entitlement grew. A suffocating wave of defeat swept her. She choked it back. She couldn't leave Damian here. It would be the death of him. Maybe the death of her. To know her brother was trapped in this life of service and forced politeness, valued for nothing more than what flowed in his veins. No, she would not allow that to happen. Not when their mother had enabled Chrysabelle to escape.

She circled around, headed toward the dais now. The arrangement of plants and animal cages made it easy to slip behind the platform. Not surprisingly, she wasn't the only comarré who'd figured it out. A few others had found the hidden spot and sought refuge from their patrons there. They nodded at her in greeting, exchanging the knowing glances that said it all: How much longer before this foolishness was over?

She made her way to the back of Damian's chair and cleared her throat. He didn't move, just sat looking at the crowd, his large form slouched in the chair like a sack of sand. 'Damian,' she whispered.

He glanced over, then went back to staring at the crowd.

'Damian, I need to speak with you.'

Without looking this time, he spoke. 'There are no comarré positions available in the Dominus's household.'

She scrunched her face up. Was that what he thought she was after? She tugged his sleeve and kept her voice low. 'If things go well, there will be after tonight.'

He twisted around to face her. 'What are you talking about?'

'Might we talk privately?' It wasn't uncommon for comarré to bear innocuous messages from their patron to that of another comarré. She hoped that was all it appeared she was doing.

With a beleaguered sigh, he dropped down onto the floor beside her. 'What is this about?'

'Privately,' she reiterated.

'Fine. Follow me.' He took off at a shamble.

She followed, wishing he could find the fire to move faster. Was this really her brother? The man who'd helped Creek kill Aliza? The man who'd had the guts to run from Tatiana in the first place? Somehow she'd expected more.

He led her into a small study, closed the door, and stood waiting, his hands on the back of a large wing chair. 'Well?'

'Damian, it's me, Chrysabelle.' He would know who she was, wouldn't he? 'You stayed at my house in Paradise City.'

His brow furrowed. 'You don't look like the Chrysabelle I remember from the Primoris Domus.'

'I'm disguised. I have friends with me and we're here to get you out and bring you back to New Florida with us.'

He blinked long and slow. 'Why would you do that?'

She wanted to take his hand but refrained. 'Because you're my brother.'

He rolled his eyes and came around to sit in the chair. 'I find it hard to believe you'd do all this out of some sense of comarré obligation.'

She shook her head. 'No, I mean you are *genuinely* my brother. We are blood relatives.'

'You can't know that. Those kinds of records are sealed.' He slumped a little lower, his posture defeated. 'I get you think you're here to help me, but—'

She stepped into his personal space, her gown brushing his knees. 'What is wrong with you? Creek told me about how you helped him get rid of Aliza, but you barely seem capable of killing a fly right now. I can't believe you ever had the wherewithal to run from Tatiana in the first place.'

With a full-body sigh, Damian let his head drop back against the chair. 'The way I feel lately, I can't believe I did either. I think she drugged my food this evening. Probably afraid I was going to make a scene at her precious ball. Like I care.'

'She can't be drugging you if she's feeding from you. It would affect her, too.'

'She's not feeding from me. Not since her Elder bought a comar a few days ago.'

Tatiana's audaciousness made Chrysabelle's hands long for her blades again. 'You are coming with us. No argument.' She pushed enough of her anger down to concentrate on what needed to be done. 'Can you manage this?'

He stared at her for a long moment. 'You're really my sister?'

'Yes. And I knew our mother.'

For the first time, a spark of life flared in his eyes. 'Knew?'

'She died at Tatiana's hands.'

The spark of life turned to fire. 'What do you need me to do?'

Chapter Forty-One

Talking to every noble who stopped her made Tatiana's patience grow thin. She did what was expected of her, answering their questions, thanking them for coming, accepting their compliments and empty words of support, but the result was that it took far too long to reach the noble she'd been watching. She kept glancing at him, but not once did he move or take his gaze from her. Almost as though he waited for her.

She liked a man who accepted her superiority, but a small bit of disappointment crept into her that he posed no challenge. At last she broke free and waded through the crowd toward him again.

His size seemed to increase as she advanced, but it pleased her to think she'd soon have the brute at her command, because there was no question that she would woo him to her bidding. Men were all very much the same, vampire or human; they all responded to the proper application of female charm.

She extended her hand and offered him the smile that had

opened more doors for her than her current position of power. 'Thank you for coming. I don't believe we've met. I suppose you know who I am.'

'I suppose I do.' The timbre of his voice was oddly familiar. Perhaps she had spoken to him at another ball. 'My ... pleasure.' Something flickered in his dark eyes, but his face remained unchanged. After a moment, he finally lifted his hand to take hers. The contact was brief and she barely felt it through the silk of her elbow-length gloves.

His cool disinterest unnerved her. 'And you are?'

'Lord Moreau. House of Tepes.'

'So we are family, then. How lovely. Do you live in Corvinestri? I think we would have met if you did.'

A muscle in his jaw twitched. 'I spend a great deal of time in Singapore.' He glanced past her and tipped his head toward where Octavian sat on the dais, Lilith on his lap and a crowd of nobles jockeying for his attention. 'A daywalker. Interesting.'

Tatiana acknowledged her family. 'Yes. She's quite remarkable.' The next sentence came out before she could close her mouth. 'I fear for her safety, though.'

Lord Moreau nodded. 'And well you should. There are many who would consider her an asset to their own families. Or a threat.'

That was all the opening she needed. She moved a few centimeters closer and let as much helplessness come into her expression as possible. At least she hoped that's how it read. Helplessness wasn't something she did well. 'There have been threats already.'

Interest widened his eyes slightly. 'From who?'

She shook her head as if the whole thing was too terrible for words. 'There is a rogue comarré in New Florida. Horrible,

horrible creature. She killed the Elder before me, you know, Lord Algernon. Sliced his head clean off.'

Lord Moreau appeared unmoved. 'A comarré killed an Elder?'

'Yes,' Tatiana insisted. 'Then she took up with the most awful anathema vampire, but he's dead now. Killed by a human, of all things. It's been on the news.' She smiled. 'I'm sure you've heard that I lifted the restrictions on electronic communications. Lord Syler is going to do the same for the House of Bathory.'

Lord Moreau nodded. 'And you think she's going to come after the child? A lone comarré.'

Tatiana leaned in. 'You don't understand what these creatures are capable of.' Her brows lifted as she looked out into the crowd. 'You have a comarré. I saw her. You must be very careful of how close you allow them to get to you.'

'I will take that under advisement.' He hesitated. 'What do you plan to do about this comarré?'

She smiled. 'I'm so glad you asked.' With a conspiratorial glance around, she started. 'I'm putting together a team of capable nobles to go after her. A team that, once successful, will be rewarded to the utmost of my power.'

'You don't need a team.' He leaned against the enormous birdcage behind him, expanding the space between them. 'I can handle it.'

'I don't think you understand how devious this comarré is.'

'I don't think you understand how capable I am.' His eyes narrowed. 'But I work alone. If you want my help, you must promise not to speak to anyone else about this issue until I've had my shot. I don't want a bunch of bumbling nobles getting in my way. Understand?'

His sudden control of the situation thrilled her. Even

Octavian rarely did much more than agree with her these days. 'I understand. You have my word.'

His mouth bent. 'Is that any good?'

'Are you implying I don't keep my word, Lord Moreau?'

He straightened and closed the distance between them until little more than a handbreadth separated them. 'I'm implying you have a reputation. And not a good one.'

She pulled back. 'No one speaks to me that way.'

'Maybe they should.' He tipped his head and came imperceptibly closer. 'Maybe you need someone around you who isn't afraid of putting you in your place once in a while. Someone who does more than ask how high when you say jump.'

His words sent a shiver down her spine and into her belly, igniting a fire that hadn't burned in centuries. Not since . . . she forced the memories away. 'My consort is the only one I need around me.'

'Then send him after the comarré.' He turned to go.

'Wait.' She grabbed his arm. Dense muscle tensed under her hand. 'I will give you a chance.'

Moreau's eyes narrowed with a look of satisfaction. 'Then I'll take care of the comarré as my gift to you. To prove my loyalty.'

She mentally shook herself. 'That's very . . . generous.'

He laughed softly, his gaze stroking the curves of her body with a familiarity that made her weak. 'The only thing that's going to be generous is how you reward me when I return.'

Creek drove faster than he should have, but a speeding ticket was the last thing on his mind. For the first time since he'd taken his position as the KM's agent in Paradise City, he actually felt the desire to do the job for more reasons than providing for his family and keeping himself out of prison.

The mayor had lost her mind. And so had the vampire who'd turned her. If this was the way all humans thought, that the answers to their problems lay in the undead life everlasting, the world would crumble faster than the KM predicted.

He skidded to a stop in his grandmother's driveway, spraying gravel as he killed the engine and hopped off the bike. Martin's truck was gone.

Annika walked out onto the porch. 'That was fast.'

He pulled his helmet off. First things first. 'How is she?'

'Resting, but doing well. She's very strong. Her friend will be back at dusk to stay with her.'

'*Strong* is an understatement.' He climbed the steps to stand beside her. 'We need to talk.'

She motioned to the low bench under the front window. He sat at the far end, not waiting for her to join him before he began. 'The mayor's been turned. At her own request, apparently.'

Annika's thin brows rose over her shades. 'That's rather inconvenient. The masters will not be happy with that news. Do you know who did it?'

'A noble.' He shook his head. 'Maybe Dominic, but she wasn't detectable as a vampire. I've never run across that, but that's a Paole power, isn't it?'

'Yes. And there aren't any of them in town.'

He snorted. 'That we know of, but then how could we?'

She nodded. 'If this new vamp is going to start siring children on a regular basis, we'll need to deal with him.'

'Understood. What are your thoughts on the mayor?'

She leaned against the house. 'What would you do about her?'

'I don't know.' Annika's question was probably a test. Didn't make answering it any easier. At least she wasn't Argent, who would have taken a wrong answer as a personal assault. He leaned his forearms on his knees and listened to the insects drone. He flexed his hands, warping the words inked across his knuckles. 'She's going to drop the curfew, which will be good, but I can't see the people who voted for her being happy about her sudden change of affairs.'

'Many will want to follow in her footsteps.' Annika leaned back. 'She did it for the power, I assume?'

He nodded. 'And because she thinks it will help her raise her grandchild.'

Annika snorted. 'She'll never lay hands on that child. I'd sooner give a snake egg to a chicken to hatch.'

He grunted. 'You've been hanging around Mr. Hoops too long.'

One side of her mouth curved up. 'I like the people here. I'm not happy Argent died, but I am glad for the promotion.'

'I can't say I miss Argent.' He slanted his eyes at her. 'You going to say anything about what happened to him?'

'I have to. But I know how to report his death in a way that leaves you blameless.' She smirked a little. 'I wouldn't want to do anything to get on your grandmother's bad side.'

'That's very . . . nice of you.'

Her smile increased. 'I'm not so bad.'

He sat back. 'Why did Argent have such a hard-on for making my life miserable?'

'I'm not allowed to discuss other KM personnel with you.'

He nodded. 'No, I guess you're not. Sorry.'

'If I were, I might tell you that Argent couldn't get past your criminal record.'

'He *knew* the circumstances that brought that record about.'

'And he didn't care.'

Creek let that sink in for a long second. 'You don't seem to have a problem with it.'

Her head dropped like she was looking at her hands. 'I understand the importance of family. Of protecting them.'

'Thanks, by the way.' He canted his head toward the house. 'For everything with my grandmother.'

Annika lifted her head. 'If she were a younger woman, I'd try to recruit her.'

'She'd turn you down.'

Annika laughed. 'Which makes me like her that much more.'

'So.' Creek took a deep breath. 'The mayor. What are the KM statutes on a thing like this?'

'You know them as well as me,' Annika said. 'The moment she endangers human life, she becomes an enemy.'

It didn't surprise him that the mayor killing Mal didn't count. 'And until then?'

'Until then, we wait. And watch.'

He nodded and stood. 'Then I know what I need to do.'

Chapter Forty-Two

If the rise in his temper was any indication, the ketamine was leaving Doc's system. At least his office was soundproofed. 'How can the marks not be noticeable when she was basically drowned in silver dust?'

'They were both covered in sand. And now they're both covered in abrasions from it. There's very little difference in the marks from the sand and the silver. Plus, with Heaven now permanently in her animal form, they'd have to know what they were looking for to find it under all that fur,' Barasa answered. 'The real damage happened internally.'

'Then what if they do a necropsy?'

Omur shook his head. 'They won't. Her father might not care enough to pick her body up himself, but I guarantee he won't want her cut up like that.'

'You're still making assumptions. I've called São Paulo twice and both times they've told me he's not available. Rodrigo Silva is either too busy to take my calls or he doesn't recognize me as pride leader. Either way, we could have a problem. I'm *not* telling him his daughter is dead by leaving him a message.'

Barasa nodded. 'I agree.'

'You might have to go to him,' Omur said.

Doc stared at the man. 'Are you insane? Talk about walking into the lion's den.'

'Jaguar,' Omur corrected.

Doc pushed to his feet. 'Dammit. We have to figure this out before it gets any worse.'

Someone knocked at the door. Doc glanced at Omur and Barasa, but they clearly had no idea who it was. 'Come in,' he called.

One of the guards opened the door. 'There's a visitor for you—'

'Move.' A wide, squat beast of a man pushed past the guard. He locked eyes with Doc. 'Are you the new pride leader?' he asked in heavily accented English.

Doc squared his shoulders, prepared for anything at this point. 'Yes. And you are?'

'Rodrigo Silva. I'm here to see my daughter.'

The minute Tatiana left, Dominic and Katsumi joined Mal.

'What was that about?' Dominic asked.

Mal snorted softly. 'More insanity. She's planning to put together a team of loyal nobles to go after Chrysabelle. The best part is Tatiana thinks I'm dead. I guess good news travels fast.' *Too bad it's not true.*

Dominic looked around before speaking. 'Things are bad enough with the mayor now. We can't have a horde of nobles infesting our city.'

Mal shook his head. 'We won't. I know how to work her. I convinced her that I was the right noble for the job and that she should give me a shot at it before telling anyone else about her plans. It was pretty easy, actually.' His mouth hitched up on one side as memories of his past life with her resurfaced like dead fish. 'Same old Shaya.'

Katsumi made a dismissive noise. 'If you're done reminiscing, can we move on?'

Mal stifled his anger. 'What did you find out?'

She nodded toward the dais. 'The woman who was seated beside Octavian is Daciana.'

'The one who was in my hold.'

'Yes. If Tatiana doesn't have the baby, one of them will or one of only two servants. A wet nurse, Oana, and the head of Tatiana's staff, Kosmina.'

'Either of the servants seem like they could be flipped?'

Dominic shook his head. 'I don't think so.' He looked past Mal. 'Carissa is coming.'

Mal turned to see Chrysabelle approaching. She dipped her head and did a brief curtsy, a show of respect for the eyes around them. 'You talked to Damian?'

As she rose from the curtsy, her disguise couldn't mask the anger in her eyes. 'Yes and he's on board. *She* has him drugged. Drugged,' she growled softly. 'She doesn't deserve a comar.'

Katsumi frowned. 'How can she feed off him if he's drugged?'

Chrysabelle looked away, checking the crowd. 'She's using Daciana's comar.'

Mal wanted to take her hand, reassure her in some way, but in this setting, that wasn't allowed. *Good.* 'We're going to get him out of here. It's going to be okay.'

She nodded, her jaw tight.

'How soon?' Dominic asked.

'Soon,' she answered, repositioning herself so they could all see the dais. 'You should get closer to the doors.' She gave Dominic a little smile. 'We'll see you on the other side.'

'On the other side,' he agreed. 'Be safe.'

Or die. 'You too,' Mal said.

With that, Dominic and Katsumi headed toward the ballroom's entrance so they could move when the opportunity presented itself. Which it should very soon.

Chrysabelle stood at his side, nervousness wafting off her in waves, her body stiffly poised as if ready to leap to her brother's aid, even though they both knew that couldn't happen. 'You'll be with him soon.'

Her gaze never left her brother. 'I hope so. Otherwise, I—'

Damian got out of his seat and approached Tatiana, who was deep in conversation with a small group of nobles. He leaned in and interrupted. The crowd noise made hearing the conversation impossible, but the change in Tatiana's expression from politely interested to obvious displeasure said it all.

Beside Mal, Chrysabelle's breath hitched.

Tatiana glared at Damian, then ignored him and went back to her conversation. He inhaled deeply, then spoke to her again. This time, she backhanded him, splitting his lip.

Chrysabelle swallowed and a shocked silence rippled out from the nobles around Tatiana, spreading through the crowd as those in attendance turned their heads.

Damian glowered at Tatiana but said nothing. She pointed toward the door. 'I will deal with you later.'

'No, you won't,' Chrysabelle whispered.

With that, Damian walked away and the crowd quickly returned to their conversations with a new, hugely interesting topic to discuss, giving Dominic and Katsumi the cover they needed to navigate the crowd and follow Damian out.

'Now we pray,' Chrysabelle said. She glanced at Mal, her calm expression noticeably forced. 'Well, I pray.' She closed her eyes and took a deep breath.

Mal watched the crowd around them, but no one paid the unsocial noble and his comarré more than a passing second of attention. Then movement on the dais caught his attention. Maybe this was the start of it. He hoped. Anything was better than the waiting. 'Chrysabelle.'

'Hmm?' Her eyes were still closed.

'Octavian's moving. He has the child and she's fussing. This might be the opening we've been looking for.'

She opened her eyes and turned to see. 'Okay,' she said with a nod. 'Time to go.'

Still seething from the embarrassment of Damian's stupidity, Tatiana almost snapped as a hand touched her shoulder. The moment she saw Octavian, she forced herself away from the volatile edge she teetered on. 'What is it?'

He shifted a fussing Lilith to his other shoulder, patting her back to no avail. 'I'm going to take her to the suite.' He frowned, his gaze roaming her face. 'Are you all right? What happened with ... ' His eyes darted toward the nobles she'd been speaking with. 'Perhaps we'll just talk later.'

She laid a hand on his arm to keep him there, then turned only enough to engage her audience. 'If you'll excuse me, my child and my consort need me.' She didn't wait for their response. 'What's the matter, my darling?' She leaned in to brush a curl back from Lilith's forehead. 'Are you hungry?'

'She might be. Oana's in the suite and Kosmina's already headed there to warm a bottle.' He jounced Lilith up and down a bit. 'I think the crowd might be overwhelming her, too.' He shook his head in frustration. 'These people. They want to touch her and hold her and—'

'Touch her? Hold her?' Tatiana squeezed his arm as horror gripped her. 'You haven't let them, have you?'

'Of course not.' He pulled Lilith deeper into his embrace. 'Let me take her to Oana; then we can discuss what happened with Damian.'

Tatiana shook her head. 'Stay with her. I'll come in a few minutes and we can talk about it in private. I could use a break myself.'

He hesitated. 'All right.' He kissed her on the cheek. 'In a few.'

As he left, she deposited her half-empty goblet of blood onto a passing server's tray, then picked up the skirts of her gown and prepared for the arduous slog to the door. She hoped the look on her face would stop anyone from approaching her.

'You're not leaving, are you, Lady Tatiana?'

At the question, she turned. 'Lord Moreau.' She lifted her chin and ignored the spark of unwanted desire his voice ignited within her. 'I must see to my daughter.'

He stared at her, pinning her with an oddly familiar look that arrowed through every carefully cultivated ounce of bravado. She hated him for that. And desperately wanted to bend him to her will. He shrugged. 'Your consort isn't capable of that?'

'He's perfectly capable.'

Lord Moreau barely moved, but he was somehow closer. 'Let him handle it, then, as I am incapable of bearing this crush much longer. How soon do you want the issue with the comarré resolved?'

Business it was, then. 'As soon as possible.'

'Do you want her alive?'

'Yes.' Even though he was going to help her, she wanted to jab at him. To prove to both of them that he was no one special. 'You won't succeed, you know.'

He smiled ever so slightly. 'You should really work on those trust issues.'

She picked up her skirts again. 'I have to go.'

'I want all the information you have on this comarré. Unless you want me to fail for a reason.'

She paused, the peculiar feeling of being bested unsettling her. She wasn't quite ready to declare this battle over. 'Fine. You may walk with me, Lord Moreau, and I will fill you in on this rogue comarré. That way when you fail, you will have no one to blame but yourself.'

Chapter Forty-Three

Hilda was gone. Lola hadn't seen her since she'd run out of the bedroom. So be it. If the woman couldn't handle her boss being a vampire, there was really no point in her remaining employed here.

Hector returned from her office and held out the phone she'd sent him to fetch. 'Anything else I can do for you, my lady?'

'No, that's fine.' She took the phone and pointed to the empty end of the sofa. 'Come sit.' The den was the darkest room in the house with its north-facing windows sheltered by large palms and overgrown palmettos. The potion Luciano had given her was keeping her awake like he'd said it would, but the sun's presence still made her skin itch. She shuddered. 'Once the helioglazing is done, I won't be such a prisoner in my own home. I hate feeling so dependent.'

Hector looked crestfallen as he sat.

She smiled at him. 'Don't worry, I'll still need you.'

Happy with that, he picked up an e-reader off the coffee table and settled his back against the sofa's high arm. His feet stretched toward her, the tops covered in a constellation of gold stars. For the briefest of seconds, she wondered how much that had hurt, but the thought slipped out of her mind as quickly as it had entered. She punched her office number into the phone and waited.

'Mayor Diaz-White's office. Valerie speaking.'

'Valerie, it's Lola. I'm working from home today. Can you let general reception answer the phone? I need you to come over here.'

'Yes, ma'am.'

Lola sighed at Valerie's terse response. 'I'm dropping the curfew and I need you to help me draft the announcement.'

'You are? That's great. What changed your mind, if you don't mind me asking? Don't get me wrong, I'm very happy you're dropping it. Just curious.'

'I'll explain when you get here. There's one more thing.'

'Sure, anything.'

'I need you to bring John Havoc with you. Can you arrange that? I'd like to make things right with him.'

She answered with a smile in her voice. 'I'd be happy to arrange that. Be there as soon as I can.'

'Thank you.' Lola hung up and held the phone to her chest. If this went as poorly as things had gone with Creek, she'd be looking for a new administrative assistant tomorrow. But Valerie wouldn't react that way, would she?

Lola stood and paced to the bookshelf that held more plaques and awards than books. Maybe John was the one she should be worried about. Vampires and varcolai weren't supposed to get along, but John wasn't just any shifter. He was a friend. Or had been.

A heartfelt apology and they'd be back on solid footing, wouldn't they?

Or was that wishful thinking? Exactly how much animosity was there between the varcolai and the vampires?

Nerves skipped over her skin along with a sudden vision of John attacking her. She shook her head and went to the bar to pour a shot of rum, wondering just how big a mistake she'd made by asking Valerie to bring a potential enemy into her home.

'Mr. Silva.' Doc stared at the man, mentally sizing him up. Rodrigo was shorter, but maybe a little more muscled. Doc definitely had him on reach. 'I've been trying to get in touch with you.'

'I already know about the challenge. Heaven called me a day ago. Told me what was going on. I know I missed the event, but I got here as quickly as I could. There is nothing I wouldn't do for my daughter.'

Doc shot Omur a look before returning to Rodrigo. 'That's ... very admirable.' Damn, this was going to suck. 'You're right that you missed the challenge.'

Rodrigo came a little farther in. 'I wish to congratulate my daughter, but first, I want to speak to you.'

Congratulate her? Ouch. 'What about?'

'This ... other woman of yours.' He sat in the last empty chair in front of Doc's desk and heaved out a tired sigh. He opened his mouth to speak, then glanced at Omur and Barasa. 'These are your council members?'

'Yes.' Doc sat as well. 'I'm in the process of replacing the third.'

'You trust them?'

So far, Doc thought. 'Yes.'

Rodrigo nodded thoughtfully. 'Good. Having men around you that you can trust is very important in our position.' He spread his hands over his thighs. 'This is how I wish to speak to you today. Pride leader to pride leader, *si*?'

Doc leaned back in his chair, still apprehensive. 'Yes. Good.'

'What I say here to you is not to be repeated outside these walls. I have your word?'

Slightly more intrigued, Doc gave a short nod. 'You do.'

Rodrigo leaned forward. 'This other woman . . . ' He sighed again. 'I understand how it is. My marriage was a political one as well. My mate was not the woman I was in love with, but love . . . ' He shrugged. 'Those of us who hold power have little room for love.'

'I don't believe that,' Doc said.

Rodrigo smiled sadly. 'You are young. You will learn. Unfortunately, my daughter has no doubt made things difficult for you.' He muttered something in Portuguese. 'Heaven is our youngest and my wife spoiled her. I know she is beautiful, but beauty is no replacement for a kind heart and a sweet spirit. She is . . . ' He raised his hand. 'I will just say she is too much like her mother.'

Doc stared at the man for a few seconds. 'This isn't the conversation I expected to have with you.'

'It is good to have this honest talk, yes?' Rodrigo sat back. 'I will confess one more thing. I never liked Sinjin. Not his politics, not his personality, not his excess of ambition. He pursued me for Heaven's hand. He was relentless. I knew he wanted only the political standing the alliance would bring.' Rodrigo frowned. 'I finally agreed. I thought actually marrying her would be the punishment he deserved. And part of me was happy to give her into someone else's hands.'

Again, Doc was left without words. What could anyone say to that?

'I know, you are thinking I am a bad father.'

'No, not at all.' Doc shook his head vehemently. 'You did what any man in your position would have done.'

Rodrigo went silent then, nodding only slightly and studying Doc. At last, he spoke. 'I know very little of you, but what I do know, I like. Perhaps our alliance will actually mean something.' He stood and offered Doc his hand. 'I am not unhappy to have you in my family.'

Doc stood but kept his hands on the desk. 'Before you shake my hand, there is something you should know.'

Rodrigo let his hand drop. A fleeting shimmer of gold passed through his eyes. 'What?'

'Heaven lost the challenge. She's . . . ' Dammit, there was no easy way to say this. 'She's dead.'

The soft leather soles of Chrysabelle's slippers made it fairly easy to trail Octavian undetected, but she still kept a good distance between them, occasionally ducking into open doors or hiding in alcoves in case he looked back. He was a vampire, after all, and the farther away they got from the ball, the less noise there was to cover the sounds of her breathing and heartbeat.

Perhaps the constant traffic of servants through the halls helped her. With so many guests staying at the estate, there was too much to be done for the servants to rest. Or perhaps it was the child's crying in his ear and the soft words he spoke to her in an attempt to soothe her. She settled down a little, but the crying only became soft whimpers and hiccupy sobs.

When he stopped, Chrysabelle darted back around the last corner and listened. A door opened and closed. *Holy mother, protect me.* With a false confidence, she sauntered forth, opened the suite door, and slipped in.

Beyond the foyer's arched entrance was a living room, and through there, another door opened into a bedroom. All empty as far as she could see, but small sounds deeper in told her to proceed cautiously. She inched forward, every nerve in her body on alert to hide or run or fight. Through a closed door in the living room, the sounds she'd heard became more distinct. More female. Two women. Most likely the child's nursemaid and another of Tatiana's servants. If Octavian had handed the baby off, where was he? If they had two adjoining suites, he could have left by another door. She relaxed and stopped hunching.

'What are you doing in here?'

She froze, the male voice behind her proof that Octavian hadn't gone anywhere. With a deep breath, she fixed an innocent smile on her face and turned. He still held the child, who had finally quieted. 'I'm sorry, I've gotten so turned around. All these suites look the same to me.' Then, as if just noticing the baby, she exclaimed, 'Oh, the baby! Look how darling she is.' Chrysabelle came a few steps closer. 'Look at those precious cheeks. May I hold her? I'd love to hold her.'

'No.' Octavian lifted Lilith higher.

Chrysabelle had expected that answer. Time was not on her side. If she tried to talk him into giving her the baby, all could be lost. Hoping she was doing the right thing, she pulled one blade free of its sheath and brandished it. The false sweetness left her words. 'Give me the child and I'll let you live.'

His eyes silvered. 'Who are you working for? Who sent you?'

'You don't need to know that.' She lifted the dagger, her heart pounding. 'The child. Now.'

He stood his ground. 'What family? Tell me that much.'

'No family. No more questions. Hand her over.'

The silver in his eyes faded. 'KM?'

'What?' She'd heard him, but doubted her ears.

'Kubai Mata?'

Caught off guard, she went still, her only movement the intake of breath. She'd never known a vampire to give enough credence to the KM to even bring them up as a possible enemy, but then Octavian had been with Tatiana at Aliza's. Maybe he'd figured out that's what Creek was. She shook her head, unwilling to give anything away. 'No.'

'You lie. I heard the skip of your pulse.'

'So what if they are who sent me? No one will believe you when you tell them that.'

He walked closer, stopping only when the point of her dagger was within striking distance. 'I won't tell them. The KM train us to reveal as little as possible.'

'You're ... KM?'

'Who do you think sent the picture of your brother and the invite to the ball?' He lifted Lilith from his shoulder and held her out to Chrysabelle.

The shock of the moment could be processed later. Right now, she needed to go. She dropped the dagger Mal had given her and untied the sash Nyssa had reworked into a sling for the baby, looping it across her body and retying it securely. Then she took Lilith from Octavian's arms and settled her into the sling.

Octavian picked up the dagger, holding the hilt toward her to take when she was ready. 'Quickly,' he admonished. 'Tatiana will be here any—'

The door opened in the next room and Tatiana walked in, Mal right behind her. Rage glinted metallic in her eyes a second after she assessed the scene before her. 'What the hell is going on?'

Chapter Forty-Four

Mal had expected Chrysabelle to be gone by now. Octavian, eyes wide in shock – or terror – still held outstretched in his hand one of the daggers Mal had given her. How Chrysabelle had talked Octavian into giving up the baby, Mal couldn't imagine. He followed Tatiana as she stormed through the living room and into the bedroom.

'I said what the hell is going on?' Tatiana shouted. 'Why is she holding Lilith?'

Chrysabelle grabbed the dagger from Octavian as she whipped out her second blade.

'Octavian,' Tatiana snarled. 'Do something!'

Octavian lunged weakly for Chrysabelle, but she dodged him, dancing farther back into the room. Tatiana reached for the top of her gown's bodice and pulled out two long, slim blades.

'You, you're ...' She jabbed one in Chrysabelle's direction, then swung around to glare at Mal. 'Is that your comarré, Moreau? Why is she holding my child? Tell her to put Lilith down or I will kill her.'

Their cover would be blown soon enough. 'Let me speak

with her.' He stepped between Tatiana and Chrysabelle. 'Get out now,' he told Chrysabelle in a low voice, throwing his arm out to block Tatiana.

With a nod, Chrysabelle started past, but Tatiana ducked under his arm. 'Octavian, grab her.'

He did, latching on to Chrysabelle's upper arm. She twisting and sliced downward, cutting through the upper sleeve of his jacket. Blood scent filled the air and his arm went limp, but the move spun her out of Mal's reach and toward Tatiana.

In an instant, Tatiana struck, her narrow blade flashing as it sliced through the top part of the sling, leaving Chrysabelle bleeding across her shoulder and the baby hanging by a few shreds of silk.

Lilith began to cry.

Mal grabbed Tatiana's blades with his hands. They bit into his palms but he yanked them away and tossed them, jerking Tatiana forward and sending her sprawling onto her belly. 'Enough.'

The shock of his actions bought them a small window of time. Blood seeping down the front of her dress, Chrysabelle ran for the door, her arms hugging the baby to her while she kept a grip on her weapons. Tatiana shoved a foot out, tripping her. Lilith was tossed free. The fall sent her wailing to a deafening level.

'Lilith,' Tatiana screamed. She struggled to crawl toward her child, but Mal planted his booted foot on her back and pushed her down. She whipped her head around, pure hatred gleaming at him from her silver gaze. She thrust her metal hand out in front of her and it morphed into a sword. 'You are about to die, Moreau. Samael protects us!'

As she positioned herself to strike, black smoke boiled in

from the foyer, gagging them with the stench of brimstone. Choking, Chrysabelle tried to reach Lilith, but before she could, the smoke parted.

The Castus stepped out and roared his displeasure loud enough that the entire estate must have heard it. 'Why have you called me? Why is my child crying?'

'Samael,' Tatiana cried. 'Help us!' She pointed at Chrysabelle. 'Kill her!'

Instead, the Castus ignored Tatiana and picked Lilith up. The baby stopped wailing instantly. He turned to look down at Tatiana. 'We gave her to you to protect.'

'I am, I—'

'You are *not*.' Samael moved forward, the skirts of shadow covering his lower half undulating like a storm cloud, faces and reaching hands moving through the murky depths.

Mal took his foot off Tatiana and backed up. He knew when he wasn't the biggest dog in the fight. At his side, Octavian sat on the floor, holding his bleeding arm and looking like he might pass out. Vamplings didn't have quite the same healing power as older vampires.

'This,' the Castus hissed, 'is over.' With that, he disappeared the same way he'd come in, a billow of smoke and stench, Lilith seated in his embrace.

Tatiana threw her head back and howled, a gut-twisting keening that brought the voices to life. Then she launched herself at Mal.

'You're going to die.' She slashed at him, her metal hand now a shorter sword.

He ducked the blow. 'Run,' he told Chrysabelle, pushing her toward the door.

She hesitated.

'*Go*.' He grabbed Tatiana's wrists. 'I'll be right behind you. I know the route.' There was no way he'd leave her alone for long, not surrounded by a host of vampires and bleeding the way she was. Some nobles wouldn't care that she belonged to someone else.

Fear shadowed her eyes, but she nodded, glancing at Tatiana. '*Hurry,*' she mouthed, then took off.

Tatiana kicked him as fringe security came barreling in a few seconds later. 'What's going on in here?' one asked.

'Go after her,' Tatiana screamed.

Another guard leaped onto Mal's back. He elbowed that one off him, then shoved Tatiana into a second one. They went down in a tangled heap on top of Octavian, who bared his teeth in pain like a wounded animal.

The moment at hand, Mal took off after Chrysabelle, her blood scent painting an almost visual trail for him to follow. Hopefully he was the only vampire running after her. He at least had to be the first one to reach her.

Accessing the mayor's property hadn't been easy, but it hadn't been that hard either. Her new security team left holes. Holes Creek had slipped right through. Now he crouched in a thicket of multicolored crotons outside the mayor's living room windows, his breathing and pulse silent in the way the Kubai Mata had taught him.

Lola reclined on the sofa, her comar at her feet, looking for all the world like she'd become the queen of something. Fool woman. All she'd done was create new problems. For him, for the city, and for the KM. Whatever the noble who'd turned her had gotten in exchange, it wasn't enough. Creek would make sure of that.

A woman he didn't recognize entered with John Havoc right behind her. Damn. He hadn't expected to see the varcolai here. Creek shifted slightly to get a better view, careful not to make any noise that might catch the supersensitive abilities of those inside, and listened hard.

John spoke first. 'Valerie told me you plan to drop the curfew. You know I think—' His eyes shifted to the comar for a second, then back to her. The muscles in his jaw tensed but behind his ever-present shades, his eyes were unreadable. 'Why is there a comar here?'

Lola smiled. 'Hector, this is my administrative assistant, Valerie, and my former bodyguard, John. John is a varcolai. A wolf.'

Hector held out his gilded hand. 'Nice to meet you.'

John didn't shake it. Valerie stayed slightly behind him, like she expected something to happen. Or John had told her to stay behind him because *he* expected something to happen. Creek pulled farther back into the bushes and held still while two guards strolled past so deep in conversation, Creek probably could have waved at them and they wouldn't have noticed.

When he looked up again, Hector had dropped his hand and was now pouting at his end of the couch.

John took his sunglasses off and a flash of wolfen blue rippled through his eyes. 'You've been turned.'

Lola laughed from her spot on the couch. 'You make it sound like a disease. Yes, I've been turned.'

Valerie gasped. 'That's awful.'

'No, it isn't.' The mayor tilted her head. 'It's what's best for the city. And it's the only chance I have of recovering my grandchild.' She kicked her feet out and stood. 'Hector, leave us.'

The comar scurried off with a speed that announced his willingness to go.

The mayor picked up a short glass off the coffee table and walked it over to the bar. 'Drink?'

'No,' John answered. As soon as the mayor's back was to them, Valerie reached out and squeezed his hand, then quickly released it. John positioned himself more fully in front of her. 'Why do you think this is good for the city?'

The mayor filled her glass about halfway, then put the decanter back in its spot. She turned and leaned against the bar. 'You know, alcohol doesn't seem to affect me quite as much as it did when I was human.' She lifted the glass, downed the contents, then set the glass aside and walked back to them.

'It's good for the city because it means I now understand all of my citizens, the human and the othernatural. Without a strong leader, Paradise City could be torn apart in the coming days. Now I am that strong leader.' She lifted her hands. 'How can that not be a good thing?'

John palmed the back of his neck. 'It can be. In many ways.'

Lola's mood shifted. 'I have a grandchild to raise. One who is half vampire. How am I supposed to manage that without understanding her needs?'

'You don't even have custody of that child. Or know where she is. And what about her father? What about his part in this?'

'Preacher lives in an abandoned church. He's in no position to raise or care for a child. And what is he doing to get her back? Nothing that I've heard. I already have someone going after her.'

'Who is this someone?'

'Dominic.'

John swore too softly for Creek to hear. 'He's the one who turned you, isn't he? He's doing this on purpose. Ever since Doc became pride leader, I knew it was just a matter of time. He's building his forces up.' He pointed at the mayor. '*This* is exactly why it's bad for the city. You'll side with the vampires now, then the varcolai will feel threatened. It will lead to war.'

Creek nodded as he lifted his phone to get a few pictures. The varcolai understood perfectly.

Lola tipped her head back as if searching for an answer in the air. She sighed heavily before looking at John again. 'For your information, Dominic didn't turn me. And I don't think the vampires will be all that happy to have me on their side after I did away with one of their own. Not that I'll be taking sides anyway. I'm looking to be a better leader. I told you that.'

John stared at her for a long, uneasy moment. 'I thought I knew you once. I thought we were . . . friends.'

'We were. We still could be. You were like family to me. You saved my life, John.'

Disgust angled the corners of his mouth. He put his shades back on. 'Whatever that was worth. You gave it away to a vampire.'

Lola went toward him a step. He didn't retreat, just put a hand out in front of Valerie. The move didn't go unnoticed by the mayor. 'You think I would hurt her? Valerie has been with me as long as I've been mayor. Since I was a councilwoman.' She tapped the space over her heart. 'I'm the same person I've always been. Becoming a vampire hasn't changed me.'

'I bet Preacher would disagree with you.' John snorted and looked away. 'You have a lot to learn. Speaking of Preacher—'

'John, I'm serious. I want things to be the way they were. I want you to come back to work protecting me. Luke too. The curfew will be dropped and we'll work on keeping peace in this city. Just having you working for me again would go a long way toward showing that varcolai and vampires don't have to be enemies.'

'Do you mean it?' Valerie asked.

'Yes.' A spasm of emotion caused her vampire features to move across her face. 'I swear on my *abuela*'s grave I do.'

A spider crawled across Creek's hand, but he didn't move. Neither did the trio inside. They just stared at one another.

Finally, John spoke, nodding reluctantly. 'Okay. But do one thing that goes against that promise and you will have the wrath of the varcolai upon you like a plague.'

She held out her hand to him. This time he shook it. 'Welcome back, John.'

'Thanks.' But caution masked his face. 'You really do need to talk to Preacher as soon as you can. He hears what's going on, that he's being left out of decisions concerning his daughter, and you'll have a whole new set of problems to deal with.'

'Understood. I will take care of that, I promise you.'

'Good.' John looked unconvinced.

Lola smiled at Valerie. 'Let's get that announcement drafted. The sooner this curfew is dropped, the sooner we can move forward.'

John stepped out of Valerie's way as she came out from behind him. 'Why such a change of heart? After everything you did, this doesn't make sense.'

Lola sat on the couch, Valerie beside her. 'I was led astray by a dark influence. A man whose only agenda is destruction. A man who is this city's enemy.'

Creek lifted his hand and watched the spider pick its way across his knuckles. He tipped his hand so the creature could find a leaf.

'And that man is?' John asked.

Lola's hands fisted. 'Thomas Creek.'

Chapter Forty-Five

Unfathomable sorrow scored Tatiana's bones, immobilizing her with the sucking loss of her child. What had just happened? She staggered to her feet, blind to the disarray swirling around her. She stumbled toward the door after Moreau and his comarré. Blood scent mingled with the fading brimstone, bringing her anger up like acid.

She would prove the Castus wrong. She *would* get Lilith back from them.

Leaving the chaos behind, she caught sight of Moreau's long black coat disappearing around a corner. She took off after him. A couple of drops of blood here and there confirmed that he was following his comarré.

Good. She would kill them both.

'Guards,' she yelled. 'With me!'

The sound of fringe obeying her was all she needed to push harder after Moreau. Her silk slippers had no traction. She kicked them off. Barefoot, she picked up speed, closing in.

Downward into the belly of the estate they descended. He was always a hallway or stairwell ahead. She'd catch a door swinging shut, just missing him. Still, she ran, Lilith's face melding with Sophia's. She would *not* lose another child. She would kill Moreau and his blood whore and prove to the Castus that she was capable of protecting Lilith. They would give her back. They *had* to give her back.

The slap of her bare soles against the hall's marble floor echoed in her ears. The fringe guards had fallen behind, unable to keep up with her. So be it. She'd take on Moreau alone. He had no idea who he was up against.

'Moreau,' she yelled ahead. 'I'm going to flay you stem to stern.'

Laughter bounced back, infuriating her. Charging her onward. How dare he spin his tale about going after the comarré when he'd been in league with his own blood whore to work harm against her. The House of Tepes would be better served by his ashes than his lies.

The marble changed to concrete. They were in the servants' section now. Lower yet and the lighting dimmed to the minimum used for storage areas.

Voices ahead. A woman. The comarré by the blood scent that mingled with the damp and dirt.

Tatiana slowed until her steps were soundless. The fringe came running up behind her. She put a hand out to quiet them and eased forward to get a look around the corner.

Moreau and his comarré stood in front of a blank section of wall. Her sleeves were pulled back and her forearms were together like a shield before her face. Maybe she was praying, knowing they'd come to a dead end. Little good that would do her.

Suddenly the wall split. A bloody secret passage.

'Like hell you do,' Tatiana screamed as she leaped toward them. She swung her metal hand up and into a broadsword.

'Blade,' Moreau shouted. The comarré handed him one; then he shoved her through the ever-widening opening. 'Close the opening.'

'Ma-Moreau,' the comarré stuttered, eyes flashing with fear. 'Not without you.'

But he turned away from her. 'You.' He pointed the dagger at Tatiana. 'We have business to finish.'

'Yes, we do.' She swung, catching the edge of a stack of crates and slicing through the bottom of one. Wood splinters sprayed over her, distracting her for a second.

He leaned back and kicked, connecting with her hip and slamming her to the ground.

'Come with me,' the comarré begged, even as she lifted her arms.

'Go,' Moreau commanded the comarré.

Tatiana jumped up, but Moreau leaped onto her. He plunged the dagger toward her chest. She twisted as it came down, catching the blade in her shoulder. Pain erupted from the pierced flesh.

The wall began to close. Tatiana shortened her broadsword into a weapon better suited for close combat.

'Damn it,' he snarled. 'That was meant for your heart.' He yanked the dagger free and jumped back as she swung. 'Next time, you'll be ash.'

Blood gushed from the wound even as the edges knit together. She pushed upright to go after him. 'I don't think so.'

He shook his head and a second later, a wisp of black smoke danced in the air where he'd been, then vanished through the wall just before the opening disappeared.

Tatiana rammed her sword hand into it. The impact jarred her shoulder and reopened the wound. She turned the sword back into a fist. In all her years, she'd only seen one vampire turn to smoke. One lying, deceitful, comarré-loving vampire. Anger forced her fist into the wall again, dislodging chunks of plaster and stone.

How was it possible? She'd seen his death with her own eyes. Howling in frustration, she fell to her knees. Rage seethed through her at the betrayal that had just been measured against her and at the way she'd been played for a fool. 'Next time, husband, you will die for real. And your blood whore with you.'

'Dead.' Rodrigo said the word like he didn't understand it. He swallowed and dropped back into his chair. His jaw hitched forward, then back into place. 'I see.'

Doc sat down as well. Heat radiated through him enough that he wondered if he should sneak a pill. 'That's why I've been calling you. I didn't want you to find out through other sources.'

Still Rodrigo didn't meet his eyes, instead staring blankly ahead. 'It was a fair fight?'

Dammit. That was not an easy question to answer. Then Barasa did it for him.

'I'm the pride physician. I'd be happy to do a necropsy if you'd like.'

'No.' Rodrigo shook his head. 'Her mother wouldn't want her cut open. I'm sorry I asked. I have no doubt it was fair.' He exhaled long and slow, looking suddenly tired and deflated.

'You've come a long way,' Doc said. 'I'll have a room prepared for you.'

'That's not necessary. There are plenty of places to stay—'

'I insist.' Sympathy for the man softened the edges of Doc's frustration with everything that had happened. And maybe a little guilt. 'It's the least I can offer you. If there is anything I or my pride can do for you, we'll do it. Your reputation as a fair leader precedes you. I would very much like to keep things good between us.'

Rodrigo nodded but sat quietly, his gaze focused low. 'Perhaps there is something else you can do for me.'

'Name it.'

Rodrigo glanced at Omur and Barasa. 'You are looking for a third council member?'

'Yes. The last one couldn't accept me in place of Sinjin.'

'I have a son, the third born. If you would take him as your council member, I would be indebted to you. Things have not gone well for him in our pride. A fresh start would be good for him.'

'You don't think he'd have an issue with me, considering his sister's death?'

Rodrigo shook his head and at last made eye contact. 'Each of us knows the way of the pride. No one enters a challenge without knowing the consequences. He will understand.' His hands loosened their grip on the chair. 'Remo is a good boy. A little troubled, but good.'

Doc wanted to know what *troubled* meant, but asking delicate questions had never been his thing. 'How ... that is ... what exactly—'

'His trouble?' Rodrigo laughed, a good sound to hear. 'His trouble is women. Too many of them. They fight over him, create problems I have to solve.' He leaned forward in his chair. 'If you knew how many angry fathers I have had to appease.' He threw his hands up. 'They all think Remo should marry their daughter. Then they expect favors from me when he doesn't.'

Doc smiled. 'So Remo's a player, huh? There are worse things to be.'

'Keep him busy with work and his troubles should be behind him. But give him no special treatment because he is my son. Treat him like you would any other member of your council.' Rodrigo raised his brows. 'Do we have a deal?'

With a nod, Doc stood and held out his hand. 'We do.' As Rodrigo rose to shake it, Doc continued. 'I am very sorry about Heaven.'

Pain filled Rodrigo's eyes again, but still he pumped Doc's hand. 'As am I. But some good has come out of this, after all, no? From this day forward, the alliance between our prides is renewed.'

'From this day forward,' Doc said. So long as Remo wasn't the nosy type.

Chrysabelle walked through the comarré tunnels beneath Lord Syler's estate, every step taking her closer to safety and farther away from where she wanted to be. At Mal's side.

Blood crusted the front of her gown and her shoulder throbbed with pain, but she was still alive. Was Mal? She knew he'd pushed her through the door to save her, but the plan had been to stay together. They could kill Tatiana another day. Like when she didn't have a horde of fringe guards at her beck and call and they weren't in the midst of a huge gathering of nobles and after Chrysabelle had a chance to spend some time with her brother.

She exhaled. Damian should be airborne by now, or about to be. She smiled. At least that part of the plan had gone well.

A scuffling sound came from behind her. She turned to see a

dark shape walking toward her from the shadows. Fear glided over her like a cool breeze. She ignored it, snagging her last blade and brandishing it. If this was her end, she would go down fighting. 'Who goes there?'

'Your friendly neighborhood vampire.'

She tucked the blade away and ran into Mal's arms. 'You made it!' A second later, she wriggled out of his embrace and punched him with her good arm. 'Why did you push me through? I could have stayed and fought with you.'

'You have family to think about now. And obviously, I didn't stay.' With a quick glance behind him, he grabbed her hand and pulled her along. 'We should pick it up a little. I went to smoke right before the passage closed. Unfortunately, Tatiana probably knows I'm not dead now.'

'You didn't kill her?' She took longer strides to keep up with him.

'I tried. Hit her shoulder instead of her heart. My choices were try again or come after you.' His mouth bent upward, his fangs gleaming dully in the dim glow of the corridor's ceiling. 'Not even a question which way that was going.'

She grinned. Words weren't really necessary to tell him what she was thinking.

His smile increased for a second. 'Hey, I have the other dagger.' He patted the hilt where it peeked from his waistband, then stared at her a little harder. 'Your shoulder doesn't look so hot.'

She glanced at the blood on her dress as they hurried through the passage. 'It hurts, but I'll be fine. She'll be searching the city for us, you know.'

He nodded, smile gone. 'Or she'll go straight for the hangars. Which is why we need to be on that plane as quickly as possible.' In the distance behind them, something clanged. His grip on her hand tightened. 'Can you go faster?'

Chrysabelle glanced back. 'Yes.'

'Then let's get the hell out of here and back on that plane so you can spend some time with your brother.'

Without another word, they started to run.

Chapter Forty-Six

From Mal's spot on the narrow metal ladder, he worked the manhole cover free and eased it aside. The dark of night would only buy them so much protection. By now, Tatiana would have guards everywhere, searching homes and businesses and no doubt watching the city's roads.

He stuck his head up. The car sat a few meters away, Mortalis behind the wheel. No one else was in sight, but they were a good distance from the estate. He grabbed hold of the sides and pulled himself up, then crouched at the edge to peer at Chrysabelle. 'All clear.'

Behind him, Mortalis got out of the car. Chrysabelle started to climb but her gown's full skirt slowed her progress.

'Here, give me your hand.' *Leave her.* He reached down, grabbed her hand, and pulled her up, a blur of white in the deep shadows of the evening.

'Thanks,' she said as she landed beside him.

'You're hurt.' Mortalis nodded at her shoulder. 'You okay?'

'I'm good. Let's get out of here.'

The fae went ahead of them and got the back door open, then

jumped behind the wheel. 'Dominic and Katsumi should be flying by now.'

'I hope,' Chrysabelle said as she got in. 'We'll know when we get to the hangar.'

Mal slid in next to her and shut the door, then leaned toward Mortalis. 'Which needs to be quickly. Our exit wasn't clean.'

'Got it.' Mortalis threw the car into gear and started forward. 'I can't drive too fast until we leave the city. That would just attract attention.'

Mal sat back. 'Agreed.'

Chrysabelle brushed at the blood covering her dress while she spoke. 'Mortalis, Octavian is working for the Kubai Mata. He's the one who's been giving Creek his intel. I'm sure of it.'

Mortalis glanced at her in the rearview mirror. 'Damn. Tatiana know that?'

Mal nodded. 'By now, probably.'

Mortalis whistled softly. 'That's the end of him, then.'

Chrysabelle nodded, but she looked lost in thought. They rode in silence until they reached the main road out of Čachtice. There, Mortalis stopped the car. He cursed in faeish.

Guards swarmed a line of cars blocking the exit. A few of the fringe had assault rifles, which would have little effect on any vampire, but many nobles had human drivers. Car by car, they knocked on windows and forced passengers and drivers out. Some guards were even getting into the vehicles.

Mal growled softly. 'Son of a priest. I was afraid this was going to happen.'

'This isn't going to make Tatiana popular with her peers,' Chrysabelle said. 'What are we going to do?'

Mortalis scratched one horn. 'You two could get out, jump the wall, and meet me down the road after I get through.'

'We'd have to skirt a long way around not to be seen, and Chrysabelle sticks out in that white dress.' Mal would do anything to keep her safe, but putting them out in the open didn't seem like the best possible solution. *Let her go.*

'Can you persuade them?' she asked.

He glanced at her. 'Not all of them.'

Mortalis looked at them in the rearview mirror again. 'We're wasting time.'

Mal frowned. 'You have a better idea?' *Let. Her. Go.*

The fae nodded. 'Yes, but you're not going to like it.'

'What?' Chrysabelle asked.

His gaze shifted to her. 'They're probably looking for an injured comarré.'

'No.' Mal slashed a hand through the air. 'She's not crossing the wall alone.' The voices booed him.

Chrysabelle held out her hand to him. 'Give me your coat.'

'I don't want you doing this.'

She raised one brow. 'You don't know what I'm doing yet.' She stretched her hand a little farther. 'Give me your coat.'

Reluctantly, he took it off and handed it to her.

'Mortalis, go ahead and get us in line. The less time we have to wait, the better.' She pulled the coat over her like a blanket, completely covering the bloody front of her dress. 'Mal, go to smoke.'

'I don't like this.' But he did it anyway, hovering near the ceiling as Mortalis found them a spot in line.

'Mortalis, if anyone asks, I'm deathly ill and you're taking me back to the plane until my patron is ready to leave.' She slipped down to lay across the seat, pulled the coat up to cover half her face.

'This isn't going to work,' Mortalis muttered.

Mal agreed, but it was too late. A guard approached the vehicle.

Drained. Empty. Numb. If it weren't for the sharp pangs of anger and loss gnawing at the edges of the fog collecting around Tatiana's heart, she wasn't sure where she'd find the energy to put one foot in front of the other. But she did. Step by step, she made her way back to her quarters. Back to Octavian.

He would explain what had happened. Tell her what magic the comarré had worked on him to make him hand over Lilith. Clarify what the Castus had said, for surely they had only taken Lilith for safekeeping. Hadn't they?

Perhaps he could also explain how Mal was still alive, because although she'd seen him die on the news, there was no doubt in her mind that Lord Moreau was actually Mal in disguise. Turning to smoke was a rare vampire trait. So rare, she'd heard of only one or two others who could do it, other than Mal, who'd gone to smoke as many times in their years together as she had scattered into wasps. She'd thought he'd lost that power when he gave up drinking from the vein.

She stopped suddenly and leaned a hand on the wall to steady herself. 'That damned comarré. That's how he did it.'

'What's that, my lady?' One of the fringe guards who'd been escorting her stopped as well.

'He didn't die,' she mumbled. 'He went to smoke. Somehow, he found safety from the sun.' She shook her head, staring at the swirls of brown and gold and cream in the marble beneath her feet. 'Because of that blood whore.'

'We need to get her back to her room.' The guard cupped her elbow. 'Almost home now, Lady Tatiana.'

She yanked her arm away from him. 'Don't touch me.'

Instead, she wrapped her arms around her body. Empty arms. Arms that should be holding her child. With a stifled sob, she marched forward.

One of the guards ran ahead and opened the door for her. She walked through and stopped, her arms falling away from her sides. 'What . . . what happened?'

Just beyond the sitting room, Kosmina and Oana stood over an irregular pile of ashes. Kosmina had a dagger in her hand. She turned swiftly. 'I tried to stop him, my lady. He was going on about betraying you and—'

'Who was? Who did you try to stop?'

Kosmina's gaze shifted to the ashes. 'Lord Octavian.'

Tatiana shook her head. 'Who did he kill?'

Oana inhaled sharply. Kosmina swallowed and backcd up a step. 'My lady, I—'

'Who?' Tatiana demanded. 'If someone was betraying me, I want a name. Now.'

Kosmina's fingers tightened around the dagger's hilt. 'Lord Octavian, my lady.'

Darkness crept in at the edges of Tatiana's field of vision. 'I don't understand. Who did he kill? Tell me.'

'My lady, I am trying to.' Kosmina stared her squarely in the eyes. 'These ashes are Lord Octavian's. He killed himself.'

Tatiana's knees buckled and she collapsed to the floor. 'No,' she whispered. 'No, that can't be.' Then the darkness swept in and mercifully took her with it.

Chapter Forty-Seven

Chrysabelle kept her head down and her eyes closed and let Mortalis handle the situation. Despite the seriousness of their circumstances, she almost laughed thinking about how Mal really had become a dark cloud above her. She tugged the coat up a little higher to cover more of her face.

The knock on the window came a few seconds later. Then the whirr of the motor bringing the glass down.

'What's the issue?' Mortalis asked.

'We need to inspect the vehicle.'

'What for?'

'Looking for someone. You and everyone inside, out. Now.'

'It's just me and my master's comarré. You can look behind me if you like, she's the only one in the car. She's passed out sick. Some kind of blood poisoning, they think. Anyway, I need to get her to the plane before she vomits again.'

'Put the back window down.'

More whirring and a little cool air kissed her ankles. She tensed, feeling eyes on her. Mal wouldn't get sucked out the window, would he? She imagined not. He seemed to be able to control his smoke form well enough.

The guard yelled to someone, 'She's alone. What do you want to do?'

Chrysabelle moaned softly for effect. If the guards pulled her out of the car, they'd have no option but to fight and even with Mal and Mortalis, the odds weren't good.

Mal's coat muffled the guards' distant conversation, so she couldn't quite make out the words. 'What's happening?' she whispered.

Mortalis stayed quiet. It must not be safe for him to speak. She heard a soft tapping and opened her eyes a slit. He'd dropped one hand behind the seat and was rapping a finger on the leather upholstery.

'What?' she whispered.

He started signing. *Guards trying to decide what to do. Not sure the outcome yet.* He stopped signing but left his hand where it was. *They're coming back.* He pulled his hand away and she closed her eyes again.

'Are we done?' he asked.

'We're sending a guard with you. You won't be able to return for your master without him. Unlock the back door.'

At the snick of the lock, Chrysabelle held back a groan, but the guard's fate was sealed. Whoever got in the car with them was about to die.

The door was opened and she felt the movement across from her as the guard settled in. Fringe by the smell of him. The door slammed shut and a gruff voice said, 'Move it, fae.'

The car rolled forward. Chrysabelle kept her eyes closed. Something – a finger, the muzzle of a gun – poked her in the leg. She didn't move.

'So what's this comarré got?'

'Blood poisoning. Had to get her out of the crowd before she infected any of the others.'

'Others? Other vampires? Is she contagious?' The gruffness turned to fear.

'Maybe. Don't know.' Mortalis was clearly enjoying this.

'She better not be.'

'I'd stay as far to that other side of the car as you can,' Mortalis responded. 'In case she throws up again.'

For effect, Chrysabelle made a little gagging sound.

The guard swore. 'Hurry up and get to the hangars.'

'We're through the gates. I guess there's no reason I can't go a little faster.' Mortalis stomped on the gas. The guard lurched into her legs and scrambled to get off her, pulling the coat off her in the process.

'What the hell? You're the comarré they're looking for!'

She opened her eyes to the barrel of a gun.

The guard kept it leveled at her but spoke to Mortalis. 'Turn this car around right now.'

A curtain of smoke formed between her and the guard. Moments later, Mal reappeared. He shook his head. 'This car isn't going anywhere. And neither are you.' He grabbed the gun out of the shocked guard's hands and tossed it into the front seat with Mortalis.

The guard tried to crawl after it, but Mal held on to him. 'Chrysabelle, blade.'

She pulled a dagger from her skirts and shoved it through the guard's chest.

His shocked expression disappeared in a cloud of ash. She sneezed. Mortalis buzzed the back windows down and the ash flew out into the night.

He glanced in the rearview, his mouth a firm line but an odd spark in his eyes. 'That wasn't as bad as I thought it was going to be.'

Mal slid back in the seat beside Chrysabelle, knocking the last of the ash from his hands. 'We're not home yet.'

Chrysabelle relaxed as they pulled through the hangar doors without further incident. Just as she'd hoped, the second plane was gone. Only Amery and the hostages remained in the building. He approached as they got out of the car.

'The laudanum's still got the vamps knocked out. Dominic took the comarré with them. She wanted to go. Damian was pretty insistent about it.'

Chrysabelle shook a little ash off her skirt. 'That's fine. I was going to speak to her about returning with us before we left anyway.' What was one more comarré in Paradise City? Maybe this one would prove a decent ally. Chrysabelle tipped her head toward the vampires slumped against the far wall. 'How long before they wake up?'

'A few more hours at least. They'll probably be stuck in here until the sun goes down again.'

'All the better,' Mal said. 'We're ready to go if you are.'

Amery scanned them. 'Aren't you supposed to have a baby with you?'

'Didn't work out,' Chrysabelle said. And at this point, she didn't really care. She just wanted to be done with Tatiana and the whole sordid mess. She'd deal with the KM when the time came.

Mortalis went to the hangar door, chucked the car keys into the night, and walked back. 'Let's go.'

Chrysabelle got on the plane first. The sooner she could ditch this bloody dress, the better. She headed straight for her bag and the clothes she'd worn in.

Mortalis stopped her from opening the closet, his six fingers splayed out on the sleek ivory exterior. 'I know you want to change, but wait until we're airborne. We need to get out of here as soon as we can, and Amery won't take off until you're in your seat. He's a stickler like that.'

'Okay.' She sat down and buckled in as Mortalis joined Amery in the cockpit.

Mal sat beside her and took her hand. 'I know things didn't go as planned, but we got your brother out and didn't lose anyone. Could have been much worse.'

She nodded. The plane started rolling forward. 'Octavian claimed to be the one who took the pictures of Damian after Tatiana had him beaten. I would have never guessed he was KM.'

'That explains how you got the child from him and his reluctance to attack you.' Mal was quiet for a moment. 'She'll kill him if she suspects.'

She sighed and stared at their interwoven fingers. 'I suppose he knew the risks going in. He let her turn him.' She looked at Mal, into those dark, comforting eyes that hadn't changed despite Dominic's disguise. 'He might have been drifting toward the other side.' She shrugged. 'The noble life has its perks.'

The forces of takeoff shoved them back. Mal brought her hand to his mouth and kissed it. 'Tatiana claimed him as consort. That's as close to being married as most vampires get.'

She broke eye contact, shifting her gaze to her lap. And what was left of her mother's wedding dress.

He let her hand go. 'Dress is kind of ruined.'

She nodded. 'I don't think Maris would mind. It was a good cause.'

'Do you ever think about . . . marriage?'

She laughed before she realized he was serious. 'That's not part of the comarré plan. Ever.'

'You're not comarré anymore. Haven't been for a while, really.'

She inhaled deeply. 'Your disguise is starting to fade. I can see your face coming through underneath.'

'Don't change the subject.'

The strands of something bright and frightening worked through her belly. 'I . . . ' Her ability to breathe had been compromised by the thoughts he'd put into her head. 'Is there a reason you want to know?'

Silver sparkled in his gaze. 'I'm not getting any younger.'

'You're not really getting any older, either.'

'Chrysabelle, you know what I mean. I love you. You love me. Why shouldn't we make things more permanent?'

'Permanent is a long time.'

'Something we both understand very well.'

'Maris and Dominic didn't work. Why would you and I be any different?'

'Because we would be. We're not them. There aren't any secrets between us.' He laid his hand over hers. 'You're trembling and your heart rate is going at the same speed as this plane. I didn't mean to scare you, so I'll just drop it.' He settled back into his seat and closed his eyes, but even she could tell he was disappointed.

'You really do love me, don't you?'

He answered without opening his eyes. 'Enough that it frightens me, too.'

His being scared made it a little easier to take. Like they were both on the same side of things, which they were, but his words just solidified how true that was. She loved him. She did. She wasn't comarré anymore and shouldn't be bound by any of those rules or standards. Didn't want to be, really. What she wanted was a life of her own, where the decisions she made came from her heart and not a head full of rules. Fingers shaking, she unbuckled her seat belt and stood.

He looked up at her, the last vestiges of his disguise slipping off his skin. 'Leaving?'

'I need to get out of this dress.' She held her quivering hand out to him and tried to keep her heart from exploding and her voice from cracking. 'Maybe ... maybe you could help me?'

His mouth opened, but no sound came out. He licked his bottom lip and blinked slowly. 'Are you asking me—'

'Yes.'

He was out of his seat a split second later and pulling her into his arms. 'It's been a really long time since I ... helped a woman out of her dress.'

'Well, it's been never for me.' She smiled at the absurdity of her nerves. 'We'll figure it out, though, right?'

Eyes shining silver, he kissed the corners of her smile and she realized she wasn't the only one trembling. 'Hell, yes.'

Chapter Forty-Eight

Behind the closed door of the plane's bedroom, with Chrysabelle in his arms, the throb of her life in his veins and the full impact of what they'd just done, there was no way Mal wasn't asking her again. So he did, inciting the voices to levels that would have been unbearable if not for the fresh blood in his system. 'Marry me.' *Fool fool fool.*

With a sated mew, she stretched lazily on the bed beside him, twisting the sheet as she turned so they lay hip to hip. 'Asking now is dirty pool.'

'That's my MO. You should know that by now.' He rolled his bottom lip in. The taste of her blood still lingered. Being able to bite her made *everything* so much better. *Worse.*

She went very quiet. He lifted his head to glance at her. Even in just the soft cabin lights, she gleamed. Everywhere. He turned and leaned on one elbow, his head in his hand, his fingers tracing the signum that scrolled across her collarbone. 'You will, you know.'

She blinked at him. 'I will what?'

'Marry me.' He focused on her eyes, making sure she understood how serious he was. 'I don't do this' – he waggled his finger between them – 'lightly.'

Her eyes narrowed to slits and her mouth bunched to one side. 'So that's an order, is it?'

'Yes.' He kissed her, then sat up and swung his legs over the side of the bed. 'In fact, I bet Mortalis is licensed.'

She bolted upright beside him. 'Holy mother, Mortalis. And Amery! Do you think they know what we've been doing?'

He wanted to laugh but didn't. 'There's a good chance.'

'We should get dressed. How long have we been in here? Are we landing? We're probably landing soon.' She yanked the sheet off him to wrap around herself. 'Get dressed!'

'Calm down. I can pretty much guarantee neither Amery nor Mortalis is going to be surprised by any of this.'

She threw his shirt at him. 'Get. Dressed.'

A knock sounded at the door. 'We'll be landing in thirty minutes.'

'We'll be out,' Mal called. 'Just getting dressed.'

Chrysabelle glared at him.

'What? You don't think Mortalis knows we're both in here? We're on a plane. Where else are we going to be?'

One hand held the sheet around her body while she rubbed her forehead with the other. 'This was a bad idea.'

'It gets better the more you do it.' Mal laughed and winked. 'You'll see.'

His pants hit him in the face.

Doc eased his weight onto the side of the bed, causing the mattress to dip slightly. Fi shifted and stretched toward him. He went still, wanting to wake her but not too abruptly.

Her lids fluttered open. 'Hi,' she whispered.

'Hi.' He smiled back. 'How you feeling?'

'Like a truck ran me over.' She yawned. 'A medium-sized one.' She rubbed her eyes. 'My head feels cloudy.' She looked around, hands spreading across the comforter. 'How long have I been here?'

'Day and a half. Barasa drugged you up pretty good so you could sleep and recover.'

She yawned again and rolled her head around. 'I don't like that. But I get it. How are things with ... everything?'

'You mean Heaven?'

She moved her head enough for him to understand she was nodding.

'Heaven's father showed up.'

Fi tensed and fear widened her eyes.

Doc grabbed her hand. 'It's cool. It is, trust me. He's not a bad guy. Nothing like I thought.'

She relaxed, blowing out a breath. 'He can't be happy.'

'He's not, but he also understands how pride law works. He knows Heaven challenged you and you won.' He just didn't know exactly how. And Fi didn't need to either.

'But she died.' Worry bracketed her eyes. 'I didn't do that. I don't have the power to do that. Not in my corporeal form.'

Doc studied her hand. So small and fragile and pale compared to his big dark one. He had two choices. Tell her the truth and let her bear the weight of someone else's sins or leave her blameless.

He looked up and forced himself to smile. 'Barasa said she had a heart defect that none of us could have known about. The fight was too much for her.'

'So ... I didn't really kill her? She died of natural causes?'

He hesitated, smiling a little broader to try to convince himself, too. 'You had nothing to do with her death.'

At least that wasn't a lie.

*

'She means to get rid of me,' Creek explained after showing Annika the pictures on his phone. 'Whether or not John goes along with that, I don't know. He's varcolai and has no beef with me, so chances are he won't, but the mayor can be very persuasive when she wants.'

'The KM do not want this city run by a vampire. They'll want her removed. Probably permanently, but I'll tell them we need provocation.' She sat on the steps that led to his sleeping loft. 'Plus I know you're not going to kill a woman, vampire or otherwise, unless you have a stellar reason to.'

He leaned against one of the garage's support columns. Annika was so different from Argent. 'I appreciate that. Something tells me that reason won't be long coming.'

Annika nodded thoughtfully. 'She'll be on the warpath for sure after she finds out she's not getting the baby.'

Creek's forehead furrowed. 'How do you know that?'

'Our operative inside Tatiana's unit was eliminated.' She smiled. 'Well, one of them was.'

'Good to know.' No point in asking for more details. 'Hey, I don't want to kick you out, but I have somewhere to be.'

Still smiling, she stood, brushed the dust off her backside, and walked to his V-Rod. 'Yes, I know. Dinner at your grand-mother's.'

'I'd ask how you know, but sector chiefs seem to know just about everything.' He grabbed his helmet and joined her on the other side of the bike.

She took the helmet out of his hands. 'I know because she invited me, too.' She plopped the helmet on over her spiky black hair. 'You're driving.'

Chapter Forty-Nine

With Mal at her side, Chrysabelle leaned against the back wall of a small mirrored room in Mortalis's home. No more than six by eight, the space had probably been a closet before Mortalis moved in. She wasn't sure what was stranger – the mirrored room or the fact that Mortalis lived one floor below Dominic's secret penthouse in the same luxury building. Made sense, though. Dominic had good reasons to keep his personal bodyguard close.

Amery shifted nervously across from them while Mortalis closed the door, completing the illusion that they were in the midst of a vast, strange crowd. The fae turned, his reflection as tense as the rest of him.

'Once we bring him in, there is no turning back. He will demand payment, whether or not he answers a question for you. If he isn't paid, he'll let it be known we brought him here without approval. And for his kind, there is no approval.'

'Where exactly are you getting him from?' Chrysabelle asked. She couldn't help but wonder where such a dangerous fae lived.

'The Claustrum,' Amery answered.

Mortalis shot him a glare that shut him up.

'What's that?' She really needed to study fae culture a little more.

'Fae prison,' Amery told her, with a look to Mortalis that said he was done speaking.

'Oh.' Her brows shot up. That was interesting, but Creek had spent time in prison, too, and he wasn't exactly a bad guy. 'What did he do?'

'You don't want or need to know.' Mortalis scowled at Amery once more. 'He can't escape this room, unless you open the door, so don't—'

'Don't open it,' Chrysabelle finished. 'We won't.'

'You might want to,' Amery said. 'This room is going to feel even smaller with a raptor in it.'

'I don't like this,' Mal muttered.

His comment didn't surprise her. She was starting not to like it either, but her desire to understand what the ring had done to her was greater. 'How exactly is this creature going to be able to help me?'

Mortalis's hands roved over his body, doing a weapons check. They slid from the hilts of the crossed thinblades at his back to a set of daggers at his wrists. 'Like I told you, he can read metal. It's more than that really, but that's the best way to describe what he does.'

Mal snorted softly. 'What kind of payment is he going to want?'

Amery opened his mouth, looked at Mortalis, then shut it. Mortalis shook his head. 'We don't know exactly, but raptors thrive on emotion.' He slanted his eyes at Mal. 'He'll want you, we're almost sure of it.'

'I'm not giving him a choice,' Mal said. 'Chrysabelle's been through enough.'

Amery laughed. 'With all the crazy in your head, the raptor probably won't even notice her.'

'Amery.' Chrysabelle gave the young fae a disapproving glare. Mal might be a little borderline, but talking about it like that wasn't polite.

'Sorry.' Amery dropped his gaze to the floor.

'Anyway,' Mortalis said, 'what the raptor wants is different every time, but he's a thief by nature, so' – he tipped his head at Amery – 'give him the stuff.'

Amery pulled out two large chocolate bars from his jacket, then held them out to Mal.

'Chocolate? Really?'

Amery's cheeks went a deeper shade of gray. 'Beignets didn't invent themselves. Sugar is a big fae weakness. Could be, he'll take these and leave you alone. At the very least, these will put him in a good mood.'

'And if he doesn't take those and leave Mal alone?' Doubts crept into Chrysabelle's head. Worries about what might happen to Mal.

'I can handle it. That thing gets one whiff of the beast that lives inside me and he'll figure out pretty quick the chocolate is the best deal.' He took the candy bars and stuck them into his back pocket, then winked at her. 'Or maybe he'll take a few of the voices with him. Seems like a win-win to me. You get your info and my head gets lighter.'

She nodded, unconvinced. 'I guess.'

Mortalis pulled a thin rod from a holster on his hip and snapped it outward. It doubled in length and the end glowed with an easy blue light. He nodded to Amery. 'Let's go.'

They turned in unison and just like that, walked through the mirrored wall behind them.

'Wow,' Chrysabelle whispered. 'I knew fae could travel that way, but I've never seen it.'

'Me neither.' He managed a half-smile. 'This is all going to work out. You'll see.'

She squeezed his forearm, his skin warm from the blood he'd had on the plane. 'I'm sure you're right.' She wasn't, but for both of their sakes, she prayed it was true.

When Mortalis and Amery stepped back through the wall, Mal sensed Chrysabelle tensing before he heard her deep intake of breath and the whispered, 'Holy mother,' that slipped out of her. Even the voices cringed.

The raptor shuffled between the fae, his ankles and wrists shackled. Slick skin the same murky gray-green as sewer sludge covered his monstrous frame. The shape and carriage of the thing reminded Mal of the Nothos, but instead of piercing yellow eyes, this creature had no eyes at all, just a sloping forehead that curved back from his wide, slit nostrils. And there was no stench of brimstone. Instead he smelled like . . . Mal inhaled again. Bleach.

'Mmm . . . gold. Sacred, dirty gold.' The raptor opened his mouth, and a three-pronged tongue flicked out from between multiple rows of teeth that curved back toward his throat. He tasted the air. 'And chocolate.'

Mortalis lifted the stick with the lighted end. 'You'll get the chocolate after you read the comarré's gold.'

The big head moved and Mal realized the raptor was nodding.

He raised his shackled arms and curled his long slender fingers inward. 'Bring her to me.'

Mortalis nodded to Chrysabelle. She pulled up the back of her loose tunic, bringing it over her head and tucking it under her chin so only her back was exposed; then she stood before the raptor and turned.

The raptor leaned in and sniffed her. 'Must touch.'

Chrysabelle stood so still Mal could barely see the rise and fall of her breathing. Her hands were clenched in the fabric of her tunic, her eyes closed in what might have been prayer.

The raptor did nothing.

'He's waiting for your permission,' Mortalis said quietly.

'Oh.' She swallowed. 'Yes, you may touch me. No,' she added hastily, remembering what Mortalis had told her about being specific. 'You may touch the metal on either side of my spine. Only.'

Amery let out a soft sigh that sounded like relief.

The raptor opened his mouth and the black tongue came out again. This time it flicked against her skin. She inhaled at the touch but after a brief flinch, held still.

Again and again, the raptor's tongue made contact with her flesh, each time raising Mal's ire. After what had transpired between them on the plane, seeing another creature, especially this abomination, touch her so intimately pushed him toward a level of jealousy and protection he'd never known with any woman.

He growled in the depths of his throat and the raptor stopped, tipped his head toward Mal, then snapped his tongue back into his mouth.

The raptor straightened to his full height, which put him half a meter from the ceiling. 'I need blood to read deeper. A drop.'

'Ridiculous.' Now the creature traveled a bridge too far.

Mortalis put a hand up. 'It's not uncommon.'

Chrysabelle nodded, flipped out the tiny blade on her ring, and pricked her finger. She held it up, the tiny ruby bead on the tip like a beacon Mal couldn't look away from.

The raptor inhaled as he bent toward her, his tongue reappearing. She lifted her hand, grimacing slightly. The tongue's three segments delicately wrapped her finger, found the blood, and retreated.

The creature was quiet for a moment. 'You are comarré?'

'Yes,' Chrysabelle answered.

He shook his head. 'Your blood is dirty. This confuses me.'

'What the hell do you mean, her blood is dirty?' Mal took a step toward the fae. 'Her blood is as pure as it gets.'

The raptor tipped his head toward Mal. 'Vampire?'

'Yes.'

The raptor mumbled something under his breath that sounded like, 'Darkness, all darkness'; then he inhaled in Mal's direction. 'Your blood is in her?'

'Yes.' Mal looked at Chrysabelle. He had no idea how the creature had picked that up.

With a small nod, the raptor continued. 'I must taste your blood as well.'

Chrysabelle's hand latched on to Mal's wrist before he could protest, the pleading look on her face making it impossible for him to object. He held out his hand and she used her ring to prick his finger as well.

'Here.' Mal shoved his hand toward the raptor and the creature licked up the offered drop.

After a few long seconds, the creature went down onto his haunches and began to speak. 'The gold is ancient. Sacred. Imbued with holy magic tainted by another for dark purposes. This gold was a ring, its circular shape a symbol of how uncnding, how indcstructible its power. But this power is what concerns you. This power is what now flows within you. This power has become part of you, greater than you.'

Mal clenched his hands into fists. 'What the hell *is* the power?'

The raptor took a breath. 'In its unadulterated form, the ring held the power to raise the undead and bring them under the sway of whoever wore the ring.'

'A zombie army,' Amery whispered.

'No longer,' the raptor said. 'Now the power is joined with the comarré's blood. Now it will raise the comarré every time she dies.'

Chrysabelle nodded. 'That's already happened.'

The raptor held up his shackled hands. 'Because you are joined with the vampire through his blood, every time you are resurrected, the power uses one of the souls trapped with him instead of a random soul.'

'The names.' Chrysabelle turned to Mal, her eyes wide and her breath ragged.

He nodded. 'Now we know why they're disappearing.' He faced the raptor. 'So as long as I have names to spare, Chrysabelle will come back to life?'

The raptor stood. 'No more questions. I will be paid.'

'Wait,' Chrysabelle said. 'These souls that the power uses, do they get released or reborn through me? I don't understand.'

'No more questions,' the raptor growled. He rolled his shoulders back, straining the shackles. 'I will be paid.'

Mal pulled Chrysabelle behind him. 'Don't worry, I'm going to pay you.'

The raptor stilled. Then his mouth drew back in a gruesome smile. 'Very good, vampire.' He swung his big head around toward Mortalis. 'Out.'

Mortalis snorted. 'That wasn't part of the deal and you know it.'

With a sharp crack, the raptor snapped the shackles and came face-to-face with Mortalis. 'You think these hold me, shadeux? I am here to escape the tedium of the Claustrum, not because you commanded it. I have done what you wished. Now I will be paid.'

'It's all right,' Mal said. 'But Chrysabelle goes with you.'

Mortalis glared at the raptor. 'Give your oath you will not leave this room.'

'My oath,' the raptor answered.

Mortalis nodded to Amery and the two of them took the few steps to the door. Mortalis opened it halfway. 'Chrysabelle, you first.'

She grabbed Mal's hand, her eyes filled with the unspoken words he already knew. He nodded and squeezed her hand back. 'Me too. Now go.'

Worrying her bottom lip, she nodded and slipped out the door. Amery followed, Mortalis behind him.

And just like that, Mal was alone with the raptor.

Chapter Fifty

'So, vampire, you offer the payment for the comarré.'
    Mal pulled the chocolate bars from his back pocket and held them out. 'Here.'

The raptor laughed. How the oddly soft sound wasn't shredded into something awful by those rows of teeth, Mal had no idea. 'Sweets. How ... sweet.' The creature latched on to Mal's forearms, dragging him closer and knocking the chocolate to the floor.

At the touch, the voices went into a dead, shivering silence, but the movement shocked Mal more than the quiet, hurtling home the reality that the raptor was now in control.

The voices crouched in the back of his brain, as far away from the raptor's contact as they could be. Even the beast trembled, cowering like a beaten dog. Mal's skin began to itch as the names crawled back along his arms until, for the first time since the names had appeared on his body, there was bare skin where the raptor's long, clawed fingers touched.

'So much emotion,' the creature hissed. 'Rage, bitterness, the desire for revenge, pain ... all of it delicious, all of it there for my taking. Enough to sustain me for a very long time.'

'Then take it,' Mal ground out.

'But I can get all of those in the Claustrum. What I want is something else within you, something rare and sweet.'

'Great. Take whatever it is and let's be done,' Mal snarled. All he wanted was to be rid of this creature and be back at Chrysabelle's side. To sink into her warmth.

The fae leaned in, his razor-toothed maw widening in what Mal realized was another smile. 'You're thinking of the comarré now, aren't you?' He tipped his head, bringing the rows of pin teeth closer to Mal's face.

The raptor's nostrils flared. 'Oh yes. I smell her in your blood. You've had her recently, haven't you?'

'You bloody—'

'I know what I shall take from you, blood eater.' His bleach scent washed over Mal as vile and wrenching as a fish kill. 'I will take your love for her.'

Mal froze. 'You can't—' Pain sapped his words, his strength, his will. His head fell back and his vision clouded. Emotion drained from him like blood spilling from a gaping wound.

A vast hole formed inside him and as the raptor released him, the voices rushed in, filling the emptiness with a raging chaos. Mal stumbled, falling into the back wall. The mirror cracked. He slid down, unable to wrench control back from the curse that had just been given free rein in his head once again. He felt himself losing ground, felt the chaos spread to madness. He pushed against it.

'No,' he whispered, but it was too late. The darkness had won.

'Thank you.' Chrysabelle accepted a cup of tea and a small plate of cookies from Velimai, but set the tray on the nightstand without touching any of it. 'I'm not that hungry at the moment.' Her stomach hadn't felt right in a week. Not since everything had happened with Mal. The stress of not knowing was killing her. Or maybe it was the possibility that he was never coming out of this ... coma or whatever he'd lapsed into.

Velimai nodded and sat in the far corner. Chrysabelle closed her eyes, but the image of Mal passed out on the floor and the raptor slack-jawed in ecstasy standing over him flashed through her head again. She opened her eyes. Watching him lie lifeless in the guest room of her house wasn't much better. At least this room was in the part of the house that had already been helioglazed.

She closed her eyes again and replaced the bad memory with the one of being in bed with Mal on the plane. She ducked her head to hide her smile. What would Velimai say if she knew about that? Her smile faded. Did Velimai know Chrysabelle had slipped into bed beside Mal these past seven nights? That she'd laid her head on his soundless chest, wrapped her arms around him, and begged him to come back to her?

A knock on the open bedroom door made her open her eyes again. 'Mortalis. Come in.'

'Any change?'

'No. Nothing yet.' She tried to smile, but what did it matter? Mortalis didn't need her to put a brave face on. She shrugged, then shook her head. 'How am I supposed to know what to do? It's not like I can check his breathing.'

Hesitantly, Mortalis reached out and squeezed her shoulder. 'I feel like this is my fault. I exposed you to the raptor. I knew what the risks were—'

'You knew that creature would do this to Mal?'

'Not exactly. I just knew the potential for things to go wrong was there.'

She went back to staring at Mal's motionless form. 'I don't regret finding out what the ring of sorrows did to me, but this . . . ' She sighed. 'This is . . . hard. What if he doesn't wake up?'

'He will. I'm sure this is just a side effect of whatever the raptor did.' Mortalis heaved out a breath. 'If you need anything, Nyssa and I are here for you.'

She nodded. 'Maybe you could talk to Damian. I'm sure he must think I'm a psychopath. I saved him from Tatiana only to ignore him in favor of the vampire she used to be married to.'

'I don't think he thinks that.'

She laughed, a sad, bitter sound even to her own ears. 'I've seen him three times in the last week. At least he's got that other comarré Dominic brought back to keep him company.' Even so, her guilt at abandoning her brother to the guesthouse was a small thing compared to what had happened to Mal because of her.

Damian told me you should take all the time you need, Velimai signed.

'Time. I'm starting to hate it.' She swallowed a nauseous rush of panic. 'If Mal . . . if he doesn't . . . '

'He will.' Mortalis walked to the windows and pulled the curtains back. 'Sun's down.'

She glanced over her shoulder. The sky was purple with twilight. 'Mal loved this time of night. When the evening was full of possibilities.'

'Bloody hell.'

She and Mortalis turned at the same time. Mal sat up in bed, a steeliness in his eyes she'd never seen before.

'Mal, you're—'

'You.' He glared at her, his eyes flashing from silver to the full-on black of the beast, then back again. IIis lip curled back. 'You did this to me.' He whipped the coverlet back, jumped out of bed, and stared down at the pajama pants he wore. 'Where the hell are my clothes?'

She pointed at the chair on the other side of the bed. 'There. Mal, why are you acting like this?'

'Acting?' He yanked the loose pants off, shredding them, then grabbed his jeans and tugged them on. 'This isn't acting. This is who I am.'

'No, it isn't.' She stood, wondering if she should put some distance between them. 'This isn't the Mal I know. You must still be sick.'

Velimai stayed in the corner, but Mortalis came to stand beside her. 'Could be some residual effect of whatever the raptor did to him.'

Mal sneered as his head came through the neck of his T-shirt. 'The raptor did me a favor.' He snatched his jacket and started for the door.

She took a few steps after him. 'Where are you going?'

'Anywhere I want to.'

'Mal, wait, we need to talk—'

He stopped, spinning to face her. 'Do we? So you can explain why you're holding me here?'

She backed up. 'I'm not holding you here. I thought you'd want to be here. I've been taking care of you.'

He laughed. 'Oh, that's rich. You, taking care of me.'

Her stomach soured at the brutal tone of his words. 'I love you.'

He rolled his eyes. 'Spare me, princess.'

A shudder built along her spine. 'You asked me to marry you.'

His face took on a hard, cruel set. 'Let's get something straight. I don't love you. I don't want you around me. And I sure as hell don't want to marry my *food*.'

'That's enough,' Mortalis snapped.

'You're damn straight it is.' Mal turned and stalked out.

Her ability to breathe went with him. Chrysabelle reached for the chair she'd been sitting on, trying to find something to keep herself from collapsing. 'I don't feel so good.'

Velimai rushed forward and Mortalis grabbed her as she started to fall.

She leaned into him. Cold sweat rolled down her back. 'What happened?'

Velimai pointed to the bathroom.

He nodded. 'Let's get a cold cloth for your neck.' He looped her arm around his shoulders and walked her into the bathroom, then helped her sit on the vanity bench. He ran the water while Velimai opened a cabinet, took out a washcloth, and handed it to him. He wrung it out and came toward her. 'Lean forward.'

She did, running on some kind of autopilot that was happy to have someone tell her what to do.

Mortalis brushed her hair aside and laid the cool cloth on the back of her neck, then he kneeled in front of her and took her hands. 'I know what happened.'

She nodded for him to continue, unable to manage much more.

'The emotion the raptor took from Mal. It had to be his love for you.' Mortalis's voice broke and she looked up at him, causing the cloth to slip free. A thin line of liquid rimmed his lower lids. 'I'm so sorry,' he said quietly.

'He doesn't love me anymore.' She closed her eyes and an image of Mal laughing in bed beside her flashed across her field of vision. Everything that had happened between them, every-thing they had been through ... none of it mattered to Mal anymore. None of it. She opened her eyes and pulled her hands from Mortalis's to cover her mouth.

Her stomach rebelled. She ran to the toilet and vomited, heaving her guts out. She sat back on her heels. Velimai kneeled beside her and handed her the washcloth, then signed something to Mortalis that Chrysabelle caught out of the corner of her eye.

She wiped her mouth and shook her head. 'Don't. Don't say that. There's no way that can be true. Not now.'

Velimai's hands stopped moving and she glanced at Chrysa-belle. *Sorry.*

But somehow, Chrysabelle knew Velimai was right. She dropped the washcloth and folded her trembling hands over her thumping heart. Slowly, they slid down to her belly.

'Holy mother.' A debilitating weight settled over her. 'I'm pregnant. How is that possible?'

'The plane ... ' Mortalis trailed off, looking slightly ill.

'I know *how* it's possible, just not how it's possible between Mal and me.' She covered her face with her hands for a moment as it hit her. 'Holy mother. This is why comarrés aren't sup-posed to sleep with their patrons.'

Velimai nodded. *He bit you, didn't he? For those few moments, he was as mortal as you are.*

Chrysabelle shook her head. 'But it's only been a week.' Her stomach rolled again and she swallowed.

You're comarré. He's a vampire. You both regenerate at an accelerated rate. Velimai frowned. *It might not be too late to rid yourself of—*

'No,' Chrysabelle shouted, her voice bouncing off the bath-room walls. She pushed to her feet even though she felt like collapsing. With a hand on her stomach, she stared down the two fae across from her. 'I don't want to hear another word about getting rid of it, and I don't want anyone knowing what's happening until I figure out what to do about this, understood?'

Mortalis and Velimai both nodded.

Chrysabelle walked out of the bathroom and sat on the edge of the bed Mal had just vacated. 'I'd like to be alone now.'

Nodding, they both left, closing the door behind them. She lay back on the bed and stared at the ceiling. Mal's dark spice permeated her sheets. She rested one hand on her belly. Pregnant. With a cursed vampire's child.

After what Tatiana had done to get a hold of Preacher's child, what would she do when she found out Mal had fathered one with a genuine comarré?

Or worse, what would Mal do when he found out? He no longer loved her. She had no reason to believe a child would change that.

She covered her stomach with both hands as fresh fear iced her skin. One thing was certain. She would protect this child no matter how much blood she had to spill.

No matter who that blood belonged to.

**Be on the lookout for the
next House of Comarré novel:
LAST BLOOD**

Glossary

Anathema: a noble vampire who has been cast out of noble society for some reason

Aurelian: the comarré historian

Caedo: an elite group of vampire assassins, most usually from the Paole family

Castus Sanguis: the fallen angels from which the othernatural races descended

Comarré/comar: a human hybrid species especially bred to serve the blood needs of the noble vampire race

Dominus: the ruling head of a noble vampire family

Elder: the second in command to a Dominus

Fae: a race of othernatural beings descended from fallen angels and nature

Fringe vampires: a race of lesser vampires descended from the cursed Judas Iscariot

Kine: a vampire term for humans (archaic)

Libertas: the ritual in which the comarré can fight for their independence. Ends in death of comarré or patron.

Navitas: the ritual in which a vampire can be resired by another, to change family lines or turn fringe noble

Nequam: a substance smoked by the fae

Noble vampires: a powerful race of vampires descended from fallen angels

Nothos: hellhounds

Patronus/patron: a noble vampire who purchases a comarré's blood rights

Remnant: a hybrid of different species of fae and/or varcolai

Sacre: the ceremonial sword of the comarré

Signum: the inlaid gold tattoos or marks put into comarré skin to purify their blood

Vampling: a newly turned or young vampire

Varcolai: a race of shifters descended from fallen angels and animals

Acknowledgments

The more books I write, the more my network of support grows. Each story raises new research questions, and answering those questions sometimes requires more brain power than my own, which is why I rely on my brother's knowledge of ships, Kimberly Menozzi's Italian skills, and Larissa Benoliel's help with Portuguese. Everyone who's helped me in some way deserves thanks, but inevitably I'll forget someone. If that's happened, please forgive me.

To begin with, I want to thank my Creator for the talents He's given me.

As always, I must thank my agent, Elaine. She's phenomenal and you should all be jealous. In truth, the whole TKA family is awesome and I'm so glad they're part of my support group.

Of course, I am so thankful to my tremendous(ly scary) editor, Devi, who lets me write the stories I want no matter how crazy. Susan, her assistant, deserves props for all her hard work, too. (She does work for the most dread editor in the biz. Just saying.) The entire publishing team at Orbit, including Alex, Ellen, and Lauren, never cease to amaze me with their talents. So good!

I'd be remiss if I didn't thank the Writer's Camp chicks, Laura and Leigh. You should probably be getting paid for keeping my fingers on the keyboard. To Rocki and Louisa, thanks for sharing this journey and always being there.

To all my readers, you guys are the reason I write. You're awesome!

Lastly, big thanks to my parents and brother for their unwavering support and to my husband for proudly pitching my books to everyone he meets. Even if he does think I use too much description.

extras

www.orbitbooks.net

about the author

Kristen Painter's writing résumé boasts multiple
Golden Heart nominations and praise from a handful
of bestselling authors, including Gena Showalter and
Roxanne St. Claire. A former New Yorker now living
in Florida, Kristen has a wealth of fascinating
experiences from which to flavor her stories,
including time spent working in fashion for Christian
Dior and as a maître d' for Wolfgang Puck. Her website is at kristenpainter.com and she's on Twitter at
@Kristen_Painter

Find out more about Kristen Painter and other Orbit
authors by registering for the free monthly newsletter
at www.orbitbooks.net

if you enjoyed

OUT FOR BLOOD

look out for

GOD SAVE THE QUEEN

by

Kate Locke

CHAPTER 1

POMEGRANATES FULL AND FINE

London, 175 years into the reign of Her Ensanguined Majesty Queen Victoria

I *hate* goblins.

And when I say hate, I mean they bloody terrify me. I'd rather French-kiss a human with a mouth full of silver fillings than pick my way through the debris and rubble that used to be Down Street station, searching for the entrance to the plague den.

It was eerily quiet underground. The bustle of cobbleside was little more than a distant clatter down here. The roll of carriages, the clack of horse hooves from the Mayfair traffic was faint, occasionally completely drowned out by the roar of ancient locomotives raging through the subterranean tunnels carrying a barrage of smells in their bone-jangling wake.

Dirt. Decay. Stone. Blood.

I picked my way around a discarded shopping trolley, and tried to avoid looking at a large paw print in the dust. One of them had been here recently – the drops of blood surrounding the print were still fresh enough for me to smell the coppery tang. Human.

As I descended the stairs to platform level, my palms skimmed over the remaining chipped and pitted cream and maroon tiles that covered the walls – a grim reminder that this . . . *mausoleum* was once a thriving hub of urban transportation.

The light of my torch caught an entire set of paw prints, and the jagged pits at the end where claws had dug into the steps. I swallowed, throat dry.

Of course they ventured up this far – the busted sconces were proof. They couldn't always sit around and wait for some stupid human to come to them – they had to hunt. Still, the sight of those prints and the lingering scent of human blood made my chest tight.

I wasn't a coward. My being here was proof of that – and perhaps proof positive of my lack of intelligence. Everyone – aristocrat, half-blood and human – was afraid of goblins. You'd be mental not to be. They were fast and ferocious and didn't seem to have any sense of morality holding them back. If aristos were fully plagued, then goblins were overly so, though such a thing wasn't really possible. Technically they were aristocrats, but no one would ever dare call them such. To do so was as much an insult to them as to aristos. They were mutations, and terribly proud of it.

Images flashed in my head, memories that played out like disjointed snippets from a film: fur, gnashing fangs, yellow eyes – and blood. That was all I remembered of the day I was attacked by a gob right here in this very station. My history class from the Academy had come here on a field trip. The gobs stayed away from us because of the treaty. At least they were *supposed* to stay away, but one didn't listen, and it picked me.

If it hadn't been for Church, I would have died that day. That was when I realised goblins weren't stories told to children to make us behave. It was also the day I realised that if I didn't do everything in my ability to prove them wrong, people would think I was defective somehow – weak – because a goblin tried to take me.

I hadn't set foot in Down Street station since then. If it weren't for my sister Dede's disappearance I wouldn't have gone down there at all.

Avery and Val thought I was overreacting. Dede had taken off on us before, so it was hardly shocking that she wasn't answering her rotary or that the message box on said gadget was full. But in the past she had called me to let me know she was safe. She always called *me*.

I had exhausted every other avenue. It was as though Dede had fallen off the face of the earth. I was desperate, and there was only one option left – goblins. Gobs knew everything that happened in London, despite rarely venturing above ground. Somehow they had found a way to spy on the entire city, and no one seemed to know just what that was. I reckon anyone who had the bollocks to ask didn't live long enough to share it with the rest of us.

It was dark, not because the city didn't run electric lines down here any more – they did – but because the lights had been smashed. The beam from my small hand-held torch caught the grimy glitter of the remains of at least half a dozen bulbs on the ground amongst the refuse.

The bones of a human hand lay surrounded by the shards, cupping the jagged edges in a dull, dry palm.

I reached for the .50 British Bulldog normally holstered snugly against my ribs, but it wasn't there. I'd left it at home. Walking into the plague den with a firearm was considered an act of aggression unless one was there on the official – which I wasn't. Aggression was the last thing – next to fear – you wanted to show in front of one goblin, let alone an entire plague. It was like wearing a sign reading DINNER around your neck.

It didn't matter that I had plagued blood as well. I was only a half-blood, the result of a vampire aristocrat – the term that had come to be synonymous with someone of noble descent who was also plagued – and a human courtesan doing the hot and sweaty. Science considered goblins the ultimate birth defect, but in reality they were the result of gene snobbery. The Prometheus Protein in vamps – caused by centuries of Black Plague exposure – didn't play well with the mutation that caused others to become weres. If the proteins from both species mixed the outcome was a goblin, though some had been born to parents with the same strain. Hell, there were even two documented cases of goblins being born to human parents both of whom carried dormant plagued genes, but that was very rare, as goblins sometimes tried to eat their way out of the womb. No human could survive that.

In fact, no one had much of a chance of surviving a goblin attack. And that was why I had my lonsdaelite dagger tucked into a secret sheath inside my corset. Harder than diamond and easily concealed, it was my "go to" weapon of choice. It was sharp, light and didn't set off machines designed to detect metal or catch the attention of beings with a keen enough sense of smell to sniff out things like blades and pistols.

The dagger was also one of the few things my mother had left me when she . . . went away.

I wound my way down the staircase to the abandoned platform. It was warm, the air heavy with humidity and neglect, stinking of machine and decay. As easy as it was to access the tunnels, I wasn't surprised to note that mine were the only humanoid prints to be seen in the layers of dust. Back in 1932, a bunch of humans had used this very station to invade and burn Mayfair – *the* aristo neighbourhood – during the Great Insurrection. Their intent had been to destroy the aristocracy, or at least cripple it, and take control of the Kingdom. The history books say that fewer than half of those humans who went into Down Street station made it out alive.

Maybe goblins were useful after all.

I hopped off the platform on to the track, watching my step so I didn't trip over anything – like a body. They hadn't ripped up the line because there weren't any crews mental enough to brave becoming goblin chow, no matter how good the pay. The light of my torch caught a rough hole in the wall just up ahead. I crouched down, back to the wall as I eased closer. The scent of old blood clung to the dust and brick. This had to be the door to the plague den.

Turn around. Don't do this.

Gritting my teeth against the trembling in my veins, I slipped my left leg, followed by my torso and finally my right half, through the hole. When I straightened, I found myself standing on a narrow landing at the top of a long, steep set of rough-hewn stairs that led deeper into the dark. Water dripped from a rusty pipe near my head, dampening the stone.

As I descended the stairs – my heart hammering, sweat beading around my hairline – I caught a whiff of that particular perfume that could only be described as goblinesque: fur, smoke and earth. It could have been vaguely comforting if it hadn't scared the shit out of me.

I reached the bottom. In the beam from my torch I could see bits of broken pottery scattered across the scarred and pitted stone floor. Similar pieces were embedded in the wall. Probably Roman, but my knowledge of history was sadly lacking. The goblins had been doing a bit of housekeeping – there were fresh bricks mortared into parts of the wall, and someone had created a fresco near the ancient archway. I could be wrong, but it looked as though it had been painted in blood.

Cobbleside the sun was long set, but there were street lights, moonlight. Down here it was almost pitch black except for the dim torches flickering on the rough walls. My night vision was perfect, but I didn't want to think about what might happen if some devilish goblin decided to play hide and seek in the dark.

I tried not to imagine what that one would have done to me.

I took a breath and ducked through the archway into the main vestibule of the plague's lair. There were more sconces in here, so I tucked my hand torch into the leather bag slung across my torso. My surroundings were deceptively cosy and welcoming, as though any moment someone might press a pint into my hand or ask me to dance.

I'll say this about the nasty little bastards – they knew how to throw a party. Music flowed through the catacombs from some unknown source – a lively fiddle accompanied by a piano. Conversation and raucous laughter – both of which sounded a lot like barking – filled the fusty air. Probably a hundred goblins were gathered in this open area, dancing, talking and drinking. They were doing other things as well, but I tried to ignore them. It wouldn't do for me to start screaming.

A few of them looked at me with curiosity in their piercing yellow eyes, turning their heads as they caught my scent. I tensed, waiting for an attack, but it didn't come. It wouldn't either, not when I was so close to an exit, and they were curious to find out what could have brought a halvie this far into their territory.

Goblins looked a lot like werewolves, only shorter and

smaller – wiry. They were bipedal, but could run on all fours if the occasion called for additional speed. Their faces were a disconcerting mix of canine and humanoid, but their teeth were all predator – exactly what you might expect from a walking nightmare.

I'd made it maybe another four strides into this bustling netherworld when one of the creatures stuck a tray of produce in my face, trying to entice me to eat. Grapes the size of walnuts, bruise-purple and glistening in the torchlight, were thrust beneath my nose. Pomegranates the colour of blood, bleeding sweet-tart juice, filled the platter as well, and apples – pale flesh glistening with a delicate blush. There were more, but those were the ones that tempted me the most. I could almost taste them, feel the syrup running down my chin. Berry-stained fingers clutched and pinched at me, smearing sticky delight on my skin and clothes as I pressed forward.

"Eat, pretty," rasped the vaguely soft cruel voice. "Just a taste. A wee little nibble for our sweet lady."

Our? Not bloody fucking likely. I couldn't tell if my tormentor was male or female. The body hair didn't help either. It was effective camouflage unless you happened upon a male goblin in an amorous state. Generally they tried to affect some kind of identity for themselves – a little vanity so non-goblins could tell them apart. This one had both of its ears pierced several times, delicate chains weaving in and out of the holes like golden stitches.

I shook my head, but didn't open my mouth to vocalise my refusal. An open mouth was an invitation to a goblin to stick something in it. If you were lucky, it was only food, but once you tasted their poison you were lost. Goblins were known for their drugs – mostly their opium. They enticed weak humans with a cheap and euphoric high, and the promise of more. Goblins didn't want human money as payment. They wanted information. They wanted flesh. There were already several customers providing entertainment for tonight's bash. I pushed away whatever pity I felt for them – everyone knew what happened when you trafficked with goblins.

I pushed through the crowd, moving deeper into the lair despite every instinct I possessed telling me to run. I was looking for one goblin in particular and I was not going to leave without seeing him. Besides, running would get me chased. Chased would get me eaten.

As I walked, I tried not to pay too much attention to what was going on in the shadows around me. I'd seen a lot of horrible things in my two and twenty years, but the sight of hueys – humans – gorging themselves on fruit, seeds and pulp in their hair and smeared over their dirty, naked skin, shook me. Maybe it was the fact that pomegranate flesh looked just like that – flesh – between stained teeth. Or maybe it was the wild delirium in their eyes as goblins ran greedy hands over their sticky bodies.

It was like a scene out of Christina Rossetti's poem, but nothing so lyrical. Mothers knew to keep their children at home after dark, lest they go missing, fated to end up as goblin food – or worse, a goblin's slave.

A sweet, earthy smoke hung heavy in the air, reminding me of decaying flowers. It brushed pleasantly against my mind, but was burned away by my metabolism before it could have any real effect. I brushed a platter of cherries, held by strong paw-like hands, aside despite the watering of my mouth. I knew they'd split between my teeth with a firm, juicy pop, spilling tart, delicious juice down my dry throat. Accepting hospitality might mean I'd be expected to pay for it later, and I wasn't about to end up in the plague's debt. Thankfully I quickly spotted the goblin I was looking for. He sat on a dais near the back of the hall, on a throne made entirely from human bones. If I had to guess, I'd say this is what happened to several of the humans who braved this place during the Great Insurrection. Skulls served as finials high on either side of his head. Another set formed armrests over which each of his furry hands curved.

But this goblin would have stood out without the throne, and the obvious deference with which the other freaks treated him. He was tall for a gob – probably my height when standing – and his shoulders were broad, his canine teeth large and sharp. The firelight made his fur look like warm caramel spotted with chocolate. One of his dog-like ears was torn and chewed-looking, the edges scarred. He was missing an eye as well, the thin line of the closed lid almost indistinguishable in the fur of his face. Hard to believe there was anything aristocratic about him, yet he could be the son of a duke, or even the Prince of Wales. His mother would have to be of rank as well. Did they ever wonder what had become of their monstrous child?

While thousands of humans died with every incarnation of the plague – which loves this country like a mother loves her child – aristocrats survived. Not only survived, they evolved. In England the plague-born Prometheus Protein led to vampirism, in Scotland it caused lycanthropy.

It also occasionally affected someone who wasn't considered upper class. Historically, members of the aristocracy had never been very good at keeping it in their pants. Indiscretions with human carriers resulted in the first halvie births, and launched the careers of generations of breeding courtesans. Occasionally some seemingly normal human woman gave birth to a half or fully plagued infant. These children were often murdered by their parents, or shipped off to orphanages where they were shunned and mistreated. That was prior to 1932's rebellion. Now, such cruelties were prevented by the Pax – Pax Yersinia, which dictated that each human donated a sample of DNA at birth. This could help prevent human carriers from intermarrying. It also provided families and special housing for unwanted plagued children.

By the time Victoria, our first fully plagued monarch – King George III had shown vampiric traits – ascended the throne, other aristocrats across Britain and Europe had revealed their true natures as well. Vampires thrived in the more temperate climes like France and Spain, weres in Russia and other eastern countries. Some places had a mix of the two, as did Asia and Australia. Those who remained in Canada and the Americas had gone on to become socialites and film stars.

But they were never safe, no matter where they were. Humans accounted for ninety-two per cent of aristocratic and halvie deaths. Haemophilia, suicide and accidents made up for the remaining eight.

There were no recorded goblin deaths at human hands – not even during the Insurrection.

I approached the battle-scarred goblin with caution. The flickering torches made it hard to tell, but I think recognition flashed in his one yellow eye. He sniffed the air as I approached. I curtsied, playing to his vanity.

"A Vardan get," he said, in a voice that was surprisingly low and articulate for a goblin. "Here on the official?"

Half-bloods took the title of their sire as their surname. The Duke of Vardan was my father. "Nothing official, my lord. I'm here because the goblin prince knows everything that happens in London."

"True," he replied with a slow nod. Despite my flattery he was still looking at me like he expected me to do or say something. "But there is a price. What do you offer your prince, pretty get?"

The only prince I claimed was Albert, God rest his soul, and perhaps Bertie, the Prince of Wales. This mangy monster was not *my* prince. Was I stupid enough to tell him that? Hell, no.

I reached into the leather satchel I'd brought with me, pulled out the clear plastic bag with a lump of blood-soaked butcher's paper inside and offered it to the goblin. He snatched it from me with eager hands that were just a titch too long and dexterous to be paws, tossed the plastic on the floor and tore open the paper. A whine of delight slipped from his throat when he saw what I'd brought. Around us other goblins raised their muzzles and made similar noises, but no one dared approach.

I looked away as the prince brought the gory mass to his muzzle and took an enthusiastic bite. I made my mind blank, refusing to think of what the meat was, what it had been. My only solace was that it had already been dead when I bought it. The blood might smell good, but I couldn't imagine eating anything that ... awful ... terrible ... *raw*.

The goblin gave a little shudder of delight as he chewed and rewrapped his treat for later. A long pink tongue slipped out to lick his muzzle clean. "Proper tribute. Honours her prince. I will tell the lady what I know. Ask, pretty, ask."

The rest of the goblins drifted away from us, save for one little gob who came and sat at the prince's furry feet and stared at me with open curiosity. I was very much aware that every goblin who wasn't preoccupied with human playthings watched me closely. I was relatively safe now, having paid my tribute to their prince. So long as I behaved myself and didn't offend anyone, I'd make it out of here alive. Probably.

"I want to know the whereabouts of Drusilla Vardan," I said quietly, even though I knew most of the goblins had keen enough hearing to eavesdrop without trying. Their sensitivity to sound, as well as light, kept them deep underside.

The prince raised his canine gaze to mine. It was unnerving looking into that one bright eye, seeing intelligence there while he had yet to clean all the blood from his muzzle. "The youngest?"

I nodded. My father had gone through something of a mid-immortality crisis about two and a half decades ago and done his damnedest to impregnate every breeding courtesan he could find. The first attempt had resulted in my brother Val, the second in me and the third and fourth in Avery and Dede. Four live births out of nine pregnancies over a five-year period – pretty potent for a vampire.

"She's missing." He didn't need to know the particulars – like how she had last been seen at her favourite pub. "I want to know what happened to her."

"Nay, you do not," the prince replied cheerfully. "Pretty wants to know where her sibling is. The prince knows." He petted the little goblin on the head as he bared his teeth at me – a smile.

Sweet baby Jesus. Even my spleen trembled at that awful sight.

Trying to hide my fear was futile, as he could surely smell it. Still, I had to give it a go. "Would you be so kind as to share my sister's whereabouts, my lord? Please? I am concerned about her."

If there was one thing goblins understood it was blood – both as sustenance and connection. Offspring happened rarely because of their degree of mutation, and were treasured. No decent goblin – and I use "decent" as loosely as it can possibly be con-strued – would turn down a request that involved family.

"New Bethlehem," he replied in a grave growl.

I pressed a hand against the boned front of my corset, and closed my fingers into a fist. I would not show weakness here, no matter how much the prince might sympathise with my plight – he was still a goddam goblin. "Bedlam?" I rasped.

The prince nodded. "She was taken in two nights ago, in shackles."

Albert's fangs. I blasphemed the Queen's late consort to myself alone. My mind could scarcely grasp the reality of it. "You're wrong," I whispered. "You have to be wrong." But goblins were never wrong. If he hadn't known, he wouldn't have said. That was their way – so I'd been taught. "Honourable monsters", Church had called them.

"Alexandra."

I jerked. I shouldn't be surprised that he knew my name. Of course he knew it. It was the posh way he said it – his voice sounded almost like my father's.

He stood before me – I was right, he was my height. The little one remained glued to his side. I had the sudden and inexplicable urge to reach out and pat her on the head, just as I had wanted to do to a tiger cub I once saw in a travelling exhibit. The comparison kept my hand fisted, and at my side. I wanted to keep it.

"Your prince regrets telling the pretty lady this news."

I turned my attention back to him. The pity in his eye almost brought me to tears. Why should a monster pity me?

"There was an incident at Ainsley's. The Vardan get tried to stab the earl, she did."

That I believed, and therefore I had to believe my sister really could be in Bedlam – where all the special barking mad went to die. Dede and Ainsley had history – a painful one.

The goblin held out his furry hand, and etiquette demanded I take it. The prince was offering me friendship, and my getting out of there alive just might depend on my taking it, treaty or no.

I nodded, my throat tight as his "fingers" closed around mine.

He was warm. For a moment – and only one terribly mad one – I could have hugged him. "Thank you."

He shook his head. "No thanks, lady. Never thank for bad news."

I nodded again and he released my hand. The goblins watched me as I turned to leave, but no one spoke. They didn't even try to tempt me to stay; they simply let me go. I think I despised them most at that moment, especially that little one who waved good-bye.

My sister was essentially in hell and goblins felt sorry for me. As far as I was concerned, things couldn't get much worse.